PRAISE FOR JO RICCIONI

"An outstanding fantasy debut, evocative and thought-provoking. Jo Riccioni combines a poet's touch with the skill of a true storyteller, making *The Branded* a compelling read."
  – *Juliet Marillier, author of the* Sevenwaters *and* Warrior Bards *series.*

"*The Branded* is a timely and passionate adventure, a story for today's women, for those who refuse to back down. With a vivid setting, and a tough and sassy female lead, Riccioni has tapped into the very pulse of the female empowerment movement."
  – *Bronwyn Eley, author of* The Relic Trilogy

"A rich and thought-provoking tale. Riccioni explores a world of distorted matriarchal structure, where fertility is a commodity. I was biting my nails the entire time. A beautifully crafted high fantasy world with a heroine that speaks to my heart and sometimes breaks it."
  – *Stacey McEwan, bestselling author of* Ledge

T0343001

Jo Riccioni

THE RISING

ANGRY ROBOT

ANGRY ROBOT
An imprint of Watkins Media Ltd

Unit 11, Shepperton House
89 Shepperton Road
London N1 3DF
UK

angryrobotbooks.com
twitter.com/angryrobotbooks
Rise or Die

An Angry Robot paperback original, 2025

Cover by Pantera Press
Set in Meridien

ISBN 978 1 91599 857 6
Ebook ISBN 978 1 91599 858 3

Printed and bound in the United Kingdom by CPI Books.

9 8 7 6 5 4 3 2 1

MIX
Paper | Supporting
responsible forestry
FSC® C171272
www.fsc.org

In memory of Uncle Luciano Riccioni (1936-2023), my first history teacher and tour guide to the wonders of the world.

PART ONE:
REIS

The Fool and The Storm

Be careful of the boy. He's a good soul born of bad. Know that if he betrays you, he will break his own heart doing it.

The buck at the water's edge is no bigger than a fleet fox. His thin antlers curve like the ribs of a slum kid back in Isfalk. He raises a wet nose, one delicate foreleg ready to run, as if he can sense me in the dense foliage downstream. I close my eyes, reach again for the sound of his tripping pulse. But I can't seem to latch on, can't subdue its beat to my own as I usually can when I hunt. Sweat beads on my lip, and my mark on the beast falters. I could blame this bastard bow, the riser far larger than my weapon in Isfalk, its draw-length longer. I could blame this suffocating heat, the humidity of the Reis jungle that hangs so close it feels like even my eyeballs are sweating in their sockets, blurring my vision. But there's only one honest reason I can't channel my skill this morning.

He will break his own heart. His own heart.

His own.

I crack my neck and feel the release roll down my spine. *Fec's sake, Nara, get a grip.* Lifting my chin, I line up again. The bow strains, string creaking, but even as my fingers release, I know my aim is wide. The buck rears as the arrow nicks its rump, but almost simultaneously there's the soft *pock* of another shot. The deer topples into the shallows, heart-shot quivering long after its body is still.

I spin around, searching for the archer. Boots crush the undergrowth, and the jungle shivers and parts. The wrangler wears a sleeveless gilet of soft leather, bronze arms dewy with sweat. Loose linen pants match the sand scarves draped around his neck, and rings of gold clamp his black curls, picking out the gilded tooling on his leather boots, the scabbard of his curved sword. He couldn't appear any more different from the stable hand I met mere months ago, bundled in patchy furs as he exercised his sled dogs across the Isfalki tundra. Now, he might be a prince of Reis stepped from his hunting lodge.

He cocks an eyebrow at me. "Bow arm a bit off this morning, Little Scourge?" He knows I never miss a shot. And he'd never miss an opportunity to bait me about it.

"Still following me like a lost puppy, Wrangler?" I tighten the strap on my quiver so I don't have to look at him, trying to ignore the angry race of my heart.

"Not such a good idea to be out here alone," he says, tone changing.

"That's one I haven't heard before. Tell me something new, why don't you?"

"I'm serious. All manner of hunters stalk the Kyder – human and animal. But if you must go exploring, at least don't do it alone." He inspects his boots, sheepish. "I thought Brim might–"

"Brim might what?" He has the audacity to look jealous. "You thought he'd be keeping guard over me as usual?" I shake my head in contempt. "Here's some news for you, Wrangler: Brim might once have been my Warder, but we're not in Isfalk anymore. I don't need permission for my movements, from him or anyone else. And I'm not about to go jumping into his arms simply because yours are taken." I shoulder my bow. "Not that it's any of your business if I do."

"Straight for the jugular. Just as I'd expect. But your assumptions are as off-mark as your aim this morning, Scourge." He smirks and I want to slap him right across that mole winking in his cheek. "What I was going to say is that I thought Brim, as a military man, would have wanted someone at your back, especially in unknown territory." He takes a breath, voice softening a little. "I knew you'd head out here at the first opportunity. It was written all over your face as soon as you caught sight of the jungle yesterday – that longing for the wilds... the need to be hunting again." He says it like he's talking of himself as much as me.

I turn my back on him, casting my gaze about the clearing like I'm scouting for game. Brim might have eventually guessed where to come looking for me when I didn't join Osha and the others for breakfast, but the wrangler knew before I was even missed. After all his lies and secrecy, it's galling that he knows me so well. I don't want him to see my anger, though. Getting angry shows I care – indifference will pain him more. I know him well, too.

"Look, Nara," he says. "About yesterday..." But he trails off, like he can't find the words to describe the events that changed everything between us.

"Yesterday?" I ask. "You mean when your girlfriend stepped aboard the *Na'quat* while I was still naked in your bed? The betrothed you forgot to tell me about?"

He sighs. "Nara, let's talk."

"No, *you're* the one who should have talked... weeks ago when we were riding through the Wasteland Plains and you kissed me."

"*I* kissed *you*? Are you sure about that, Scourge?"

I snatch a breath. After everything he's done, he dares suggest I was the one who made the first move. "Go to hell, Wrangler."

"Tempting, but keeping an eye on you is a far worse fate, I think."

"I don't need anyone keeping an eye on me, least of all you! Fecs alive, if I'm to be a prisoner here, too, I might as well have saved myself the journey from Orlathston. Or from Isfalk, for that matter."

"You're not a prisoner here." He frowns like he's offended. "You can go where you like."

"Really? Is that the truth, Wrangler?" It takes all the willpower I possess to gentle my voice and quiet my rattled breathing. "So, I'm free to do what I want?"

"Have you ever done otherwise?" He folds his arms and scans the clearing as if my being here is a case in point.

"Alright, then. Does that mean I can ask a favour?"

My change in tone takes him by surprise and his expression slips from suspicion to hope. Perhaps he can't quite believe I'd give him the chance to earn my forgiveness, and yet he seems to long for it anyway. I draw close, close enough to trace the neck of his gilet with a finger. "There's something I want, Nixim." His pupils dilate when I say his name and turn my face up to his. "Will you do it for me?"

Voice a low rumble, he answers, "Your will, my hands, remember?"

"I remember." I bite my lip and his breath hitches. "So, what I want," I say, stabbing a finger in his chest, "is for you to skip on back to your lyfhort and leave me the fec alone!"

His shoulders drop and he lifts his face to the blue sky peeping between the jungle's canopy. "I guess I deserve that."

"You deserve a whole lot more than that."

We freeze at the sound of the undergrowth being trampled nearby. A husky voice calls out, but its owner is no man. The slender woman who emerges from the trees has thick black curls escaping her sand scarves. The thin sleeves of a fitted chemise boast athletic arms. When she shoulders her weapon, I realise the heart-shot that felled the deer was hers. The wrangler isn't even carrying a bow. If I was in any doubt as to who this woman is, the little mole to the side of her mouth settles it for me. She's the wrangler's sister – one of the two women I rode behind in sullen silence for hours on the journey inland yesterday.

She makes a quick exchange in Reis with her brother, before running kohled eyes over me from boots to crown. Her face had been shrouded during our ride across the desert, and now, up close, I notice her skin is a shade darker than the wrangler's, her stare even shrewder. The colour of her irises is complicated, like his – an inner ring of pale brown, changeable as the evening dunes we'd crossed on the long ride from the coast. When she adjusts her quiver, the underside of her wrist shows a delicate branding peeking from beneath her cuff.

"Hra kim, sha Azza Ni Azzadur," she says boldly, a note of challenge in her tone. I flounder at the Reis words, determined not to look at the wrangler for help. "Azza Ni Azzadur," she repeats.

"Sorry, I…"

The mole hitches above her lip. "It is my *name*. I am not interrogating you."

"You know Isfalki," I reply. "You barely opened your mouth yesterday, so I assumed–"

"Perhaps I had nothing to say." She shrugs, but it's clear she's the type of woman who has plenty of opinions, even if they don't reach her tongue. Her Isfalki is accented but good, and I'm wondering where she could have learned it this far south when she asks, "So, do you have one too?"

"One what?"

"A name." She draws it out as if I might be simple. But when she glances at the wrangler, I see her eyes are alive with amusement.

"Oh… yeah… I mean, I'm Nara," I say, feeling all kinds of stupid.

"Rest easy, Nara Fornwood. I know who you are. My brother has told me all about you." Under her scrutiny, the wrangler busies himself with his water flask, taking a long drink and squinting off through the trees. But when I stare a beat too long, he meets my gaze, emotions scudding across his face as quickly as clouds across the taiga – regret, guilt, frustration. I don't care to know which. I sip from my own water skin, trying to be as casual as I can with resentment pulsing on my tongue and anger burning up my cheeks.

His sister hums softly at our silent exchange. "My brother," she muses, "still trying to tame the storm, I see."

"My sister," the wrangler retorts, "still spouting ridiculous proverbs, I see." And with that, he hacks peevishly through the foliage and is swallowed by the jungle.

Azza's chuckle at his departure has a smoky hoarseness to it that belies her neat frame. "It is a Reis saying: *The fool who tries to tame the storm eats only sand.*"

"You think *I'm* the storm... the trouble that needs to be tamed?" I take an indignant breath. "Bit of an assumption when you've known me, what... one whole day?"

She lowers her chin with a look that warns not to take her for a fool. "Nixim has never been very good at staying clear of trouble, and you, Nara Fornwood, are trouble. Anyone with eyes can see it." She frowns. "But there is more resting on your arrival in Reis than my brother's heart."

Her words hit the pit of my stomach – not the put-down, but the threat of the unknown. The weight of what it means to be here kept me awake for most of the night, tossing with worry for Osha. She's my main concern, she always has been. And yet, on the wrangler's advice, I've brought her to a land we know nothing of, looking for answers to an ability she won't even admit to possessing, both of us ignorant of what getting those answers might cost.

"I couldn't care less about the heart of your brother," I tell Azza. "But I do care about my sister, and he's told me fec-all about what the Reis intend to do with her. So, any light you want to shed on that would be gratefully received." Not the most diplomatic request for information, I'll admit, but at least I asked without putting my arrow to her throat.

We lock eyes for a moment, and I can feel her appraising

me. "You Isfalki," she says, heading off in the direction of the felled deer, "you talk too much when you hunt."

As if the wrangler wasn't enough, now I have his poxy sister to deal with.

The Sister and The Betrothed

"We call them *turcas* in Reis," Azza says when I follow her to the river. "They are plentiful in the Kyder." She pulls out her knife and field dresses the small deer with the quick, capable hands of an experienced hunter. Her technique is different from mine, and I watch her, engrossed. When she's almost finished, she says, "As children, my brother and I would spend days tracking them here, camping out and running wild. He loved this forest."

"Don't indulge me with *talk*," I say, but she smiles as if seeing straight through me.

"He did not choose to leave Reis or become a Seeker, you know. It was our father who sent him off to hunt for Pure girls like you and your sister." She grunts and I can't tell whether it's in disapproval or the effort of her work. "My father thought such a quest would give Nixim purpose, encourage him to fully embrace the traditions and beliefs of our people."

"Yeah, *that*," I scoff, angling my head so she can better see the branding scattered across my stubbled scalp. "He wasn't exactly searching for girls like me." The fine blue freckles of the Brume virus, evidence of my susceptibility to disease, identify me as a common Brand, unlike my sister, Osha. Her unblemished skin sets her firmly in the camp of the Mor minority – Pure women in great demand across the Continent as breeders of stronger, healthier offspring.

To my surprise, Azza barely glances at the markings. "I hear

16

you are struggling to believe our prophecy?" she says instead. The wrangler must have confided in her, and I find myself resenting the idea of them discussing me like I'm some kind of problem to be managed.

"One Pure woman with magical powers to cure the Branded and return peace and happiness to the world?" I fold my arms. "It's a children's bedtime story... and I'm hardly a child."

She treats me to that husky laugh again. I'd expected anger, an argument. Perhaps I'd even wanted one – a distraction from my bitter disappointment with her brother. But, far from being offended, she's entertained. And that annoys me even more.

"Look, I'm sorry if I can't naively swallow your belief in this Elita, or whatever you call her. But if you're angling for someone to be the prophet of your little sect, you can think again about my sister." I'm being churlish now, maybe even dangerously provocative given our situation as guests in her homeland, at the mercy of customs I don't understand. But attack is what I know best when I feel threatened.

I think about Osha and her healing gifts, about the new life growing inside her. My grandmother made me promise to look after her, as if she knew Osha would be the one to need it. And now we're out of the Settlement, out of Orlathston, I'm not about to let her be manipulated into another cultish prison – one where she might wear a crown, but a prison all the same. "I'm sure you can find a home-grown princess who'd enjoy wearing the robes of prophet queen a whole lot more than my sister. Why don't you ask Nixim's girlfriend?" I scoff. "She seems ready-made for the role."

An image from yesterday's journey inland from the *Na'quat* visits me sharp as a stitch in my ribs: the wrangler's betrothed, mounted on a stallion of pure white, her sand scarves fringed with silver coins that jangled in the breeze. Her riding manta was made of a gossamer fabric, shot with threads that caught the sun like veins of gold in rock – impressively impractical, but dazzling all the same. Underneath it, her toned legs were

clad in supple, well-worn leather, and the curved blade on
her hip had a scabbard scuffed from use. Even I wasn't fool
enough to believe she was all decorative vanity – her riding
skills proved that. And yet her hand, when she mounted her
horse, had reached for Nixim's shoulder, and all through the
long trek around the edge of the desert she'd inclined her head
to speak only to him.

"You refer to Hira?" Azza interrupts my thoughts. "I see you
have not forgiven her for yesterday's antics."

"It was a cheap trick with the horse."

"That is Hira, to the bone. She enjoys childish games."

"It didn't feel childish. That colt could have broken my neck."

Azza's soft hum has something knowing in it, as if she
understands far more of me than I do of her.

The horse I'd been given for the journey was a magnificent
beast, surely meant for royalty, not an orphaned Brand in
shabby hunting leathers and worn-out boots. He turned out to
be skittish, constantly chomping at the bit and demanding to
be given his reins. I could taste his impatience foaming on my
tongue, feel the nervy twitch of his flank in my own muscles, but
I couldn't seem to sway him calm. By comparison, the mounts
of Osha, Brim, Haus and the Maw were like docile nags, bowed
by the merciless sun and a heat that could crack skulls.

The entire day I wrestled that animal along the edge of the
Storm Sands and across the arid plain inland from the sea,
until we ascended a ridge. At the summit, Hira finally halted
our party, watching a point ahead of us with anticipation. At
first, all I could see was a rock massif in the distance, eddies
of sand swirling here and there. But gradually, as the sun
dropped, shadows began to form – shadows that turned into
the silhouettes of hundreds of tents and gers sheltering in the
lee of the plateau. There, in the stone, the shapes of windows,
doors, crenelations and ramparts slowly appeared. An entire
fortress had been cut into the rock, everything the colour of
sand, until dusk embossed the city onto the landscape.

"Cha Shaheer," the wrangler announced. "The Shadow City of Reis." As if the name was a starting bell, Hira heeled her mount, teeth flashing white as she trilled a wild burr and galloped off, tossing Nixim a look of pure challenge over her shoulder. He hesitated at my horse's flank, but I wouldn't look him in the eye. I wanted none of the race that was afoot, least of all at his invitation. His horse whinnied impatiently, and the next moment I was watching him chase his betrothed across the sands. A kick to the ribs if ever I'd felt one.

"Poxes if I'm going to be left behind like dead carrion!" Brim called out. Haus, Osha and the Maw followed his lead, galloping into the growing dust trail. My colt reared in complaint, then yanked the reins from my grip and lunged after them. I'd been grappling him to an unsteady trot for so long, his speed felt fluid and easy, his adrenalin metallic on my tongue, pulse a hungry drum. For the first time since hearing that knock on the door of the captain's cabin, I felt strong again, full of purpose... I felt myself.

But Hira couldn't have predicted how I'd handle the horse. She couldn't have known about my sway over animals.

"The race across the hearthsands at dusk is a tradition," Azza tells me now as she cleans her field knife. "The Shadow City may be our beating heart, but the Reis come from nomadic roots. As children we are given saddles before boots. I believe Hira intended the stallion to test your... *mettle*. That is the Isfalki word, no?"

"Stallion? That horse was a colt. Haus said he couldn't have been broken in more than a week – his shoes were still shiny! Hira didn't want to test my mettle. She wanted to see me on my arse."

"Perhaps," Azza says. "Yet she failed, did she not? You mastered the animal. Were you not satisfied with the results of the race?" Those big eyes bore straight through me again. It's almost as if she's guessed how naturally I fell into the beast's rhythm, into the bellow of his lungs, the beat of his hooves,

how we'd become one and the same creature. We'd set a
fearless pace across the plain, flying past the Maw and Brim,
and then Haus, who'd likely reined in his horse to keep abreast
of Osha. When I flanked the wrangler, I ignored his shouts
– encouragement or warning, I didn't care in that moment.
All that mattered was the race and the gates of Cha Shaheer
and getting there first, before the woman who'd jangled like
a bauble the entire journey from the *Na'quat* – a woman who
clearly considered me so far below the level of a threat she'd
barely acknowledged my existence.

The stone walls of the city loomed ahead, dusted pink in
the last light. Under a giant archway built between two rock
faces, we thundered to a stop, neck and neck. Hira swung in
her saddle as our horses danced around each other, gifting me
an exhilarated grin clearly meant for Nixim. I was faced with
her beauty up close for the first time. Sand scarves dislodged
by the ride, her flawless brown skin was offset by long hair that
made my throat tighten. Not jet black like the wrangler's or his
sister's, but a shimmering platinum, the colour of spider silk in
a dewy dawn.

"Hira spoke to you under the gates of Cha Shaheer," Azza
says, interrupting my thoughts. She's busy binding the feet
of the turcas, but she can't quite disguise her curiosity, which
makes me suspect there's far more than my pride and a horse
race at stake here. "What did she say?"

"She told me I rode well *for a Sky-Eye*. It's the nickname the
Hrossi give the Isfalki because of our–"

"And what was your reply?" Azza interrupts, making it
clear she's worldly enough to know a little slang without my
help.

"I told her I was a Fornwood Solitary. I wasn't born behind
the walls of the citadel. I'm no Isfalki."

Azza pauses her work for a moment. "That was an
unfortunate response."

"Why?"

"Hira is a Pure, as you probably guessed. You might as well have said you were riddled with disease. She will be sure to tell the whole of Reis that you are branded *and* feral."

"Then she'd be telling the truth. It's what I am." I tap the branding above my ear with a shrug, but I can't help remembering the way Hira's lips had thinned at my grubby leathers, the nicks and scars on my hands from fighting. By the time she got to the shaved strip of my scalp, it wouldn't have made any difference if I was a branded Solitary or a Mor from Isfalk's Founding Four – I was no more her competition than the shit from her horse. "Welcome to civilisation, Nara Fornwood," she'd announced.

"Apologies," I shot back, "we haven't been introduced." I matched her tight smile with one of my own. "Nixim failed to mention you."

It was the truth, after all. Not my fault she hadn't liked hearing it. She'd ignored me, barking orders to an approaching stable hand instead.

"Hira can call me a feral, if she likes," I tell Azza. "I can hold my own when it comes to slinging insults."

"My brother warned me your tongue is as sharp as your sword." She grunts, and it's not from shouldering the turcas. "But I know Hira. If you have slighted her, she will make sure you pay for it."

"Look, I've got bigger things to worry about than your brother's girlfriend–" I begin, but she holds up a finger to shush me. Poxes, what is it with these high-handed Reis women? When I follow her line of vision, I realise she's spotted another turcas, about sixty paces downriver, a doe this time – the mate of our felled quarry. The deer lowers her head to drink, unaware of our presence. Azza leans quietly against the trunk of a palm tree, easing the burden of the buck. "Perhaps you will have better luck with this one, Nara Fornwood?" she whispers.

Without thinking, I nock an arrow and line up the shot.

She wants to challenge me? Okay, then. I turn my thoughts inward, listening for the doe's heartbeat, calling to it with my own. It's there, tripping inside me, but it grows halting and faint every time I try to press dominance. I remember the dreams that plagued me last night, not just fears for Osha's physical safety, but terrors about our skills – nightmares in which my sister's sway grows ever stronger the more she denies it, while mine slips away like sand between my fingers the harder I grasp.

Azza remains perfectly still, watching me with such intensity, the shot starts to feel less like a challenge than a test. Suddenly I'm nervous, afraid of failing. Afraid of not failing. "The mark's too far," I mutter. "Stupid bow's throwing my aim." Shame burns my cheeks at the excuse.

"You do not aim with your bow, Nara Fornwood. We both know it."

I snatch my gaze from the deer to stare at her. Does she know about my skill? Has the wrangler told her? "Quiet yourself," she says gently, the previous note of challenge gone. "Hone your mind to your purpose."

The words sound vaguely familiar, her light touch on my wrist reassuring. I draw the string and set my sights, doing as she says... doing what I do best. With lowered lids, I pinpoint the heat, the smell, the very breath of the creature. The doe's heartbeat hammers inside me now, clear as the peck of a sapsucker in the Fornwood, and I leap on it, growing her thirst and keeping her distracted at the water's edge. The arrow sings through the trees, a clean hit. I might be smug if I wasn't too busy staunching the gush of blood from my nose.

Azza doesn't comment on the shot. Instead, she unwinds her sand scarf, offering it to stop the flow. "Do you always bleed when you hunt?"

"I'm not sick, if that's what you're bothered about. It just happens from time to time."

"When you sway?"

I swipe angrily at my nose. "So, your brother tells me nothing yet blabs everything to you?"

"He did not have to... *blab*. I saw it for myself with the colt yesterday. And again now." She studies my branding for a time. The Blood-wife told me the skill to sway only developed in Pure women... and yet here I am. I can't tell whether Azza is perplexed or shocked – her face would do well playing cards in any Isfalki tavern.

"You going to speak or just keep eyeballing me?"

Her frown deepens. A second later her lips twist in understanding. Her Isfalki really is good.

Still, she ignores me, walking off towards the felled doe. "You're just like your brother, you know," I call after her. "Or is being broody and secretive something they teach at school here in Reis?" I stomp through the dense foliage, trying to juggle the scarf at my nose, my bow and quiver. "So I'm a Brand and I bleed when I hunt. Big deal. It's hardly going to kill me."

She tugs my arrow from the deer and hands it back to me. "Come, Nara Fornwood. Let us finish our sport. Some breakfast might sweeten your mood."

"Fec's sake, my mood is perfectly fin–"

"As fine as it was before you and Nixim arrived?" She cuts me a look, eyebrow raised. There's no getting anything past this woman. I stride ahead so she can't see me gathering my thoughts, trying not to return to that night aboard the *Na'quat*. The wrangler and his lyfhort have thrown me off my game, but they're none of my concern now. Protecting Osha must be foremost in my mind. Azza can sweeten my mood all she likes, but corner something *feral* defending its own and you're going to get bitten. She's a hunter. She should know that.

The Shadow City

The jungle thins before a rocky gorge and we find the wrangler sitting atop a boulder, waiting for us. He's deep in thought, but startles at our approach, stepping up to heft the doe from my shoulders. I shrug him off. "Seriously?" He sighs.

"Yes, seriously. You sell me to Wasteland traders, shackle me in a sled wagon, then abandon me to the fighting pits of the Cooler. Now you want to play nice?"

"It'd be refreshing if you let me for once, Scourge."

"Why would I do that? As you keep reminding me with that ridiculous nickname, I'm not very nice. And I can carry my own fecking game, Wrangler."

Arms crossed, he looks up at the blue sky for a moment, cursing in Reis before striding ahead in the direction of Cha Shaheer.

As far as I can tell, the gorge we're navigating is the only natural passage through the crater-like massif that forms the Shadow City. At dusk yesterday, when we rode under the stone arches of the northern gate, Cha Shaheer had seemed a citadel built of living rock. But now, approaching from the south and with the sun fully risen, its volcano-shape is clearer to see, the fortress settlement a patchwork of flat rooftops and courtyards descending to a central agora and marketplace. The buildings are half hewn from the stone, half built atop it, and at its highest point the weathered gilt cupola of a temple glimmers like a second sun. Workmanship like that surely makes the city ancient, even by Old World standards.

I follow the wrangler's route through streets alive with the day's business, stopping only when Azza calls for me to drop the turcas outside what looks like an abattoir. When the butcher emerges, tying on an apron, I notice that he's tall and strong, and he has no brandings on his face or hands. Back in Isfalk, dressing meat was no job for a Pure, not unless they'd been exiled to the Brand village and forced into menial work for a crime or misdemeanour. I'm curious to know why someone immune would lower himself to perform such labour, but I'm also in no mood to strike up edifying conversation with either of my companions. I've been gone too long from Osha already, and much as I hate to admit Azza's right, I could use some breakfast.

When I'd skirted the marketplace on the way to the Kyder it was still dark and empty of wares and people, but now the square is lined with carts selling all manner of produce and food I've never seen before. My stomach grumbles at the smell of cooking and my tongue grows more parched at every hawker with a steaming urn or cart of pressed fruit. We pass saddlers and metalsmiths, papermakers and scribes, chandlers and embroiderers – some noticeably branded and others not, but all freely mingling. It's easy to imagine I've walked back over a hundred years to the thriving and carefree streets before the decimation of the Brume, to a time when the immune were not raised above the infected majority, a time before the concept of Branded and Pure even existed.

The wrangler watches me digest it all. "What were you expecting, Little Scourge? A few starving nomads in patched-up tents? Women being traded for camels on the edge of the Storm Sands?"

I don't get to answer, for a shout rings out above us. "Nixim!" In a flurry of white robes, a young girl almost throws herself down the steep steps that zigzag their way from the temple. "Nixim!"

"Saqira?" the wrangler answers, the word almost winded from him as she launches herself into his arms. He swings her round in a stream of Reis exclamations, then sets her down and looks her over, his face full of joy and an indulgence I've never seen in him before. There's a likeness between them – her hair a mess of wilful black curls above fallen sand scarves, something teasing about her smile. She can't be more than fourteen – the same age he was when he came to Isfalk.

"Look at you, Bu!" he says. "How did you get so tall?"

"Probably the same way you got so hairy, brother."

I press back a smile, realising a moment later they've switched to Isfalki for my benefit. Poxes, is everyone in the wrangler's family better educated than the whole of the Isfalk Council put together? And to think I once accused Nixim of being less cultivated than his dog. He draws Saqira close for another hug. "A shave would be good," she adds, pinching his chin. He knuckles her in the ribs, mussing up her neat robes, until she squeals for mercy. Such sibling games seem so domestic, so normal, it strikes me briefly that I've had little chance to see the wrangler's real nature, beyond the dictates of the Settlement and the dangers of the Wastelands. I push the thought away. What concern is it of mine now?

"I'll have you know I bathed *and* shaved last night," he tells her. "Where were you, anyway? Couldn't be bothered to come out and greet your long-lost brother?"

"I wanted to, but–" She glances over her shoulder.

Hira is descending the steps with far more grace than the younger girl before her. This morning she wears robes of metallic silk that fall like moonlit water, and when she draws close I notice her kohled eyes are framed with lashes tipped in silver. Their application must have taken as long as my hunting trip. The entire ensemble is a sight to behold, but mostly serves to tell the world she has servants waiting on her every whim. I can hardly be critical of that: back in the Settlement, Osha and

I had Frida to dress us – at least before I was thrown out of the citadel. The thought stirs up worries for my old friend.

Hira greets the group, remaining on an upper step. It displays her appearance to full effect, while also allowing her to look down on me. She's good, I'll give her that. A moment later, however, she surprises me by lowering her head before Saqira and kissing the hem of her reis-chafi. "Sa ga-lil, Eirafa," Hira says with solemn ceremony. The girl places a palm on Hira's crown and impatiently rattles off a few words in return.

"Eirafa?" the wrangler asks. "A High Seer... already?" Hira answers in Reis and Nixim frowns, as if to remind her that conversing in a tongue guests cannot understand is the height of ill-breeding. "She can't have been initiated yet, surely?"

"She was integrated into the High Seer Circle during yesterday's rite. It is why she could not venture out to welcome you." Hira looks at me as she says it, ensuring I reap the full benefit of her perfect Isfalki. It has the intended effect – I feel like an uncultivated boor for speaking only one language, and most of that in curses. "My mother is delighted with her," Hira continues. "Saqira's visions are stronger than an Eirafa twice her age."

A shadow passes over the wrangler at this news. He told me about the Seers in Reis when we crossed the Wasteland Plains. Searching out Mor women like Osha for them to read was part of his mission as a Seeker – the very reason he brought us here. But I wasn't expecting his younger sister – a girl barely past childhood – to be one of their oracles, and apparently, neither was he. Azza gives him a pointed look, and he says no more on the subject.

Over the wrangler's shoulder, I notice Osha making her way towards us from the citadel's main keep, Haus not far behind. My sister's cheeks, usually rosy, are pale this morning and her step a little slower than usual. To anyone else, she might simply appear tired from the long journey yesterday. She disguises her pregnancy well for now, but it weighs on her, mentally more than physically, the father of her child uncertain. She's sworn me to tell no one of her condition, especially Haus, and it feels like yet another deception in the fog of lies we've been sailing through since we left Isfalk.

When she draws up beside me, Osha tilts her chin to the bow and quiver slung at my back. "Couldn't wait one day to get a weapon in your hands?" she murmurs, before greeting the group with a smile.

"I couldn't sleep. I left you a note," I say, reaching for her hand, already seeking forgiveness. I feel the instant spark, the warmth that spreads through me whenever our skin joins, but she won't squeeze back. She's angry I stole out while she was still sleeping. I shouldn't have, not when we know so little about this place, not when she's still being sick from the child. After the nightmares about our skill, I spent most of last night pacing my room, worrying about her and our future here. By the time morning came, I was desperate for a little peace. All I wanted was a few moments of that old solitude, the simplicity of nature, a brief chance to remind myself of the girl I used to be... before the Wastelands, before the Cooler... before the wrangler. And, weakly, I gave into the urge.

"Osha Fornwood?" Saqira asks, breaking my thoughts. The introductions are over and she's studying us with keen curiosity. "Are you and your sister twins?"

"So they claim," Hira answers. "I suppose even the same year has both a summer and a winter." Her focus darts between our faces and it's obvious which season she is casting me as in that analogy. It's like we're back in Isfalk being inspected by Father Uluf all over again. Osha does squeeze my hand now – restraint, not reassurance, in the message.

"Interesting. Do you experience winter here in Reis?" my sister muses, tone innocent. "I thought being so far south it would be hot all year?" Hira doesn't see fit to reply, and I can't help noticing the wrangler's lips twitching in amusement.

Osha turns to Saqira. "To answer your question, yes, we're twins."

"Your hair," the young girl gushes. "I've never seen..." And, as if it's the most natural thing in the world, she reaches towards Osha, palm out ready to touch it. I flinch instinctively, but it's Haus who blocks Saqira's path. The girl freezes, blinking in confusion. She seems no more threatening than the doe I just felled, but after Orlath and the Cooler, I'm grateful for Haus, for knowing he wants my sister's safety as much as I do. He's a comfort when we know so little of the customs of this land, these Seers and what they intend for Osha.

The wrangler guides Saqira aside. "The chat will have to wait, Bu. We need to get cleaned up and we're hungry."

"Cook is preparing ma'kata in the kitchens, especially for you," she says, crossing her arms. "Whenever I ask him to make it for me, the answer is always *no, too time-consuming, run along now*. But you ride through the gate, and nothing is too much."

"Just as it should be," Nixim teases.

She draws an indignant breath. "Father claimed the north would teach you a lesson, but your head is bigger than ever."

"How else can I fit my brain in it?"

She laughs and leans into him, slipping her arm around his waist. He stoops to kiss her hair. She couldn't have been more than eight or nine when he left Reis, but they behave as if he's never been away. Perhaps she's the reason the wrangler understood my bond with Osha, how much I hated our separation in Isfalk, my need to protect her. But then I remember how he played on that bond for his own motives, winning my trust so that Osha would follow me here, and I harden my heart again.

"Father has been asking after you," Saqira tells her brother as we walk towards the keep.

"My mother and he are busy arranging the feast, Nixim," Hira adds. "The messenger you sent from Orlathston arrived weeks ago and the whole of Cha Shaheer has been in a frenzy of preparation. The southern tribes have journeyed here specially for the gathering."

The wrangler's face falls.

"Come now, Nixim Ni Azzadur," Hira says, "you did not think your return was going to be as easy as a race across the hearthsands and a soak in the saman?"

A muscle feathers in his jaw. This fuss around his arrival tells me he's no ordinary Reis heading home after a long stay in the north, and he's not rejoicing at the attention. I remember his words in the cabin of the ship. *I don't want to arrive either.* I'd thought it was because he wanted to stay with me, just the two of us, but it's obvious now he had other reasons for not wanting to rush ashore. A bead of sweat runs the length of my spine, cooling the memory of his arms, his lips, his breath on my skin. That night is dust now, blowing across the Storm Sands.

We pass into a large natural courtyard where servants hurry to different parts of the keep and guards cross their horses to the stables nearby. All kinds of activity sounds through the windows above – pots clanging, a female voice yelling orders, rugs being beaten, the vague strains of music on the air.

"You find our people readying for the festivities," Hira tells us. "No celebration can surpass a gathering of the Reis clans."

"All this for the return of Nixim?" Osha asks me under her breath. I answer with a nervous shrug.

"We celebrate the homecoming of Nixim Ni Azzadur, yes," Hira explains, "but we also prepare for the High Seer reading to come." Her gaze travels Osha from head to foot, dubious. "The people hope that the Elita will finally be declared."

A deep cut forms between my sister's eyebrows. I've wanted to tell her for weeks about the prophecy and the assessment of the Seers here in Reis. I tried to talk to her about her healing gifts back on the Wasteland Plains – whether she could feel the quickening of it, the ability to sense another's pulse, as I do with animals when I hunt – but she'd refused to listen, telling me I was talking nonsense. So, I kept my vision at the Bloodwife's cottage to myself, sharing nothing about Frenka and what she told me of Sways. I haven't brought up the subject

since. Besides, Osha's had so much else to deal with already –
her condition, her nightmares of Orlath, the fear he could be
the father of her child. I wanted to spare her the burden of
yet another worry, at least until I was certain what was ahead
of us. But now my time is up. If my sister doesn't learn about
Sways and the Seer reading from me, she's going to learn it
from someone like Hira.

I run a hand behind my neck, longing only for a bath, a little
food, and a dreamless sleep. Ahead, a stable boy crosses our path
leading a horse I recognize – the colt I rode from the *Na'quat*.
He's back to his usual tricks, wide-eyed, and side-stepping
erratically. He jostles into a servant carrying an urn and at the
sound of the jug clattering to the ground, the beast rears straight
into the path of Saqira. I catch her as she reels backwards and
the moment our skin touches, I feel a jolt like static through my
arm. There's that compulsive pull I'd experienced with Mother
Iness back on the Roundhouse stage, and again with the Blood-
wife in her cottage on the Edfjall. Saqira stills and her cheeks
drain of colour, turning white as her robes. Her eyes flutter
from side-to-side, as if in a waking dream, irises filming over
with a milky pearlescence. It only lasts a second, but it's enough
to remind me of the sand krait the wrangler had killed on the
Wasteland Plains, and I recoil in shock.

Haus is at my shoulder, steadying, calming, but Saqira's eyes
have already returned to their warm hazel. No one seems to
have noticed anything more than the upset of a frisky horse.
No one except Saqira. Her gaze is locked on my branding.
Drawing the wrangler close again, she whispers in his ear. He
takes her arm and leads her away, and I'm left feeling like I've
corrupted her somehow – a dangerous book she's cracked open
in secret, my mind exposed to her, plain as words on paper.

Playing Princesses

"Narkat? What is it? What happened?" Osha calls.

She's followed me back to our quarters high up in the citadel. "Nothing," I say, slowing to let her catch up on the stairwell cut centuries ago from solid rock. "I'm in no mood to meet any more of the wrangler's family, that's all."

It isn't exactly a lie.

I lean against a casement offering views back over our journey here – the rocky tableland we crossed, the smooth contours of the Storm Sands, and in the north-west the vaguest glimmer of the sea on the horizon. I imagine the *Na'quat* moored and creaking, lazy as an old dog in the sun, and a gush of longing washes over me.

Osha catches my face in her hands, frowning. "What? I'm just hungry," I tell her, pulling away to continue up the stairs. She climbs behind me in silence, understanding I need time and privacy to confide what's on my mind.

High-ceilinged and airy, the room we've been given is a refuge from the heat and bustle of the Reis streets far below.

Rooms, to be precise, for this is no shared dormitory back at the Mor school; here we have a full set of interconnected chambers at our disposal. Tiles of abstract designs make the walls colourful and busy, but the furniture is simple – low daybeds and floor cushions, plain gauze curtains rippling gently before an arched terrace running the length of the apartments. I draw back one of the sheers and step out, taking in the view south past the city. A valley spreads beyond the gorge, a broad river cutting between cultivated plains, the lush pockets of the Kyder on either side. It seems as fantastical as an Old-World fireside tale, as if Cha Shaheer is the magical gateway to a forgotten paradise, a land of plenty hidden by the Storm Sands.

"It isn't what I was expecting at all," Osha says, shoulder brushing mine as we lean over the balcony. "I mean, in Isfalk people always said Reis was barren, its people nomadic, barely surviving on the edge of the desert, but..." I know exactly what she's doing – skirting around her concern, warming me up, approaching gently. She nods towards our lavish quarters. "Somehow, I don't think your wrangler works with dogs here."

"He's not *my* wrangler."

"Nara."

I shift beside her, not wanting to go down this route. The real conversation we need to have is about her. But I don't have a chance to begin. We hear someone moving about the rooms. A serving woman is spreading platters of food across the low tables – fresh fruits I don't recognise, nuts, some kind of cheese, and flat bread. There are boiled eggs drizzled with sauce and a variety of small cakes – more choice than we've ever had in one meal, even at Morday feasts. It comes on the wrangler's orders, no doubt. "Definitely not a kennel boy," Osha mutters.

I'm no longer hungry. When the woman pours drinks that smell alcoholic, I take a cup from her. It's smooth and goes down far easier than Isfalki kornbru or the bitter dramur vit of the Wastelands. She offers me a refill and I notice the brandings on her hands. They're dark and twisted thickly along both forearms, matched by a lick up her neck like a blue flame. Clearly the Reis are not as pedantic as the Isfalki about the appearance of their servants. The woman is short in stature, but she has as much brawn as any Ringer from the Cooler, and like many of the Brands I saw in the streets this morning, she seems in good health.

I knock back a second hit of the liquor, a consoling warmth starting to seep through me. A little numbness will ease the confession ahead. My sister watches warily but bides her time, waiting for me to speak. When I was unconscious aboard the *Na'quat*, Nixim must have told her about the mesmer and how the Reis use it to induce visions because Osha had asked me about it afterwards. I told her the snake's venom had shown me Brim's uncle, Lars Oskarsson, talking to our Amma, claiming he'd brought us across the desert to live with her, insisting we move to the Isfalki citadel under his protection once raiders started sweeping the forest, killing Solitaries. And I told her how I'd seen our grandmother murdered by Isfalki Warders, not the Reis, as we'd always believed. Osha was dubious back then, and I haven't even begun to explain the Elita prophecy and everything the Blood-wife told me about Sways. I gird myself for the task ahead, pouring another shot.

Once the servant has left, I can't put it off any longer. I tell Osha everything. It spews from me in a breathless confession, the liquor lubricating my tongue.

Afterwards, when there's no more to say, my sister is pale and quiet. "Are you shocked? Angry that I brought you here without telling you the full story?" Osha still won't answer. "I mean, this Elita prophecy... the idea that you could be singled out as Reis's possible prophet healer... it's ridiculous, of course," I babble into the silence. "I told the wrangler as much, but... Osha? Say something." I want a reaction, any reaction. She only rises, walks the length of the room, deep in thought.

The Reis woman reappears, fussing around us with glasses of hot tea. I let out an audible groan, but Osha thanks her, then asks her name. I screw up my eyes in frustration. "Takia?" my sister repeats, accepting the tea. "Thank you, Takia."

The servant reaches to clear the bottle of wine, but I snatch it from the table. "Yes, thank you, Takia," I tell her. She gets the hint and leaves the room with a sniff in my direction. "That's typical of you, O."

"What is?"

"I break the news that you're the prophet priestess of a desert kingdom and you're more interested in getting to know the brandservants."

She turns her back on me. I want it to be in anger. Anger has been my constant companion since watching our grandmother slain and our cottage burned down when we were eight years old. Since learning I couldn't be a Warder guard because Mors had to breed babies as a vocation. Since finding out I was a Brand and being separated from the one person who has been my constant, my home. Anger is easier to deal with than my own guilt. But my sister has always been adept at swallowing her emotions, never letting them command her. She's the better version of me; the version I should strive to become.

"O? Please."

"It's illogical," is her first response, as if she's reading a theory of healing in one of her Old-World manuscripts, or questioning the methods of apothek Fenderhilde in the Isfalk archives. "This prophecy, the very idea that anyone could cure through some kind of sixth sense, rather than skill and learning – it's childish, nothing more than superstitious wishfulness in the face of sickness and death."

My sister: the philosopher, the academic. Of course, this would be her reaction. For Osha, empirical evidence is everything when studying disease, its symptoms and cures. But I've felt the skill. It's *primed* in me now when I'm near animals, just as the Blood-wife said it would be the more I became aware of it. And I know Osha has a version of this gift in her too.

"Crackpot prophecies aside, O, I've seen you when you treat patients. The way you fall still, as if everything around you quietens and grows far away. All your other faculties joining together to become this new sense, honed to your subject. At least, that's how it is when I hunt. You feel it too, don't you?" She shakes her head, but I must be chipping away at her because there's a note of desperation in the movement. "Why won't you admit it?" I reach across and take her hand. She looks down as our skin touches. "You feel that? The spark, the warmth? It isn't just the closeness of twins we feel. It's an instinctive connection. Like calling to like. I felt it with the Blood-wife. I felt it with Mother Iness in Isfalk. And I felt it with Saqira just now. It's because we have this skill... because I believe what the Blood-wife told me is true. We're Sways."

"Do you know how insane you sound right now?" Osha says breathlessly. She tugs her fingers from my grasp. "Do you realise how much you're scaring me with such nonsense?"

"You're scared because you know it's not nonsense. I was scared, too. I was in denial for so long. It's something we can't explain. Something we don't know how to control. Of course that's scary! But the wrangler said there are people here in Reis who might be able to teach us more about our skills and how to wield them properly."

She stops pacing, gnawing on the inside of her lip, vulnerable and uncertain.

"O?" I say gently, and her face crumples. She can't lie anymore. "Tell me you feel it. Tell me I'm not going mad, Osha."

Blinking tears from her eyes, she takes a shaky breath. "Even if it is true, even if we have this skill, the idea I'm some kind of Chosen One is absurd!"

I scoff in agreement, but relief floods me at the line she's tentatively crossed. "Come now, don't put yourself down – you'd make a great Elita," I joke, trying to lift the worry etched on her face. "I mean, healing aside, you're a born diplomat... you charm everyone you meet and turn the most fearsome Waster chief into a lovelorn pup." She shakes her head to stop me. "You ask servants for their names, for Mother's sake. Even when I deserve to be slapped, you can't bring yourself to do it. I think the Reis would be lucky to have you." I grin at her, but the hand resting at her belly is sobering.

"Osha," I say, serious now, "if they do decide you're this *Elita*, and they could teach you to grow the sway inside you... do great things with it... would it be what you want?"

"Hypothetically?" she asks, which makes me smile. She may have admitted she feels the sway inside her, but she's not buying into the rest of it yet.

"Hypothetically," I answer.

She lowers herself to perch on the edge of the divan, smoothing her forehead under her fingers. "How can I say yes when we understand so little about what it means? But how can I say no when it might change the lives of so many Brands for the better?" Healing the Branded has always been Osha's calling, the reason she spent her nights in the Isfalk archives poring over forbidden texts for cures and remedies. She swallows, studying the markings on my scalp with a worried look in her eyes. Her palm has returned to her stomach again, and I can guess the direction of her thoughts.

"You're thinking about the baby – that it might be branded, like me." Only children of two Pure parents are guaranteed to be born stronger and resistant to disease. That's why Isfalk controlled the pairings of Mor women. But both Haus and Orlath are Brands. "You know the child is as likely to be born Branded as Pure." I tell her. "But that isn't a death sentence."

She stiffens. I knew she'd baulk at any mention of the baby or its father, but I wish she'd confide in me, let me offer comfort about her fears.

"Don't make this all about me, Nara. You brought us here because you want answers about our parents and where these come from." She slips the pendant from her neck and looks towards my matching one. "You say *I'm* obsessive with my research and my herbs, but the mystery of these is everything to you, isn't it? It always has been."

I rub at my jaw, guilty as charged. Her medallion glints in the sunlight from the terrace, the glyphs around its spiral winking cryptically. "Doesn't it bother you that we don't know our own history, or who we are?" I ask. "We're like a story with no beginning."

"Does it matter? Surely, it's who we might be in the future that counts? I don't want to go backwards, Nara." She takes my hand, her grip adamant. "I don't want the kind of life we had in the Isfalk citadel. And if this," she raises our laced fingers, the energy tingling between our joined skin, "if this means I have a chance to cure the Branded, to create some better kind of world in the future, then, yes, I'll open my mind to it."

Her words surprise me. Something has slotted into place for her. For the first time I suspect it isn't me who has convinced her to risk hope over common sense: it's the child she carries.

"Tell me how it feels when you heal people," I say. We've never spoken of it before, and now I need the comfort of her confidence, of knowing she's like me, that she feels her sway as I do.

She mulls it over, taking her time. "Sometimes, when I touch the sick, it's as if I can smell, or even *hear* the ailment in them. It was like that with Haus and his headaches. I sensed his pain at the first touch..." Her cheeks flush at the mention of the chief, but she shakes it off with a toss of her head. "But, Nara, when I treated the Branded in the Settlement, I wasn't healing them with magic." Her voice turns cynical. "I'm no spae-wife. It took diagnosis and prescription, years of learning herb lore and physik. I'll always have faith, first and foremost, in what I know and can see." She pauses and I hold my breath. "But if this skill – this *sway*, as you call it – can help me improve the lives of the Branded and fight diseases I have no cure for, then I'll trust Nixim. I'll learn to wield it, if he thinks I can."

"And the Seer reading?"

She nods. "Whatever it takes."

I lift a hand to her cheek, marvelling at my sister's pure, unmarked skin, the flush across her high cheekbones, her full lips. Yet it pales compared to the beauty I see within her now.

How are we so different? How can she consider with such measured reason and generosity something that goes against her very nature, her values. "I've never had your patience, O. I wish I did."

She shakes her head. "You have your own strengths, Nara. Vitality… courage…" She lifts a finger to trace the scar at my neck – a gift from Iness's ghosthawk. "Your determination is like a fire burning inside you. People can't help but be drawn to it." Her eyes are full of love, and a trust that's almost unbearable. I'm too raw to handle it right now, too uncertain of myself, of the wrangler and Reis, and what I've walked us into.

"Burning determination, huh? I think you mean *stubborn*?" I finish off my glass. "Although I am pretty determined to spend the afternoon with this." I reach for the bottle.

Osha sighs. "At some point you have to let him explain, Nara."

"Who?"

"You know who," she says, tired of my games.

"The wrangler has nothing to explain. I've got bigger things to worry about than him."

She turns my chin, so I'm forced to hold her gaze. "Having feelings is not a weakness, Narkat. It's our vulnerability that keeps us human."

"Yeah, well, vulnerability isn't going to do you any favours in a fight," I say, jerking away.

Brim taught me that. He'd pick on my weaknesses whenever we trained back in the Fornwood. But it was the wrangler who first pointed out how to correct them, how to play to my strengths and keep my defences up – the very tactic I failed to use in my relationship with him.

"You should know something about Nixim," Osha says, not ready to drop the subject of my feelings. "When you were unconscious aboard the ship, he didn't leave your side for three days. I had to bring him food and remind him to eat. He barely let anyone come near you."

"Well, he had no right."

"No right?" Osha frowns in reprimand. "No right to care about you?"

"Not when he's promised himself to someone else, no."

"Oh, his betrothal," she drawls. "I guess that's as good an excuse as any to push him away."

"He made a vow to another woman, O, and he lied about it."

"Did he lie? Or did he simply not tell you?"

"It's the same thing!" I snap, but heat floods my chest remembering how the wrangler had broken our kiss, trying to talk, while I was only interested in undressing him.

"For Mother's sake, Nara, he couldn't have been more than fourteen years old when he came to Isfalk. If he was already betrothed at that age, surely it was his parents' doing – some obligation or a longstanding alliance between families. Are you saying he should uphold their promise now, after years of being away? That he should follow duty and expectation? You were so good at that yourself, weren't you, back in the Settlement?"

I groan in frustration. I've no hope of defending myself against Osha's logic, so I pivot for the attack. "Listen to you, sis. The expert on love."

"What's that supposed to mean?"

"You preach to me, but you haven't so much as looked at Haus since we ran from the Cooler in Orlathston. He's desperate for a gentle word, any kind of explanation, but you offer him nothing. Are you going to let *him* have the right to love *you*?"

"That's not the same," she shoots back.

"Isn't it?" I glance at the hand covering her stomach. She scowls and snatches it away. "You still haven't told him?"

I try to make her hold my eye, but she won't. "The child you carry might be his, but you push him away. You won't give him the chance to decide for himself if he wants–"

Osha rises suddenly, walking onto the terrace and putting an abrupt end to the conversation. I love my sister, but sometimes she manages to outrank even me in her pig headedness.

We don't speak again until the sun has set. It's Takia who reunites us. "Saman," she announces, standing over the divan where I'm sprawled. I'm still in my hunting suedes, stewing in resentment and another bottle of the excellent Reis wine. "Come." Takia's lips stretch in distaste at my grubby gilet and blood-stained fingernails. "You wash now." It isn't an invitation. She's evidently been assigned to us because she knows some basic Isfalki, but I suspect her tone would be brusque in any language. I give her a mocking salute, but when I rise, the room spins. I manage to recover my footing before Osha emerges from her bedroom.

We follow Takia through chambers we haven't yet explored, to a set of double doors. She throws them open with a flourish, and I stand blinking in the reflections of sunset on a long rectangular pool of water. A small domed roof sits above it, but on three sides the keyhole arches of a terrace are open to the pink sky, the noise of the city somewhere far below. "Saman," Takia declares proudly.

"Mother's love!" Osha sighs. "That's a sight for sore eyes."

"And a sore arse. Why the poxes didn't she show us this last night?"

Osha covers my ungratefulness with a smile as Takia hands us towels. The truth was that, after arriving, we'd had a quick wash to remove the sand and dust, wanting only a little food and a place to lie down. Now, I almost fall over myself in the hurry to kick off my stinking boots and leathers. The water smells spicy and inviting, and when I jump in, the warmth of the day's heat feels like an embrace. I surface, thinking of the Moon Pools, another world, another lifetime away, and yet still under these same stars that are beginning to dawn in the arches of darkening sky.

Osha gets into the pool slowly. Without her clothes, I can see how her breasts have swollen in the weeks we've been journeying, and her tummy has begun to tighten like a drum. She cups it instinctively as she lowers into the water, and I'm reminded of my vision at the Blood-wife's cottage – the image of a young Mother Iness crossing the desert, hand protecting her belly in just that manner. When Osha catches me looking, she draws her palm away. "Don't," she says. "I don't want to talk about it. Can't we simply enjoy this bath and pretend for a little while that we're… I don't know," she gazes around the saman, "…maybe that we're southern princesses and this is the night of our return home after a long journey across the sea." Games of make believe were often the way we'd mend childhood quarrels. It's her version of an apology.

I offer her one of my own. "I can pretend, O," I tell her gently. "You know how good I am at pretending."

Kha Nixim

Takia comes into the saman three times, trying to entice me out of the water and into the silk robes she's laid out for the evening's entertainment.

Osha has already dressed for the homecoming feast, but I refuse to be hustled and cajoled, especially to an event celebrating the wrangler. In the end, Osha tires of waiting for me and descends to the party with Haus and Brim, on a promise that Takia will sober me up and deliver me herself. Takia can promise all she likes, but while the wine lasts, I have no intention of budging. I'm as wrinkled as a crone and not sure whether I'm drowning my sorrows or closer to actually drowning, but when she holds up the shimmering green dress like some kind of bribe, I can't help snorting. There's even embroidered slippers to match. "Forget it, Takia," I tell her, indicating my scars and bruises. "Even you can't turn *this* into a silk purse."

"Perhaps not... but she's paid to try." I nearly choke on a mouthful of wine. Nixim stands at the edge of the saman, arms crossed. I sink to my neck in the water. "Oh please, Scourge. I have seen it all before. Bashful doesn't look good on you."

"Well, entitlement doesn't look good on you, Wrangler."

It's a lie. He's changed from his hunting leathers into evening clothes that suit him so well, they must have been specially made. I imagine an attentive seamstress selecting the bronze linen of his tunic to match the inner ring of his eyes. Perhaps it was Hira herself who chose it. His loose pants are gathered at the ankles, edged in thread that glimmers in the light of the torches, but his tanned feet are bare, the skin so rich against the tiles I have the urge to touch it. Poxes, why did I drink so much?

"Come on," he says, "you're clean enough, now, don't you think?"

"But not quite drunk enough." A ridiculous snigger escapes me. I fumble for the bottle at the edge of the pool, but he takes it before I can get there. Gold flashes on his finger.

"Well, well… is that your *betrothal* ring?"

He sighs, pulls up the legs of his pants and sits on the step of the saman, ankle-deep in the water. "It's a family heirloom, since you're asking. I'm kind of obliged to wear it now I'm home." He takes off the ring and passes it to me. The engraving is of the Gildensfir, the spiral the Reis call the Halqa. He told me it stands for the endless cycle of life, death and rebirth – the symbol of balance, the symbol on my pendant.

"How quaint! The icon of your little cult." I toss the ring back to him, then dunk myself under the water, trying to clear my head and find the edge of my previous anger. The wine may have eased the pain, but I need to keep a hold of my wits around him. When I surface, he's still watching, eyes languid. We're silent for a while, perhaps each hoping the other will speak first.

"Nara–" he begins.

"Are you some kind of Reis prince, Wrangler?" Suddenly I want this on my terms and I want answers.

"Not a prince, no." He hesitates. "My father is the Kham-elect of Cha Shaheer."

"So, that means he rules here?"

"An elected ruler, yes."

"And Hira? She's the princess, I suppose."

"She's the daughter of his Khadib – his chief advisor." He fidgets, sitting on his hands as if he doesn't know what to do without reins or a weapon in them. It makes the muscles of his chest flex through the opening of his shirt. I look away.

"I tried to tell you aboard the *Na'quat*. My betrothal to Hira was arranged long ago. We grew up together... our parents thought it suitable and... well, I was too young to know any better." His tone turns impatient. "If you'd come down to the feast, you might actually learn something instead of sulking here making assumptions, as usual. My father wants to meet you."

He waits, but I don't move, only shivering a little now in the cooling night.

"Feeling a bit chilly there, Scourge? I should have told you, evenings in the desert get *very* cold." He cocks his eyebrow, but he doesn't need to: the irony is blatant. Back in the Waster camp, it was me holding him to ransom in the icy river. Now I'm the one freezing my tits off.

"Stop calling me Scourge. It's not my name. And I'm not getting trussed up for your fancy homecoming feast only to be gawked at and judged and found wanting."

"Oh, but I think you are," he says, still smiling. "Takia takes her orders very seriously. She's going to sober you up and turn you into such a silk purse, it'll be the lady Hira looking like a sow's ear by comparison."

"Dream on, Wrangler," I scoff. "They're your fantasies, not mine."

I turn my back on him and swim to the other end of the pool, only to hear a sudden splash. He's in the water, fully clothed and wading towards me.

"You're coming down to the feast, Scourge," he says, tone ominous, "and you're going to charm everyone."

"I don't have a charming bone in my body and you know it."

"Copy your sister, then. She's doing an excellent job already." He backs me into the side of the pool, hands on the lip of the tiles, arms boxing me in.

"You've given them Osha. I'm not going to make any difference."

I shiver as he steps closer, hips pressed to mine. He lifts the back of my thigh so I feel the heat of him between my legs. "You'll make a difference to me," he murmurs. Half of me wants to knee him in the jewels, the other half wants to wrap myself around him until he's lost in me again the way he was aboard the ship.

"I'm so sorry," he says, warm breath skimming my neck. "I tried to tell you about Hira, but you were so... distracting. Can you forgive me, *Na'quat?*" And that name in his mouth, *my* name, the very name he gave his ship, takes me straight back to the captain's cabin and everything we did to each other that last night together. It almost ruins me.

Almost.

"Nixim," I whisper in his ear. "You think getting between my legs empties my head? Have a little *respect.* And don't try to play me with my own moves." I throw him off, drawing back my palm, but he catches my wrist. Wrenching free makes me lose my footing, and he seizes my hips. "Get your hands off me, Wra–" Before I can finish, he's jacked me out of the water, delivering me straight into Takia's arms. She traps me in a towel, her brawny embrace tight as swaddling as she bundles me out of the saman.

"You filthy... lying... son-of-a-trull!" I yell at the wrangler as he hurries past in a trail of dripping linen. He has the audacity to mime a kiss at me before he slips through the door.

In the dressing room, Takia releases my arms and looks me over distastefully. "Does that bastard spend all his free time thinking up ways to humiliate me?" In response, she pushes me to a sitting position on the bed and begins to towel my scalp so roughly it hurts. I shrug her off and she grumbles something in Reis. "What's *your* problem anyway?" I mutter, but the flexing hocks of her forearms make me wonder whether it's wise to get on her bad side.

"Stupid," she says through gritted teeth. "Very stupid girl."

I pull in my chin. "*Me*?" Obviously brandservants are free to speak their minds in the Shadow City. "Why am *I* the stupid one?"

"Every girl in Cha Shaheer dream of Nixim Ni Azzadur. Yet he turns his face to *you*?" She assesses my half-naked body as if I'm the runt of an already deformed litter. "Stupid, ugly *and* blind," she concludes, sucking her teeth.

Mother's tits, is the whole of the Shadow City in love with the fecking wrangler?

The Feast

I'd imagined the feast would be held in the main keep of Cha Shaheer, or in the great domed temple we'd seen lighting our way across the sands when we'd arrived. But Takia leads me back to the desert plain.

She's done a decent job of straightening me out, making me drink several cups of dark, syrupy tea that delivered a brutal jolt of clarity... and remorse. I follow her without complaint until we reach the camp of tents and gers. It has doubled in size since the previous evening. Dozens of fires burn across the plain, the smell of spitted meat mingling with smoke. Takia weaves a path between groups of people who recline on rugs and cushions, too busy making merry to give much attention to the roving dancers and musicians, let alone the wiry little foreigner passing in the shadows. It feels like the whole of Reis has gathered here, one great nomadic clan celebrating life and freedom under the vast swathe of stars – so different from the mood of the Isfalk Settlement, with its confines and restrictions. Hira was right: it is a sight to behold... and then I remind myself why they're all here. The vast weight of what the Reis expect of Osha returns to roost with ominous clarity. I shiver in the cold night air, wishing Takia's tea hadn't been quite as sobering.

She stops in front of an open-sided tent, easily the size of Isfalk's market square. It's fringed in a pelmet of golden tassels and laboriously embroidered panels. I take a deep breath –

this must be where the leaders and elite of Cha Shaheer are gathered. Without ceremony, Takia shoves me under the canvas, then hurries off to join the festivities. Who can blame her? If I had to forfeit a feast to play nursemaid to a mouthy drunk, I'd dump me too.

Inside the tent, guests lounge on bolsters set over a patchwork of carpets. Low tables are spread with more dishes than I've ever seen before, filling the air with tang and spice. A group of dancers jostles past me, clad in what look like shimmering underthings, showing off the training in their toned limbs. Some are Brands, but a few have no visible marks at all on their faces or hands. They might even be Pureblood. But Pures as mere entertainers? I scan the guests again. Many of the men are wearing sleeveless linen tunics, open at the chest, and the women scantily draped gowns revealing plenty of skin. All look and behave like Pures, but a good many of them display their brandings for all to see, as if they are little more than decoration. Again, I'm struck by how healthy these Brands seem, how fit and strong. They're nothing like the small, sickly inhabitants of the Isfalk village.

I try to keep a low profile as I search for Osha, but the further I enter, the more people are crammed in around me. I can't see Haus or Brim, and with everyone almost horizontal, even the Maw's towering size is lost to the crowd. Picking my way between noisy groups, I begin to notice heads craning, my own gaze returned with even greater scrutiny by some of the revellers. *I'm* the oddity at this gathering, I soon realise – the girl with the cropped red hair, the foreigner who has refused fine silks and slippers in favour of leather pants, a cotton shirt and a fur-lined waistcoat to keep out the chill of the desert. Takia tried every trick in the book to get me into those silks, taking great delight in showing me my own clothes soaking in a tub of dirty water. When I demanded she replace them with something similar, I was treated to the full brunt of her outrage – an interesting translation of Reis profanities involving goats and my mother. I got the gist, but it didn't make me change my mind about the dress.

"I refuse to get wrapped up and bejewelled like an offering," I told Takia. "I'll play Nixim's game, but it'll be by my rules."

To give the woman her due, she did very well sourcing my current outfit at such short notice. Although, under the scrutiny of such an elegant audience, I realise now just how much I stand out – something feral, something of Orlath's fighting pits lingering about me still, no matter how long I soak in the saman.

I lift my chin and square my shoulders, searching for Haus or Brim, desperate for back-up. When I spot them, I find even they have taken advantage of the sleeveless tunics and loose linen pants of the Reis. Traitors.

"Where in Mother's name have you been?" Brim says, taking my elbow and steering me to a quiet space. "This feast is unbearable. When I'm not being interrogated by Reis leaders about Isfalki politics, I'm being seduced by their bored daughters. And half of them are–"

He stops short.

"Brands?" I offer.

His eyes flick to my scalp and he frowns. "I'm sorry, Nara, I didn't mean to–"

I shake my head to stop him. He's my oldest friend and he's known me as a Mor for most of our childhood. He's still getting used to me being a Brand. Poxes, so am I. "It's just that... well," Brim flusters, "it's still a surprise to be approached by branded women in that way... to see them behaving like Pures." My stomach sinks, but how can I be offended when I'm just as shocked as he is to witness Brands mingling so freely with the immune?

"You can hardly blame them for flirting," I say, running my eyes over his open-necked tunic of sky-blue linen. The pale contours of his chest are visible beneath. "You look pretty fine as a Reis." He pulls up the baggy pants awkwardly and rolls his eyes, but his cheeks shine at the compliment.

"And you look–" He stops, apparently reconsidering what he was about to say. "The same as ever." He clears his throat. "Maybe a bit cleaner?" That's what I love about Brim – his honesty. "Come on," he says, nodding for me to follow. "Osha's been asking for you."

We weave our way to the centre of the ger, where a fire smokes up through an opening in the canvas. I soon spot a tumble of red hair flaming against golden silk. Osha is resplendent amongst a group of Reis, Azza and the wrangler among them.

When she spots me, my sister glares. I'm late. Again. I mouth her an apology, but my gaze is already slipping to the wrangler. He's changed into jet-black linens, his skin glossy in the heat of the fire. For a brief second, my core wrings at the memory of it, smooth and brown under my fingertips, his smell of leather and steel and wind off the ocean. Before he can look up and catch me staring, Hira leans into him with a bright laugh, and the moment is gone. I should thank her for giving me that slap of reality.

Hira rises and the music stops, the entertainment clearly hanging on her command. The dancers clear the performance space and she steps into it, utterly confident, drinking in the admiring looks of the audience like a bloom in water. She milks the silence for a moment, before a languid melody starts up on a reeded pipe. A few bars later, a drummer begins a slow, ominous beat.

Hira circles her hips. Her silk pants, as if designed with this in mind, sit low on her waist, and her cropped chemise is backless and sleeveless, tied at the neck and shimmering like mercury over her breasts. The fabric seems to draw all points of light to it as she moves, making everything else a little duller in comparison. Her platinum hair is uncovered now and upswept to show off as much of her naked skin as possible, smooth and seductive as the dunes of the Storm Sands. In Isfalk, only a woman with a flawless complexion would reveal so much skin or call such attention to herself. Only someone who was Pure. Not that I'd imagined Hira would be branded – her manner is too similar to the most entitled Mor back in the Settlement. But with Reis surprising me at every turn – Pures and Brands rubbing shoulders so freely before my eyes – I'd relished the idea my intuition might be wrong, that Hira and I were equal in that one regard: our marred skin, our tainted blood. Evidently, we're not.

The music grows steadily faster and Hira spins, keeping time, each turn of her head coming back to where the wrangler sits, unable to take his eyes off her – the shape of her bare arms, the flat plane of her stomach with its winking jewels, the silks that billow around her legs as if she's surfacing from a pool of moonlight. No one can keep their eyes off her, not even me. She's spellbinding – I'm not liar enough to deny it. Just as the drumming reaches fever pitch, with Hira a vortex that sucks every hint of sexual desire her way, the music stops abruptly. She holds her final pose like a professional, her only movements the rise and fall of her diaphragm, a trickle of sweat snaking from her forehead, a loose tendril of hair swaying at her cheek like a finger crooked towards Nixim.

The tent erupts in applause and Hira's face lights with pleasure. She reaches for the wrangler, pulling him up by the wrist, and he stands beside her, nodding with good nature, though his eyes flick over the audience like he's searching for someone. Hira must notice it, too, for she tiptoes to press her lips to his, demanding his attention. A second of awkwardness stiffens the wrangler's body, before he recovers and a murmur of approving *ahhs* goes up from the gathering. What a couple they make, all bronzed skin and toned limbs, his dark curls the complement to her pale ones, as natural – as *inevitable* – as night and day. If learning of their betrothal was a stab in the guts, bearing witness to their popularity is a twist of the knife.

When Nixim sweeps the crowd again, I duck behind a tent joist, aiming to leave, but the wrangler's voice stops me. "Father," he announces, "there's someone I'd like you to meet. Allow me to present Nara Fornwood." The large man seated next to Azza stares directly at me. His dark curls are limned with the ash of age and gathered in gold rings behind his ears. When he smiles, he shows broad white teeth and a mole that dances in his cheek, as familiar as the back of my hand. I'm looking at the wrangler thirty years from now.

Nixim is suddenly behind me, his palm on the small of my back. I nudge it away. "Nara, this is my father, Haxim Ni Haximdur, Kham-Elect of Cha Shaheer and the Seven Clans."

It's such a mouthful, I hardly know what to say.

Thankfully the Kham makes the first move. He touches one hand to his heart, the fingers of the other to his lips. "I have heard much about you, Nara Fornwood." His Isfalki is heavily accented, but his voice is deep and rich, and I understand now where Azza inherited hers. "My son tells me of your skill in swordplay, your courage and your... what is the Isfalki word... *charm*?" I dart a look at the wrangler. He keeps a straight face but those brown eyes glitter just like his father's. To my mortification, my cheeks flash hot.

"Charm isn't one of my greatest qualities, Kham," I say. "It isn't something I've been inclined to study."

"Along with punctuality, it seems," Hira mutters, loud enough for everyone to hear. She folds her legs elegantly beneath her, looking not at me but towards another woman in the party, as if seeking her approval. She is older than Hira, but her hair, worn in a coronet braid is the same colour and there's enough similarity in the shape of their faces for me to gather they're mother and daughter, despite the difference in their skin tones. For Hira's mother is as icy pale and blue-eyed as any Isfalki Mor. Her looks seem as misplaced here among the Reis as mine are and yet she behaves as if at home, an air of authority about her that is easily the match of the Kham's.

She surveys me, brows pulled together at my coarse clothes, the massacre of my hair, like I'm some insect that has blown into her wine. I hold my chin up as long as I can until, skin prickling with disquiet, I shift in my boots. When she finally speaks, it is to scold Hira. "Come now. Our guests have had an arduous journey here. Give them some allowances, daughter, before you start examining them and finding fault." Her eyes flick to the site of my branding and I get the impression she'd like more than anyone to examine me.

"Well spoken, Phibia," the Kham says, but she barely turns her head to him. If she is his chief advisor, then she's one who has no doubt of her influence.

"Tomorrow, Hira will take our visitors to relax at the Golden Saman," the woman announces. "Afterwards they can browse our markets." She pauses, then adds pointedly in my direction, "Some of them require new clothes."

The wrangler coughs in amusement. "With respect, Phibia Khadib, I'm not sure Nara would care to spend the day shopping." My blood throbs in my throat, furious he thinks he knows me so well... even if he is right.

"Is that so?" Phibia answers, mouth hardening at being corrected.

"I will take Nara Fornwood hunting again, if she prefers," Azza offers. "I believe she would rather have a bow in her hands than pore over silks in the suk." Poxes, what is it with these two, speaking on my behalf? I open my mouth, but think better of contradicting them. I'd rather brave another round in Orlath's fighting pits than risk having to spend the day with the wrangler's girlfriend.

"Is my daughter correct?" the Kham says, taking in my leathers and boots. "Would Nara Fornwood prefer to hunt for dinner than dress for it?"

I want to answer that Nara Fornwood is fecking tired of being spoken about in the third person. But I nod in agreement. Turning to his advisor, he says in a cajoling tone, "Let them explore Reis as they choose until they are settled." And to my surprise, he folds Phibia's fingers inside his own and brings them to his lips. It appears she's his right-hand woman in more ways than one.

"As you wish, Kham," Phibia replies.

Azza rises from her cushions to toss another log on the fire, and I can't help noticing the smug look she sends Phibia's way, as if she's scored a point in a game only they were playing. She brushes the log dust from her hands onto delicate silk pants.

"Really, Azza Ni Azzadur," the older woman says, "try to remember your place. We have people for such tasks." She lifts her chin to a brandservant who hurries over to fuss unnecessarily with the fire.

"How could I ever forget my place, Phibia Khadib, when you remind me of it at every opportunity?" Azza takes the jug the servant has set down and proceeds to top up the liquor in Phibia's cup, completing the service with a mocking bow. For a moment the air between the two women vibrates like a plucked string, and as Azza returns to prod at the fire, I see her throat working in a way that's all too familiar – she's swallowing back anger.

"Now, now," the Kham says, breaking the atmosphere, "this is a feast, is it not? Our guests should be shown how we celebrate here in Reis."

"Kham, forgive me, but might I speak?" Osha's is the last voice I'd expect to interrupt the Reis leader. "Your hospitality is very generous, and my sister and I are beholden to you." She fingers the hem of the golden sand scarves pooled in her lap, gaze running nervously over the gathering. "It might be best, however, if Nara doesn't mix too much with the crowds here. I hadn't expected such integration… That is, in Isfalk, we were sheltered behind walls and Nara has barely been exposed to sickness and contagion. She is a Brand, as you see."

"Osha!" I silence her, mortified that she would be so transparent now, of all times. She may be trying to protect me with all the goodness of sisterly love, but she's just made every single person in earshot turn and look for my branding. I might as well be wearing a sign saying *Runt*. Hira smirks into the fire. But my sister won't be distracted.

"I've read a good deal of Old World physik and the suggestion is that exposure to–"

"Osha Fornwood," the Kham interrupts in that rumbling voice, and it's as if the entire tent quietens to listen. "Your concern for your sister is as it should be. But do you think Cha Shaheer disease-ridden? Primitive? That we Reis are barely one pox away from the dust of the desert?" He raises a bushy eyebrow, as if he's been privy to the tales spun by gossips in the taverns of Isfalk. "Look around you. Are my people weak? Unhealthy? Suffering?"

Cheeks pink, Osha casts her eyes around the feast, to the dancing and laughter in the camp beyond. "No Kham," she concedes. "They seem quite the opposite, in fact. I'm merely taking precautions–"

"As I've told you, Father," the wrangler interrupts, "the healing arts are considered a kind of witchcraft in the north, so Brands avoid disease at all costs. Osha's worry for her sister is a natural result of that, since Nara is more susceptible to infection."

I've never heard him so rational, so formal. He's like a different person in front of his father.

"You brought her from the Orlathston Cooler, no?" the Kham scoffs. "The girl survives that pit of disease, and her sister worries about Cha Shaheer?" His laugh barrels around the tent and the Reis nearby respond in kind.

"You should know that Osha's a talented healer, Father," the wrangler says, changing tack. "She's never been able to practice freely in Isfalk. I thought she might like to spend a few days with our own apotheks, at liberty to study the body and its diseases. There is some time before..."

He trails off. Before what? Before they cast her to their Seers? Before they put her through her paces as a Sway? Before they control her life?

Osha's eyes widen, but not at what I'm imagining. "Is this true, Nixim? There are apotheks here who practice freely, out in the open?" She's taking the wrangler's bait as greedily as a starved snowjack. "And I'd be allowed to visit them?" The wrangler looks to his father, who consents with a tilt of his head. Osha grins, unable to disguise her enthusiasm. The thrill of discussing medical principles with other healers in broad daylight, instead of poring over manuscripts alone in the bowels of the Isfalk archives, is too much for my sister. "I can't tell you how much I'd like that, Nixim," she says, almost breathless with gratitude.

The wrangler cuts me a look. Does he think I'm a fool? That I can't see through his motives? Delighting my sister with the very thing she's longed for most in her life so that I'm indebted to him. Of course, her happiness makes me happy, but the fact that he's behind it riles me beyond words. "Nixim can give you a tour of our infirmaries, too," Azza tells Osha. "You will learn that our healers are able to treat many of the most common fevers and poxes left in the wake of the Brume virus. It is why the Branded live long and healthy lives here in Reis, just like the Pure." Her voice rings with pride, but her focus now falls on Phibia. "They aren't shunned for their blood or made to live in ghettos, as they are elsewhere in the Continent, and Cha Shaheer thrives because of it. That is my mother's legacy, is it not, Father?"

"Indeed," the Kham replies. "Indeed." But his attention has waned, distracted by a new platter of food.

Phibia shifts among her cushions, knuckles white inside her pale manta, as if trying to gather her patience with Azza.

"Infirmaries? I'd like to see those very much," Osha says. "I wasn't expecting to find such freedoms in Reis, let alone be given the indulgence to explore them." She says it with her usual grace and charm, and I'm sure she's instantly back in the Kham's favour. I've always known I could learn a trick or two from Osha's diplomacy, but this time I'm left worrying that my sister has been swept away in the tide of her obsessions. Why is no one talking of the real reason we're here? The more the topic of the Seer reading is avoided, the more ominous it feels. I think of Saqira's brief touch. If a flutter of hands had such a draining effect on me, what toll will a proper reading take on Osha, especially in her condition.

"It is settled, then," the Kham says. "Nixim and Azza will show each sister what they most wish to see in Cha Shaheer." He rises and stretches a palm across his ample belly. "And now *I* wish to see more roast turcas... then play a little bone dice."

As he finishes, Phibia grabs his hand, speaking to him in Reis. It is Azza who responds, the spittle of her vehemence illuminated in the firelight. The two women glare at each other. Phibia draws breath to retort, but the Kham physically intercepts the argument, his answer terse and final. Whatever his decree, it causes a complacent smile to spread across the Khadib's lips. Azza drops her eyes to the flames, stony-faced, chastened, but not apparently surprised. "Osha Fornwood will be read when the full moon gives greatest clarity to our Seers," the Kham says. His Isfalki is for our benefit, but his tone is impatient, as if at an argument he's already tired of moderating. "I have made my decision, daughter, and you will accept it." The group seems to shift among the cushions as everyone recovers their bearing.

"I suggest you rest," Phibia tells Osha smoothly. "Seer readings can be taxing, but less so if you approach them of your own free will and with an open heart." She offers a smile, as if she hasn't just made a veiled threat, as if she hasn't inferred Osha will be read whether she likes it or not. It makes the skin of my scalp tighten, my spine prickle with unease.

The Kham departs for one of the campfires outside, where meat is being carved from a spit. He seems unperturbed by the discord between his daughter and his chief advisor, taking the opportunity to wind his way between the crowd, chatting with a cook, joking with serving boys. Their beaming faces reflect that he's a popular leader, not just respected but beloved. Phibia trails behind him, but she's far more imperious and less natural with those around her. She engages only with certain Reis of her choosing, and there's a pattern among them – they all appear to be well-dressed, elegant, and Pure.

Azza mutters into the fire, something that sounds very much like one of Takia's colourful curses.

I lean towards her. "So, the Khadib – not your favourite person, I take it?"

Azza draws a wary breath. "Phibia has been in our lives since I was a child. She has taught me many things." I shift awkwardly, thinking I've read the signs wrong and have let my mouth run ahead of me as usual, but Azza continues. "Phibia has always been... how do you Isfalki put it? *The snow in my shoe?*"

I chuckle, surprised. "Only a real Isfalki would say that. Where did you learn–" but I break off, following the line of Azza's sight to Phibia, her white hair, her milky skin almost luminous as she moves through the crowd. Her Isfalki wasn't just good, I realise now. It was fluent. Unaccented. "Wait. Phibia is from the Isfalk Settlement?"

"Did you not recognise one of your own?" Azza says.

"I wasn't expecting to find another Isfalki this far south. How the pox did she end up here?"

"The same way you did, I believe. Through the Wastelands and down the desert coast."

"She was *traded*?"

"I cannot tell you. She rarely speaks of her past." Azza scoffs softly. "Phibia prefers to work on the future."

"What does that mean?" I ask, looking again towards her father and his advisor.

"Forget it," Azza mutters.

I want to ask her more, but she gazes into the flames with such sadness in her eyes, I don't have the heart to press her further, however much she's provoked me today.

A few moments later, Azza is on her feet. "Come, Nara Fornwood," she declares, her tone all determination and challenge. "A Reis homecoming feast is no time to be sober."

"Be careful, Az," the wrangler warns as she takes two cups from a tray. "You don't know the trouble this one can cause when she's drunk." He rubs a finger along the scar still visible above his eyebrow, a gift from the bar brawl at *Helgah's* all those months ago.

"That fight wasn't my fault," I toss his way. "And no one asked you to get involved that night."

"You wouldn't remember what you did or didn't ask me to do that night, Little Scourge," he says with a filthy wink. Cheeks flaming, I snatch the drink from Azza and slug it back with a wince. Right now, I need more alcohol like the wrangler needs more arrogance.

"You're going to regret that," he sing-songs as his sister refills my glass. He could predict the manner of my own death, and I swear by Elixion's cock, I'd run towards it just to spite him.

"Here's to regrets then, Wrangler." I raise my glass to him. "These days I've got so many I've lost count."

And now it's him wincing as I knock back the shot.

A Lesson in Prejudice

I wake with a jolt, head pounding like I've done a bout in the Cooler. Light streams through the balcony drapes making me squint as I shuffle tentatively about the apartments.

Osha is nowhere to be seen, her bed empty. Slowly the events of the homecoming feast return to me, and I remember the wrangler's promise to take her on a tour of the infirmaries. Fec's sake, how much of that Reis wine did I sink last night? Didn't seem to keep the dreams at bay, though – images of Osha's sway gathering like a terrible storm while mine scatters as sand before it. The clammy sweat on my skin this morning isn't only from my hangover.

Takia appears with breakfast – which she tells me is lunch – but I can't swallow a bite. I end up pushing it aside, opting for a plunge in the saman instead – a vain attempt to shock myself sober. The heat of the day has already settled in the water and I can hear the bustle of the city rising up from the streets below – the call of stallholders in the markets, the tap of a stonemason's chisel, the teasing of children at play.

I wrap myself in a robe and perch in one of the pool's arched windows, my head jangling.

"Hell's poxes!" a voice carries over the wall of the saman. I lean over the casement and peer down. Immediately below is a small amphitheatre I hadn't noticed before – a patchy ring of sand surrounded by a half-circle of tiered seats, their stone rendered smooth from centuries of sun, wind, and human touch. In the centre, Brim kicks up dust, dodging an opponent who lunges at him with a staff.

"Why so slow on your feet, Captain?" Azza taunts, landing a smart thwack across his bicep. Brim's torso is bare and glistening with sweat – they've been training for some time already. "Perhaps you are thinking too hard before you strike. Or else you drank too much last night?"

Brim bristles and I know it's more at the criticism than the hit. His mouth sets with purpose as he stalks towards her. "To be fair, you have the home advantage, Mor Azza. I'm not used to this heat. But it wouldn't be good manners to thrash my host in our first training session, would it?"

She laughs her husky laugh, but I can tell she's already gearing up for the offensive. I watch, fascinated, as she spins, footwork a practised dance, swinging the stave firm and fast into Brim's guts before he can dodge or block. He bends double. It takes little more than the shove of her boot to see him sprawled in the sand. Fecs alive, the wrangler had said she was good. I hadn't quite imagined she was *that* good. "You should know, I am not one of your precious *Mor*, Captain Oskarsson," Azza says, crouching over him. "You can dispense with the chivalry." She offers him a hand, and the coiled branding peeks from her cuff. Brim must see it too, for he draws back his chin in surprise. Azza drops her arm, disconcerted, and Brim seizes her distraction to swipe at her ankle with his stave. She loses her footing, toppling backwards onto her arse beside him.

"And you should know, Azza Ni Azzadur, that I'm no longer an Isfalki Captain," he tosses at her. "Don't assume I'll play fair."

Brim rises and brushes off his pants, grinning as he extends his own hand now. I remember him doing the same to me when we trained back in the Fornwood, not so long ago... a lifetime ago. So much has changed since then. The sight of him now, shed of his Warder uniform, sweat-slicked and covered in sand, makes possibility unfurl inside me like a new leaf.

Could things be different between us here in Reis? Could he look beyond my branding and love me for who I am below the skin? I remember bathing with him at the Moon Pools, the way he'd gaze at me through the sulphurous mist, and I feel that familiar longing in my throat, not easily forgotten. Now, the sight of another woman's hand in his stings like sweat in an open wound.

"Nara!" he calls up, spotting me on the balcony. "Finally back in the land of the living."

"Only just," I say.

"You look like the last goat in the suk," Azza observes. I'm guessing it's a Reis insult. The last animals left at market are usually sick or runts.

"Trull's tits, woman, how can you train after what I saw you drink last night?"

She scoffs. "That, Nara Fornwood, was barely a nightcap. We Reis suckle on ryki with our mother's milk. Or did they not tell you about that in the Isfalki taverns?" I cut her a look. Baiting definitely runs in her family. I don't contradict her, though. I'm beginning to realise they talked only shit in the Isfalki taverns.

"You still taking me hunting or what?" I ask.

She squints up at the high sun as if to emphasise my tardiness. "Get dressed and eat something. Dusk in the Kyder is not as easy as dawn for our sport, but I have heard that Nara Fornwood likes a challenge?"

I don't answer. I get the impression Reis is going to be nothing but a challenge.

We set off on foot in the late afternoon, Azza leading us along the suk road towards the gorge – the southern boundary of the Shadow City. Brim and the Maw come with us, but Azza tells me Haus is riding out with her brother to camp overnight with some of the Reis clans.

I'm pleased at this development. Haus needs time away from Osha as much as I need it from the wrangler. Punch-drunk from my sister's rebuffs, I'd found the Ringer champion tending his wounds outside our quarters, still game to take another round of cold-shouldering on Osha's return from the infirmaries. "What you need, Chief, is to hold your own reins for a bit," I told him. The innuendo wasn't lost on him, for he blinked those pale lashes at me. "Go. Get lost for the night. If I know my sister, she'll worry so much about where you've gone, the relief when you get back might just crack her."

Shadows lengthen as we pass the suk and all manner of Reis cross our path on their way home for the evening – stallholders with unsold wares, goatherds and horse-wranglers heading back to grazing land, hawkers closing up the food carts that line the route. A gang of small boys tail the spectacle of the Maw, pointing at the span of his hands and measuring his boot prints in the dust. But when we pass a vendor selling sweetmeats, they change tack, assailing Brim in Reis and tugging him to the stall by the hem of his jerkin. He looks to Azza for help.

"They want you to buy them kurcha," she says. "How easily you turn from predator to prey on the streets of Reis, Captain Oskarsson. Clearly, they thought you the weakest target." He makes a face at her and she laughs, tossing coins to the boys who instantly release Brim. This growing rapport between him and Azza makes my throat tight. I swallow, distracting myself with the colour and noise all around us.

Cha Shaheer is so full of life, so chaotic and vibrant, it makes Isfalk seem no more than a cold and prudish outpost tacked onto the frozen reaches of the Continent. Passing the marketplace, Brands and Pures walking side-by-side, it strikes me again that this is what the Old World might have been like, how it might have sounded and smelled. All this industry and abundance, all this freedom taken for granted as people went about their business, unhampered by the segregation and restrictions of their skin, of their blood. I take a deep breath. If

I couldn't hear and smell and feel the energy of Cha Shaheer pulsing all around me, I'd imagine I'd dreamt it up in my sleep.

"Nara, try this," Brim says, offering up the sugary pastry Azza has bought him. "It's truly incredible."

I take a bite. He's right – it's sweet and rich. The Isfalki would trade their own mothers for something so indulgent. But I frown at him. "Mmm, not sure about that. Let me have another taste–" I clamp onto his wrist as he tries to snatch his hand away, finishing what's left of the pastry in one greedy mouthful.

Brim winces. "Cock's poxes! You little…"

Azza is watching us, curious. "Back in Isfalk," Brim explains, "whenever we cut school to go hunting in the Fornwood, I'd steal a couple of pies or some cobs from my family's kitchens. Nara always claimed her share tasted off or was stale, and asked for a taste of mine to compare. Of course, I'd oblige and… well, you just witnessed the trick for yourself. I rode home hungry most of the time."

I shake my head at him. "You're the idiot, falling for it over and over again!"

"Yeah. Stupid, huh?"

Azza is watching him with those shrewd eyes. "Perhaps it was not the trick you fell for, Captain?"

"Ah now, Azza Ni Azzadur, don't give me away," Brim says, sheepishly.

"Not I," Azza replies. "You have done that all by yourself."

What? Have I missed something here? Have I been missing something this whole time between me and Brim? When I look at Azza, the knowing twist of her mouth makes me feel like a fool. I wasn't tricking Brim out of his lunch when we were children – he was *letting* me eat it, sparing my pride through the game. At the Mor school they took food from Brands to feed us privileged breeders, but I was hungry a good deal, especially as Osha and I gave much of our food to Frida and her family in the village. The Reis fare we've been eating makes me realise just how meagre an Isfalki table was, even on feast days in the Pure citadel.

I scan Brim's face – his fair hair growing out of its close crop, the line of his jaw, usually as clean and straight as his sword, a little stubbled now. Our argument on board the *Na'quat* comes back to me.

I can't turn a blind eye to the challenges of loving someone like you, Nara.

How is it impossible? Because I'm a pain in the arse? Because I never do as I'm told? Because I shaved my head?

Because you're a fec!

That word in his mouth, *fec* – that was what had stayed with me. But Brim had been telling me he loved me. He'd said it was difficult, not impossible. I'd been the one to say that, to accuse him of being a Settlement man to his very bones. Was I wrong?

He holds my gaze for a moment, before he reaches over to brush my chin. "Sugar," he explains.

"Oh." I swipe a cuff across my mouth, and I don't know whether I'm more confused at Brim's touch, this sudden revelation, or how the wrangler's sister is reading my burning cheeks as if all my old longings are suddenly written on my skin.

"Are we hunting or reminiscing?" she says abruptly, and I'm grateful for it. "Come, the light will not linger."

We push on, but when the Maw falls behind at a stall selling ryki, I'm glad when Brim offers to retrieve him.

Azza must hear my sigh of relief, for she cuts me a look. "What?" I snap. "The mere smell of that liquor breaks me into a sweat right now."

"Indeed." Azza chuckles. "Although, you seemed somewhat *sweaty* before the ryki cart."

I ignore her, squinting towards the gorge. A unit of mounted soldiers approaches, heading into Cha Shaheer. Their sand scarves are dusty, and their breastplates and greaves of hammered bronze have seen action, if not recent. The sheathed swords at their hips are curved in the Reis style.

"Azza Ni Azzadur." Their captain nods, and I'm shocked to see she's not only a woman but one whose cheek is emblazoned with some of the darkest brandings I've seen since my encounter with the slum children in the Fornwood all those months ago. The two women grasp forearms and Azza listens while the captain talks. When she's finished, the woman glances in my direction. Azza strokes the horse's shoulder contemplatively for a moment before she shakes her head, that throaty laugh sounding somehow confidential now.

"What was that about?" I ask when the captain and her riders are gone.

"They are Ghumes, our border patrols. They watch for ships of raiders targeting our southern farming settlements. I know their commander well."

I stare after her.

"Are you surprised, Nara Fornwood, that Captain Alrahim is a woman? Or that she is a Brand?"

There's no point being disingenuous, she knows the answer is *both*.

"In Isfalk, stronger and fitter Brands might get jobs serving our forces as mess hands or armourers," I say. "Dog wranglers, in your brother's case. But only Pures can fight or hold office."

"And why is that?"

"Because they're more suited to military roles, of course. They're healthier, stronger."

Her smile is thin, as if she's tired of hearing this argument. "You imply, then, that the Branded are weak? That you yourself are inferior?"

I close my mouth, indignant. When applied to myself, my own logic makes me balk. Hadn't I dreamed of becoming a Warder? Hell's poxes, I'd never considered myself weaker or my abilities compromised. Not until I was *told* I was a Brand. I think of Teta San and the Maw – their size and strength, their skill, despite being branded. And I think of the wrangler and Azza herself. Any army would be lucky to have them. I claim

I'm not an Isfalki, but how quickly I regurgitate the Settlement's assumptions. How ingrained are they in me, when I thought I was so *different?*

"Open your eyes, Nara Fornwood," Azza says, gaze sweeping the people all around us on the route through the gorge. Noisy school kids – Branded and Pure – race to swim in the river, already unbuttoning matching tunics; a farmer, Pure as far as I can tell, pulls an empty produce cart alongside a woman whose hands are lashed with brandings; a Pure mother nurses her blue-cheeked infant under the shade of a palm. Many of them acknowledge Azza when they spot her, the couple with the cart even chatting as we pass, and I begin to understand her status in the city. She's more than just the daughter of the Kham; she must walk regularly among them, for the esteem they show her is earned, not commanded.

"The Branded seem different here than in Isfalk," I say.

"How so?"

"They're bigger, for a start. Healthier-looking... less..." I shrug, searching for the right words.

"Less hungry?" she suggests. "Less indentured?"

"I was thinking, maybe the Brume wasn't as severe in Reis as it was in the north? Perhaps you Reis weren't exposed to the full brunt of diseases left in its wake as we were."

"The Brume!" Azza barks a sardonic laugh. "How you Isfalki like to make the Brume responsible for all society's ills."

"But wasn't it? I mean, it weakened Brands to disease. That's why they need protecting, sheltering."

"Do they?" She sucks in a long breath as if to draw patience. "Tell me, what did they teach you in that Mor school?"

I worry the inside of my lip, wondering at her agenda, but when I look at her I see she's genuinely curious. "We learned that the Brume epidemic spread through the Old World over a century ago, after the Comet Winter. Only a lucky few survived, and of those even fewer were pure-skinned – untouched and unaffected by the diseases that raged in the Brume's wake."

"So Isfalk separates the strong from the weak, the chosen ones from the sinful. That is what your church believes, does it not? That Holy Mother intended the Great Malady to raise the blessed above the infected?"

"I don't know why you're asking," I say. "It's obvious you already know what the Isfalki believe."

"I am asking because I want to know if *you* believe these things to be true."

I cross my arms and fidget under the scrutiny of her gaze. "I don't know... I mean, the stuff about Brands being sinners is Uluf's typical priestly shite, I guess. But the fact is, the Brume wasn't fair. Some were left marked, their blood tainted, more vulnerable to disease and birthing weaker children. Whether you like it or not, that separated us."

"No, Nara Fornwood," Azza fires back, voice firm. "The Brume did not separate us. The prejudice of mankind did that." She studies my face, gauging my reaction.

"Look, it wasn't always so extreme in Isfalk, you know," I say, wondering why I'm being defensive of the colony that cast me aside, that traded me and my sister like commodities. "In the beginning, the immune nursed the infected, protected the weak... that's how the Settlement began. The Pure were guardians and defenders."

"And this is what happens now in your isolated northern colony? The strong defending the weak?" The look on my face must be answer enough, for she continues. "The Brume outbreak killed hundreds of thousands across the Continent. But the deadliest disease is what survivors made of its legacy." We've caught up to the schoolkids, now dive-bombing into the river, the celebration of their freedom from school brash and carefree. "You will learn, Nara Fornwood, that the only real difference between people is in the way they are treated, the opportunities they are given. Reis is living proof of it. You yourself are proof of it."

"I don't think it's as simple as that."

"You were brought up with the privilege of food, care and education, were you not?"

"By mistake, yes."

"And do you not feel as capable as any Pure?" When I shrug my assent, she smiles. "Which proves my point. The Branded in Reis seem stronger and healthier to you because they are. They have been allowed to be. Here, the marked do not go hungry. They are educated and given treatment when they fall sick. They have the same opportunities as the Pure." She points to the kids in the water. "He might become a farmer or a teacher, she might be our next army general or even elected Kham." She makes a soft hum, growing pensive. "My mother held that role, before she died. Perhaps Nixim told you?"

"You can safely assume your brother has told me nothing," I say, and amusement plays about her mouth.

"As Kham, my mother worked for years growing Cha Shaheer's infirmary and schools, ensuring the Branded had opportunities and the freedom to choose. Much of her work laid the foundation for Reis to thrive as it does today. She always told me: *Think not of the pain of the past, but the hope of the future.* That was her credo."

Azza's eyes kindle with admiration as she talks of her mother.

"Was she a Brand, like you?"

Azza falls silent as I glance at the blue-black tendrils peeking from her cuff.

"Ah, this." She pushes back her sleeve, giving me a full view of the spiral winding up her forearm. It is formed from tiny specks, like pollen carried on a breeze, the lines reminding me of those I'd traced around the wrangler's shoulder, the brandings that merged perfectly with the halqa tattoo under his bicep.

"Nixim and I had our brandings crafted before he left," Azza says, shaking her head at the memory. "I was not more than fifteen, he thirteen. We were rebellious and grieving. You must understand, we had just lost our mother."

"*Crafted?* Wait. You're telling me this is ink?" I reach for her arm, but she draws it away. "Your brandings, Nixim's brandings – all of them – they're nothing more than tattoos?"

She lowers her eyes. It's the first time I've seen her look sheepish. "You assumed we were both Brands?"

"Of course I assumed you were Brands! Where I come from, the Pure don't deliberately mark their skin to look like fecs!" I strangle an incredulous laugh, anger following hot on its tail. "Cock's poxes, I don't know what to believe any more."

"I suppose that was what we intended all along – to blur the lines between the Pure and the Branded, to stop people making assumptions."

"Well, you sure as hell reeled me in," I snap, but it's the wrangler I want to rail at. When I discovered I was branded and they me cast out of the Isfalk citadel, I think deep down it was a consolation knowing he was inferior, like me, that we were equals. Now, our positions have fully reversed – he's entitled, revered, Pure, while I'm the Brand. I feel further from him than ever.

Azza says, "It was idealistic, immature… even offensive. I see that now. But back then, we told ourselves we were proving a point. What did it matter what was written on the skin?" She runs her fingertips across her branding – her *tattoo*. "*Ros sang e akham.* It is a Reis saying: *Blood and bone become ever dust.* It is true for everyone in the end, is it not?"

"In the end, maybe, but why would you deliberately mar your skin like that? Having grown up in Isfalk, that's pretty hard to get my head around."

"To understand our motives properly, you must know about my family… and about Reis politics." She sighs. "It's complicated. Perhaps another time."

"What is it with you and your brother for keeping people in the dark? I do have a brain, for fec's sake. I think I can keep up."

A grin breaks slowly across Azza's face. "Your tongue is from the gutter, Nara Fornwood. But I see why Nixim likes you."

"Honestly? I couldn't give a pox for what your brother likes and doesn't like right now. Tell me everything he hasn't. I want to understand."

Azza rubs her knuckles along her jaw, uncertain.

"Please," I ask gently, and she nods as if she knows exactly what that small word costs someone like me.

"There have always been certain Pure families in Cha Shaheer who believe in their own superiority," she begins. "Those who think only they have the right to lead and govern. It is not so unlike Isfalk, or so I am told." Her expression grows hard as she continues. "Phibia stirred up their beliefs, giving them purchase. She has undone much of my mother's work, returning elitism and division to Cha Shaheer."

She pulls down her cuff, covering the tattoo. "Nixim and I had them inked the year our mother died. Our father was Kham and Phibia had just been made Khadib. Under her influence, he insisted I join the temple as a handservant to its Seers, when all I'd ever wanted was to work in the Forum with him and continue my mother's civic legacy – her dream of building Reis into a prosperous integrated colony." She looks up at me with a sad smile. "At the same time, Phibia made my father promise Nixim to Hira, claiming the union of their children would be a power match that would secure the vote of Pure elitists in upcoming elections. My brother was resistant, and so my father – at Phibia's suggestion – agreed to send him away to become a Seeker. Phibia's argument was that such a mission would instil in Nixim some much-needed respect for the Reis religion and its prophecy, while the sacrifice and danger involved in a Seeker's life would teach him obedience and give him a chance to prove his worth." Azza folds her arms, shaking her head.

"She wanted the two of you separated, didn't she?"

"You are astute, Nara Fornwood, when you want to be," she says, but I'm too engrossed to retort, gesturing for her to hurry up with the story. "I suspect Phibia also wanted Nixim removed from the influence of my mother's supporters. Even though he agreed to the betrothal to placate her, she still convinced my father to send him away. A few days before his journey, my brother and I went to the suk together and had our brandings inked. My father's reaction to them was terrible enough, but you should have seen Phibia's. She was horrified. Incorporating the Halqa into his design was both ironic and masterful on Nixim's part – Phibia could hardly complain about the symbol or the fervour he feigned for a cause she'd forced upon him. But the fact that he'd marred his Pure skin, well..." Azza laughs, that gravelly sound I'm starting to find contagious. A moment later, however, she's staring off into the distance, preoccupied. "It was not easy for my mother, building what we have here in Cha Shaheer, overcoming ignorance and prejudice. There are those in Reis who still believe in Pure entitlement, that immune bloodlines should remain undiluted, and that only the Pure are worthy of holding power. The old ways still linger..."

"Like a bad smell?" I offer.

"A little worse than that, I feel." Her expression darkens. "You saw Phibia and my father at the feast?"

I remember the Kham's hand around his advisor's, how he'd brought her fingers to his lips. "Her work with him extends far beyond her official duties, I'm guessing."

"Do not think too badly of him. My father was not always so misguided. As a younger man, he was a lot like Nixim – brave, confident... trying to tame the storm," she adds pointedly. "He was born of old blood, you understand, a clan of Pures who prided themselves on their lineage. My mother was a Pure healer of great reputation but no family line – outspoken, idealistic, already campaigning to better the lives of Brands in Cha Shaheer. When he fell in love with her, he took on the disapproval of his entire clan. But they complemented each other. Her deeds and good judgement made her popular among the masses, while his name gave her credibility with the Pure clans. He supported her to become the next Kham, and when she passed unexpectedly" – Azza touches her fingertips to her heart and lips, lowering her lashes for a moment – "my father was elected to take her place."

I can almost imagine the rest without her explanation, but I listen absorbed while she completes the picture.

"Once he became Kham, Phibia worked tirelessly to become Khadib. And since then, she's slithered her way not only into my father's bed, but into his mind and heart." Her eyes narrow and glaze, as if she's imagining the Khadib's pale head on her father's pillow, whispering in his ear. "He mourned my mother for a long time, but as soon as he had the first stirrings of lust again in his loins, that siren swayed them in her favour."

"*Swayed* them? Phibia's a Sway?"

Azza nods. It suddenly makes sense – at the feast there was something about the Isalki Mor that was both compelling and set my teeth on edge. She had the same magnetic charge about her as the Blood-wife and Saqira, except in Phibia's case there was something sinister about it – closer to what I'd experienced when Mother Iness grabbed my wrist on the stage of the Roundhouse.

"Phibia is not only a Sway," Azza says. "She is High Seer at the Golden Temple of Cha Shaheer. She will be the one to read your sister."

A droplet of sweat snakes between my shoulder blades in the heat, but I feel suddenly cold, clammy. "That woman makes my skin crawl. I don't want her anywhere near my sister."

"I'm afraid, Nara Fornwood, we do not have a choice."

The Healers and the Hrossi

The day of Hira's promised tour of the Golden Saman sees me in no great hurry to get out of bed. Takia bangs around outside my door nevertheless, and when I can take it no longer, I haul myself upright and stomp through our quarters, looking for Osha. Her chamber is empty, her bed barely rumpled.

Manuscripts and scrolls brought from the Cha Shaheer libraries are scattered on the low tables of the lounge room and around the floor nearby, interspersed with a mess of ink wells, quills and parchments. We've only been here for a handful of days, but Osha has already made herself at home, the scene not unlike the alcove in Isfalk's abandoned archives where I'd find her burning candles late into the night. How liberating it must feel for her to study out in the open, to leave her books and notes around for anyone to see, to discuss her theories and findings freely with other healers. As Takia begins to tidy the space and stack the manuscripts, I get a fleeting sense of vindication, a feeling that, despite the Seer reading hanging over our heads, bringing my sister here might not have been such a terrible idea. Osha needed to come to Reis for more reasons than I could have ever imagined.

"I wouldn't do that if I were you," I tell Takia as she removes a quill resting inside a codex. She regards the manuscript, frowning over an illumination of what looks like a nest of snakes, but which on closer inspection is the human gut. "Believe me, I know from personal experience that Osha gets very grumpy if you lose her place." The Reis woman sniffs, returning the quill. "Do you know where she is, by the way?"

Takia gives me the shoulder. She still hasn't forgiven me for the night of the feast and seems to be taking it as a personal slight that I refuse to wear the silks she lays out for me every morning. I can get nothing out of her, and when Osha doesn't return for breakfast I set off to look for her myself, adamant I'm not enduring a tour of the city with Hira alone.

It's easy to get lost in the endless tiled corridors of Cha Shaheer's main keep. I'm reassured I'm headed towards the centre of the city when I end up on a promenade overlooking the hotchpotch of canopies that form the suk. The shouts of hawkers rise, raucous as the wild birds of the Kyder, the busy alleyways crowded with moving heads – a riot of coloured sand scarves. As I return to the corridor, I hear footsteps, the familiar jingle of jewellery. I duck back outside and pin myself to the wall. Peeping through the archway, I see Hira and a bevy of attendants heading in the direction of our rooms. Brim meets her, coming the other way.

"Ah, Captain Oskarsson," Hira minces sweetly. "I come to take Osha on a tour of our city, as promised."

"Only Osha?" Brim asks.

"The other sister may come too, of course… if she wishes it." The *other sister*. Nice.

"Well, I just came from their quarters, and no one answered."

"I see." Hira sounds disappointed.

"I'd offer to find them for you, but I think you know this maze of a fortress better than I do."

The Reis girl's affected amusement tinkles down the corridor. "And I believe you know their characters better than I, so perhaps you might help me guess where to look first?"

"It would be my pleasure." Brim is either genuinely pleased to be of service or he's a diplomatic liar. I'm hoping for the latter. "And should we fail to find them," he continues, "I, for one, would be delighted to see the Shadow City with you, Mor

Hira." He offers her his arm. I release a breath of relief that he's saved me from her, but that use of the Isfalki honorific, his focus on her Pure blood, makes something flip in my chest like a fish on the ice. Disappointment, jealousy, exclusion – perhaps all three. I almost want to retrace my steps and commandeer Brim in the corridor just to spite Hira, to prove his loyalty to me goes beyond *skin*. But I won't risk the prospect of a day in her company, even with Brim as a buffer, so I let them pass.

"That's a dangerous move." I nearly yelp in shock at the voice over my shoulder. Nixim leans against the wall as casually as if he'd always been there, admiring the morning. "Hira won't forgive being stood up."

"The last thing I want is a city tour with your betrothed, Wrangler. I'm sure even you can understand that."

"She's not my betrothed."

"Really? Does she know that yet? Because at the feast she kissed you very publicly to resounding cheers. And I distinctly remember her telling the crew of the *Na'quat* she was your lyfhort." His full lips grow thin and he has the decency to look ashamed. "You know what, I couldn't care less what I've walked into between you and Hira. I've got bigger things to worry about... and right now that's finding my sister."

"She's at the infirmary libraries. You might have guessed–"

"I know. That's where I'm heading!" I turn and walk off, but when he lets out an amused grunt I can't resist turning round.

"The infirmaries are that way." He cocks his head to the end of the promenade where a set of steps accesses the streets below. "Come on."

"I'll make my own way, thanks."

"As you like." He shrugs. "But if you want to see her sometime this week, I suggest you let me show you the quickest route. The streets of Cha Shaheer are trickier to navigate than your moods, Little Scourge."

I draw a slow breath, trying to stop myself from taking the bait. He does have a point, though: I've got no idea where I'm going and, knowing only a word or two of Reis, asking for directions will be a long shot. Reluctantly, I follow his lead. My only retaliation is to stay a good five paces behind him as he walks, making conversation awkward. His frustration amuses me at first, but when he gives up trying to talk, I realise I'm left watching his shoulder muscles torquing under the fit of his tunic, a mesmerising patch of sweat seeping between them in the sweltering morning. His black curls catch his collar as he turns to acknowledge people in the street. They part for him to pass and I catch the breathy whispers of young women behind their sand scarves, the less coy admiration of older matrons. It seems everyone in the city knows exactly who Nixim Ni Azzadur is. Everyone except me.

At the edge of the suk, he pauses at a stall, chatting to the vendor who hands him a fruit I don't recognise. I'm obliged to stop too, loitering at the next stand along while he peels and bites into the pink flesh. I try not to notice the juice on his lips, his tongue chasing a drip on his chin. *Fec's sake, Nara, pull yourself together!* But before I can turn away, he's tossed one of the fruits towards me. My hands go up reflexively to catch it and he grins. Cock's poxes, why didn't I let it smash at my feet? It's a test to see how closely I'm watching him. The scheming bastard.

"That's a mangelo," he calls out. "Perfectly ripe. You should try a bite."

Ignoring him, I hand the fruit back to the vendor, then cross my arms, making a show of waiting. He sets off again, eating and strolling without a care in the world – a benign prince surveying the thriving kingdom laid out at his feet.

"You're enjoying this immensely, aren't you, Wrangler?" I call ahead.

He answers without turning. "What's not to enjoy? It's a beautiful morning, mangelos are having a bumper season, and I haven't tasted one in seven years... so, yeah, I'm enjoying myself. Plus... you can't keep your eyes off me."

"Not by choice, you cocky son-of-a–"

"Sure about that, Scourge?"

"Can you just hurry up? You said if you showed me the way it *wouldn't* take all day to get to there."

He finishes the fruit, stopping at a fountain to rinse his hands. When he begins walking again, he picks up his pace, striding down the crowded thoroughfares, threading between market stalls and ducking down alleyways like he's never been away. I almost have to jog to keep up. After half an hour, I'm breathless, sweaty, and about to flip the finger at his game, when he takes a sharp right up ahead. I round the corner only to run straight into a wall – a wall made of him.

One hand catches my shoulder, steadying, the other grips my waist – all kinds of unsteadying. The fruit on his breath smells so sweet I get a stab of hunger.

"That's a cheap trick, even for you, Wrangler," I tell him. But I don't pull away. Right now, I want to taste that mangelo more than anything in the world.

"I'll resort to cheap tricks if I have to," he says, voice low, lips parted, staring straight at mine. And my mutinous body wants to close the gap, fingertips resting at the fine dip of his throat. It would be so easy to give in, but my desire trips on something jagged inside me – self-respect or self-preservation, I'm not sure which. I surprise us both by placing his palm over my heart, making him feel how it drums erratically, like the hooves of fleeing quarry.

"Feel that, Wrangler?" I whisper. He nods slowly. "I'm not so sure my heart can take another kicking from you."

Every muscle in his body contracts, as if I've drawn my sword and slashed him. He steps away, wiping the back of his hand across his mouth.

His eyes are flat, distant, as he says, "I'll take you to Osha."

* * *

My sister isn't in the infirmary libraries. Instead, we find her on a ward.

Hewn of thick sandstone, the Old World buildings are set within a covered colonnade of keyhole arches. Inside, the wards are cool and dim, sheer drapes billowing at the windows and sectioning off quarters where patients convalesce or are treated by men and women in neat, blue robes. At the centre is a quadrangle filled with greenery and the sound of water gushing in a fountain. There's an aura of calm efficiency about the compound, clearly established as an oasis for the sick. It makes me think how different our lives would have been had we grown up here; how different the lives of so many Brands if Isfalk allowed the treatment of disease in sanctuaries like this.

We're greeted by one of the attendants in blue. The wrangler speaks to her in Reis before making his excuses. "She'll take you to Osha. I have business with my father today," he says, avoiding my eye. Watching him leave, I can't tell whether I'm relieved or disappointed at how much my honesty affected him. So much for Osha's advice to be more vulnerable.

I follow the woman down a long corridor, voices drifting to us from beyond a curtain at its end.

"It is a problem. We have seen no sickness like it before in Reis," a female voice says in accented Isfalki. "The *Codex of Reis Dur* and the *Diary of Hamshek* – which I translated for you yesterday – detail similar symptoms, however."

"And the suggested treatment?" I hear Osha ask.

"They differ vastly."

When I enter the room, my sister is standing over a woman who is in the late stages of pregnancy. Three Reis healers in green robes talk across the patient's sleeping form, the edge of authority about them suggesting they're the apotheks Osha has been meeting over the past few days. Through the archway beyond, Haus is loitering in the shade of the quadrangle, whetting his dagger against a sharpening strap. He's close enough should Osha need him, but out of her way should she not.

The group greets me as I enter, but I can see my sister is engrossed, anxious not to be interrupted. I move to join Haus in the colonnade and the healers immediately continue their discussion, the woman whose voice I'd heard in the corridor translating the comments of the others into Isfalki. Haus lifts his chin when he sees me but carries on sharpening his knife.

"Still no joy, Chief?" I ask.

He doesn't answer, pouting in concentration as he moves the blade along the strap. I study his pale eyelashes lowered to the task. They've always seemed too long, too pretty, for the cut of his jaw, the scruff of stubble on his cheeks. His mood tells me Osha has not softened towards him in the time he was away, as I'd hoped she might.

"I'll talk to her, alright?" I say. "Just give her some more time. Orlath put her through a lot."

I realise my mistake as soon as I've said it. To Haus, Orlath's name is a lash on an open wound. His gaze snaps to mine, a muscle flickering in his jaw, and suddenly he's no longer the young chief staring longingly at my sister across the campfire, no longer the smitten Hrossi who offered up the reins of his horse along with the solemn braid-promise of his heart. It's the Cooler Ringer I see in him now, the mask from the arena, grim, single-minded – the face not of Haus, but of Lynstum. *Lightning Strike*. In the ring, he was known as the ultimate dealer of deaths – quick, clean, merciful. But I'm certain that if the Waster overlord were to cross paths with his champion fighter now, Orlath's dispatch would be anything but merciful. Love hasn't made Haus blind. He saw the bruises and marks on Osha's neck before we escaped the Cooler, and he must have guessed Orlath helped himself to more than that, despite their bargain. But does Haus suspect Osha's condition? And if she won't tell him about the child, should I? Pretty soon, I won't even have that dilemma – Haus will be able to see it for himself.

The Hrossi stands and paces the colonnade, eyes scanning the fountain but likely seeing some other vista, far away.

"Chief?" I say gently. "Talk to me?"

His jaw continues to grind away in silence for a while. But pretty soon he can no longer hold it in. "The waiting... here in Reis... and Orlath," he tries to explain, fists working at his sides. "I want to..." But his frustration and his lack of fluency trip him. He barely needs to say the words. His intentions rise off him clean and sharp as the smell of the metal being honed. Haus is a man of action, born in the saddle, with a sword in his hand. But more than that, I suspect he can't leave a debt unpaid. It's the very reason he took Osha and the other Mor straight to Orlath in the first place – to honour his feudal dues. Now, though, that debt flows the other way. Orlath broke his word when he harmed my sister, and Haus's Hrossi honour demands revenge. "When I look at her..." he tries again, staring at Osha through the archway, "I see his hands, his lips... his teeth..." He closes his eyes and growls out a breath. "I want to... I *must* go back."

"To Orlathston? To finish what was started between you and Orlath?"

He nods and I notice the lines that have gathered around his eyes. I understand for the first time how much this has been consuming him. I thought his sullenness was from mooning over Osha, that it was she who'd been putting obstacles between them. But now I see that Haus himself might also be the problem, contemplating his revenge on Orlath every time he looks at the woman he loves.

"I hear you, Chief. I have unfinished business with that sick fec myself." The faces of Annek, Dalla and Sigrun lit by the fire on the Wasteland Plains still haunt me. "How can I leave the other girls at his mercy in that stinking harem? We made a promise we'd go back for them, remember? But here I am feasting and hunting and taking leisurely soaks in the saman." Guilt winds me like a punch to the throat and, sensing it, Haus takes my forearm.

"Then we go back. Together."

"It's not as simple as that, Haus. You know we need back-up forces, horses, weapons... we need a ship! And I don't like our chances of negotiating all those things from the Kham until Osha has been read by his damn Seers. It's the only thing these Reis seem to care about right now."

He begins pacing again, until I catch him by the wrist and make him sit beside me on the low wall of the fountain. "Just a few more days, Chief, okay? Let's get past this prophecy bullshit and we can start planning, yeah?"

I'm making a promise I might not be able to keep because, honestly, I have no idea what Osha's reading will bring or how friendly the Reis will be towards us when it is over. But seeing Haus tormented like this pains me, not just because I know he longs for my sister, and she for him, but because I owe the Hrossi my life. And I fully intend to pay him back.

All I can think to do right now, though, is distract him, just like he did me back in Orlathston. After my fight with Teta San, I'd clung to the sound of Haus's voice in the dark, his words echoing down the wall of cages, grounding me, keeping me sane.

"Haus, back in the Cooler you promised to tell me something," I say, tone calm and steady. I wrap his calloused fist in mine. And without even trying to hear it, the fierce *lub-dub* of his pulse jumps in my ears, syncopated against my own. Instinctively, I take a breath to slow it, rein it in. I use my sway to grow the peace I know is there within him, that stillness he shared with me when I was so close to losing control, the cool-headedness that made him a leader of men at such a young age. "Do you remember when I asked you how you could bear it – all the bloodshed and death?" He grunts in acknowledgement. "And you said to think of my happiest memories – my grandmother giving me my first bow... riding with Brim in the Fornwood... playing with Osha in the snow as children. I was blessed to have so many, you said, because you had only one. But you wouldn't tell me what it was."

He nods, remembering.

"You told me I had to win my fight first. But we escaped the Cooler before I could, so…" I pause, waiting to see if he'll let me divert him this way. "I think you owe me a memory, Chief. What was your happiest time?"

His eyes dart to Osha through the archway, her face focused intensely on the patient. She lifts her head briefly, frowning as the Reis healers discuss the illness.

"Well?" I prompt him.

"Wait," he says, raising his chin towards my sister. And I watch as Osha's hand creeps not to her pendant as it always used to when she was deep in thought, but to the back of her hairline, drawing forth the thin braid and twirling it subconsciously around her fingers. Her red locks are intertwined with Haus's brown ones – their braid-promise. His face lights up, as if he's watching some small miracle, smiling to himself as he touches his own braid in response. It's his talisman of hope, I realise now, and for a brief moment my sister's gaze finds his. There's such longing in the clench of her eyebrows, such desire in the set of her mouth, it gives me the impression that Haus knows my sister better than she knows herself, that he understands her heart would never be given lightly. He trusts she'll come back to him if he waits long enough, and no one knows patience like Haus. He learned that first-hand in the Cooler.

I press him no more about his memories. It's plain as daybreak – his happiness lies in those braids.

"I've already explained, our most accomplished infirmary Sways have laid hands on the patient." The Reis translator's voice rises as Osha reaches for the sick woman. "The illness resists mental influence and we are uncertain if the fever is contagious, so it would be best–"

Osha ignores her. Through the archway I can hear the patient muttering feverishly at Osha's touch. The woman's skin has a bruised tone to it, oddly familiar. Stillness slips over my sister like a mantle and her eyelids lower. It's as if she's yoking all her faculties to that greater sense – her sway. Within seconds, she's keenly alert again, searching for Haus through the archway. He lurches towards her, sensing her fear.

"What is it, O? What's wrong?" I ask.

She draws a quick breath to gather herself. "I think this woman might have frost fever."

It was the sickness I caught on the Wasteland Plains. Osha had never seen the symptoms before and had mistreated them. Haus had been the one to save me, just as he had most of his crew who'd contracted frost fever the winter before. My sister begins to explain to the Reis healers that Haus knows the woman's illness and how to treat it, but as soon as the Hrossi enters the room the apotheks stiffen, unable to keep the discomfort – no, the *distaste* – from their faces. The translator holds up her palm. "The unskilled are not permitted to treat patients here," she says coolly, taking in the brandings on the chief's neck, the nicks and scars on his bare arms, his braid-promise bound roughly in its leather thong. Evidently, she could tolerate his presence in the garden, but she's drawing a line at the treatment room. I get the impression this line is less about Haus being unskilled, and more about him being a Hrossi. Reis has its share of prejudices, it seems, just like Isfalk.

"I don't understand," Osha says. "I'm telling you this man might heal the woman. He saved most of his crew from this very contagion and he has first-hand experience of treating its symptoms."

The apotheks respond all at once in their own tongue until the translator holds up her hands for silence. "With respect," she tells Osha – a sure sign she's about to show none, "my colleagues find that hard to believe. Wastelanders are better known for taking lives than saving them, and Hrossi men do not present with the skill."

"Skill or not, my own sister lives because of this man's care," Osha argues. "When I was unable to read her illness, he diagnosed it immediately. It responded only partially to my abilities, the rest was due to his knowledge of herbal compounding."

"Still, the Hrossi is not permitted to treat patients here," the healer insists.

Osha tugs her copybook from her pocket and riffles angrily through the pages. "Frost fever *is* contagious, make no mistake. You may have eliminated many diseases from this city but unless you want a new outbreak among your Brands, I suggest you follow Haus's methods." Panting a little, she finds the notes she wants and thrusts the book impatiently at the translator. "You'll need to source the herbs noted here... and you're going to have to do exactly what he says."

The translator remains doubtful. When she makes no move to follow her instructions, Osha rounds on her: "It's interesting," she says, masking the anger in her voice with nonchalance. "I was led to believe that the Cha Shaheer infirmaries were founded on enlightened learning and unbiased inquiry – the bedrock of a truly civilised society, or so Azza Ni Azzadur claimed. I'll be sorry to report back to her that Reis healers sacrificed a woman and her unborn child today because of some elitist rule about unskilled healers. And I'm sure the Kham would be devastated to think a contagion was allowed to run amok in his city all because of narrow-mindedness."

The apotheks are quiet as my sister's threat is conveyed to them. Pride aside, it's obvious they have little desire to be held accountable to the Kham for an epidemic they might have prevented. The translator leaves first, a sudden flurry of green robes and barked orders, Osha's book open in her hands. The others quickly follow suit.

"What the fec, O," I tell her. "You were magnificent!"

"Oh hush," she says, "you know how I hate the word *fec*." She glances up at Haus through her eyelashes, but he clearly agrees with me for his face is filled with awe and he seems unable to remove his hand from where it has found hers at the patient's bedside. Osha doesn't draw away. She takes in every detail of him now, and he blinks back at her in return, a whole conversation passing between them without words. Osha might be the first person to have acknowledged Haus as something more than a scarred Ringer, more than a barbarian trader – the only person to value him for what he might know beyond swords and horses and fighting.

If Haus was lovesick before, I don't think he has a hope in hell of being cured of my sister now.

A Defensive Strategy

As the Seer reading draws closer, my nightmares about our abilities become even more vivid and complex. I dream I never had the sway skill, that it was all in my imagination, while Osha's powers grow apace. Sometimes, in my dreamscapes, my sister stands as tall as the Golden Temple of Cha Shaheer, crowned in a ring of glyphs like some ancient goddess, glowering at me in all her fearful glory. "You're weak," she thunders. "And you're late."

I don't know whether to laugh or cry when I wake, but I certainly don't tell Osha about the nightmares. She distracts herself with the care of patients at the infirmaries during the day and her studies at night, while I kill time hunting or training in the amphitheatre below the saman. I rise at dawn to spar with Haus, Azza and Brim, before the heat thickens the day and makes us sluggish. Some mornings the Maw can be roused to join us, but he's like an old man kicked from his bed, surly and slow, until the ryki arrives at lunchtime. The wrangler is noticeable for his absence. Five days have passed since he led me to the infirmaries, and as much as I tell myself his whereabouts are no business of mine, it vexes me he's disappeared without so much as an explanation.

"Your brother doesn't feel the need to train, then?" I ask Azza one morning. The mole on her lip twitches. "Don't give me that look. I'm only making conversation."

I lunge for her right flank, but she predicts the attack, masterfully deflecting my stave. Before I can recentre, she spins, her own staff caning the backs of my knees, and I slam onto my side with a grunt. "Mother's tits!"

"Your emotions make you rash, Nara Fornwood," she says as I spit sand from my mouth. "You should keep thoughts of my brother out of the training ring."

"Oh, please. I barely think of your brother!"

"Then you will be *barely* interested to know he has left Cha Shaheer. He visits our mother's clans in the south."

I swipe sweaty palms down my pants. "So neither of you thought I was worthy of being told that information?"

"He said I should inform you only if you asked. He thought you would not."

I get up and shake myself off, seething. Another test of the wrangler's, this time to see if his absence bothers me. Now Azza will tell him it does.

I take up my stance, furious and jittery – the worst combination. The Seer reading is tomorrow night, and once again the wrangler has dumped us in the middle of the action, then promptly shown his heels. No one in Reis will give me anything but the vaguest information about what the reading entails for Osha, and I'm starting to feel manipulated and trapped.

I launch my offensive while Azza's back is half-turned, aiming straight for her head. It's a cheap shot, but I can't help myself. She veers aside, eyes flaring at the intensity of my onslaught. Our weapons crack in the dawn quiet, the grunt of her effort satisfying as I follow up my initial gambit with a second thrust, and a third, in lightning succession. From the tail of my eye, I see Haus and Brim stop their own sport to watch us, surprised at the serious turn of our engagement. Azza stumbles and I press my assault, dealing a blow to her left hip. When my stave catches the side of her head, I'm rewarded with a hiss of breath behind gritted teeth, a blossoming of red above her eye.

"Nara!" Haus shouts. "Enough!" But my blood is so fired up it burns all reason to a cinder. Azza has only one hand on her stave, the other nursing the gash in her brow. I take the opening and lunge with a strike that's sure to send her to the ground. It never makes contact. She blocks my weapon with hers. A second later, her fist meets my face in a stunning left hook. Stars explode and pain roars. I hurl my stave across the arena in frustration, cursing the woman with every foul expletive I can conjure.

Brim runs to my side as I sink to the sand. "What the pox happened?"

"She broke my fecking nose, that's what happened!" I finger the bent bridge.

"Mother's love, you were on fire, Nara! One minute you were sparring and the next it felt like we should place bets. But how many times have I told you never to rule out the offside. You should have seen that left hook coming–"

Haus cuts through Brim's excited babble with a grunt, passing straight across the arena to Azza. He staunches her eyebrow with a cloth, glancing back at me, thoroughly unimpressed. Mine were dirty moves – Cooler moves. He showed me half of them. But we're not in the Cooler now, and he trusted me to know the difference. I'm suddenly embarrassed at my loss of control, embarrassed I launched myself at Azza without due warning, and I'm mortified that Haus witnessed it.

"Here, lift your chin, let me see," Brim says. He cups my jaw in both hands and draws me close. When I see him wince, I know it's bad. "Not so much blood, but yeah, it's broken," he confirms. His thumbs stroke my cheeks, and despite the pain, he feels grounding somehow, his eyes as familiar as the taiga sky in summer, his face as reassuring as childhood. "Sit tight for a minute. I'll get something for the pain." He rises to find a servant. Knowing how I've disappointed Haus, how I've made Azza lose all respect for me, I almost want to cry at Brim's care. He's always been there, however bad my behaviour, however much I screw up.

Damn the fecking wrangler! This is his fault. Azza was right – I need to keep my emotions out of the arena. Now I'm going to have to swallow my pride and apologise – both to her and Haus.

The chief approaches while Brim is busy with the servant. He squats on his haunches and looks down at me through those long lashes. "Stupid," he declares. Great. He and Takia can form a club. I spit blood in the sand at his feet. He reaches across, covers my nose in his fist and resets the bone with a grisly crunch.

"Mother-fecker!" It's more a gurgle than a cry, blood clotting my throat. "You could have warned me!"

"As you warn her?" he says, tilting his head to Azza. I struggle to my feet and straighten my shirt, trying to gather some self-respect. To my surprise, Haus rests his palm on my shoulder and squeezes, a gentle question of sorts. I nearly fold with shame.

"I know. I know," I burble. "I lost control. I underestimated her – no way did I think she'd throw from the left." He's silent, waiting. "Alright... I was wrong to advance on her when she wasn't ready. I'm sorry I did it, okay?"

Haus shakes his head, frustrated and amused at the same time. "Stupid for these things, yes. But stupid most for seeing an enemy when you can see a friend."

Osha tends my nose as we sit under the arches of the saman. Her hands are not as gentle as I know them to be, but when I wince in complaint, she pointedly turns my chin to Azza. The wrangler's sister has her back to us, leaning over the balustrade as she watches the others spar in the arena below. The air between us isn't exactly balmy – her eyebrow needed two stitches, and Osha is prompting me for a proper apology.

I press the bloody sponge to my nose, a pathetic excuse to delay the inevitable.

"You're a child," she mouths, shaking her head. I can't bring myself to answer her, which means she's probably right. Eventually she breaks the tense silence. "The woman with the frost fever is well enough to go home tomorrow, thanks to Haus's instructions."

"I would like to have seen the faces of those apotheks," Azza announces, surprising me. "It is not often our Sways find their skills subservient to the herb lore of a *barbarian*." She eyes Haus over the wall of the saman. He's sobering up the Maw under a bucket of iced water, laughing as the giant growls like a bear woken from hibernation. "I heard Haus gave the woman a Hrossi tonic?" she asks Osha.

"Lucky her," I scoff. "Horse piss for breakfast." I mimic a dry heave. "I'll never forget the memory of that brew. The smell alone is enough to raise the dead."

"And yet you live to whine about it," Osha reminds me.

"I think some people here might be rueing the day you forced me to drink it." I slip Azza a look. "I'm a fecking ingrate. I deserve a lot more than a broken nose." The Reis woman blinks at me for a moment. When it comes, her slow grin is a relief. She may be prickly and arch, but she doesn't hold a grudge and my respect for that only reinforces my shame. She shakes her head at my pained frown, telling me to forget it.

"Our healers in Reis set too much stock on their sway," she tells Osha. "Their skill has kept sickness and disease at bay in Cha Shaheer, but they do not like to admit there are still contagions they know nothing of, or patients with symptoms that resist their powers. And they forget the great trove of apothek in our libraries, the oral wisdom of our nomadic tribes and the peoples beyond our borders." She crosses her arms over her chest, watching the Maw warm up with lunges and shadow swings. "They think the Hrossi know nothing but fighting and horses and scavenging. And yet the plains people have weathered the Great Malady and its subsequent diseases for over a century. The Wastelanders did not survive by accident."

I mull over her words. The past few days Osha has been regaling me with how much she's learned in the infirmary, its libraries and archives. She's even admitted to feeling more aware of her own powers by watching gifted Sways tapping into theirs. That's a radical development for someone like my sister. But Azza's criticism of the Reis healers sets me on edge. In Isfalk, bigotry and intolerance was on display for all to see – here in Reis it lurks in cracks and fissures, like rot in the city's foundations.

Perhaps it's human nature to be selfish and destructive. Perhaps we can never truly escape that aspect of ourselves.

I think of Phibia wresting the reins of power from Azza at the feast, getting her way with the Kham over the Seer reading, and everything that awaits us tomorrow night comes crashing urgently into the day. Osha is convinced her powers are nothing compared to other Sways in Reis. She's approaching the reading as a duty to our hosts, wanting to get it over and done with, so she can get back to her studies under the other healers. But what if she's wrong? What if the Seers claim she *is* the Elita? Will we be separated again? Will she be trained so her powers grow? Or will she become Phibia's puppet, a pawn to be manoeuvred as the Khadib sees fit?

There's a shout from the arena below – Haus and the Maw engaging. The morning breeze from the Storm Sands is hot and dry, making the men squint as they circle each other.

"Haus is a good man, I think," Azza remarks as she watches him dodge the Cooler giant's infamous swing.

"No," I tell her. "He is the best of men."

"He knows a great deal about healing as well as fighting, I understand."

"He does," Osha says. "My grandmother taught me about the properties of Fornwood and Wasteland simples, but Haus is showing me Hrossi compounding – the mixing of roots, plants and berries. I'm studying the composites that plains people use in their decoctions and tinctures." Osha twirls her lyf braid around her fingers, deep in thought, and I sense the lecture to come. "Haus's frost fever tonic, for example, is an anodyne as well as an inhibitor. He often talks of compounds the Hrossi believe can repel disease before it takes hold. Sometimes, I wonder–"

She jumps to her feet on a snatch of breath. The Maw has landed a hit across Haus's cheek, drawing blood despite the blunted swords.

"It's a scratch," I tell Osha. "They're mucking around." I cup my hand and call down to Haus in a nasal voice, "You give the Big Man a chance to wind up that swing and he's going to use it, Chief." We watch for a while as the Maw tries to overpower Haus again and again, but the Hrossi's defence is solid now, pre-empting him at every turn. "Poxes, Maw! Get your hand out of your pants. Why are you letting him pussy-foot around you?" The giant grins at my heckling, but Osha scowls. "What?" I ask her.

She considers my swelling nose, crossing her arms in irritation. My sister will never understand the point of a sport that spills blood and causes pain. She's spent her whole life trying to prevent both. I touch her wrist, encouraging her to sit back down beside me, but she remains at the balustrade. There's a groan of effort below, as Haus defends against a barrage of cracking strokes from the Maw. Osha freezes. She appears to be watching the fight, but I know that look, the way her eyes flicker from side-to-side as if busy calculating sums. My sister is elsewhere, deep in some new method of healing, the line of a codex, her own notes. Her face shines with sudden realisation.

"You were saying?" Azza prompts. "What do you wonder?"

My sister returns to the moment, waving her hand nonchalantly. "It's nothing – a vague theory."

"What, O?"

"Well, I just wonder whether all this time I've been trying to treat diseases after they've spread, when what I really need to do is *that*." She points down to the sands.

"That?" Azza asks in confusion.

"*Defend*... Defend against the infection first," Osha says, as if it's obvious.

"You mean treating patients before they get sick?"

She looks at me steadily. "Yes."

"But which disease?" Azza asks. "There are so many."

"Against the only one that matters," she replies. "Against the Brume."

"Surely that horse has already bolted?" I say. "You can't protect the Branded from something we already have. It's in our blood."

"It is, Narkat." She frowns at me a little sadly. "But tending that pregnant woman with the frost fever seeded an idea, and watching Haus just now... it's only a theory, but..."

Azza sits up. She and Osha exchange a look. "What do you need?" Azza asks. I feel as if they're already on the same page, while I'm still fumbling to open the book.

"If I could have time to research in the Reis archives, to study Hrossi compounding in greater detail and make some tests, I might be able to see whether my idea has any credence."

"What idea?" I ask, still in the dark.

"Children. I think the answer lies in children... babies, specifically."

"A defensive treatment, to prevent them *inheriting* the Brume?" Azza says.

I look at Osha. Her face is already alive with the possibility of it.

"Imagine if there was a compound that could shield babies from the Brume at birth, before they were weakened by its attendant diseases. Even if we couldn't eradicate the Brume itself we could make it powerless within a generation. Amma always told me we've only scratched the surface of herb lore and the healing potential of the natural world. There's still so much to learn." She takes a breath. "I'm aware it might be nothing but an ill-conceived conjecture," she says, trying to calm her eagerness, "but I won't know unless I have the chance to try."

Azza nods at her slowly. "The Reis have a saying," she muses. I roll my eyes, waiting for another trite pearl of local wisdom. *"Arkam ak neet skorham bharsus.* The difference between nothing and something is effort."

"That one's glib, even for you, my friend," I tell her. She offers me a grin and for the first time I notice a slight chip in her front tooth. The imperfection – more than the smile – eases the guilt still churning in my stomach. We all have flaws and, Mother knows, mine are too many to count. Maybe she'll go easy on me? Regaining Azza's trust is going to take more than a few cheap jokes, but at least she seems open to me trying. I turn to look for my sister's approval, but Osha has already disappeared inside to her manuscripts.

That night, Osha studies late in the infirmaries. I don't disturb her or bring her back to our rooms to rest, understanding too well that keeping her mind busy is the way she keeps her nerves at bay. I've done exactly the same thing, except with action – returning to the amphitheatre to train with Haus for most of the afternoon. Now night has drawn in and we've lost the light, I perch in the arched casement of the saman, waiting for Osha's return. The evening is deceptively calm and seductive, the sweet scent of blossoms drifting up from the trees in their urns below, the soft breeze beguiling as a calm before the storm.

I can't help my thoughts turning to the Wrangler. Why hasn't he returned yet? What's he doing in the south that's so secretive?

"Nara?" a man's voice calls from the entrance to the saman. My heart bucks like a snowjack. But it's Brim's outline in the shadows, not Nixim's. He steps into the light of the torches, hand rubbing the back of his neck awkwardly. The blue of his eyes still has that touch of northern glaciers, his skin the paleness of the snow-swept Fold, at odds with the desert night.

And yet he seems changed somehow. His brow is furrowed and he shifts on his feet, as if carrying a weight on his shoulders.

"What's wrong, Brim? Or are you checking up on me?"

He makes a soft noise in his throat. "All these miles we've travelled and you still think of me as your Warder?"

"You know you were always more than that to me." He looks up, something bright washing over his expression.

"Nara... I..." he begins, but when he sees my expectant look, he seems to think better of what he was going to say and trails off. He leans against the casement.

"I never thanked you for saving me from Hira's tour," I say, grappling to fill the silence that is growing heavy. "I'm sorry I disappeared. I just couldn't face an entire outing with her. She did make a point of telling me how much fun you had together, though." And I almost kick myself for letting my jealousy seize the moment, ruining what might have been the start of something about the two of us, and us alone.

"She's not as bad as you make out, you know, Nara. Hira's pretty intelligent. She can be quite entertaining, if you give her the chance."

"Yeah, if you're a Pure, maybe." I scratch the branding above my ear, the hair growing back where I'd shaved it aboard the *Na'quat*. "Even if I could get beyond her personality, it's her politics that leave me cold. You do know what she and her mother stand for, right?"

"I've heard all that," he says with an impatient wave of his hand, as if it doesn't concern him. "Haven't we fought enough over politics back in Isfalk, Nara?" He steps closer.

I take a breath, surprised at his sudden movement, even more so when he covers my hand with his own, then lifts my palm to his lips as if it's always been his. "You know, I still feel as I always did about you." Skin on mine, I sense his pulse calling to me, steady and familiar, like a tune I've known for as long as I could remember. It's the path homewards, a childhood scent, the taste of Amma's cooking. It's security and ease and comfort, all rolled into one. But something in me pushes it away, suddenly frightened, full of doubt. Could we ever be truly equal? He's a Pure. I'm a Brand. But I am also a Sway. The thought snakes through my mind, making me shiver. Has Brim's connection to me come from my own desires all along? Was I the one turning his curiosity to friendship, his friendship to love? I snatch back my hand.

"You say you feel the same, but how can you when I'm so different now?" I touch my branding. For once he keeps his eyes fixed pointedly on mine. The marks on my skin used to bother him so much. I can't help feeling he's avoiding them now to prove a point, to show me – to show himself – that they don't affect him any longer.

"Can I ask you something, Brim–"

He doesn't let me finish, raising a hand to cup my jaw and pressing his thumb to my lips instead.

"I can't ignore it anymore, Nara. All these unknowns about your parents, your lineage, even the fact that you're a Brand. I've realised it doesn't alter how I feel." He speaks in a rush, as if slowing down might make him forget the words he's rehearsed, or worse, make him change his mind. "I've had so many chances all these years to tell you, but I let the Settlement and its rules, being a Warder, an Elix heir – I let it all get in the way." He takes a hurried breath. "So, I'm telling you now before I lose my chance, before I lose you… to someone else." I let him pull me closer and the warmth of his chest through his clothes, his familiar smell when I feel so unmoored, so uncertain, is like home. His mouth lowering to mine, his hands heavy at my waist, the urgent way he grips me was the stuff of my dreams all those lonely nights in the Mor school. It seems so inevitable, so fated now, I can't stop myself.

Why, then, does the kiss feel so wrong? Why are his lips not the right fit? His tongue the wrong taste? The press of his body the wrong shape?

I draw back gently. His arms tighten. "Brim, please. I–"

"My turn to interrupt something, it seems." The wrangler stands at the edge of the saman, arms folded across his chest. I lurch away from Brim, fingers pressed to my lips, swallowing back a healthy dose of shame that I have no reason to feel. Brim breaks into a smug grin at the sight of Nixim.

"Wrangler–" I begin.

"No explanations needed, Scourge. I'm *nothing*, remember? You told me as much aboard the *Na'quat* and that's abundantly clear now. It'd be hypocritical of me to expect anything more, after all *my* lies, *my* deceptions, wouldn't it?"

"Nix, wait–" I reach for him, but Brim catches my wrist. "Cock's poxes, Brim!" I spit, wrenching from his grasp. "Get off me!"

"Truly, I only came to tell Azza I'm home," the wrangler says.

"Then maybe you should try *her* quarters?" Brim points out with a withering smile.

"Precisely."

The wrangler strides from the room, avoiding my gaze.

With a flash of bitterly injured pride, so does Brim.

The Seer Circle

The dome of Cha Shaheer might be tarnished and cracked up close, but the grandeur of the Golden Temple still conjures the opulence of the Old World. In the daylight, its tiled courtyards and well-tended paths of espaliered fruit trees are a bright oasis of calm, a glimpse into a long-lost era of peace and prosperity. But now, in the dark, the mood is very different. Ancient braziers smoke along its colonnaded circumference and a miasma of incense belches from their vast iron baskets, making it difficult to see the temple's entrance.

Hira has been tasked with officially delivering Osha to the reading ceremony. Despite my protests, a line of temple acolytes separates me from my sister, their white robes making a ghostly procession through the dim grounds.

Azza takes my elbow, drawing me back. "Do not concern yourself. Phibia appeases her daughter with these ceremonial honours," she says. "Hira would give anything to be as powerful a Sway as her mother and sit in the Seer Circle, but for all her pride and high-handedness, she has not inherited the skill. Tonight, she plays temple attendant."

"But Saqira sits in the Circle? You said she'd be part of the reading?"

Azza nods. "Saqi's skill showed itself to be strong from an early age, before she could learn to mask it. Phibia likes to keep potential threats to her own power close. She's more likely to control other women with the power if she gets to them young." It reminds me of the tactics of another Sway I know – Mother Iness.

"But what about you? Don't you have the skill like your sister?" Azza looks away, her lips clamping shut and I can see I've broached a prickly topic. "You said Phibia pressed your father to make you a temple attendant, but you don't wear the robes of one as Hira does."

She scoffs. "Phibia can keep her temple rituals and prophecies. She knows I want nothing of them. It's part of the reason we do not see eye-to-eye."

I want to ask her more, but we've arrived at the entrance to the inner sanctum – an expansive grille door, elaborately wrought. Like the dome, its gilt is pitted and flaking with centuries of exposure to the elements. The same heady clouds of incense waft through it, obscuring the dark interior. Hira hasn't spoken a word all the way here, her face funereal, as if any kind of chatter might lessen the significance of the ceremony that's about to unfold. But when I step after Osha across the threshold, she puts up a hand to stop me. "This place is not for your kind, Nara Fornwood. The Circle is for Seers and those to be read. Only the Pure may be granted admission."

"I go where my sister goes, that's the deal," I tell her. "Take it or leave it."

"It's fine, Nara," Osha intervenes. "I'll be alright." But her face is wan with nerves. Gone is the flush of exhilaration she'd been unable to disguise while testing compounds with Haus over the past few days.

"If you've changed your mind, you don't have to do this, O. I won't let them force you."

"Stop, Nara," she answers firmly. "I want this over and done with." She still thinks the whole thing is a misunderstanding, that she can't possibly be the woman the Seers are looking for. Perhaps she's right. But what if she isn't?

I release my frustrations on Hira. "Anything happens to her in there and I swear, daughter of the Khadib or not, I'll hunt you down."

"Understand this, Nara Fornwood," Hira replies, leaning in so close only I can hear. "The Kham might make a show of his sympathies for your kind, but he won't compromise his blood. And neither will Nixim." She scans my branding, her lip curling. "The Pure are too powerful for him to cast his lot with fecs."

Hira knows her words are vinegar on an open wound. I want to shove them back down her throat, but instead I let them wash over me. There's more at stake here than my own injured pride.

"Hira," Azza barks. "Your mother is waiting. Be a good girl and run along."

Stony-faced, Hira grabs Osha by the wrist and tugs her inside. I hover, debating whether to go after them, but my sister shakes her head. "Leave it," she mouths. The feeling of being separated from her sets my teeth on edge. It brings back too many memories – Osha being led away from me on the Roundhouse stage, Orlath's men dragging us apart in the Hrossi settlement.

I lunge after them, but Azza seizes my elbow. "Let her go." She pulls me towards a stairwell. "We can watch everything from up here."

Ascending the steep and winding flight of steps, we reach a viewing gallery that opens out just under the dome itself. Here, a crowd gathers to watch the sanctum below. I see the Kham on the other side of the balcony, surrounded by his retinue, the wrangler among them. So, Nixim returned to watch, then? But not with me.

Azza finds us a prime viewing spot. At first, the haze from the braziers is so thick I can make out nothing but the breathy hiss of Reis prayers hanging in the air, as if the space below is a vast pit filled with sand sirens. My skin chills at the sound, while the cloying scent of incense takes me back to the Pairing rite in Isfalk all those months ago. My breath quickens and that familiar fear of being trapped begins to crawl through me. Have we journeyed this far only for Osha to be thrust into yet another ceremony, bound by rules and rituals, prodded and peered at, up for public scrutiny?

I try to stay focused on the spectral silhouettes of the acolytes that begin to emerge between the braziers below. As the haze shifts, I see the shapes of women seated in a circle in the centre of the prayer space. Their chants rise, amplified by the dome above, the underside of which is painted with shimmering glyphs from the Old World, their chipped gilt winking in the light of the torches like fish in a rockpool. My eyes water from the incense and the lettering begins to dart and wriggle, growing more like snakes chasing each other's tails. With a jolt, I clutch my necklace. The glyphs are forming a single character above me, an all-too-familiar symbol – the Halqa of my pendant – rising clear as sunlight under the dome.

It comes to me then, shocking, frightening – the necklaces Osha and I have worn since birth are the revered icon of an ancient temple on the other side of the Continent, and I have no idea why we have them. When I turn to ask Azza, she quietens me, drawing my attention back to the space below. Phibia has made an unearthly entrance through the haze. Long white robes show off her athletic height, and her silver-white hair is loose and free of head-dressings, blazing down her back, bright as the tail of a comet. Saqira, following a few steps behind, walks alongside a third Seer. They hover at Phibia's shoulders, making a spectral trinity as they approach the Seer Circle. And there, cross-legged in the middle of it, Osha calmly waits, her red hair even more luminous in the grey fog of incense.

The temple falls silent, just as the Roundhouse used to when the Pairings were announced. And watching Phibia hold court in all her lofty glory, Reis's politicians and leaders looking down on the proceedings, awaiting a verdict, something dawns on me – this isn't just a religious rite. It's as political as any Pairing ceremony in Isfalk. Phibia has Reis holding its breath. The hope of the Branded resting on her say-so. No wonder Azza wants nothing to do with the ritual – she and her mother spent their lives empowering Brands, while this prophecy is a step backwards, encouraging them to believe in the coming of a Pure saviour as the only answer to their condition. It formalises branded frailty – branded weakness. Now I understand Azza's attitude towards the prediction, and I see why the wrangler had been so conflicted when he'd first told me about it on the road to Orlathston.

At Phibia's nod, acolytes approach the seated women of the Seer Circle. They're carrying oversized fans of translucent vellum and the glyphs illuminated on the sheer leather wink as they walk an arc, fanning the smoke from the braziers across the proceedings. My lungs constrict from the rising fumes that smell herby and aromatic. I hear Osha coughing and when I squint through the stinging smog, I make out my sister kneeling before Phibia, her head suddenly thrown back, mouth slack as if in sleep. Her arms are held by Saqira on one side and her counterpart on the other, while Phibia cups Osha's face in both palms, as a mother might before kissing a child. But even from here I can tell there's no tenderness in her touch. The Khadib is hungry, readying for the kill, like any good hunter… and my sister is the quarry.

In a panic, I thrust away from the balcony, elbowing through the crowd for the stairs. "Nara Fornwood!" Azza calls out.

"She's hurting her, can't you see? I shouldn't have let her anywhere near my sister."

"Wait!" Azza yells, chasing after me as I take the stairs two at a time. "Do not enter. You must stay away from Phibia." But I'm already opening the grille to the inner sanctum and running inside. Two acolytes catch me by the arms just as I'm about to break the Circle. Phibia and Osha pay me no heed, still locked in their strange embrace, a visceral tension connecting them.

In that instant, I know she's reading my sister, assessing the strength of her Sway. I feel the flinch of Phibia's apprehension, as if she's been clawed by some small animal, can sense her doubt like a scratch she's trying to press closed. And then it's gone. She exhales, and her shoulders drop in relief. I need no help to understand: my sister isn't The One. Osha isn't the Elita.

The Khadib releases Osha's head – a flippant dismissal. Coupled with everything that's gone before, it makes me furious. I wrench from the acolytes and launch myself at Phibia, gripping her forearms in tight fists, but the moment our skin touches, a jolt slams through me like a charge of lightning. I snatch a breath, drawing deeply on the smoke that fills the circle. My lungs almost seize and my vision telescopes. Phibia seems far away and intimately close all at once. She jerks back from me and for an instant I catch the utter shock on her face. And then I'm flung wide, far out across the last stars of an ombre sky, my stomach swooping, my eyes blinking hard against a dazzling fingernail of sun rising on the horizon. The fringe of a sand scarf flutters against my cheek in the dry wind.

Just like the visions that have come before, I hear the jangle of weapons and bridles, the creak of leather, sense the focus of several hundred men and women unified in a single purpose. Except now I recognise the people and the place. Azza, in full Ghume armour and greaves, rides at my side. Behind us is a Reis army, gathered on the ridge we'd climbed when we rode to Cha Shaheer – an army with *me* at the helm.

Spread below us on the plain, the enemy camp is barely stirring, fires down to their embers, horses just beginning to shiver from sleep. They aren't the sleek desert mounts of the Reis, but hardy, brindled beasts, well-suited to the motley warriors sleeping around the ashes, wrapped against the night's chill in only patch-worked skins. For these are riders used to a cold far more punishing than the Storm Sands. These are convoys hardened to the howling winds and snows of the

Wasteland Plains. And those sleeping near them under the silver furs of their capes were born for colder still. For this is a camp of Wastelander *and* Isfalki warriors, joined together in one vast force, outnumbering the troops at my back by three to one.

My mouth turns dry, my throat as desiccated as the plain below. The ranks behind me shift and murmur, soldiers about to lose their confidence. A lone cry tears through the dawn, almost shredding the remnants of my resolve along with it. Iness's tiercel. I try to forget the bird is the crone's spy, listening instead for the flutter of its avian heartbeat. It focuses me, holding the hawk's pulse in my chest – animals are familiar territory, they're what I know best – and I meld its restless rhythm to the drum of my own. There's a flutter as the ghosthawk comes to settle on my arm, and without thinking, I fall into its yellow eye. The silver-haired woman appears reflected there, just as she had in my vision at the Blood-wife's cottage, and this time I have no doubt who she is. It isn't Iness's younger self as I'd once thought. The physical resemblance had misled me. The pale face that crosses the Storm Sands is Phibia's. And as I stroke the bird's brindled breast, something locks into place, something I understand instinctively – Phibia is Iness's daughter.

My chest constricts with a sudden weight I can't seem to shift. Doubt, fear and inadequacy begin to ripple through me, all the confidence and purpose I've drawn from the army at my back melting like ice in my fist. The hawk's talons tighten on my forearm and I can no longer feel my fingers. I cry out in pain. And I realise then that Phibia is with me in this vision, just as the Blood-wife and Iness had been, except she's not only seeing what I see, she's swaying it. *Look what I can do*, her fingers say as they constrict my racing heart. *See how much better I am at this than you?* Her breath taunts my seized lungs. *How pathetic you are, little fec, dabbling with a freak gift so far beyond you!*

I dig deep trying to master my pulse, but it's already fractured into too many rhythms, unruly and erratic. My throat tightens, the image of my army and the camp on the plain turn watery at the edges. I try to stay it, try desperately to hold on to the vision, but I feel like I'm drowning, like I'll never be able to draw breath again.

A hand reaches for mine and I'm dragged through weightless black, the only light coming from the gilded glyphs on the underside of the temple, guiding me upwards. I gulp and swallow like a drowning woman breaking the surface. Phibia swims into focus, examining her outstretched hands. Her fingers and gown are splattered with blood, and I realise it's mine, my nose gushing all over her white robes. Instead of disgust, her face is alive with realisation... and fury.

Azza cups the back of my head. The shape of her telescopes to some distant horizon, those little golden symbols swimming all around her. And the whispered prayers and chanting stops. Everything stills. I hear Reis words – a voice angry and demanding, but I'm too tired to care anymore. The silk of the carpet is so soft... soft as a snowjack against my cheek, and my body is numb from cold, so cold... like I've been sleeping in the Fornwood snows overnight.

"Stay with me, Narkat... Look at me!" the wrangler demands and I remember the feel of those arms all too well. "Hey, stay with me, okay?" But I'm too exhausted. I want to sleep. I want to forget the glimmer of the temple, the choke of incense, the chaos of that hated vision. I only want to breathe the sharp, clean air of the Fornwood and be left alone in peace.

Weakness and Power

The faces are blurred and shift with the light, slipping from my grasp as quickly as my dreams.

Daybreak – Osha.

Sunset – Takia.

Midnight – Azza.

Hands make me drink when I'm not thirsty and douse me in icy water when I already feel as glacial as night on the permafrost. Once, kicking for consciousness and struggling for breath, I'm lifted to a casement, to the cool, dry air of the evening desert. "Breathe," a voice whispers across my skin. I catch the scent of autumn woods and kasta nuts. But my hands find only bunched sheets, my body a twist of damp restlessness.

Fragments of conversation in the night. "What's wrong with her?" Osha's panicked fingers at my neck, my wrists. "I can't read it."

"Move her to the infirmary with the other sick Brands."

"This is no Brand sickness, Hira, and you know it."

"She's not being moved anywhere." A door slams, angry footsteps retreating.

"Brim?" I croak. But the palm that engulfs mine is the wrangler's. I know because the texture, the shape is stamped on my memory. The warmth of it feels so good, I'm too exhausted to push him away.

* * *

It might be days later; it might only be hours. Sultry afternoon light plays across the tiles. I want to sit up, but my body feels like it has no substance, my head light enough to float away on the breeze that comes in from the terrace. I lie silent, watching the figures outside through the billowing gauze curtain, listening as their voices settle into particularity.

"What do you want me to say, Az?" The wrangler sounds regretful and annoyed at the same time.

"I want you to say you were a fool for bringing them here." His sister paces the balcony. "She might have bled to death! Her sway is strong – Saqi felt it when she first arrived, I saw it in the Kyder, and you suspected it all this time. We could have kept her hidden. But, no, you brought her to Cha Shaheer, right under Phibia's nose."

"But I wasn't sure. How else could I confirm what she was without you two laying hands on her? Phibia would never have known if you hadn't let Nara run into the inner sanctum!"

"Please… don't fight." Osha stands between the bickering siblings. Her presence is the reason they're talking in Isfalki, not Reis. "It's no one's fault. Nara has always done what she wants. She's so adamant she has to protect me. I think our grandmother drummed it into her."

"I mean it when I say I'm sorry, Osha," the wrangler tells her, voice low. "I thought Nara was–"

"What?" Azza barks. "Please do not say you thought either of them could be the Elita, Nixim?" She scoffs. "Holy Mother's Chosen One? Effa of the Wasteland Plains? Pick a myth! Or have you been in Isfalk so long you've started to believe the religious nonsense spun by purists to keep the Branded quiet?"

"Stop, Az," Saqira says gently.

"Forgive me, Eirafa. Am I being too blasphemous for your tastes?" I've never heard Azza sound so cynical, so angry.

"Nixim does not understand how powerful Phibia has become in his absence," Saqira says. Moderating between her brother and sister, she suddenly sounds so much older than her years, as if the cheeky young girl racing down the temple steps was some kind of act she reserves for public appearances.

"She was powerful enough when he left," Azza complains. "Did she not make our father rekindle faith in that mindless prophecy? Did she not revive the Order of Seekers to search for the Elita? It was not piety that motivated her to do so. Hunting down other Sways is a convenient way of finding those with the potential to become more powerful than herself. She needs to know who she can control and who she must eliminate."

"*Eliminate*?" Osha says, but Azza hasn't finished scolding Nixim.

"Cha Shaheer is living proof the Branded do not need any Elita to save them. They are perfectly capable of saving themselves when given the opportunity. Or have you forgotten, brother, what our mother achieved in this city through integration?"

"Of course I haven't forgotten, Az. You talk like I'm not on your side. I've always been with you and her cause."

"You have a strange way of showing it, delivering a woman with such skill straight into Phibia's hands."

"Where else was I to bring her? Nara and Osha know so little about their abilities. I thought in Reis they could at least be trained to realise their potential." The wrangler sounds agonised, genuinely rueful now. "I believed Nara was stronger than she proved to be–"

"She *is* strong. That's precisely the problem," Azza says. "I told you after I saw her hunt in the Kyder, her sway is more concentrated than anyone's I've sensed since our mother's – stronger than mine, perhaps even stronger than Phibia's. But she is *wild*, Nixim – unschooled and undisciplined. How did you expect her to fare against a trained Tathar at the height of her sway? If Saqi hadn't been there to pull her out of the vision, she might have bled herself dry trying to withstand that woman!"

Silence. Only the mundane sound of cartwheels on cobbles, the shouts of hawkers rising from the streets below. I don't want to move. I'm overwhelmed by their words. I have no idea what a *Tathar* is but I'm desperate to know the truth, to hear what they say about me when they think I can't hear.

"In the temple, when I touched her and saw her vision, she *was* trying," Saqira says. "But it was like when I used to play dress-ups in Azza's hunting boots – they were too big, I'd run too fast, and they'd trip me up. She hasn't grown into her power. It's why she bleeds."

"But she can learn to control that, right?" Osha asks. "Nixim, you said Azza can teach her. That was why you brought us here, wasn't it?"

"If Azza can't train her, no one can," the wrangler says, but his sister doesn't answer, turning her back on him and surveying the city below.

Saqira exhales impatiently. "Azza prefers to keep her skill hidden and unused, just as our mother did–"

"Saqi," Azza says, as if warning her off a topic that has caused arguments before.

"Every Sway has their area of strength," Saqira continues for Osha's benefit. "For some it is influencing the animal mind. Nara has already become very good at that. For others, like you and the apotheks, it is reading the human body and helping it to heal. Then there are those of us who can go a step further, seeing into the mind of another person, our touch allowing us to access visions of their past, their present, sometimes even their future. In the temple, we Seers use a little help with that."

"What help?"

"Krait's mesmer, usually. It's in the incense we burn during readings," Saqira says.

"But how is it that my sister has a connection to animals *and* she has visions?" Osha asks.

"Occasionally, a Sway grows into their skill to find they have more than one gift. They may favour the primary ability they develop in childhood, as Nara favours hunting, but they can be trained to access others. In even rarer instances, such Sways are gifted with the ability to influence human emotions, as well as read them. In Reis these women are called Tathars and, as my sister mentioned, Phibia is one of the most powerful examples. She hunts Sways under the guise of seeking the Elita, but she does not do so for any religious reason. Rather she uses the prophecy for her own political agenda, seeking to control those with the power to threaten her. That is why the Elita will never be declared."

Saqira clears her throat and looks for approval from her older sister, evidently trying to impress her with words I suspect have come straight from Azza's own mouth. It is plain to see Saqi idolises her. "Phibia believes she is the only Tathar in Cha Shaheer," Saqira adds, that cheeky tone returning briefly. "She does not realise another hides under her very nose."

"That's enough, Saqi!" Azza barks.

The young girl gives a breathy laugh, unsurprised at the rebuke. "My sister is ashamed of her gift. She deems it a form of supernatural trickery. Dangerous. Deceitful."

"You know very well that is not what I think, Bu," Azza says, mastering her temper. "It is more complicated than that."

"Then train her, Az," Nixim pleads. "Help Nara realise her potential, even if your principles mean you deny yours."

"We don't have much choice, sister," Saqi says. "I told you, I was there with Nara inside the vision. She saw a foreign horde amassed on our borders – an allied force of Wastelanders and Isfalki – and she was leading the Reis army against them. Perhaps she is to be the hope of the Branded, after all? The best hope for any Reis who wants to protect our mother's legacy."

"That vision is only one version of a possible future, Saqi," Azza says. "We still possess free will to choose as we see fit."

"I know. But I am with Phibia more than you," the girl replies. "I work closest to her in the temple, remember? And I believe she will use *her* free will to overtake Reis. Her ambition will make Nara's vision come to pass. An attack on Cha Shaheer is going to happen, in spite of what you or Nara Fornwood *choose*."

"But I don't understand," Osha interrupts. "Why would Phibia need a foreign army to overtake the city when she already holds considerable power here?"

"She holds *elected* power," Azza corrects. "Power given by choice can be taken away again. And it is not only Cha Shaheer Phibia cares about. Our most fertile farming territories in the south are her goal. Dominating them means she would control the country's major food source. But the clans who work the land there, and the Ghumes who protect it, are known to be loyal to our mother's cause."

"That's why Saqi is right," the wrangler says. "We need to use Nara's vision to our advantage."

"How?" Osha asks.

But Nixim's answer is for Azza. "You told me when I arrived that our father no longer sees clearly because of the Khadib. His decisions are influenced more and more by her prejudices. If we can't make him believe what she's plotting, the defence of Reis falls on us. I've begun to rally some of our mother's supporters among the Seven Clans and those Ghumes that are loyal to you and Captain Alrahim. But it isn't enough, Az. If Phibia gets support from the north she will certainly overpower us."

Azza paces for a moment. "You believe we need to defend the whole of Reis, not only our hearthsands?"

"I'm saying we may need to prevent the arrival of Hrossi forces and that means a pre-emptive strike."

"Attacking Orlathston?" Osha is the first to say it, her voice unsteady.

"You hope to defeat the Hrossi overlord in his own capital, brother?" Azza scoffs.

"We do have two of his best weapons on our side," her brother answers. "Haus and the Maw. Every waking moment since leaving Olathston, Haus has been plotting to avenge himself on Orlath. All he needs is the resources at his disposal." I understand then that the wrangler has already been negotiating with the Hrossi chief about a return north. My vision has merely given him further justification of that decision. "If talks with our father fail, we must have a second strategy – a strike in the north. Controlling the Wastelands before Phibia does and cutting off the route to Isfalk is our only hope." Through the curtain, I can see the wrangler studying his sister's reaction. "Az, I need you with me on this." It's her approval he wants most of all. His shoulders sink in relief when Azza finally gives a reluctant nod.

"But talks with our father come first, Nixim," she says. "War must be our last resort."

The wrangler catches her hands between his, cementing their agreement. "Az," he says, making his sister hold his gaze, "one last thing. Nara must train to realise her potential as a Sway. I need to know she can protect herself should Phibia…"

He trails off, perhaps to spare Osha.

"Should Phibia come for my sister's blood again?" Osha continues for him.

The wrangler nods at her, frowning. But he turns back to Azza, tone private now. "Please, Az. Train her… if only for me." His words seem to soften something in her. They soften something in me.

Azza pulls from his reach and steps from the bright balcony into the shadows of the room. She's the first to see I've regained consciousness, and that I've been listening. Studying my face, she cocks an eyebrow.

"Will Nara Fornwood let me train her? That is the question."

Lies and Influencing

Watching the evening shadows creep across the city, I try to process everything that has happened, everything I've heard.

Osha is preparing soup for me like I'm some convalescing patient in danger of breathing their last; I can hear the Maw playing rune jacks with the Ghume guards Azza has stationed in the corridor; and I suspect Haus has disappeared to the stables, busying himself among the horses, as is his habit. We're all biding time, waiting on a knife's edge for the return of Saqira and Nixim, the outcome of their talks with the Kham. But there's one person who's noticeable for their absence. I haven't seen Brim since the night we kissed. He wasn't there when I woke after the Seer reading and it grieves me. I have to set things right with him... even though I have no idea where to begin.

"Something troubles you, Nara Fornwood," Azza says, sitting beside me in an archway of the terrace.

I scoff at her. "You want to chat about what's on my mind? Shall we start with the power-crazed Sway who just tried to kill me? Or the gift that nearly bleeds me to death every time I use it? Perhaps we can shoot the breeze about sailing back to the deranged tyrant who abused my sister and put me in a fighting pit? Take your pick."

She nods in sympathy, but there's a twinkle in her eye. "And your Elix Captain? Your thoughts do not turn to him?"

I blow out my cheeks in frustration. Am I truly so easy to read? "Yes, I'm a bit worried about him, if you must know."

"You care for him greatly, do you not?" she asks gently, carefully.

"We grew up together and we've been through... a lot. But he's still my best friend... Do you know where he is?"

"Captain Oskarsson is on a mission this evening. Hira came asking for news of you, and I know Phibia will send spies if she does not get it. Brim offered to dine with her and Hira tonight. He will ensure Phibia still thinks you fight for your life. He'll keep her distracted. That way, Saqi and my brother can speak to our father alone, without her meddling presence."

The news conflicts me. I'm incredibly grateful to Brim, but also worried for him, and a little jealous he's spending so much time with Hira. Azza sees it. "Your Captain is a loyal one, I think?" she says. "My brother must... how do you say it in Isfalki?... *watch his back*?"

But I won't be baited into a discussion of my feelings. It's a petty distraction and I see through it. "And what about you, *Azza Ni Azzadur*? Are you loyal? Trustworthy?"

"Do we still talk of your captain?" Perhaps she noted my jealousy the day she sparred with Brim in the amphitheatre.

"No, fec the men. I'm talking about you and me. You've been lying all this time about who you really are... what you are. Your family has a habit of that, don't they?"

She stiffens as she leans against the stonework. "I did not lie to you, Nara Fornwood."

"But all this talk of the Elita and the prophecy, and you and Nixim never even believed it yourselves?"

"Not revealing my opinions is not lying. In thinking the way we do, my brother and I oppose many of the most powerful Pures in Reis, not just Phibia. It is not something to be discussed with strangers on a whim."

"Then what has this whole journey been for? Why did Nixim bring us here? You *knew* Phibia would never declare Osha the Elita... or anyone else for that matter."

She brushes the sand scarves from her hair, takes a preparatory breath. "The continuation of the prophecy is useful to Phibia. The Elita will supposedly cleanse the blood of the marked, returning the Branded to the health and prosperity of the Old World. But do you not see how the coming of a Pure saviour implies the Pure are superior, how it divests Brands of any belief in their own strength and abilities, and keeps them subservient... *weak*?" She straightens now, framed in the arched casement, Cha Shaheer spread out before her. Her passion is a restless pulse in her neck. "The prophecy is nothing but political propaganda framed as spiritual belief. My mother knew it and she worked to quash prophecy fanatics. But since her death, Phibia has done the opposite, encouraging the religion to grow again. As I said, it suits her agenda."

The soft colours and gentle sounds of evening sit at odds with the turmoil churning inside me. All this time I believed Osha was the gifted one, the one with the real skill... the one who needed protection. But now it's me with the latent power – the one Phibia might kill. The ground is constantly shifting under my feet. I feel uncertain about everything, vulnerable, out of control. So, I do what I always do – I attack.

"It's not just the prophecy." I turn on Azza. "You lied about your branding and now you've lied about your skill, too. You could have told me at any time when we were hunting in the Kyder. You could have *shown* me you were a Sway."

"I blocked you from sensing my abilities, but I did not lie," she insists. "There is a difference."

I want to press her so much more, but there's a sudden commotion within, quickened footsteps, a door banging. We hurry inside to find the wrangler, more unsettled than I've ever seen him before. He paces the room, palm smoothing his temple, trying to gather his thoughts.

"Brother?" Azza prompts.

"It's worse than you warned," he tells her. "Father wouldn't even listen. He's no longer the man I remember as a child." Ghumes arrive in the doorway and the wrangler issues hurried orders in Reis.

"Nixim?" Azza asks, panicked. We're hanging on his every word now.

"Father's opinions are warped by Phibia beyond rescue. She knows that Nara's vision has shown us her plans for a foreign alliance."

"Surely she was not present when you tried to warn Father what Nara saw? You spoke to him in private?"

"Of course I did. But she burst into his chambers in the middle of our discussion. One of Father's personal guards must have fetched her as soon as we entered his quarters. The Kham's Watch is now the Khadib's Watch, it seems."

"And Father would listen to nothing you said?" Azza says. I can hear how desperately she wants to be contradicted.

The wrangler lowers his chin. "He asked me how I could have sunk so low... how I could have let my head be turned by a–"

He breaks off, cutting me a look under heavy brows.

"By a *fec*," I finish the sentence for him.

"We fought and he made terrible accusations. Phibia has made him believe Nara is an Isfalki spy." The wrangler forks his fingers into his hair, squeezing at the roots. "Saqi and I could have used your help," he tells his sister, accusation in his voice. "You might have tried to... to sway him."

"Do not lay that at my feet, Nixim." Azza shakes her head, but she's conflicted, I can tell. "I will not sink to that krait's methods. I will not be like her. I made a vow..." she begins, before thinking better of it. "It is too late. If Father is lost, we must follow our contingency."

"Then we move," Nixim agrees. "And we do it now."

"What? Where are we going?" I clasp his sleeve, suddenly realising we're on the run. *Now* means *immediately*. "For pox's sake, Wrangler, tell me what's happening?"

"It is not safe here anymore. We have to move north and hope that Haus can secure us a stronghold there." He speaks quickly, catching me up on a plan he's clearly already set in motion. "I've organised ships for the forces loyal to us, carrying them north to Orlathston. Azza will take you and Osha aboard the *Na'quat*. We need to get you out of Cha Shaheer as soon as possible."

"What about you?"

"I leave for the south. I'll sail with the southern clans and join you in a few days." My heart drops to my stomach. He won't be coming with us. "You've gathered all your essentials?" he says, turning to Osha.

"I sent everything ahead to the ship this morning, as you asked," my sister confirms. She has the decency to answer my look of betrayal. "Nixim told me to be ready to leave at a moment's notice. You were still recovering. Be angry at me if you like, but for Mother's sake, stow it for later. We need to hurry." And she turns her back on me to help Takia grab clothes and riding mantles.

The wrangler takes Azza by the shoulders, searching her face. "Now is not the time to hide your skill. You'll stand by your promise? Osha will help you manage her. Do this for me, Az?" I've never seen the wrangler so fierce, so determined. After a beat, his sister says, "I will train Nara Fornwood. Rest easy, brother, and be safe." He seems satisfied enough with that, even if I am not.

"Nixim, wait," Osha calls, panicked. "Where's Haus?"

"At the gorge with the Maw. They have horses at the ready."

Osha hurries to shove a few quills and copybooks into bags.

"Is Brim with Haus?" I ask the wrangler.

It's the first time he stands still, studying me now, as if looking for clues. He catches my elbow and pulls me through to the terrace, away from the others rushing about the rooms. No torches have been lit and the darkness is suddenly intimate.

"Your first concern in all this is still for Pretty Boy?" he asks, voice low. The note of self-doubt in it tugs a little at my heart.

"My first concern is for myself and my sister," I answer, stubbornly holding his gaze. Now, fleeing Cha Shaheer, the threat of war imminent, it doesn't seem the moment for lies – either to him or to myself. I'm struck by the thought that I don't know when I'll see him again – that I might *never* see him again. It makes me angry. Angry and panicked. "Poxes, Wrangler, *you* could have been my first concern. But you never tell me the truth… you won't trust me or confide in me… you think I need to be *managed* by your sister–"

"Nara, stop. I've never lied to you. Not once."

"But you've let me make all the wrong assumptions. What about Hira–"

"Stop. Enough."

He steps nearer, still scanning my face, as if hoping to see some shred of the way I looked at him that night aboard the *Na'quat*. He's so close, it would take nothing to lean into him, to find him again… if he wants to be found. But neither of us makes the move.

He sighs in frustration. "Things are… complicated," he says.

"Are they? They didn't seem very complicated when it was just you and me that last night on the ship. Sometimes things can be beautifully simple. Or have you forgotten?"

"It's not me who's forgotten." He lifts a hand, as if he wants to slide it along my jaw and draw me in, his expression tentative, hopeful, despite the urgency all around us. "But you're so bloody stubborn, Little Scourge!" he says, making a fist of his palm. "You're going to let me leave with that vision of him kissing you turning over and over in my mind? Knowing that he's your first love? That he's what you've wanted all along?" He drops his hand, shaking his head.

I recognise that flicker of pain in his eyes; it's the same pain

I've felt every time I've seen him with Hira. It's a loose rock on the uncertain path ahead of us, but it's one that I have the power to kick away. All I have to do is reach out for him. But my mind seizes on the two of them at the feast, so handsome, so perfectly matched, their kiss delighting the adoring crowd. I can't help myself. "Does it feel different with a Pure? Is it better?"

"What?" His mouth falls open and he steps away, face turning stony. "I don't know, Nara, does it feel different with a Prince of Isfalk? That's what Brim Oskarsson is, isn't he – an heir of the Founding Four?"

It's the first time he's used Brim's proper name. Part of me wants to confess, *Who? I don't even remember who Brim is when I'm with you.* That part of me wants to see the mole jump in his cheek again, wants to fist his collar and feel his tongue warming the permanent chill I've felt ever since leaving the bunk we shared at sea... ever since seeing him with Hira at the feast... ever since the vision in the temple. That half of me wants to cry out. *Shut up, Wrangler, and put your hands on me!*

But the other half – perhaps the stupid half – suffocates that voice into silence.

We stare at each other for a long moment, scavenging among the wreckage of fear and pride and hurt for a route back to that night aboard the *Na'quat*, but the sounds of the others rushing about inside becomes too urgent to ignore.

"So you'll let Hira and Brim be the last names on our lips?" he says. "Not even a goodbye kiss?"

"You waiting for an invitation?"

"Yes."

That's so typical of him to put this on me. But I won't be the one to give in, to show weakness and need. "You'll be waiting a long time, then, Wrangler." He tries to mask the sting, but his shoulders sink in the moonlight, like I've stolen a little of the breath from his lungs.

"Here," I say, taking a coin from my pocket and tossing it to him. "A parting gift." It's the gold piece Lars Oskarsson gave me the night I was exiled from Isfalk, and it glints for a second in the space between us. He catches it and looks down at the Halqa symbol – the match of my pendant, the match of his tattoo.

"What's this for?" he asks.

"To play *Lady Luck*." I shrug, aiming for the nonchalance I've seen Ghume guards feign when they play the game of chance outside our door. But I can't quite keep the note of bitterness from my voice. "Halqa-side up can be Hira, plain side up can be me. Might help you decide."

"Is that how you decided? Has Pretty Boy won the toss over me?"

I hesitate. Inside, a voice is yelling, *There is no toss, Wrangler. You win every time.* But I won't give him the satisfaction of knowing it, not when he won't come to me, not when my broken heart still demands payback. "Maybe," I tell him.

"Then I'm glad love is such a game for you, Nara." And his use of my real name, the coldness of it in the same sentence as that word *love*, almost breaks me.

"Nix, wait–"

But I'm too late. He's already striding from the terrace and into the chaos beyond.

Everything seems to happen too fast after that.

We're stealing down corridors, dim passageways, and crude steps leading through the bowels of the city – a network of Old-World catacombs and caves. I barely have time to lose my mind over the confined spaces, to pant in panic through the dim and musty tunnels, for we're running – away from Phibia, yes, but also away from any chance I might have at fixing things between myself and the wrangler. And the dawning sense of my own self-destructiveness is distraction enough from any other petty fear I might be grappling with.

When that old dread of being trapped finally does catch up and my frantic lungs feel like they're about to reduce me to my knees, vision blackening at the edges, Osha tugs me on by my sweaty hands. Suddenly we're outside in the cool night air, beyond the city's defences, surfacing between a chasm in the gorge. Haus waits for us in the darkness, the Maw and a retinue of Ghume soldiers behind him. And then the wrangler is there, speaking quickly to Azza in Reis, and I want to sob in relief, to shout out that I take it all back, that there is no coin toss, no Lady Luck. We make our own luck, and I will always choose him. But before I can speak, he swings up into his saddle and I'm left watching his dust trail racing south, a Ghume unit chasing after him into the night. Nixim didn't even spare me a second glance.

Azza steadies my horse, Haus, Osha and the Maw already mounted. Everything feels wrong – parting with the wrangler this way, but also leaving Cha Shaheer itself. It's like something is binding me to the Shadow City. *Don't look back.* Amma's words ring in my head. She knew my nature so well. She knew I'd always look back at the hard things, the things others turned their faces from. Amma trained me to hunt, to stare death in the eyes, after all. And I understand that terrible tug of Cha Shaheer now. I don't want to run from Phibia – I want to *face* her. There's something she knows about me, some answer I need, but I'm moving further and further away from it. It nags as I tighten my reins, as I cast about me for the reassurance of familiar faces – for Osha, Haus, Brim. "Wait," I call out. "Where's Brim? Why isn't he here?"

"We have to go," Azza answers, not looking me in the eye.

"I won't leave him again," I say. "We have to wait." When I'd argued with Brim on the Wasteland Plains, parting ways with him had felt like I'd cut off an arm. I turn to Osha. "Where *is* he? He should be here."

My sister's face is pale in the light of the waning moon. "The Ghume guards searched for him, but he couldn't be found."

"Azza, hold on. Just a bit longer," I plead. "I know he'll come." But in my heart, I'm not so sure he will. That last look of bitter disappointment I saw on his face when the wrangler interrupted our kiss and I pushed Brim off me – it might be too much pride for him to swallow.

Azza circles my horse with her own. "I am sorry, Nara Fornwood. There is no more time." And without waiting for my response, she whips the rump of my mount with her reins. He launches into the desert darkness straight as an arrow, and I'm too confused about Brim and the wrangler and Phibia to fight it.

The steady rumble of hooves, the suck of lungs, the drag of wind in my face is freeing. But flee as we might, I can't get away from that chill deep inside me. It takes material form now, a familiar shape at the edge of my vision. High above our dust trail, a lonely night shadow circles, too distant to hear, too far for me to call down, but I see it there – the ghosthawk, Mother Iness's bird.

Isfalk following. Isfalk watching. Isfalk waiting.

PART TWO:
A HROSSI DEBT

Back Aboard the Na'Quat

"Focus, Nara Fornwood," Azza snaps. Her practise sword slaps me sharply across my bicep and I drop my guard.

In a blink, she's in my face, blunt steel pressed to my neck. I stumble against the gunwale with an irritable shrug of surrender, and she sighs, evidently as tired of me as I am of her. It's bad enough we've been on the decks training since sunrise and I still haven't landed so much as a hit on her; now I have an audience. Up in the rigging, half the crew of the *Na'quat* appear to be watching me take a beating, while the Maw, playing rune jacks against the rise of the quarterdeck, winces every time Azza sends me sprawling across the boards. "You allow your thoughts to stray, Nara Fornwood," Azza says.

"You reckon?" I try to tame anger with sarcasm. How can my thoughts *not* stray? We nearly lost everything in Orlathston, escaping with barely the shreds of who we once were. Now we're voluntarily sailing back there, straight into the hands of Orlath – the sick fec whose primary entertainments were abusing my sister in his Mor harem and watching Haus and I brawl for our lives in his fighting pits. We're lucky our body parts hadn't ended up as trophies on the walls of his keep.

On top of the delightful pastime of revisiting those fears, I'm still worried sick about Brim's whereabouts. And, yes, the wrangler's. Is it foolish to hope that they joined up and travelled south to recruit Nixim's supporters together? Osha is hopeful, but Azza avoids my eye when I speak of it. This is our fifth day at sea and there's still been no sign or word. Nixim's ships should have caught up with us by now, even if the wind was against them. In typical wrangler style, he's keeping us guessing.

Haus is the only one who appears to sail on steady seas. Azza grows to rely on his counsel, just as I have. He's convinced her to stay the course, heading for his hearthlands and the support of his clan. As my confidence wanes with each passing day, the chief's seems to grow, believing he can muster clans of Wastelanders against the Hrossi tyrant and certain the wrangler will follow through on his word to boost a rebel army with his own. If we succeed in a takeover of the port city, Haus tells me we'll control the Continent's trade routes, as well as the gateway north, cutting off supplies to Isfalk, just as Nixim planned.

And yet, listening to him discuss strategy with Azza, the sheer scale of the plan in which Osha and I are now embroiled is suddenly overwhelming. It feels like only yesterday we were girls fleeing raiders in the Fornwood, and now we're players in an uprising to control the Continent. So, when Azza accuses me of letting my thoughts *stray*, I want to laugh in her face. My mind isn't getting side-tracked by petty distractions – it's being assaulted and sacked by a barbarian host of worries almost every moment I'm awake. And when I sleep, my dreams become a warped version of those worries. I feel out of my depth on every count.

"Raise your sword, Nara Fornwood," Azza commands. "Let us go again."

I shake my head. I'm tired. Physically and mentally. But I'm mostly tired of her high-handedness. I knew she'd stand by the promise she gave her brother, but I hadn't expected training to start the first morning we were at sea. And she's had me on the decks at dawn every day since, with nothing to show for it. I can't access my sway, I'm still bleeding every time I try and, worst of all, I still haven't landed a decent hit on her.

Wiping the sweat from my lip, I turn to walk away, but she grabs my wrist. As soon as our skin touches, I feel it – that quickening, that warm tingling like blood recirculating in a dead arm. And then intense pain, as if she's taken her dagger and is trying to skin that arm. It steals my breath and I sink to my knees.

"Is that it?" she bites out. "Your best effort?" She mutters something to herself in Reis.

To my surprise, it's Haus who intervenes. Calling Azza over to the wheel, they exchange words I can't hear. Afterwards, she lays down her weapon, sauntering to the water bucket. "Very well," she calls over her shoulder, "rest now, Nara Fornwood."

I baulk at the command. "You know, you can save your breath and call me Nara," I pant. "You don't need the Fornwood bit all the time."

"I think it is you who needs to save your breath." She watches me rub at my arm, the pain of her mental assault still lingering. "Talk less, block more." When she approaches, I flinch. But slow and gentle, she lays her palm on the back of my neck. I feel the quickening again, this time easing the pain, flooding me with confidence, inviting me into her trust. The feeling's similar to what I felt with the Blood-wife, what I feel when Osha takes my hand, except much more certain… stronger.

"How do you do that?" I ask, unable to disguise my wonder.

"You could do it, too, if you focused."

She begins to walk away and now it's me snatching her wrist, closing my fingers around it – straining to hear her pulse. Her skin is balmy in the ocean breeze, her blood flowing even warmer beneath it, pepper and cinnamon against the tang of salt spray on my tongue. The steady lub-dub is compulsive, drawing me to it. I latch on like iron filings to a magnet, and a vision washes over me – two hands, spreading a map across a table. Their shape is oddly familiar, one finger pinning down the corner of the parchment, another tracing place names and borders. I try to push further into the image, to discover the owner of these hands, or what the chart reveals, but the connection between us suddenly dissipates. Azza's mind turns blank as the winter Fold, and I shudder at the cooling of her skin. It feels like I'm knee-deep in the snow, the door to a fire-lit hearth slamming shut in my face.

"Well, shit," I say, deadpan. "Talk about the cold shoulder."

She looks away, impatient. "*That* is what I'm trying to teach you, Nara Fornwood."

"What, to be an icy bitch?" I can't help being pissed – my first breakthrough in days of training and she still won't cut me some slack.

"Call it what you will," she says, stiffening at the insult. "I prefer the term *defensive strategy*. It is how I prevented you from sensing my skill when we first met, and it is why Nixim has pressed for *me* to instruct you." She lifts the end of her sand scarf and swipes under my nose. "Unless you intend to bleed to death first."

"Why does it happen to me, anyway?" I sniff. "Osha doesn't bleed when she heals."

"Osha is a gifted Sway but she does not have the breadth or depth of your skill." She sits down next to me, leaning against the gunwale. "Your visions and the force of the energy Saqi felt in you at the reading all suggest your abilities run deeper than your sister's. Your sway drains you."

"Because I'm already weaker, I suppose?" I tap the side of my head, the site of my mark. "Because I'm branded and you're both Pure?"

She looks me square in the face, her kohl-rimmed eyes as unfathomable as the ocean around us. "Listen to me, Nara Fornwood. You do not bleed because you are a Brand. You bleed because you are unschooled. All Sways exhibit such limitations when they come into their abilities as children or young adults. Fainting, fitting, nose bleeds – they are common. I had a mother to teach me how to overcome that stage, but you have never had the benefit of another Sway guiding you.

I believe if you had..." she hesitates for a moment, "... if you were trained... you might learn to do more than *see* inside a person's head. You might learn to..."

"To do what? Influence their thoughts? To become a Tathar, like Phibia? Like you?"

She stares me down. "Then you heard what Saqi told your sister?"

"About the Sways with pumped-up abilities, yeah." I roll my shoulders with exaggerated cockiness. "You think I'm one of these *Super Sways*?"

"Your performance so far makes it doubtful," she fires off, annoyed that I'm making a joke of it, that I'm wasting her time. I see myself reflected in those big eyes – a brash little misfit, terrified of this vague and unbiddable power that makes me see things that aren't there, that makes me bleed... that makes me swagger and bluff to cover how out of control I feel. "No one can predict the full capacity of a Tathar's gift, Nara Fornwood," Azza says, her voice gentler now she's seen through me. "My mother once told me only a portion of the Tathar's power is hereditary – the potential passed down a female line to one rare daughter or granddaughter while skipping all others. The rest lies in your own efforts – how hard you train the skill. The more aware of it you become, the easier it is to access and the stronger it will grow."

"Like a bow or sword technique? You learn the method, you train the arm, and the muscles get more intuitive."

"A little simplistic, but yes." She rubs a knuckle across her lips, hesitantly. "You should be aware, Nara Fornwood, that not all Sways who can glimpse inside a subject's head are able to influence their thoughts and memories as a Tathar can. Most Seers can only bear witness to a person's past or future.

"Like Saqira, you mean?" Azza studies her palm, almost embarrassed. "She puts you on a pedestal, you know," I say. "Even I can see it." Uncomfortable with my observation, she glances away. "You'd rather Saqi idolised you as a politician or social reformer, not a Tathar?"

"We should get back to work."

I've been too personal, drawn too near to the argument I overheard between the sisters on the balcony. But if she's to be my teacher, why shouldn't I know more about Azza and her abilities?

"Who taught you to block other Sways from your thoughts?"

After a beat, she gives in. "My mother. That was her forte. Nixim thinks a defensive strategy is your best chance of survival against a Tathar at the height of her Sway." She gets up, straightens her tunic. "But sitting here talking about it will not see much progress."

I lean my head against the ship's rail, cutting Azza a look. "How can you teach me to wield my abilities when you're so ashamed of yours?"

She blanches for a second time, then leans over the rail, staring at the churning sea. "I am not *ashamed* of my skill. I simply choose to not let it define who I am."

Curious, I get up too, resting on my elbows next to her. "But it is who you are, surely?" Azza's expression grows faraway for a moment before turning blank again. "You know, Azza Ni Azzadur, we have a saying in Isfalk." I clear my throat. *"If you don't trust me, how the fec am I supposed to trust you?"*

She laughs at last – that husky rumble I haven't heard in a while. "You made that up, I think?"

"Yes, Azza, I made it up."

"Very well." She takes a moment to watch the gulls hover and dive the ship's roiling wake. "Being a Tathar is problematic for me in a way Saqi struggles to understand," she begins. "When our mother died, I was... I was like a ship without a rudder. I clung to her legacy as my guide – she always stressed the importance of intellect, integrity and good deeds above any power of sway. Saqi was much younger than me, so Phibia was more involved in her upbringing. When Phibia pressed for her to join the Seer Circle, my father agreed, and so did Saqi. My little sister may seem young, but she has her own mind, as you heard for yourself." She lets out a breath of amusement. "Phibia thinks she controls her, but she does not realise that Saqi spies for us."

"*That's* why she stayed behind." Being trusted with this confidence pleases me as much as the information itself, and Azza knows it. She smiles.

"Phibia is ignorant of my skill. I've kept it blocked from her since I was a child," she says. "My mother called the technique *parikshan* – shielding – and made me practice from an early age. After her death, when I witnessed Phibia's rise to power and her desire to dominate other Sways, it became strategic to me – a matter of self-preservation. Now, as you see, Saqi and Nixim pressure me to use my abilities more and more."

"But if you're so passionate about protecting her achievements, why don't you?"

Her jaw tightens, teeth set, as if it's a long-standing argument she must physically brace herself to counter. "If I use my sway, does it not make me exactly like Phibia? Would I not be influencing people to do *my* will instead of allowing them the freedom to make their own choices? Sways with the healing skill, like your sister, are admirable, but influencing the actions and emotions of others as if they are puppets is not a *gift* – not one I am proud to use, anyway. My mother dedicated her whole life to building a Reis in which everyone has the power and the possibility to better themselves. She never used her sway to do it and she made me promise I would continue that legacy. It is her ideal I uphold, the path I've always tried to follow."

Promises. I think of the vow I made to Amma to protect my sister. I understand the pacts we make with the dead, the hold they have over us. I understand Azza's ambivalence to her skill. The Blood-wife warned me being a Sway was a double-edge sword, something the wise might consider a curse as much as a blessing. But I also understand everything Reis will lose at Phibia's hands – the Isfalk she is seeking to replicate in a land of such freedom, such opportunity for all.

"With all respect to your mother, Azza, did she ever have to face a megalomaniac Purist gathering an army of foreign invaders at the gates of Cha Shaheer?" Azza blinks at the bluntness of that image. "Don't you think the protection of Reis is what she would have wanted you to uphold first?" I press on. "Your grand principles aren't going to do the Branded any good if Reis is turned into another Isfalk. And if my vision is correct, Isfalk is where Phibia's loyalty lies."

Azza's gaze snaps to mine. "Why do you say that?"

"Before I left the Settlement, I made Mother Iness's bird come to me. It showed me a woman crossing the desert. At first, I thought it was Iness in her youth. But then the face became clearer. It was Phibia. I'm certain she's Iness's daughter – the resemblance is too uncanny. And I saw something else, too. In the vision, Phibia was pregnant."

Azza grows restless as my words sink in.

"What is it?" I ask her.

"There were rumours in Cha Shaheer, when I was a girl. Perhaps they were true…"

"What rumours?"

"The gossips said Phibia was an Isfalki Mor, brought to Reis as a trade. Some claimed she was already with child when she arrived and began living with the eastern clans."

"So, it was Hira she was carrying in my vision?"

"No. Hira was sired later by the Kha who took Phibia as his wife – she inherited his darker skin, his looks. He was Kha of a Pure clan, and a powerful voice in the Cha Shaheer Forum. A match with a northern Mor of Isfalki blood was a coup for him, a status symbol. He is dead now. Conveniently."

The implication shocks me. "You think Phibia killed him? Is she that mercenary?"

Azza folds her arms and raises her eyebrows. "You tell me, Nara Fornwood. Phibia made you bleed like a sacrificial goat in the Golden Temple. Did it not feel like she was capable of killing?"

We both know the answer to that. I chew the inside of my lip. "If she was pregnant when she arrived from Isfalk, where is that child? Did it survive?"

"I do not know," Azza says. "But I think I know the person who might."

Galley Tales

"Takia?" I say, incredulously. Azza leads me below decks to the galley where the servant prepares our meals. "Really?"

"Yes, Takia. We have a saying in Reis: *If you want to hear the secrets of a Kha, listen first in his kitchens.* Takia once worked in Phibia's."

I was surprised, and not a little disappointed, to discover the servant was to sail with us to Orlathston. Now, the idea that I might have to beg her for information is galling to say the least. "I don't think Takia likes me very much."

"Of course she does not like you," Azza scoffs. "Takia was Nixim's nurse-maid. She dislikes any woman who might come close to exceeding her in his affections. And on that count, you are the first."

Azza's eyes glint with mischief as she watches me flush, knowing her words give me both pleasure and pain.

When we enter the galley, Takia is preparing a stew. Knife raised mid-chop, she blanches at the intensity of our focus, sensing that something is afoot and she is at the centre of it. She recovers enough to put the knife down, and I'm thankful when she busies herself making herb tea while Azza chats to her in Reis. Gradually, though, the servant stiffens at the questions and her expression grows suspicious, her uncertainty directed at me. I imagine word of the scandal at the temple spreading among the citadel staff as they scrubbed the blood from Phibia's clothes and my own. Takia must see me in a new light – the fec who took on the Khadib.

"She tells me she was friendly with one of Phibia's handmaids some years ago," Azza translates. "The woman was a brandservant who came with Phibia from Isfalk." But as they continue to talk, Azza's face begins to fall, and the tone of her questioning turns insistent.

"What is it?" I ask. "What does she know?"

"The handmaid told Takia that her mistress gave birth just weeks after arriving in Reis. Not one baby but two."

"What?" My heart kicks, pulse hammering in my throat. "Phibia had twins?"

Azza nods. "She sent them away just after they were born."

"Away? Where? What was wrong with them?" My questions trip over each other, urgent, frantic. I can feel terrible suspicions winding around my lungs and knotting tight, squeezing my breath.

"She says Phibia felt some kind of shame over the babies. Perhaps they interfered with her new match with the Kha and her introduction to the Pure clans of Cha Shaheer she sought to rise within. It is believed she sent the infants back to Isfalk."

"To *Isfalk*? Why Isfalk?" It can't be. Plenty of women have twins, don't they? Osha and I aren't the only ones in the whole Continent. It's a coincidence, that's all.

"Takia claims Phibia arrived in Reis with another Isfalki – a Warder captain," Azza continues, but I almost want to stop her. If she doesn't translate Takia's words, I can remain oblivious, I can keep at bay the rawness creeping through me that such a woman might be my mother. And not only that – she just tried to kill me. "The Warder stayed until the children were born, then returned with them to Isfalk."

"Who was he – the Warder?" My voice cracks on the question. I fist my pendant, the Gildensfir cold against my palm, as cold as my heart is growing.

"She does not know."

But I believe *I* do and I want Takia to deny it. I grab her arm, trying to keep the tears from my eyes. "What was he like, Takia? The Warder – what did he look like?"

She clamps her lips together, forehead knotted, my violent reaction making her close up. Azza slowly removes my hand and nods her reassurance to the servant.

"Tall... tall man," Takia stutters in Isfalki. "The hair... here," she draws a line from her forehead to her crown, "like *Bar'quan*."

"Bar'quan?" Azza confirms and Takia nods. "She says his hair had a streak, like lightning." But I hardly need the translation. I can already picture the pure white bolt across Lars Oskarsson's crown, as clearly as when he handed me the Reis coin on the steps of the Roundhouse all those months ago.

I can't sleep. I can't eat. I can't train.

I can think of nothing but Phibia, as if the woman has already infiltrated my mind even from across the sea. Could she truly be our mother? At every turn I see proof of it: the Halqa symbols around our necks since birth; our age tallying with the time she arrived in Reis; my vision at the Blood-wife's – how Oskarsson claimed he brought our mother across the Wastelands with us *in her belly*; how much shame my branding must have caused a woman like Phibia – shame enough to send her babies away.

"You're jumping to conclusions, Nara," Osha tries to reason with me that evening in our cabin. But in the light of the ship's lamp her expression doesn't match the conviction of her words. "There are too many questions that still remain. Why would Oskarsson keep our identity from us? Why did he take us to live first with Amma in the Fornwood instead of allowing us to join him in the Settlement? And your markings must have come from one branded parent. If Phibia so despises Brands, why did she fall pregnant to one?"

"But the coincidences, O. Don't you see?" The cabin grows smaller somehow as I pace. I feel like an animal caged. "I have to talk to that handmaid of Phibia's. She would know more than Takia does."

"If she knows, she's taken it to her grave," Osha answers. "Azza already told me the woman died years ago."

I strangle a groan of frustration. This is why I had that feeling when we fled Cha Shaheer – the sense that, if I left, I'd never find out the truth – a truth only Phibia knows. This can't be the end. I won't let it be. The Khadib hasn't seen the last of me. Deep in my bones, I know that we're going to meet again. We have to.

Osha puts her hands on my shoulders, pressing me to sit. "You need to look forward," she says, nudging my chin in the direction we are sailing, "not backwards to Cha Shaheer. Our focus is Orlathston now, remember? Get some rest."

But I can't sleep. My mind turns circles through my thoughts like a mill – the Hrossi conflict ahead, the wrangler so far away, Brim missing, and Phibia, my *mother*, segregating Brands and Pures, turning Reis into another Isfalk. I toss and turn in the narrow bunk for what feels like hours until, finally, the dreams come.

Orlath watches Osha writhe in a childbed pooled with blood. The more drenched the mattress becomes, the more my sister sinks into it, disappearing from view. Soon all that is left is the baby she has birthed – a boy. The hands cleaning him belong to Haus. He passes me the child, who sleeps peacefully in the crook of my elbow while I go about my usual day aboard the ship – training with Azza, eating with the crew, climbing the rigging to watch for the wrangler's arrival. I manage it all one-handed, until the seas grow restless and the ship crests a giant wave. The baby wakes, squalling louder than the elements all around us. His mouth is wide. So wide I can see the tiny, filed teeth crammed inside. He's the image of his father.

I jolt awake to find myself taken hostage by my sheets. I unravel them, but sleep is impossible after that. Finding Osha's bunk empty, I climb above board. On the quarterdeck, the silhouettes of a man and a woman are silvered in moonlight. I stop my breath, straining to hear their exchange, but I can't make out the words, only the fitful rise of their voices over the shush of the ocean – accusations and defences, attacks and parries – a lovers' quarrel. Osha reels away, a flash of amber hair. Haus draws her gently back into the circle of his arms. A sob, a murmur of comfort, the press of lips before she retreats again, leaving him alone at the wheel, rubbing the back of his neck and lifting his eyes to the night. I catch a Hrossi curse, one I recognise all too well from my days in the Cooler.

Did my sister tell him about the child? Her belly below her clothes is unmistakable now, but she keeps it well hidden under furs, her medicine bag slung across her midriff during the day. And when I press her to tell Haus, she swallows back her tears and makes me vow again and again not to betray her. Haus is all she longs for and yet the closer we get to Orlathston, the more adamant she becomes – as if she senses the young chief sees only Orlath's hands when he touches her skin, Orlath's lips when he kisses her, Orlath's child when the time arrives. I've told my sister that Haus is miserable without her, that he wants only her, however she comes. I saw it on the Wasteland Plains, I saw it in the Cooler, and I see it now. But she won't listen. This denial of love and happiness for the sake of blood – how futile, how pointless and misguided it is. Did Phibia do the same? Did she fall in love with a Brand – our father? Or did he force himself on her? Is that why she hates Brands so much? Is that why she sent Osha and I away when she got to Reis? Did she give us up for a fresh start with her new Kha, for the reputation of his Pure bloodline?

As much as I want to deny it, perhaps everything comes down to blood after all.

Stolen Jewels

The *Na'quat* follows the coast north for two more days without spotting another vessel. It's not until the morning of our eighth day when the crew sights several ships chasing our tail from the south. Azza holds a thin brass instrument to her eye, and I watch, fascinated, as she uses it to scan our wake. "Five or six of them," Azza calls to Haus at the wheel. "They fly the flag of the southern clans." Haus makes the order to stow our sails so the other vessels can close the distance.

"Did I not tell you, Nara Fornwood?" Azza smirks at me. "Nixim follows trouble." I attempt a withering smile, but my heart flits like a bird on a branch at the prospect of seeing him.

"How you can you even see that far?" I ask, trying to pull myself together.

"Here," she says, handing me the length of brass and showing me how to hold the glass to my eye. "Look for yourself."

When I focus the eyepiece, the ships seem no more than eighty paces distant rather than tiny specks on the horizon. The wrangler might be on one of those caravels, but so too might Brim. I haven't lost hope that he was simply delayed fleeing Cha Shaheer and managed to join Nixim in the south.

I lower the instrument and blink at Azza, impressed. "It is called a skub," she says. "I've had it since I was a child. My mother gave it to me when I shot my first turcas buck." I look through the small aperture again, scanning the decks of the closest two ships, searching for a familiar dark head.

I chide myself, looking again for a blond one instead. Guilt rushes through me remembering the way Brim and I parted, that broken kiss, the offering of his heart that I pushed so roughly aside as soon as the wrangler appeared. I hate that I've disappointed him, that he might think of me badly.

"Striving for Brim's approval is second nature to you," Osha had said when I told her Brim and I had quarrelled. "Even in the Mor school you never thought you were good enough for him. You do realise that you strive constantly to win his regard, even though you do not want his heart."

"That is not true," I'd fired back.

"Which part? Not striving for his approval, or not wanting his heart?"

I was silent then because, as usual, my sister already knew the answer. But old habits are hard to break.

Perhaps Azza guesses the run of my thoughts, perhaps she feels guilty for leaving Brim behind too, for she takes the skub from me and says, "Come, Nara Fornwood. Those ships will not be alongside us for two or more hours yet, and we have work to do." She grabs my hand and pulls me across the decks, ignoring my weary groan. "Most Sways have their entire childhood to master what we are attempting to achieve in a matter of weeks."

I should admire Azza for her tenacity, be thankful for it. She's trying to teach me how to stay grounded now when I access my powers, how to keep my pulse calm and steady, focusing on tiny changes I might make to block her intrusions into my thoughts. But I'm still a poor student. My nose bleeds almost constantly, making me dizzy, and I'm finding our mental drills far more exhausting than any of the physical paces Brim or Haus ever put me through. Understanding my love of action, she starts me off with swords or staves, and we spar to disarm each other, but only with the objective of getting close enough to touch skin. For that is when the true battle begins – a struggle to manipulate the pulse of the other, to wrestle it into submission until the mind follows and the opponent's thoughts are broken open like ripe fruit. But so far it's only ever been Azza doing the breaking, reading my thoughts, until my nose gushes with the effort of trying to stop her.

With the ships on our tail and the wrangler and Brim playing a tug-of-war in my mind, my focus on training is non-existent this morning. Azza finally gives up when one of the vessels draws alongside us. Haus calls for the crew to lower a gangplank to bridge the decks and I lean against the gunwale, searching for the messy curls of the wrangler. But it's Captain Alrahim who steps aboard first. Azza greets her in Reis, but I'm too busy scanning the wheel and the quarterdeck, even the rigging of her ship. "Where are Nixim and Brim? Are they on the other ships?"

Azza doesn't answer, preoccupied with a letter Alrahim has placed in her hand.

"What is it? What's happening? Where is he?" I ask, unable to wait for her to finish reading.

"Nixim's not coming. He sent this," Azza says. The blood has drained from her face and she reaches to clutch the rail, Captain Alrahim's arm shooting out to steady her. The note hangs open in front of her and I wish I could read the curled script.

"Azza?" I press.

"It is my father–" She breaks off, mouth quivering with barely wrangled emotion. "Saqi sent a messenger south to Nixim. He writes that the Kham is dead."

"What?"

Her eyes pool as she clutches the captain's hand. Alrahim steadies her, arm at her back.

"The healers say it was his heart, but…" she palms away angry tears, "…there was nothing wrong with his heart."

I struggle to find the words to console her, fearful it will release a deluge of other emotions in me. The news is shocking, but not unfamiliar. Powerful people die with suspicious frequency around Phibia.

Azza's voice grows hard. "Phibia's husband, my mother, and now my father – all gone, removed from Phibia's path when they became inconvenient."

I rub my temple, as if it might straighten out my thoughts.

"Phibia will not let anyone stand in the way of her ambition," Alrahim says.

And yet, she let me live. Why didn't she rid herself of that inconvenience too – the terrible shame of a branded child? Did she draw the line at murdering a newborn? Did she feel some jot of tenderness towards me?

"There is more," Azza says, clearing her throat of emotion. "Nixim writes that Phibia's guards now control Cha Shaheer and its army. Many in Reis are questioning the Khadib's military rule. For this reason, he stays behind to continue gathering her dissenters to our cause. He anticipates Phibia marching forces to exert her control over the south, but he hopes our success in securing Orlathston might intercept any support the Khadib was planning to receive from the Hrossi. He sends Captain Alrahim and units under her command to affect the Orlathston campaign, which he entrusts now to Haus and myself. If successful, he asks Haus to reciprocate the favour in Reis."

I digest it for a moment, lungs working overtime, jaw clenching so hard my teeth hurt. This news is a hard blow for Azza, for us all, but I can't help the worm of resentment that uncurls inside me when I think of the wrangler not showing up. How many times has he left me in the lurch before now, right when I need him – when we all need him most. For a brief moment, Azza looks almost as deflated as I feel, but she swallows it back masterfully.

"What do we do?" I ask her.

"Do?" she questions. "We do as he asks... as we promised we would." Regardless of whether we can take Orlathston with the numbers at our disposal, her self-control, her resolve as she discusses the new situation with Captain Alrahim and

Haus is a sight to see. Despite all my fears, I can't help but admire her. She's a born leader.

Just as the three descend to begin planning their strategy below decks, I catch Alrahim's arm. I can't help myself. "Brim? Is he not with you? Did Nixim say if he'd seen him?"

She shakes her head, making it clear she has no news.

"I don't understand. How could he simply go missing? Where is he?" I ask Osha.

"Brim can take care of himself, Nara."

But with his last known whereabouts being Phibia's personal quarters, I'm not so sure he can.

With the current winds, our crew estimates that the journey to Orlathston is still a three-day sail. Over the course of that journey, Azza takes breaks from long strategy meetings with Haus and Alrahim to thrash my butt above decks. Any grief for her father, for her usurped home, for her absent brother, all seem to have run off her like rain on canvas, or else she keeps it tight inside her. Meanwhile, I'm no closer to blocking her intrusions into my thoughts and I'm getting more drained and anxious with every passing day.

Azza says nothing of my progress and I don't dare ask. Sometimes I think I'm going backwards, my skill so amorphous it feels like trying to shape sea fog or catch the salt spray. I try my best to keep her out of my head, away from my most private reveries, but I know in moments of weakness she's already read my worries for Brim, my regrets over the way we parted. When yet another mental wrestle sees me on my knees, nose spouting down my front, I lose patience, pushing her helping hands away. "Poxes, Az, I'm trying my best!"

"Are you?"

"Give me a breather, at least."

"The time it takes you to breathe will be the very moment a Sway like Phibia chooses to strike." Her big brown eyes search my face as her fingers wrap around my wrist. And I feel her steady pulse, the warmth of her presence all around me, inside and out, creeping through every pore and cell of my being. It's suffocating. I try to focus, to block her by tamping down my emotions, letting my thoughts turn monochrome until they fade from my mind, like dreams in the daylight. But she's too good, too adept.

"If you honed your defence as much as you hone your thoughts to that kiss with your Warder Captain, we would be making more progress," she barks.

"Mother's tits, Azza. Stay out of my head!"

"Heed my lessons, Nara Fornwood, and you will be able to keep me out yourself."

I get up, swiping my nose irritably. "Think of him again," she demands.

"What?"

"If the Elix heir is where your thoughts run, then think of him… But this time, keep me out."

I frown, wary of having her inside my head once more, picking over my past for her entertainment, but in the end I do what she says. I conjure Brim's pale eyes, blue as the glacier at Tindur Hof, his hair the colour of ripe wheat, that way he always runs a hand behind his neck whenever he's frustrated with me. Azza's fist tightens around my arm, and I sense her like the charge before a storm, her shadow on the periphery of my thoughts. I try to push her back, but before long I'm remembering the Moon Pools and the way Brim would undress, dragging his shirt over his head by the scruff of the neck, the scar of an old wound along his ribs that I'd helped Osha to stitch, hands barely able to keep steady at the feel of his warm skin. And I recall the way I'd pull these images out late at night when I couldn't sleep, polishing them until they shone with new hues, coveting them like stolen jewels I could never keep… the way I'd touch myself thinking of him.

And suddenly, Brim is there before me, reaching out. "Nara," he says in that exasperated tone.

"Poxes, Brim, what took you so long?" I rush towards him, noticing now that his face is ashen and drained. When I take his hand, it's warm and sticky in mine, and looking down I see there's blood – not my own, for a change, but his. I let out a whimper of panic, mopping at him with my cuff, only to discover his wrists are slashed, steady arterial pumps splattering across the decks. I think of Phibia, see her pink lips smiling, the only brush of colour among her pale face and hair. But the knife that has cut Brim is in my hands, not hers. He drops to his knees and I cry out, light-headed and unsteady on my feet. Doubts creep through me like ants under my skin. I can't save him – he's bleeding too much and I'm no healer. I'm good only for hunting, for killing things. I'm nothing but a Brand, unschooled, compromised, weak – that's what Saqira had said, wasn't it? I'm barely strong enough to stand on my own two feet, let alone face off against one of the most powerful Tathars in the Continent. I should just give up now. Lie down here on the briny decks with Brim and let myself bleed...

"What the fec!" I cry, snatching my hand from Azza's and backing away. "What *was* that? What did you do?"

"I am showing you how she will bend thoughts, Nara Fornwood – how Phibia will grow your worst doubts and fears, until you believe they are the truth. She will enter your head and work your memories in a heartbeat, making you see not your own reality, but hers. Your skill, as it stands, is little more than a jester's trick compared to her mastery." She exhales raggedly, closing her eyes as if in exhaustion at the work ahead of her.

My breath is ragged, not just from shock but indignation, like a child unfairly thrashed. My face burns with shame and rage, knowing Azza witnessed my pimply pining for Brim. "Those were *private* thoughts. You had no right," I accuse her, desperately needing to attack after feeling so defenceless. "It was a teenage crush. I don't feel that way about Brim anymore."

"That is my brother's business, not mine, Nara Fornwood," she says. And, despite her frustration at my lack of progress, I notice a hitch at the corner of her mouth.

"What's so funny?" She shakes her head. "Tell me!"

"Is that what it felt like, your first love – stolen jewels?" She makes a sad humming noise in the back of her throat. "That is… criminal."

"Fec you, Az!" I spit.

Her husky laugh rumbles from her, so contagious that, as much as I fight it, a snort of amusement escapes me. Before I know it, we're both bent double, holding our stomachs and wiping tears from our eyes. Given the news we've had, the danger ahead of us, it feels wrong to be laughing, but that's what fuels it even more. I'm in sore need of light relief and it feels good to be pulled apart for fun instead of for my failings and mistakes. It feels like the baiting of the wrangler and I miss it so much. I miss *him* so much it suddenly winds me like an elbow to the gut.

When she straightens, Azza says, "You know, the Reis have a saying–"

"Of course they do." I roll my eyes.

"The finest jewels are worthless if they cannot be worn."

"Right." I offer her an exaggerated nod as if she has imparted some shining pearl of wisdom. "So, your brother – is his love a jewel I might wear?"

She grins. "Perhaps. Nixim is complicated. Somewhat more rough-cut than your Warder Captain." She eyes the short hair growing back over my branding, the nicks and scars I earned in the Cooler. "But rough cuts seem to suit you, I think."

Head lowered, I defend against her probing with an attack of my own. "And what about you, Azza Ni Azzadur? Do you have no jewel you covet?" I flick my eyes to Captain Alrahim on the forecastle.

Her face drops and I think I've overstepped the mark, until she grins. "Did I ever tell you that you ask too many questions?"

I nod, but I'm quiet now.

The absence of the wrangler seems to make the impossibility of what we're trying to achieve come home to roost.

"Az?" I ask, wanting her reassurance. "Do you think Nixim will succeed?"

"You mean in recruiting our army?"

"Yeah."

"He will do it," she says. "The majority of the Seven Clans are still loyal to my mother and my brother is very good at influencing people to do what he wants."

Her confidence bolsters me and my stomach settles a little. "Nixim is no Sway – men cannot be, it seems – but I wonder sometimes whether he inherited a little of the gift of our mother's blood. He has a charm for enticing people to follow him."

I thumb my own chest. "Case in point." Tentatively, I add, "You didn't think to go with him? To use your sway to recruit more forces?" She sighs, disappointed with the question. "Alright, I know, I know... it's not the way you operate... it would be coercive. Too much like Phibia."

She smiles, but it's a sad one, hinting at something else that bothers her.

"You don't think Nixim's army will be enough, do you?" I venture, guessing at her expression. "My vision – the enemy forces gathered below the tableland – we were outnumbered."

"You know my opinions on visions. They are only one possible version of the future."

"But it might be true – admit it."

"Perhaps."

"Then what do we do?"

She levels a look at me, determined, challenging. "We train harder. And we fight better."

"But what if we're not enough, Az? What if Orlath wins? What if Cha Shaheer is lost to us? All those Brands – what will happen to them? All your mother's work–"

"Too many questions, Nara Fornwood." She holds her palms up to me as she would a spooked horse. "No one can know all those answers." She lays her hands on mine, and I immediately feel a surge of her warmth licking through my veins, as if I've just knocked back a shot of dramur vit. The knots in my belly ease, my breathing slows, and I want to stay like that, letting her sway me, eyes closed, drawing on her strength, her confidence. But eventually I feel her sliding away. When she sees the disappointment in my face, she says, *"Where there is no answer, exploring the question must be enough."*

"Poxes, Az, I'm starting to think you should write a book. *The Wisdom of Azza Ni Azzadur.*" Her laugh feels like a reward. "Can I ask you one more question?"

"Do I have a choice?" she says.

"No." I take a breath, a little embarrassed. "The name of our ship, the *Na'quat* – what does it mean in Reis?" She frowns. I imagine it was the last thing she was expecting me to ask, given my previous interrogation. "Your brother renamed this ship, but he never told me what it meant."

"And why do you ask this now?"

I fold my arms across my chest, willing myself not to blush. "It's very close to my nickname in Isfalki – *Narkat*. My grandmother gave it to me. It's a type of northern snow cat the Isfalki call the *scourge of the snows.*" Her face lights up with understanding and she nods, as if finding her brother's name for me entirely apt. "You know Nixim vexes me for sport. So I'm thinking his version – *Na'quat* – means something bad in Reis, like... I don't know... *poxy trull* or *hell hound* or *cantankerous bitch*?"

Azza raises her eyebrows for a second and then holds her belly as she laughs.

"What? What does it mean? Tell me – I'm a big girl. I can take it."

"In Reis, *Na'quat* is what seafarers call the constellations," she says, pointing two fingers toward the heavens. "Literally, *the moon and the stars.* It is a fine name for a ship because that is how sailors chart their way." Her eyes hold mine. "But if one person were to call another *Na'quat...*" She runs her tongue between her bottom teeth and her lip, waiting.

"Oh... *Oh.*" I turn away quickly, so she doesn't see my cheeks burning. "Okay."

All this time, I was accusing Nixim of mispronouncing my name, and he was telling me something else entirely. So typical of the wrangler. I head below deck, eager to unpack this new information alone. Knowing what the wrangler truly meant every time he called me Na'quat gives me a rush of warmth that stays with me far longer than Azza's sway.

An Unwanted Gift

As we get closer to Olathston, we're hampered by rain. Thick lashes beat down, and the ocean heaves and sulks like some whipped beast of burden. At the first break in the downpour, Azza thrusts a stave in my hand and drags me out to the decks.

"There is no time for sulking in our hammocks."

I grunt, forced to shake off my tiredness as she immediately begins to attack. Parrying and defending for most of the first half hour, I get scant chance to mount my own offensive. There's something wild and aggressive about Azza today – despite our confidences of late, I can tell that her nerves are starting to wear thin. But I have begun to make a little progress. I don't bleed as much when I access my skill, and sometimes, if I catch her off-guard, I get a glimpse into her moods brooding below the surface of her skin. As soon as I do, though, she pounces on me, deflecting the invasion. I struggle to copy her, to shed my emotions and thoughts so I can block her manipulations, but I never can, and we are running out of time. She had bigger hopes of me. I read it in her for the briefest moment yesterday. Her disappointment hurts more than the stave she's just sliced behind my thighs, making my knees buckle.

I drop to the puddling deck on all fours. The rain begins to pelt again, so hard that it runs in channels down my hair and into my mouth. I can only just make out her hand as she reaches to grab for me. I shy away, not ready for her touch, not ready for her presence in my head again. I suspect that today she's in no mood to be merciful about what she might see there.

She lunges towards me once more and I spin from her. "Take my hand. We must keep trying," she shouts above the hissing rain.

"Back off for a bit, Azza."

"Take my hand!" she spits, following it up with a stream of Reis words that I can guess are even more salty than her mood. I've never heard Azza swear before.

"If that curse involves goats and my mother, Takia has beaten you to it."

Azza blinks the water from her eyes and squints down at me with a look that could rend stone. She seizes my wrist, her nails digging into my skin so hard they draw blood.

"What the fec, Az!" Before I can blink, she's there in my head, slamming through my memories like she's looting a house. I try to block her, breathing through my hurt and anger, white-washing my emotions. I imagine my memories turning pale as winter, until they melt away like spring ice. But she's too strong. She's there beside me when Amma gives me my first bow; she's there as I run from the blazing cabin; there when Brim carves the face of the whipping boy on our training tree; there in the sled on the way back from the Blood-wife's, her brother's thighs warm at my back; there watching him swim in the river on the Wasteland Plains; there when I pull him from the burning Cooler; there in the captain's cabin...

"Stop!" I cry out, but no sound leaves me. I take a ragged breath and stagger to my feet. "Fecking stop that!" Fury burns the skin of my chest and neck, and everything I've tried to quell – all my indignation and injustice and resentment – comes washing back through me in a surge, making my skin tingle and my bones feel like I've been struck by lightning. "I didn't ask for any of this. I didn't want to be a Sway. This isn't my fecking country, or my battle. But as long as I'm here, this is how you get me – wild, unschooled, undisciplined. Tough shit! Stay the fec out of my head!"

She stands before me in the rain, panting almost as much as I am.

"Very well." She nods once and turns her back to me. I try to tame my breath, to tamp down my rage.

"Az," I say, softer now, anticipating the regret that will set in as my blood cools.

"My efforts here are done, Nara Fornwood. You must face Orlath as you are – a Fornwood Solitary with a gift for brawling. Nothing more." And the way she gives up on me cuts more than all my failures put together.

The Ghosthawk

Being an island fortress surrounded by Hrossi settlements on either bank of the river makes the Orlathston campaign fraught with challenges. But Haus has clearly been plotting it for weeks, if not since we first fled the Cooler.

His strategy surprises and frustrates me – we sail well past Orlathston, mooring our ships in a remote cove several days' journey up the coast, closer to Haus's hearthlands in the north-west. From there, we ride to the capital, allowing Haus and the Maw to gather supporters, horses and weapons as we travel. It's an exercise in patience, demanding a good deal of campfire talk and drinking of dramur vit while the young chief ingratiates himself with his kinsmen and listens to their grievances against Orlath.

The whole plan takes weeks longer than I was expecting, but Haus's insistence is based on forward-thinking, even I can see that. If we attacked Orlathston immediately and were successful, our Reis forces alone would not be enough to hold the city in the long term. Haus is effectively securing as much of his homelands as he can, and frankly I'm surprised at his success. Either sympathies were waning with the Hrossi overlord and the feudal demands of his reign before we arrived, or Haus is more popular than I thought. Perhaps both. It's a boon for our campaign that I was not expecting, and while the young chief had been quietly counting on the support of his local clans, he had not understood the extent of the growing antagonism towards Orlath among the northern Wastelanders – a discontent that was primed for a leader to harness, it seems. If Haus wants this role I'm unable to tell, but the further south we travel, the more it's thrust upon him as word spreads of Lynstum's return, the Maw at his side, and the redheaded Pure woman he fights for – the likeness of Effa herself – surely a blessing and sign of the change to come. More and more Wastelanders join our cause.

Another unexpected bonus on our travels in the north-west is Osha's opportunity to talk to Hrossi healers in the settlements we pass through. Haus introduces her to a bright-eyed crone called Shessa, the spae-wife of his home clan and a mother to him after his own died. She and Osha follow our convoy by wagon, detouring to medicine trails to gather herbs, roots and seeds, and discovering the unique practices of other healers along the route south. My sister is utterly engrossed, barely surfacing from her studies of tinctures, philtres and compounds with Shessa, scribbling notes in her journals by firelight late into the night. I think how different this journey is from the first time we made it – in chains in the back of a wagon sleigh – and yet my fear at approaching Orlathston is all the more concrete now I know what is ahead of us.

"Does it pain you to be going back there?" I ask Osha one night around the campfire. "To know you might see him again? If we don't succeed–"

"Hush!" she says, shaking her head at my negative talk. "Going back doesn't scare me. What terrifies me is the thought of Annek, Dalla and Sigrun still trapped there after all these months, what he might be doing to them, how they will be suffering. I promised I'd return for them, Nara."

Shame washes through me at her words. I remember the girls' faces in the firelight, looking at me with such trust, such faith as we decided to turn our backs on Isfalk. But I only led them from one kind of prison to another – one that was so much worse.

"Here I am obsessing about Phibia and my skill and who I really am, when they're suffering at the hands of that sick fec. I'm so selfish, O."

The mention of Orlath makes her flinch, and I can't help searching out the scars on her neck. She angles away self-consciously.

"I'm sorry for what he did to you," I whisper.

"Don't be. I don't worry for myself. It's Haus I think of. I'm afraid for him. Afraid his thirst for revenge will make him take risks and do something stupid."

"Osha–" I take her hands. "Haus is the least stupid man I know. How do you think he survived so long in the Cooler? That doesn't just take brawn, it takes brains, cunning… mental fortitude. Every time he fights, he does it with a strategy. It's what he taught me in the ring. He's not going to do anything without thinking it through first." I stroke my thumbs over her knuckles. "But, O, if he's going into battle, don't you think you should talk to him? He deserves–"

"He deserves what? Used goods? To be raising the child of his enemy? To feed and protect and sacrifice himself for a bloodline that isn't even his?"

"You don't know that for sure."

"I know he deserves more than that. More than me."

But when I look at her twisting that lyf-braid between her fingers, the flames of the fire limning her hair in gold, she takes my breath away, and I'm not so sure she's right.

Osha opens the well-thumbed copybook resting on her lap. I recognise this particular journal from her time spent taking notes in the Isfalk archives. "There's hardly any space left in there now," I say, but wanting to keep her on the topic of Haus, I broach slyly, "Who would have thought the wisdom of Wastelanders now sits alongside those of the infamous apothek Fenderhilde?"

"And why would the Hrossi not have something worthy to teach?" She darts a look at me, her expression defensive. "Haus saved your life when you caught the frost fever."

"I didn't mean it like that, O. I'm not belittling him. He has my respect above anyone's. It was more a criticism of *us*." Her face softens a little. "I'm just saying it wasn't so long ago that we looked at Wastelanders like they were shit on our boots. What could barbarians teach us civilised Isfalki? But when I fell sick, you hung on his every word."

"You would have died if I didn't. What Haus and Shessa teach me is just as important as anything I've read in a codex or manuscript – perhaps more so because it's never been written down. Everything they know is passed on orally."

"Yeah. Haus told me the Hrossi don't read or write." I remember his fascination watching Osha scrawling in her notebook on our way to Orlathston, the trouble he went to sourcing her ink and quills on the Wasteland Plains.

"Their lack of literacy hardly matters because of what they retain in their collective memory," Osha says, eyes glazing as she drifts to that place of curiosity and wonder I've seen her occupy for hours at a time in the Isfalk archives. "Did you know each Hrossi clan is a guardian of specific traditions and knowledge, depending on the geography of their hearthlands? So, a clan from the northern plains, for example, might hold the key to the properties of faenger root and haver bark, while a western clan might know cloudberries or islav moss or black poppy. They pass this knowledge down to their children in their foraging songs."

I shake my head. "Haus didn't go into so much detail about his heritage when we were in the Cooler. But then *we* weren't taking long walks alone together in the forest."

My sister chooses to ignore me. "Each clan prides itself that they are the depository of their hearthland's lore, passed down through generations. And as they survive the maladies and poxes that beset them, they only increase that knowledge." Osha's face is animated in the firelight. "The Hrossi aren't scavengers, Nara. They don't pick at the remnants of the Old World, as the Isfalki like to make out. They have their own history and culture and learning. They're like walking almanacs of practical lore and it only makes me want to keep journeying through the Wastelands, writing down the healing treasures their spae-wives guard in their heads. Who knows, the answer to the Brume itself might be hidden among them."

"Woah... how times have changed," I say. "Osha Fornwood, the student of apothek and physik entertaining the *flim flam* of spae-wives."

"I never call it *flim flam*."

"Back in Isfalk you used those exact words."

"Did I?" she muses. "How things change. How *we've* changed."

"We have, but right now we've much bigger things to worry about than visiting Wasteland spae-wives." I reach over and take the journal from her hands. "You and that baby need more rest." Setting it out of her reach, I make her lie down next to me, pulling the furs over us both. We're silent for a good while in the dark, lulled by the hissing embers, the snores of the soldiers, the soft nicker of the horses all around. Just when I think she might be asleep, Osha says, "I lied before, Nara." Her whisper is low enough not to wake me in case I'm asleep. "I *am* scared to go back to Orlath's island again... I'm terrified of seeing *him*." I want to reassure her, but I stop myself, making my breathing slow and deep so she thinks I've nodded off. A few moments later, I feel her push back the blankets, hear the soft scuff of her feet around the campfire. And I smile to myself, knowing where she's going even before she slips under Haus's furs. My ruse to get her to defend him and the Hrossi paid off. I'm glad she seeks his comfort instead of mine, and I'm glad he's there for her. But most of all, I'm glad because when she's in his arms he can have no doubt at all about her condition now. I know Haus – he'll be a father to that child, whether it's his or not, bloodlines be damned. He'll be a father to it simply because Osha is its mother.

I think of Phibia sending her children away, of Iness exiling her own daughter for the sake of blood, and I'm desperate to know more, to understand these bonds that tether us together. I get up and prowl through the camp, moving between the gentle forms of the horses in the dark, trying to absorb their calm. But when I hear the ghosthawk's pitchy scream slicing through the night, it feels like I've called forth the bird with the sheer will of my desire. The dark kite of its shadow circles above me, descending until I can hear the fluttering of its wingtips in the clean air, until I raise my arm, as instinctively as I did in my vision. I snatch a breath when the bird settles, its talons tight on the suede of my coat, watching it chatter and preen for a moment until its yellow eye settles upon me. Fear creeps through my body like an icy draft. This is Iness's bird. I've never taken its sight before in any conscious way, only in my visions. What if Iness is watching me through its searing eye, spying on our movements, our plans? The bird's pulse dances with mine for a moment, while I debate these things, but then I make the leap, subduing its rhythm to my own, feeling its instincts and thoughts like something physical, sharp and metallic as a knife on my tongue. I know in my gut that I've made the tiercel mine. It will do as I ask. Its vision engulfs me like diving into a hole cut in the ice, dark and bracing and fathomless, but when I emerge on the other side, I'm soaring high above Isfalk, its citadel hunkered like a sleeping dragon on the edge of the frosty Fold. The western gate is rising with a grinding clank and then in a tumult of hooves, hundreds of mounted Warder guards spew from within. This is no reconnaissance party or defensive unit chasing raiders from our borders – a job I longed to be tasked with once upon a time. This is an all-out expedition, a campaign force, sleigh wagons of supplies and weapons following in their wake. This is Isfalk on the war path.

I release the hawk, and as it flaps into the night I rush to rouse Haus and Azza.

"You are certain it was Isfalk?" Azza asks.

I cut her a look. We've barely talked since coming ashore. She still hasn't forgiven me for throwing her lessons back in her face.

"They rode south?" Haus asks.

"No. That's the thing – they came from the west gate, as if–"

"They cross to the ocean," Haus finishes for me.

"If they head for ships, their destination is not Orlathston," Azza says. "It is Reis. They move at Phibia's command."

"Then my vision in the temple might be true. Phibia is boosting her army with Isfalki soldiers?"

Despite her doubt about the usefulness of the Sight, Azza nods reluctantly. "We stay true to our plan. We focus on denying Phibia the Hrossi support she might be expecting." Turning to Haus with a determined look, she says, "We must secure Orlathston without delay. I need to return our forces south as soon as possible – my brother is going to need them."

The Overlord and The Ringer

I'd imagined our attack on Orlathston would be a siege of the island fortress, but word must have reached the overlord of an insurgent host moving down from the north because, not a day's ride from the capital, Orlath's army meets us on the Wasteland Plain. I scan his forces through Azza's skub. They line up on the horizon, banners snapping defiantly in the wind as if Orlath thumbs his nose at his Cooler Ringer. As if he's saying, *You think I would hide like a mouse and not come out to greet you, Lynstum?*

Thankfully, Osha is not here to witness a battle on the open field. We said our farewells two days ago when the spae-wife convinced her to rest at one of the huts along the medicine trails, tempting her with the promise of harvesting a galbo root unique to the area. Shessa said its pain-relieving properties were second to none in treating the wounded and that was motivation enough for Osha to stay behind. Although it's my guess the crone is wise to her secret. From the moment Shessa first met my sister, I'm certain she saw the mood, the stance, the behaviour of a woman with child. And her distraction with the galbo root is intended to make Osha rest and save Haus the pain of trying to focus on a bloody battle with his lyfhort looking on.

The wind in my face is dry as we scan the host spread along the horizon, my throat even drier, laced as it is with the smell of fires, horse shit, and unwashed bodies carried from the camp.

I look to Haus in the grey morning light, his expression stony, unreadable. And for the first time, I realise he's facing the prospect of killing his own countrymen. I trust him implicitly. He would never do anything to betray Osha, or me – he has more honour than that, more honour than any man I've ever met. But Azza is not so sure. She doubts Haus. I can hear it in her criticisms.

"A head-on attack is more concentrated," she contradicts him in the strategy tent as we rehearse our tactics for the last time. "Circling Alrahim's forces to the east to attack on the flank means dividing our host in two. It will weaken us and put my Ghumes in more danger." She stares down the Hrossi chief.

The prospect of battle, of seeing her people confront death, is eating at her, and my vision of Isfalki reinforcements strengthening Phibia's threat to Nixim has her scared.

"I will not sacrifice Reis blood for nothing, and especially not for some bleak Wasteland settlement," she says, her mouth a mean line. "I require your word that Hrossi forces will support our campaign in the south as soon as Orlathston is secure."

I've never seen prejudice and selfishness in Azza before, and it is an ugly thing to witness now. It makes me squirm, remembering my own intolerance when I believed I was a Pure, the superiority inherent in me.

The Hrossi chief is silent.

"Don't do this, Azza," I say. "You don't know Haus. He said he'd support Nixim and he'll honour that." Even Captain Alrahim gives Azza a disappointed look.

"I must be certain of him," she continues, eyeing the Ghume captain a little desperately. "In the heat of battle, will he truly be able to turn on the overlord who once commanded his loyalty? I won't have my people risk all for nothing." She paces impatiently, Haus watching her in silence. Then slow and steady, as if he's approaching a panicked horse, he takes her palm and lays it along his wrist. She freezes for a moment at his touch, the whites of her eyes flashing. When her pupils flick from side to side, I know she's reading his mind, just as she's done so often with me in training. Who knows what images she sees? Perhaps they're from his time in the Cooler, a childhood of abuse at the hands of his lanista father, the slaughter of his friends for the sake of entertaining Orlath and the Hrossi masses. Or perhaps it's something else, for I suspect Haus has endured much worse than what I've learned of his past. Whatever it is she witnesses, Azza's face crumples, her huge eyes growing tender, a flush of shame burning up her cheeks.

"Very well," she says, finally in command of herself again. "We follow your strategy, Chief Haus. I give you my trust. Do not disappoint me." But she holds my gaze as she says the words, as if she means them for me as much as Haus.

When we're making the final checks of armour before moving out, I lay a hand on the Hrossi's arm.

"Wait, Chief," I say, preventing him from mounting his horse. "I need to know something. My sister... did she... I mean, do you know?" I mangle the question, conscious that I'm breaking Osha's trust. But the gentle squeeze of his fingers around mine is answer enough. "So you will stand by her, even if the child is not yours?"

His exhaled breath fogs in the chilly air of the plain.

"It's just, if I don't make it... if I don't come back... I need to know that you'll look after her, Haus. That you'll look after both of them."

I can hear the desperation in my voice, but I don't care anymore. There's too much at stake to worry what he thinks of me, and he's seen me in much worse states. To my surprise, I feel his arm snaking around my shoulders, drawing me to him in a tight hug. His bulk is solid and reassuring, furs soft and warm under my cheek.

"Always too many words... not enough belief," he says.

"But the child," I press. Somehow, it's the only thing giving me hope, right now, knowing it will survive – that Osha and her baby will be there to carry on, even if I am not. "I need you to promise me you'll look after them. If Orlath comes for her–"

He straightens at the mention of Orlath. "He will not touch her again," Haus growls. "Not while I have breath."

I catch the movement of his hand at his neck, winding Osha's braid over his knuckles. "We make the promise, she and I. Mine is hers, hers mine, *body and soul*," he says with great patience, as if I'm a child who cannot grasp the first principles of sharing. "We are lyfhort. Everything she is, everything she has, is mine to love, to protect. You understand, Nara Fornwood?"

I do. Blood of his blood or not, I know now he'd give his life to protect my sister's child. And that's all the answer I need. I pull out of his arms, nodding as I squeeze his shoulders. Haus mounts his horse. He has removed one doubt from my mind, but my thoughts trip on so many others. The failure to train my skill makes me feel insubstantial, the shell of something I know I should be, with Azza's final words on the *Na'quat* echoing in that empty space inside me. *You must face Orlath as you are – a Fornwood Solitary with a gift for brawling. Nothing more.* I can't help wishing the wrangler was here. I'd give anything now to hear his aggravating voice at my shoulder, for the distraction of his barbs, to be the reason that mole twitches in his cheek.

Narrow your stance, Na'quat. Or do you prefer Scourge of the Snows? Perhaps the Isfalki name panders more to your pride?

His taunts are like the spark from a flint, catching and flaring in my mind.

Fight as the person you are, not the one you think you should be. Focus, Nara. You can do this. Hone your mind.

Can't stretch to a goodbye kiss?

I should have. I should have promised. I should have told him everything and not been so proud, so stubborn. I should have said he drove me mad because I was mad for him. Why is it only now, with death staring me down, that I can admit I love him? Now, when it's all too late. He could have told me too, when he had the chance in Cha Shaheer. He could have sent me a message with Alrahim. He could have been *here*. Now neither of us may survive to say those words and it makes me angry. So angry.

But that's good.

Anger is good. Anger is something familiar and certain.

Anger is my old friend.

Battle is chaos. I never realised it, all those years I yearned to be a Warder soldier. It is filthy and feral, mean and desperate. Haus may have had a strategy, but whether it plays out amidst the blood and body parts, the felled horses and strewn weapons, the rain that starts to sheet across the plain turning grass to mud, dirt to bloody puddles, I can't tell. Soldiering isn't glory and greatness or principles and purpose as I'd dreamed it was ever since I first held Brim's sword when I was ten. Soldiering is selfishness and shame and regret. If I once believed a military life would be more meaningful and fulfilling than that of a Mor mother, the Battle for Orlathston corrects that delusion. Children are hope. War is only regret.

Haus makes me follow Azza and her Ghumes to attack on the eastern flank. The element of surprise plays to our favour for a while, but before long the campaign feels less like two sides in battle and more like a rabid wolf fighting itself. Two hours in and I've been unhorsed, I'm drenched with rain, blood and sweat, and fatigued to the bone. A Hrossi horseman catches me off-guard with a kick to my back. Pain lashes my shoulders and I lose my sword. I wheel about, managing to yank the rider's boot from his stirrup. The vast grey stallion rears, his rider dwarfed in the saddle. Intricate tattoos curl up his neck and over his shaven scalp, one eye patched in leather to mask the gift Nixim left him in the Cooler.

Orlath.

The Hrossi keeps his seat, grinning down at me with those pointed teeth. His henchmen close in. I'm unarmed, but not defenceless. I've one weapon left – my old friend fury takes control. With a feral scream, I run full tilt at Orlath's horse, grabbing his furs and launching myself up behind him in the saddle. The beast rears again, but not before I have my fists around the overlord's neck, skin to skin. His pulse rolls through me like logs down a hillside, fast and arrhythmic but strong enough to make my very bones thrum. And when I tame it to my own heartbeat, images flicker across my sight like sunlight through trees on a speeding sleigh. Annek and Sigrun paraded through a hall of drunken soldiers, Dalla stripped, her limbs bruised and shaking as she steps into a bath… and then a sight that makes my blood run cold… Osha's hair trapped in Orlath's fist, bite marks weeping on her throat.

"You sick fec," I grit through teeth clenched so hard I feel them crack. Rage makes his pulse slip from my grasp, and I flounder to regain it. All I can think of is squeezing my fists tighter around the bastard's neck. Orlath chokes as the horse bucks and skitters, trying to throw me, and by the time he elbows me in the stomach, I'm barely holding on. One of his men slashes my back. My armour takes the brunt of the blow, but I tumble to the dirt, cowering, hands fending off the trampling hooves overhead.

When I dare raise my eyes again, Orlath couldn't care less about me. His sights are set on the man who stole his flame-haired Mor, his lucky charm, his Effa incarnate. Haus has broken the ranks of Orlath's guards, the overlord and his champion slowly circling each other as if to feel the full weight of a moment they've been imagining for so long. Orlath grins but Haus's face is a mask of control, revealing nothing. To my dismay, Haus jumps down from his horse, hefting his warhammer and bracing in the sparring stance I'd witnessed so many times in the Cooler. He shouts in Hrossi and Orlath's sneer flickers uncertainly around the faces of his men. As if shamed by the chief's words, the overlord reluctantly dismounts. But before he's even turned to Haus, he takes a swing with his sword. The young chief ducks it, then side-steps, his axe his only weapon. Orlath attempts a second blow, but his movements are hampered by his shield and Haus dances circles around him. In a fit of rancour, Orlath hurls the buckler at Haus. It's a fatal mistake. Haus could slice an apple from a tree with the accuracy of his axe arm; no sword alone will deflect its force. Yet he bides his time, as if he's back in the Cooler drumming up the audience in a frenzy of excitement... just as Orlath taught him to. The overlord braves a two-handed strike to Haus's head. He misses, and the momentum of his overweight broadsword sends him stumbling to his knees. Haus is on him in an instant, grabbing him by the hair from behind and pressing the blade of his axe to Orlath's neck. When I look to Haus's face, I expect to witness triumph, vengeance, even fury. But the chief's expression doesn't even show hatred. There's only a terrible weighted sadness to the line of his mouth as he presses the honed edge to Orlath's skin, like he's remembering the necks of other, much worthier men beneath his blade.

Orlath's lips move. I know the shape of that word. I've heard it formed on a hundred tongues in the stands of the Cooler. *Lynstum*. Except now it's a plea, almost shameful in the mouth of a man so unused to begging. Haus doesn't answer it. Everything stills, as if time wants to record the moment for posterity, but in the space of that breath, everything turns to chaos and Haus misses his chance.

Orlath's men close in. Haus spins to defend an attack from his right, just as the Maw breaks the ring, the huge bulk of his mare forcing other mounts aside. Steel flashes, armour cracks, horses scream, wild-eyed. I lose sight of Haus completely, grabbing the sword of a fallen Hrossi to defend myself. That's when Azza cuts through the fray. Seizing my arm, she swings me up behind her in the saddle, hacking through the melee to ride us to a position of safety. Trembling and worn down by the battle, I can't be anything but grateful to her.

Azza uses the skub to track the Maw's contingent. "The giant pushes our lines forward," she says. "Haus is with him."

"Let me see," I ask when my hands feel steady enough. She gives me the glass. Once I've seen Haus, I scan for Orlath, eventually spotting a group of riders breaking rank and fleeing the battleground. Within the shield of their protection, the Hrossi overlord gallops across the plain, a streak of bloodied furs, racing for the refuge of his island fortress.

One Clean Stroke

Our forces run through the Wastelands surrounding Orlathston as quick and lethal as a bush fire driven by a hot wind. Some of the home clans loyal to Orlath fight to retain their settlements, but they're no match for the training of the Ghume forces and don't share the fervour of Haus's insurgents, who secure the villages and routes to the north and east in a matter of weeks. But Orlath did have the strategic foresight to establish his stronghold on an island in the river, and it only takes a few units of his henchmen to hold the fortress against a unilateral attack from hundreds of Hrossi and Ghumes. Firebombs and blazing arrows are catapulted at our boats as soon as we attempt to come ashore, and it soon becomes clear the only thing blocking us from a full sweep south is control of the island and the port it commands. The battle for Orlathston threatens to evolve into a drawn-out siege for an island not much bigger than the Isfalk citadel and a trading port the span of the Fold.

I come across Haus at sunset on the northern banks of the river, the charred remains of the Cooler across the water, a black smudge against the pink sky. "Admiring the wrangler's handiwork?" I say, hoping to draw him out, but he doesn't take the bait, preoccupied with yet another failed assault of the fortress. He sent word for Osha and Shessa to join us now the fighting is confined to a siege, and I'd hoped their arrival might improve his mood. But his joy at reuniting with my sister, the way I caught his palm snaking briefly to her belly – the fact that she allowed it – hasn't offset the unrest I see now in his eyes, the invisible weight that stoops his shoulders.

"Chief?" I repeat, but he only grunts, drawing himself from his thoughts as reluctantly as a drunk from the tavern. I know where his preoccupations run – Azza grows more restless with each passing day. She worries for her brother, wants to return south with her Ghumes, and I sympathise. I long to see the wrangler safe as much as she does, but unless we hold the island and the port, Haus cannot spare Hrossi warriors for a campaign against Phibia. Orlath could regroup and take back the Wastelands, and everything the young chief has achieved here would be for nothing. Azza knows it is not fair to ask that sacrifice of Haus, but it doesn't stop her frustration seeping through our camp like the growing damp of persistent drizzle.

"Haus?" I press again, squeezing his hand. He draws it away, but not before his pulse floods my senses and I catch an inkling of what his mind is truly plotting... fearing. His brown eyes hold mine, wide and imploring through those long, feminine lashes.

"Do not tell Osha. Do not tell anyone," he pleads. And holding his fingers to my open mouth, he finishes, "And do not fight me... this is my decision."

I know Haus well enough to understand that when he asks something of me, of anyone, there is a damn good reason behind it. And so I bite back my disdain, my fears and arguments, and return with him to the strategy tent to listen without comment while he goes through the motions of planning the next assault on the island with Alrahim and Azza.

When our meal is over and our tactics agreed, we depart for our own beds. I catch the Hrossi chief's shoulder before he makes for my sister's tent. "Don't," I say, a single word all I can manage. He tips his chin towards my hand, acknowledging me but not wanting to turn around, not wanting to hear my arguments that his scheme is madness. "If you are going to do this, don't say goodbye to her," I tell him. "She'll read it in your face. She'll know... And she will never let you go." He stiffens in surprise, but then he nods. He looks towards the river, prowling silent and ominous as some vast snake in the night, fear tightening the corners of his mouth.

"Thank you," he whispers, and I know he's grateful I haven't tried to stop him, grateful the only thing I've talked him out of is his instinctive need to see my sister one last time. "Take care of her."

"No," I tell him flatly, and he spins to face me. "You damn-well knocked her up, Chief. Come back and take care of her yourself."

His grin is slow but genuine. We know it may not be the truth, but neither of us cares for the truth. He makes to draw his hand away, but I clasp it firmly in both of mine. "Wait," I tell him – one final order. And I fall still, my eyes half-closed so I can focus on his heart, his racing pulse. I try my best to steady it, to play down the fear that increases its rhythm, and bolster his courage instead, but I can't do it. My own dread makes my skill fail me. I'm not disciplined enough, not strong enough to give him the one thing he needs. And once again, I regret giving up on Azza's training, turning my back on my potential from sheer pig-headedness and pride. "I'm sorry," I say, but he only presses his shirt to my bleeding nose to stop my apology. I pull him into a hug. "One clean stroke, Lynstum," I whisper in his ear. "One stroke, you hear? And then come back to us."

I'm woken that night by Osha's soft moans. "O?" I call out in the dark, thinking to wake her from her nightmare, but she isn't sleeping on the stretcher bed beside mine. She's standing in the open flap of the tent, bent over double with pain.

"What is it? What's wrong?" I rush to her side.

"Cramps." She draws a breath through gritted teeth. "I think the baby is coming early."

I don't answer. Osha is over halfway through her pregnancy but if the baby is born now, it will not survive. Neither of us speak the fear. Instead, I grab her by the elbow and try to make her sit on the pallet. "Shall I fetch Shessa?"

Before she can answer, she grabs a pitcher and vomits into it.

"Shessa already gave me pain relief," she says, wiping her mouth.

"Poxes, O, how long has this been going on?"

"All day."

"Why didn't you tell me?"

"Just fetch Haus," she groans. "I want Haus."

Fecs in hell! She's been disguising her condition with furs and oversmocks all these weeks, keeping the chief at arm's length. Now – the night he's risked his life on a solo mission – she finally demands his presence and I'm sworn to secrecy.

"Let me help you, O." I reach for her hand, hoping to read her pulse, to reassure myself of the child's, but she draws away, putting up her palm to stop me.

"Get Haus," she repeats, frantic.

The Maw appears in the opening of the tent. She'd obviously woken him to find the chief, but the giant now shakes his head at her. "Where *is* he, Nara?" Osha wails. "He's always near. Something must be wrong." Unsure what to tell her, I look to the Maw. Helplessly, he offers me his skin of dramur vit.

"Fat load of use you're going to be," I tell him, swiping the skin and pushing his vast bulk back through the flap.

"Nah–ra," Osha groans through a contraction. I wheel around, but she holds up her hands once more.

"No! Don't touch me."

"Why not?" Seeing her in such pain and being unable to help is worse than feeling it myself. I break out in a cold sweat, my breath coming thick and fast. "O, *please!*"

"Find Hau–" She can't even finish, stumbling to the trunk at the end of her bed. Groping about the herbs and roots, the phials of liquid and powders, she unearths a spoon, and tries to measure out a dose of black liquid. Her hands shake so much, she gives up and slugs it directly from the bottle.

"What the hells is that, O?" I bark. "What did you just drink?"

"A distillate... pavera milk... mixed with... other things. It s-stops–" Her eyes roll back into her head and her breathing steadies, the tension in her face melting. She remains conscious just long enough for me to catch her. I lay her down on the bed and the touch of our skin flares through me. I hear the downward spiral of her slurring pulse, sense the pain behind it, the twisted struggle at the core of her body. And somewhere below her own, I hear the child's heartbeat tripping quickly. It reminds me of the flutter of hazewings in the Fornwood – so fast and fevered they live only for a day. My skill isn't primed to heal, but even I can sense that something is very wrong. It nearly kills me that I can't help her. There's only one person who might.

I swallow my pride and run to fetch Azza.

By the time she's at my sister's bedside, Osha's curls are matting on the damp pillow. She's half awake, but too weak to even push our hands away. Azza palpates her neck and then the skin of her belly. The thought that Osha might slip away, her pulse too weak to read, makes me rigid with panic. "Haus is coming!" It's all I can think to say to comfort her. "He's coming, O, I promise. Just hold on, okay?" And she manages to blink slowly, her dry lips forming something like a smile at the lie. I don't want it to be a lie. Fecs, why did I let him go? She needs Haus now. What if he doesn't make it back? What if she doesn't make it? How will I ever live with myself?

Azza frowns at my panicked breathing and pushes me towards the tent flap. "Get some air, Nara Fornwood, and let me concentrate." I want to argue, to refuse to leave, but

I know that I'm not helping anyone breathing down Azza's neck. I regret my own lack of skill, regret pushing Azza away when she might have taught me to save Osha myself. Blinking back tears, I step outside to pace beneath the black sky. The ghosthawk is there, somewhere in the night. I can hear his cry. It's too dark to see his familiar diamond shape, so I listen for the beat of his wings. His pulse, vague at first, grows like distant thunder, then drums down, a steady rain. If only I could read humans as easily.

"Hello, my friend," I coo to the bird as he settles upon my arm. The grasp of his talons, that piercing eye, his nervy preening feels less savage to me now. "Where is he, then? Show me Haus." Yellow irises pin mine and I succumb, shedding myself into the tiercel's vision like falling into sunlit water. When I catch my breath, I become aware of a figure rising from the depths of the river, dripping wet. Haus cuts silently through the dark bullrushes to the banks of Orlath's island. The moonless night protects him from the sentries on the fortresses' gates and perimeter walls, but as he steps into the glow of the torches, I realise his intention isn't stealth or subterfuge. He's going to declare himself, show his hand openly, and be walked straight into the besieged fortress.

There's a fuss among the guards as they seize him, a superior hurriedly raised from sleep to verify that the solitary warrior on Orlath's doorstep truly is the great Ringer, Lynstum. Haus is marched under the infamous façade decorated with heads and body parts in their weathered armour, and straight into Orlath's hall. I remember the vast space from our first meeting with the overlord as prisoners, but in the night-time, the torches barely beat back the shadows of the cavernous chamber. The ghosthawk settles in one of the high windows long-void of glass, and I catch the dull gleam of the throne cobbled together from Old-World gadgetry scavenged from the plains. I see it now for what it is – a throne of detritus made for the tinpot overlord of a remnant empire.

The men hold their blades to Haus's neck, shifting their weight from foot to foot, eyes flitting between each other nervously. They've taken his weapons, but anyone who had seen Lynstum fight might have known to bind him. The guards realise their mistake too late. One drops silently to his knees, throat cut by his neighbour's sword, the hilt of which jabs back now to wind its owner in the guts, sending him doubling over. Haus commandeers the helve of the weapon, finishing the other two men before the fourth can get back to his feet. There's a hissed breath, as if the guard has registered the fate of his comrades, but when he staggers, I see with the hawk's precision the sound is a death rattle, the last gasp of a man facing his maker. One clean stroke.

Haus runs, clinging to the shadows of the hall and snaking between the surrounding buildings, until somewhere deep in the Cooler, the hawk loses his tail. All is quiet for far too long. And then I hear a high-pitched cry, the slap of bare feet on paving, followed by the ring of steel. A woman, naked except for a sheet pressed to her front, comes screaming onto a balcony, Orlath in unlaced pants following after. Haus backs him up to the stone balustrade, their silhouettes lit by a solitary torch. The hawk settles on the roof above, and I can hear Orlath's low voice, the Hrossi words nonchalant, conversational – he's cornered, playing for time. Haus doesn't answer. He looks down on the smaller man, face cryptic. Is it hatred that blazes inside him, the need for revenge? Or is it pity Haus feels – pity for Orlath's greed, his misuse of power, his manipulation of men whose love he might have commanded through respect instead of fear. It's difficult to tell. For this isn't the face of Haus. It is the mask of Lynstum, the Ringer Champion.

Do it, I will him. *One clean stroke, fast as lightning. Do it. And come back to us.* But Orlath says something that makes Haus hesitate, and the overlord takes his chance. Steel glints at his open leathers. There's a struggle. Haus grunts, veering backwards, and I spot the cause. Blood bubbles from the hilt of a poniard lodged at his collar bone.

Orlath doesn't stop to admire his handiwork. He runs for the chamber. Haus staggers after him, a trail of blood in his wake. I hear the clang of steel, the grind of swords within. There's a clatter, like a table overturned, and two pewter goblets skittle through the casement. The smell of liquor rises into the night, then burning. Flames spit and flare as drapes catch fast. There a wet cry, a thud, and a bloodied arm falls across the threshold. The ghosthawk's scream shreds the night in two. Startled into flight, it lifts into the blackness, away from the smoke and fire. I don't have the strength within me to sway the creature beyond its instinctive fears.

A shudder of dread brings me back to myself, the beat of the bird's wings already distant above me. Fecs, what just happened? Was it Haus or Orlath who fell? Glimpsing only part of the action suddenly feels worse than not seeing any of it. I hurry back to my sister. I can't help Haus, but I can be there for Osha.

Inside the tent, Osha lies very still, eyes closed. Breath seizes in my lungs.

"She sleeps," Azza reassures me.

I exhale in a rush. "She was in so much pain, Az... Mother's love, I thought..." I lower my head to the bed, shivering in shock. "The baby?"

"It lives."

"How did you stop her labour?"

"How do you think?" Azza levels me a look that says I might have stopped it myself had I bothered to learn how. "Osha will need rest from now on. She is in no condition to be scouring the plains looking for herbs or losing sleep attempting to cure the Continent of the Brume." Her tone makes clear she blames me for Osha's lack of care.

"Her pregnancy was not my secret to share. She made me promise–" But Azza is already stepping through the tent flap.

I catch her arm. "Thank you, Az… for saving her. And the child." I want to add that I'm sorry for the way I behaved on the ship, that I'm sorry for being ungrateful and proud and stubborn. But my mouth won't form the words.

She lifts her chin in acknowledgement, but her eyes remain stony. They feed the guilt that's been taking root within me since the battle on the plains. Had I been a better student, had I listened and worked harder, I might have swayed Orlath on the battlefield. He might not have escaped, we might have avoided a siege, and I might not be waiting for Haus to return, wondering whether he gave his life because of my failures, my mistakes. Regret settles like lead in my bones.

For the rest of the night, I watch over Osha and keep a silent vigil for Haus. When the first pink rays cut through the flap of the canvas, my sister wakes. She immediately asks for the chief.

I squint back out at the dawn. The thought of him not returning, of never seeing my sister again, never holding her child, makes acid of my stomach – burning away words. I shouldn't have let him go. I should have told him it was a foolish plan. I should have gone with him. So many things I should have done.

"Do you think–" Osha begins weakly. "It's just, I told him about the child. He was… he said he was happy. He said he didn't care if it wasn't his." She shakes her head and tears track her cheeks. "But I'm scared, Nara. I think he might have gone to find him, to hunt Orlath down."

I busy myself making food so she can't see my face.

"Look at me, Nara." She waits for me to turn. "You don't have to confess it. I know the truth. When I'm in his arms, when he kisses me, touches me, how can he not see Orlath? How can he not remember how Orlath dishonoured him?"

"How can he not see *you*, O?" I plead. "He didn't go to find Orlath for his own honour, he went for yours! Everything he does is for you and the child. Let him honour you."

"And if he doesn't return?" she says, desperate now.

"I know Haus. He'll return." *If he's alive.* I wish my heart felt the conviction of my words.

Before I get the chance to put myself through the wringer of regret again, there's a noise on the other side of the canvas. A figure stands at the flap.

"Mother's love, Chief." I exhale deeply.

Haus's leather pants are dripping wet from the river, his furs running with blood. He sways a little as he stands, outlined in the dawn light. I grab his shoulders to steady him and something falls from his fist to thud in the dirt. When I pull him inside, Osha tries to get to her feet, immediately focusing on the wound at his neck, but Haus, scanning the scene, is already on his knees before my sister. His Hrossi whispers might be a prayer, a curse, or both at once – I can't tell, I'm too busy watching him press his forehead to her belly, watching her snake her hands through his hair. He draws back suddenly, aware of his filthy state. His fingers tremble and he chokes back his disgust. "I... need to wash–" his voice cracks, but my sister tugs him back to her, a fierce possessiveness in her expression that is too intimate to stay and watch. I slip from the tent, almost tripping over the object Haus has discarded at the entrance. It's a wet sack.

"What is that?" Azza asks. The camp guards must have told her of Haus's return and she has come to find him.

I lift the sack and shake the hessian on the dirt between us. The contents roll free. It takes me a few blinks to register what I'm seeing. A shaved head, tattoos swirling up the scalp and under-jaw, an eye-patch dislodged to reveal a scorched and empty socket, thin lips parted in a rictus of tiny fangs.

"Holy fec." I shudder, but I can't look away. I want to grind those hellish teeth into the dirt, even though they seem no more threatening now than a kitten's.

"Haus got his revenge," Azza mutters, toeing the severed head with a combination of awe and disgust.

"A clean stroke, by the looks," I say. "More than Orlath would have given him." The thought that this could have been so different, that it might have been Haus's head mounted above Orlath's gate – while I did nothing to prevent it – makes me retch. I spit in the dirt. The only thing holding me together is pride – not for myself but for Haus. My friend remained true to himself, true to Lynstum, quick as lightning, and merciful to the end. Life could so easily have made him otherwise. And I can only marvel that he didn't let it.

On the other side of the river, smoke is starting to obscure the fortress in grey plumes that are rapidly turning black. Azza watches the fire with shrewd eyes, understanding the opening Haus has made for us into the fortress. "Your Hrossi chief has honoured his promise, Nara Fornwood. We must press this advantage while the island is leaderless."

I nod my agreement. I have a promise of my own to fulfil. "We should hurry. If Sigrun, Dalla and Annek burn alive in that harem, Osha will never speak to me again."

Our Mor

My terror of returning to the Cooler had grown into nightmares the further we journeyed into Hross. But those old fears pass like storm clouds petering into spring rain. Without his absolute leadership to answer to, Orlath's cronies fall apart, driven by the very jealousies he seeded in them to prevent any unified front against him. A few clansmen manage to flee to their hearthlands, but the majority bend the knee sooner rather than later, and the island is ours within a day.

We find the entrance to Orlath's harem locked from the outside, its high stone walls partly shielding it from the fire that had started in the overlord's quarters. Our soldiers wrangle nearby flames, but coughing and frantic cries from within make me worry the women will suffocate if they aren't freed quickly. The harem's guards have long since fled with the keys, and it becomes clear there's nothing for it but to break down the gates. Haus organises a joist to be pulled down and used as a battering ram while Alrahim coordinates two lines of the strongest Ghumes to make the assault. But female voices cry out in various dialects over the walls – pleas for help, or terror at the prospect of a new onslaught of abusers.

"Annek!" I yell above the tumult. "Annek... Dalla... it's me, Nara. If you're there, move the women away from the gates." But no answer comes back in Isfalki, the cries gradually growing fainter. Unable to bear it, I join the Maw and the other soldiers on the ram. "Fec's sake, how long does it take

to batter down an old door? They're suffocating in there!" The
giant only grabs my forearms, correcting my grip on the wood,
showing me how to set my shoulder before the next strike.
Just when I think I've ground my teeth to stumps and my
bones feel pummelled loose in my skin, a great crack rends the
air. With one last thrust the door splinters off its hinges, smoke
and ashes billowing with the force of its fall.

The first thing I make out is a woman, tall and athletic,
striding through the haze. Her face is blackened with smut but
I'd recognise the determined line of that mouth anywhere.
"Annek!" I shout, but she is too distracted to hear me. She seizes
a broken chair leg like a club, then breaks into a run. The Maw
intercepts her path but Annek takes a swing at him, undeterred
by his size. I always knew she was a brawler, someone I'd
want on my side in a fight. She lands a hit across the Cooler
champion's cheek, the contact surprising them both. They stand
across from each other, panting, before the giant seizes the club
to avoid a further thrashing. At the same time, Annek pulls a
dagger from her robe and lunges for the Maw's throat. He veers
back, dodging it, but the whites of his eyes flash at the near
miss. A beat later he's flicked the blade from her hand, like he's
batting away a troubling mosquito. Annek raises both arms over
her head, waiting for the blow, as if being struck is something
she's grown used to. The Maw only catches her wrists and draws
them gently to her sides. For the first time since I've known
him, the Ringer makes a conscious sound – a long low rumbling
that gathers momentum from deep within his chest. It takes me
a moment to realise he's laughing.

"Annek! Wait! It's me – Nara." I rush to catch her shoulders
before she braves another attempt on the giant.

"Nara?" She scans my face, as if to check it's truly me. "I
heard a voice. But I wouldn't believe it was you. I'd given
up hope..." She looks over her shoulder to the other girls
gradually appearing from their hiding places. "Sigrun always
said you'd come back."

The younger Mor steps from the haze, coughing and grimed. "Holy Mother!" Sigrun cries, dropping the pewter candlestick she was intending as a club. "Nara!" She lunges towards me and I'm enveloped in a frantic hug.

"And Dalla? Is she here too?" I can't be happy until I find them all alive and safe.

"She's here," Annek says. She looks to a spot where a woman in soot-streaked robes lurks behind a courtyard pillar. "Dalla?" I say approaching her. But there's something changed in the highborn girl, I can sense it as soon as I draw close. Her shoulders are rounded and she seems smaller somehow, like a dog cowed by the boot. She studies me for a moment, arms crossed, and I think of the first time we met in the wagon sleigh crossing the Wasteland Plains, the way she'd looked at me as if I was little more than shit on her shoe. How changed she is now.

"Dalla," I try again.

"Is it really you?" Her voice is a cracked whisper.

"Yeah. It's me."

She lifts her chin, blinking back tears. "You took your fecking time."

The five of us stay up into the early hours of the morning – Osha, me and the three Mor. We talk, we listen to each other's news, and we drink dramur vit. Lots of dramur vit. Not to celebrate, but to console, to loosen our tongues and then to fill the gaps of silences no words can occupy. Dalla remains quiet, the campfire crackling and flickering across her face, pale as a ghost in the shadows. We could have taken more comfortable lodgings inside Orlath's fortress, but the girls wanted to get off the island – to put the memory of that prison behind them as soon as possible. Besides, Annek claims, being around a campfire again feels like our time on the Wasteland Plains, and I understand why that might mean so much to her – to all of us. It was the first time we understood the lie of the home that had raised us… the first time we decided not to return to the oppression of Isfalk and to cast our lot with the Hrossi instead. That decision was a double-edged sword, but at least we made it for ourselves – a first act of defiance for most of these women. And that felt more like a gift than a punishment.

Annek tells us a little of how they were treated in the harem. She and Sigrun were passed to Orlath's chieftains, Annek fighting it at first, until she realised that compliance was the only way to freedom. She explains how she made herself a favourite with certain Hrossi clansmen, trading their gifts with servants in exchange for supplies, and even securing outings with them beyond the harem walls, all with a view to plotting an escape. Only Dalla, I gather, was taken exclusively to Orlath's chamber. Only she experienced anything close to what had happened to Osha. She won't speak of it, but the marks about her neck and face tell me enough. I grieve for her. I grieve for them all, and I blame myself for the fact that I couldn't save them, that I didn't come back soon enough. Guilt eats away at me – how sorry I'd felt for myself as the Brand among them, how I believed I was slighted because of my skin. But these Mor were dealt the harder fate – they became pawns to be sacrificed in the Continent's power games.

Osha reaches for Dalla's hand, a force in her grasp as they study each other in silence. I sense a solidarity pass between them, a growing fortitude in Dalla that has nothing to do with Osha's sway. Despite the highborn girl's prejudice, her condescension to me when we'd first met, I'd have never wished her such a fate, not even when she drove us to distraction in the sleigh wagon. But she's not alone in her pain now and neither is Osha. It's a small consolation, I guess.

Sigrun, always the quietest but most observant in our group, asks when Osha's baby is due. My sister blushes under the scrutiny of the women, but when she realises she's fooled none of them, she answers.

"I have two months to go, perhaps less... I can't be sure."
She stares into the fire. It feels like progress that she's finally
spoken openly of the child, but I can sense she doesn't want
them to pry too deeply.

"What I don't understand is how none of *you* ended up
pregnant in that fecking place," I say, deflecting the topic from
Osha.

Dalla's eyes dart to mine, accusing. It was a tactless question.
I almost wish she would dish me one of her serves as she used
to, but she stays silent.

"Sig convinced a guard to smuggle us some bloodwood,"
Annek answers.

"What?" Osha turns to Sigrun in shock. "You brought a
gravid purgative into the harem under Orlath's very nose?
That's instant death for anyone involved." She's as surprised
as I am that it would be Sigrun, the youngest and most timid
among them, taking such risks. "How did you do it?"

Sigrun turns away in shame, but Annek catches her chin
and holds it high, as if to remind the younger girl to be proud
of her actions. And I understand the kind of *convincing* Sigrun
must have performed for a guard to risk his life over women's
herbs. How Orlathston must have changed her. How it must
have robbed her of trust and love and innocence. And yet, she
refused to become helpless. She kept on fighting. They all did.
While I was battling to survive the Cooler, these girls were
doing just the same here, using what strategy and weapons
they could. It's not for me – it's not for anyone – to judge them
for that.

I look into the faces of each Mor in turn. Sigrun chews her
lip, Annek squares her jaw and Dalla stares into the flames, fist
tight around the vit skin – perhaps the most changed of them
all. "I have something to show you," I say.

Osha face hardens, understanding my intent. "You might
want a swig of vit first," she tells the girls as I back into the
darkness to retrieve the hessian sack.

Orlath's head rolls before them in the dirt, tattoos lit by the embers, one eye socket a hollow shadow. Sigrun jerks back with a soft cry and Annek sucks a breath between her teeth. But it's Dalla's reaction that interests me most. She doesn't flinch, as if that response has long since been lost to her. Instead, she hands me the vit skin, gathers her furs around her and rises to inspect the gory remains.

"Who did it?" she asks blandly.

"Haus," Osha replies.

Dalla nods as if it explains something. "He didn't deserve it," she says. "Orlath didn't deserve that." And for a moment I'm confused, shocked that she might take Orlath's side.

"How can you say that?" I ask.

Her wide pupils are blacker than the night. "He didn't deserve a clean death," she mutters. "He deserved so much worse."

And with one strike of her boot, she kicks the head into the fire, withdrawing to her tent.

The Quickening

Within days, Azza is preparing ships, weapons and supplies for the journey back to her brother in Reis. It is too soon for Haus to leave Orlathston – *Hross*, as the city is now renamed. But for the campaign south he pledges as many Wasteland warriors as he can spare – his contribution more than matching Alrahim's Ghume forces. The Maw agrees to lead them, and Azza seems satisfied.

As for the Isfalki Mor, Dalla cannot contemplate staying in Orlathston. She boards as soon as the ships are ready. Annek joins her. That doesn't surprise me; I'd always recognised a kindred spirit in the tall Isfalki woman – the yearning for freedom and adventure sparkling in her eyes at the sight of the open sea. But Sigrun chooses to stay behind, fascinated by Osha's healing work and her studies of herb lore under Shessa the spae-wife. My sister will not leave Haus, and neither Azza nor I will contemplate letting her travel after nearly losing the child. And so, there's only me left to walk the line between leaving or staying behind.

"I thought I'd find you mulling about here," Osha says, startling me in the charred arena of the Cooler. We've both avoided entering the amphitheatre, but returning to its ruins feels somehow necessary now, like drawing back the curtain on our nightmares to shrink them in the sunlight. It was on these sands where Teta San thrust my knife into her throat, where I fought Brim, where Osha was forced to watch her lover risk his life for a virtue that had already been stolen. But it's also where the wrangler opened the cages of Ringer fighters and set fire to the stands. It's where his arrow shot Orlath in the eye – Orlath, whose body now bloats at the bottom of the Heitval inlet, the feast of crabs and eels.

Osha's hand on my arm draws me from my thoughts. "You act like there's even a decision to make."

"I know. Of course I'm going to stay here with you."

"No," she says on an exasperated breath. "Because of course you're going back to Reis."

I pace the ring, shaking my head. "How can I? You're my family – the only one I've got. We've never been that far apart, and I promised Amma–"

"Amma is gone, Nara. Life moves on. Besides, if I must be *looked after*, Haus will be the one to do it and, frankly," she arches an eyebrow, "he does a much better job of it than you ever have."

"Isn't that the truth?" Sulkily, I toe a boot in the ashy sands. "Leaving you feels like I'm cutting off a limb."

"And turning your back on the wrangler won't?"

I press my lips together. She knows me too well.

"My bull-headed little sister," she says, taking my shoulders and making me meet her gaze. "It's your turn to swallow the advice you gave me. Let go of all these barriers you're putting up. Let go, Nara, and let him love you."

The simplicity of it makes me bury my face in her neck. "I was so terrible to him when we parted in Reis. I let him leave... I let him face death without so much as a word of goodbye... I thought it was a weakness to tell him how I really feel–"

"He already knows, Narkat."

"How can he, when I've been the mother of all bitches to him?"

"He knows because... well, I made sure he knew."

"What?" I pull out of her arms. "You told him I love him?"

"Yes," she says, sheepish. "Because you do and because he needed something hopeful to carry with him on that awful mission."

"Osha!" I turn on her. "How could you? I kept your secret about the baby from Haus just like you asked me to, and yet all this time you were blabbing your mouth to the wrangler about me. Holy fec, his ego's big enough already. He doesn't need it boosting!"

"Believe me, Nara, with you he needs it," she says, arms crossed. "Anyway, you never asked me *not* to tell him."

I swipe a palm over my face, growling my frustration at the derelict rim of the Cooler. All those times I thought I'd scored over him, and he was holding my sister's trump card to his chest. "Cock's poxes!" The birds wheel in the circle of sky above me, screeching and cawing their laughter.

"Perhaps this makes it a little easier to leave me?" Osha says. I keep my back to her, sulking. When she draws close, she knuckles me in the ribs. "Come on, Narkat. Let's get you packed. Azza needs you with her."

"No, she doesn't."

"Yes, she does. Training you on that voyage back to Reis is going to be her only distraction from worrying about her brother. And Mother knows, you need the practice. So, you're going to have to swallow that great wad of pride stuck in your throat and apologise to her."

"Apologise?"

She nods. "I need someone looking out for you, Nara... someone who isn't a mute ex-Ringer with boozing and brawling as his only gifts."

"The Maw has other gifts," I tell her.

"Really?"

"Yeah... like not blabbing."

"Nara." She sighs. "Just apologise to Azza."

I know she's right, but I'm not sure Azza will bury the hatchet with me just yet. Osha must see the apprehension on my face. "Don't worry, she'll forgive you. Everyone always does."

"You sure about that?"

She nods. "Must be because of your charm."

I wrap my arms around her. "What am I going to do without you, O?"

"You won't be without me." She takes her pendant from inside her dress and taps it to mine. "You and me, sis, remember?" The childish habit might have brought tears to my eyes if the sentiment wasn't marred by another feeling – a creeping dread every time I think of the symbol. The Halqa draws me back to Reis almost as much as my desire to see the wrangler, but I'm terrified of learning why we carry it about our necks, terrified of confirming that the Khadib – Azza and Nixim's arch enemy – might be our mother. But I need to hear it from Phibia's lips. I need to know who I am.

Dalla and Annek find their sea legs a few days into our voyage. It fascinates me to see Dalla helping Takia prepare food in the galley, preferring the servant's company to the soldiers and crew above decks. And then I remember Dalla's fondness for her family's cook, Cyrus, back in Isfalk. I begin to suspect that Takia gives the highborn girl tasks and chores to deliberately distract her from her dark thoughts and nightmares. Slowly, as the days pass and the sea air brings some colour back to her pallid cheeks, I notice some of the archness and vitality return to Dalla's manner. She even seems to have found the energy to bicker with Annek again. It almost feels like old times.

"Takia and I could use your help washing dishes and preparing supper, you know," Dalla complains to Annek one evening. "Or are you going to prance around with swords and lock eyes with that hulking beast for this entire journey?"

"I'm not *locking eyes* with the Maw," Annek retorts. "For a start, I'd get a crick in my neck if I tried. Besides, I'm too busy making sure I don't get knocked out by his stave to be flirting with him!"

The Maw has been teaching Annek to fight, sometimes roping me into the exercise so she has a more size-appropriate sparring partner. It hasn't escaped me how much she revels in the training, how natural her skill is with weapons, or how much it seems to peeve Dalla every time the Ringer corrects her grip, or squares her shoulders, demonstrating the proper defensive stance.

"Does he have to be so hands-on about it?" Dalla mutters as the giant shoves Annek's feet apart with his boot, pressing a palm to the small of her back to adjust her hips. "He's not breaking in a horse."

"I think I can handle it, Dal," Annek calls out. "And I hate to tell you this but... we're already broken in." She circles the Maw, drawing heavy breaths. "If we'd been trained to defend ourselves, perhaps we'd have had a bit more say in that matter." She moves in for a strike and parry sequence under the Maw's silent scrutiny.

"Speak for yourself," Dalla sniffs. "No one's broken me in."

The comment warms my heart, as if the old Dalla is flickering somewhere beneath the surface, ready to flame to life again like a stoked ember beneath ash.

"What are you smirking at?" she barks at me. I shrug, but she knows I've seen her assessing the flex of Annek's thighs, the sheen of sweat on Annek's biceps, Annek's forearms clasping the Maw's after they've sparred together. Dalla is jealous. It's as clear as the sails of the *Na'quat* imprinted on the blue of the sky. "I'm not smirking at anything, princess," I say. "I was only wondering when you're planning to come clean with her?" I lift my chin towards Annek.

"Come clean about what?"

I give her a look that tells her not to bother pretending. She fumbles with the copper she's been scouring and it clatters to the deck. Annek looks our way, briefly concerned.

"What would you know of it?" Dalla hurries to pick up the pan.

"Not that much, really. But, for what it's worth, I think you'd get a favourable reception."

"Is that right?" she says, voice caustic. I nod. "And what of that ridiculous man mountain?"

I scoff at her description. "The Maw has one true love and that is the soft swell of a full vit skin. Do you really think she'd be taunting you in the middle of sparring if her objective was to impress *him*?"

Her face softens suddenly, as if she'd never considered that possibility. "Really? You think she bickers with me because…?" And the note of vulnerability, of hope in Dalla's voice makes me warm to her more than I ever thought possible.

"It's why she's always done it, Dalla. Haven't you realised yet?" And I think of the wrangler, our baiting and bickering. How long has it taken me to realise the same thing?

Annek looks across from the water bucket, frowning at our tête-à-tête. "What are you two whispering about?"

Dalla's head cocks and the angle of her lashes, the tease in her voice when she speaks brings back memories of her drinking vit around a Wasteland campfire. "If you'd bother to do something useful," she answers Annek, "I might tell you."

"Something useful? Like what?"

"Let's see. Takia's given me a list." Dalla counts on her fingers. "There's the galley to scrub, potatoes to peel and the stew to make." She gives Annek a long look. "Am I supposed to strip all the cabin beds on my own?"

Annek runs a tongue under her bottom lip, trying not to smile. "Well, then," she says, handing her weapon to the Maw. "I guess that's enough training for today."

Three days later, I'm sparring on the forecastle with Annek, when Azza intercepts without warning, gifting me a slap under the chin with the flat of her practise sword.

I've been trying to say sorry to Azza all this time, but she's been working me so hard – mocking me with jabs like this one, tripping my footwork, intercepting with an attack when Annek does not – that resentment is once again taking over remorse. "If this is your way of showing you're still crabby with me, it's not very subtle," I say, rubbing my jaw where it burns.

"It is my way of telling you to lift your attention and stop being lazy. The Reis have a saying, Nara Fornwood. *Slow feet, sore head.*" She lunges again, but I dodge it this time.

"The Solitaries have a saying, too, Azza Ni Azzadur." I spin behind her, repaying the blow with a hit to her thigh. "*Why hold a grudge, when you can hold a sword?*"

"I did not think Fornwood Solitaries were known for their swordsmanship."

"Yeah, well, they're not known for their proverbs either – you're not the only one who can make shit up."

She almost laughs, but our sparring takes over. Mid-play, she clobbers the shield from my grasp with her own and both bucklers clatter across the decks. It's deliberate – she seizes my wrist and I feel her presence engulf me as it always does, searching my mind like she's running through its corridors, throwing open doors. Rage catches like a flame, heating my blood.

"Let your anger control you, and you will be trapped inside your failure," she snaps.

"How can I not get angry? You're ransacking *private* thoughts!"

"Empty your mind as I showed you, and there would be nothing to ransack... Block me."

I draw a long breath, trying to think of the calmest moments in my life. Bathing in the Moon Pools; dozing by the fire in the Fornwood cabin; hunting on the tundra – a horizon of glacial blue trimmed with the pink of dawn, the wind so cold it burns everything else away. That last image feels cleansing somehow, reducing my thoughts to basic survival. My pulse slows, my chest grows lighter and my mind empties, clean as the ice plains. But it is not a blank page, as Azza described. Need and hunger drive my focus, just as it did growing up. I'm a hunter; I'll find my quarry or I won't eat. Azza isn't in my mind anymore, but I can hear her blood pumping a steady beat in my ears. I latch onto her pulse, wrestling with its rhythm until it succumbs to mine. The sway quickens within me... and her mind cracks open like a lit doorway in the dark. I see an airy, high-ceilinged room with ornate tiles in blues and golds – somewhere high up in Cha Shaheer's fortress. Open casements look out across the gorge river, the Kyder lush and green in the distance. A desk is at the centre of the space, covered with parchments and scrolls, and on it I see those hands again, pinning down a map, tracing borders with a finger, just as I'd glimpsed before in Azza's head on the journey to Hross. With a start, I realise they are Brim's hands, his short blond hair and broad shoulders leaning over the desk. He's deep in conference with a woman whose white hair is braided around the back of her head in the way of Isfalki Mor, her robes pristine white. Phibia.

"What are you doing here, Brim?" It's Azza's voice, interrupting them as she enters the chamber. Her tone is stricken as she takes in the scene with quick darting looks – the maps, the proximity of Brim and the Khadib, their hushed confidences.

"We're getting to know each other, aren't we, Brim?" Phibia answers for him. "You didn't tell me, Azza Ni Azzadur, how bright and charming young Captain Oskarsson is. He reminds me very much of someone I used to know." And the Khadib's fingers fold affectionately around Brim's on the desk. "His experience in the Warder army promises to be very useful."

The vision blurs at the edges and I blink, but I'm hungry for it, angry, resentful and desperate for news of Brim after all this time. When I sense Azza grappling back control of her pulse, I press my advantage again.

"I must talk with you, Captain," Azza tells Brim, watching Phibia with wary eyes. But Brim continues to be engrossed in the map, as if Azza hasn't spoken.

"As you can see, the young Captain is preoccupied," Phibia says, her hand still brushing his on the table.

Azza bows her head at the older woman and backs out of the room.

The rhythm of our pulses trips and fractures now, and the vision blurs, slipping from my grasp. When I'm back in my own head, on the decks of the *Na'quat*, I wrench my hand from Azza's with a wince as if she's lit a flame between us. I slip backwards on the briny deck, sprawling on my arse at her feet. Azza takes a few steps back, too, and we stare at each other, the wind whipping the breath from our open mouths. "You confound me, Nara Fornwood," she says, her voice barely audible above the elements. "One moment you can barely block me, and the next you break straight into my most private memories." She studies my face, but has the decency to show a little shame, as if I've come across her naked before a bath.

"You've known all this time," I say. "Phibia got to Brim. She swayed him, didn't she?" Azza doesn't answer. "Fecs in hell, Az, why didn't you tell me?"

"There was no time. I thought you would not leave Cha Shaheer without him."

"Damn right I wouldn't have!" I get to my feet. "Would you abandon your best friend to the mercies of that mind-warping bitch?"

Her face hardens. "No. I abandoned my father and sister to her instead."

I shut my mouth, avoiding her quick, intelligent eyes, but I'm still fuming, knowing now more than ever that I have to go back to Cha Shaheer for Brim. I have to learn how to face that scheming krait – I have to learn how to do it for him.

"He's my oldest friend, Azza, don't you understand? He's never abandoned me and I won't do it to him. I owe him."

Her expression softens. "It pained me to leave him too–"

"Then why didn't you help him when you saw them in the study? Why didn't you use your own sway to draw Brim away from her?"

"And risk letting Phibia know what I am after all these years? No!" Her sympathy is gone, her tone determined again. "My secret is my greatest weapon against her. And I will not give that up for one man, however much he is your *friend*. There are other lives at stake here."

I look at the set of her face – resolute, focused, controlled. "I wish I could be more like you," I tell her, "but I'm not." Azza wants to teach me to access my skill by denying my feelings, wiping my thoughts. But it was hunger and need that quickened my sway just now. And it was a whole range of emotions – anger, resentment, the desire to protect those I love – that allowed me to stay inside her vision when she wanted to push me out. Without those passions, what would drive me? Perhaps there will always be something wild, impulsive and consuming about me. Perhaps that's my strength after all.

I straighten my jerkin and roll my shoulders. Rain starts to lash the decks. Through it, I sense Azza watching me, uncertain.

"Pick up your sword," I say, blinking at her through the rain. "I have more ransacking to do."

The Tathar and The Fec

As we draw closer to Cha Shaheer, Alrahim navigates the fleet out to sea, to avoid being spotted from the coastline. We sail south of the landing where the wrangler brought us ashore on our first trip to Reis. If my vision is correct and Iness is sending reinforcements to join Phibia's cause, Azza believes that is where they will make anchor and disembark. So we establish our forces well south of the capital, making camp under cover of jungle even thicker than the Kyder. Scouts ride out immediately to find the wrangler and tell him our position.

"So we're supposed to just sit and wait, not knowing if he's dead or alive?" I ask Azza. I'm thinking of Brim as much as the wrangler, my focus torn.

Azza lays a hand on my shoulder as I pace beside the campfire. "I, too, am anxious for news of Nixim. But war is a waiting game and patience wins it." Her eyes are liquid black in the flames, penetrating, before she looks away, chewing the inside of her lip.

"What is it?"

"I owe you an apology, Nara Fornwood."

"Er, shouldn't that be the other way round?" She shakes her head and I can see she's serious. "Really, an apology from Azza Ni Azzadur? This should be good."

She rolls her eyes at me as she reaches into the pocket of her waistcoat and withdraws a small fold of paper. "This was inside the letter Captain Alrahim gave me on the voyage to Orlathston. It is from my brother... but it is for you."

"For me?" I watch her hold out the note, something shame-faced in her expression. "You mean you've had this for weeks and you're only handing it over now?"

"It was not to be delivered to you unless you'd made progress with your training. That was Nixim's explicit instruction. He wanted to ensure you were not distracted by... other things."

"Oh, he did, did he?"

"Alrahim tried to change my mind. She said news of Nixim might spark you enough to see some results. But then you gave up our sparring and the attack on Orlathston was imminent and I... I thought it best not to give it to you."

"Fec's sake, what is it with you people making decisions for me? Am I still a child?" I snatch the letter from her and stride to my tent. Throwing myself on the stretcher bed, I examine the folded paper. On the outside, the words *Little Scourge* are written in untidy script. Inside, the ink is even blotchier, as if the lines have been scrawled on the move.

If you're reading this, my sister has worked you hard enough to see some progress in your skill. I'm sure you've thanked her with many a charming turn of phrase. Even so, I'd trade places with Az in a heartbeat if I could. I'm surprised to discover your venom is easier to bear than being parted from it.

I miss you, Na'quat.

And I hate the way we said goodbye.

There. Am I being honest enough for you now?

My throat tightens, and I have the stupid desire to lift the paper to my face, to see if it still smells of his skin. It's as close to a love letter as I'm ever going to get from the wrangler. It slugs me right in the heart... and between the legs. Poxes, did he know when he wrote it that I'd be savouring each word? Is that why he didn't want me *distracted*?

As Azza has probably told you, my progress recruiting among the Seven Clans is slower than I'd hoped, given my father's death and the new urgency of our campaign. I try not to get defeated or despairing. Instead, I imagine you growing your skill with my sister and I'm thankful for it. So thankful that she's teaching you to defend yourself. You asked for none of this, Nara. I thrust it upon you, and you trusted me when, by rights, I should have told you more – done more – to earn that trust. I don't have the time or the talent to tell you how I feel in this letter. Only know that I regret not asking for that kiss when we parted. I mean it when I say you guide me, my Na'quat, even if you think you don't. You've always guided me.

Your Wrangler.

PS. Tell Pretty Boy if he so much as comes near you again, I'll slice off his jewels and feed them to my dogs.

I read the words over and over. They weren't what I was expecting and the thrill of his honesty is a giddy rush, like too much air in starved lungs, or bright sunlight after a dank prison. His declaration makes me honest with myself: it's all I've ever wanted to hear from the wrangler – that I'm important to him, that he needs me as much as I need him.

And yet that final postscript nags at me, spoiling my joy. Nixim believes Brim sails with us. Azza had known the truth. If I didn't read it in her thoughts, she knew I might suspect it from this letter.

"You read this note!" I accuse her across the campfire. "It wasn't sealed and you read it. Tell me, was it Nixim who wanted me to keep my eye on the fight, or was it you?" She doesn't speak so I guess the answer. "You meant to keep me ignorant of Brim, you wanted to keep me hoping he was still with Nixim."

"It hardly matters, now," she says, avoiding my gaze. "You learned the truth with your skill – you read my memories. That is a better result."

"But you could have told me the truth."

"What good would it have served? We were at sea. You could not have saved Brim."

"But I might have before we left Cha Shaheer!"

I run a hand over my face, full of regret. I should have gone back for Brim as soon as I knew he was missing. He didn't abandon me on the Wasteland Plains, even when I tried to force him to. He followed me to Orlathston despite all the risks. "I might have guessed he was in danger when he didn't come, that something – or someone – was preventing him from being by my side." I level an accusing look at Azza. "I should have listened to my instincts and trusted what I know about Brim."

Azza shakes her head. "Nara Fornwood," she says in a scathing voice, "you confuse your precious instincts with the truth."

"What do you mean by that?"

"It means, instincts can lie. What we think we know of a person can change. And you are quick to accuse others of deceit, but you never examine the lies you tell yourself."

"Mother's love, Az, I don't have the patience for your riddles tonight. If you've got something to say about Brim or about me, then say it. Otherwise, I'm going to bed."

She remains silent.

I clutch the letter in my fist, and storm back to my tent. It is not Nixim who preoccupies me now, but Brim. I can't stop seeing the image of Phibia's hand on his in the Cha Shaheer fortress. He's still there, under the influence of her sway. What will she make him do? And what will become of him when he's no longer of use to her? Will his fate be the same as the Kham's, the same as Azza's mother? I can't simply abandon my oldest friend to that murderous krait. Wild, impulsive and dangerous as it may be, I know what I must do. I've known it ever since fleeing the Shadow City – I must face Phibia myself and get Brim out of Cha Shaheer before war erupts in Reis.

It takes time for the camp to fall asleep, and singling out a horse from the pack without alerting the watch to my movements is much harder than I imagined. But thankfully the mare I've saddled is swift and silent, responsive to my sway as she picks out a dappled trail through the jungle. I hear no sound of being followed.

When Alrahim had told me we were two days south of Cha Shaheer, she was calculating the movement of troops. As a solitary rider, my guess is I could reach the city before dusk tomorrow, if I push my mount and keep rests to a minimum. The mare makes steady progress through the night. But riding alone, my thoughts prey on me. Am I strong enough to free Brim from Phibia, if that's what it comes down to? Facing the krait terrifies me, but it feels inevitable somehow – fated to happen after the showdown in the temple. The nosebleeds have finally stopped when I access my skill now, and I have been able to keep Azza out of my head, breaking into her thoughts once or twice. Our last day aboard the *Na'quat,* I had even made her kiss Alrahim's cheek during a break from sparring, much to the Captain's red-faced delight. Azza, however, wouldn't speak to me for the rest of the journey. She'd argued the stunt was childish and meddling. "You told me the seed of desire had to be there for a Sway to influence it," I'd argued. I had felt a little guilty... for all of two minutes. But truly it was only payback for how she'd spied on my old pining for Brim, how she'd kept news of him from me, and how she'd withheld Nixim's letter.

Still, one or two manipulations don't make me a Tathar. I know I have so much more to learn, but there's not enough time. There never has been. I have to return to Cha Shaheer as I am. I must at least try to get Brim away from the fortress and Phibia's influence or I won't be able to live with myself. I was so dishonest with him about my feelings for the wrangler, so dishonest with myself. I only hope Brim can forgive me. I only hope Azza and Nixim can.

By dawn, the forest is thinning a little, and by late afternoon I've reached the hunting grounds of the Kyder, following the line of the river towards the Shadow City. The mare is lathered in sweat and blows heavily beneath me. As soon as I find a spot,

I wade her into the shallows and rub her down while she drinks. At dusk, the gorge is so peaceful and calm it's hard to believe armies amass on either side of it, that the clean waters here might soon turn red with something other than the reflection of sunset. I push the thought from my mind. I can only focus on the task ahead – getting Brim out of Cha Shaheer. Whether or not I succeed, the battle will rage without me.

I cut back under cover of the Kyder to wait for nightfall. Tethering the mare, I scatter a few oats from my saddlebags onto the forest floor. It's the only feed I can offer her after our long ride, but it's better than nothing. If I make it out of Cha Shaheer, I may need her again. Whispering for her to wait for me, I head back out to the gorge and begin to climb the boulders in the dark, hoping to the Mother I've remembered the location correctly. I make a few wrong turns at first and have to scramble back over rocks, sliding and nearly breaking my neck in the dark. But then it's there before me, the black slash of the crevice opening into sheer sandstone – the entrance to the catacombs Azza had led us through when we fled the city. I come across one of the torches we discarded on our flight out and I light it, barely able to stop my hand from shaking as I hold the flame before me. The passageway of living rock around me is chill and dank compared to the air outside. My breath grows erratic as I enter and I have to give myself a talking to. *You've been through these tunnels before, Nara. They're a means to an end and you owe it to Brim. You're seriously going to let a narrow space defeat you before you can get to the main event?*

I distract myself by studying the markings on the walls. I hadn't noticed them on the way out of Cha Shaheer – too busy running. The glyphs and strange pictographs are from some ancient time long before the Brume, long before the Old World, I suspect. Who were these people all those centuries ago? How did they live; how did they die? The images flare before me as I hurry past, their struggles real, too – disease, war and hardship. But I also see celebration, love and children.

It gives me an odd sense of comfort somehow, knowing that whatever the outcome of the war ahead, whatever happens to me – to this measly body and uninspired soul – there will be survivors, always survivors clinging to that life-force Amma said was in us all. I think of Osha's child, and the gut-heavy fear I've carried inside me since my exile from the Isfalk citadel blossoms with the tiniest tendril of hope. That child will survive – other children will survive, even if I don't. *Think not of the pain of the past, but the hope of the future.* Azza's voice rings in my mind – a voice I don't want to hear, a voice that would only damn me for what I'm doing right now.

I push on, through the bowels of Cha Shaheer, following the winding passageway upwards, until at last it branches off into several directions and I know I've reached the fortress. I try to recall the haphazard corridors and walkways that lead to the upper rooms where Osha and I stayed. Brim's quarters were only a short walk from ours. But the keep is silent and dark now, so different in the dead hours that I struggle to remember the route. I'm forced to retrace my steps more than once, ducking around corners or into the shadows of alcoves whenever a night watch passes. In a few hours staff will begin filling these passages, rushing about the morning's chores, increasing my chances of being noticed.

I hurry on through the maze of stonework until the twists and turns bring me to Brim's door. The handle is unlocked and I slip inside without knocking, fearful of waking a servant. But the rooms are unlit and silent, empty of life. I search his bedchamber anyway. The casement shutters are closed and I dare to light the small candle by the bedside to check for signs of his presence. The bed clearly hasn't been slept in, but his belongings and clothes are still here, meaning he hasn't left Cha Shaheer. I riffle through his things, looking for clues. His boots, his weapons and his armour are missing. I know Brim – his sword is as precious as a limb and he'd never go anywhere without it. But why the boots and armour? He hasn't worn them since we first landed in Reis – it's too hot. So, where in Hell's poxes is he? And what is he doing dressed for a fight?

I decide to check our own quarters. Perhaps he's sleeping there in case one of us returns. But those rooms are also dark and empty, the saman reflecting the last stars like a square of night sky fallen to earth. I have one last option before facing the inevitable – Saqira. Going to her places us both at risk, but she's my only ally in the city.

I head in the direction of the Golden Temple, hoping to snatch a moment alone with her in the Seers' quarters before the rest of the city wakes, but I draw back just in time to avoid two guards stationed in the passageway. Even in the dim light of the wall sconces, I can see that their sleeveless surcoats are embroidered with the symbol of the Halqa. They are well-built in their armour, their faces and arms unmarked. Only Phibia would ensure her personal guards were Pure, and only she would have such an ornate and well-protected entrance to her private rooms. Is Brim on the other side of those gilded doors? If I could reach him before anyone else wakes, I might release Phibia's sway over him and we could flee the Shadow City together.

I find a recess to watch and wait. Minutes, hours slip by and my heart starts to sink – I should be making my way back to the tunnels now if I want to escape unnoticed before daybreak. But if I return alone, my only achievement will be pissing off Azza – and Nixim – when they find out. There's another thought flickering at the back of my mind, too, one that I haven't openly admitted to myself until this point – did I come here hoping to rescue Brim, or was it because I wanted to confront Phibia, to face her on the offensive before she could attack me and those I love? That's always been my style, after all. If I use my sway against her unexpectedly, as I did with Azza, what might I discover about the coming battle, about her planned tactics and greater strategy? But, equally, what might Phibia discover about our own?

I think of what Azza said before I left. Am I confusing my instincts with the truth? Am I lying to myself right now? Is it Phibia's military secrets I want or her personal ones? *Be honest with yourself, Nara Fornwood.* The voice in my head sounds remarkably similar to Azza's. *What you want Phibia to show you is yourself.*

It's the truth. Phibia has become the key to all the unknowns in my life. She's the one person who might tell me who I am, who I belong to. Coming back to Cha Shaheer wasn't only about finding Brim. It was about finding myself. I squat on my haunches in the shadows, feeling selfish, treacherous, destructive. I've risked Azza and Nixim's whole campaign for the chance to get those answers. I shake my head hard, as if I can physically loosen the guilt from my mind. I don't want to examine it now. I can't. There isn't time. My only focus is seeing if Brim is behind that door.

The guards seem to have come to an agreement – one sinks to the floor, head propped against the wall, stealing a quick nap, while the other paces, keeping watch. When he turns on his heel to retrace his steps, he's close enough that I can see the dampness glistening at the back of his neck, can smell meaty sweat and the stale smoke of a pipe habit seeping from under his armour. He gives a grisly roll of his shoulders, cracking his spine before he shuffles off once more. It's been a long night – he's hot and tired and craves sleep as much as his sidekick. That's his weakness; that is what I must sway. But can I do it at will?

My hands tremble violently as I wait for the guard to pass again. He's almost upon me when he pauses, withdraws a pipe from his surcoat and turns to one of the wall torches to light it. I'm on him before his taper even catches, reaching from behind to pull him into a headlock, and muffling his mouth with my sand scarf. I feel his pulse leap in his throat and my own blood answers – calming, reassuring, comforting. It's easy to slow his heart, easy to encourage his mind to reach for the rest he desperately wants. The man drops to his knees so fast I struggle to catch him before he thuds to the tiles. "Sleep," I whisper over his stale snoring. "And when you wake up, for fec's sake, quit smoking. You might get kissed more." The other guard stirs, smacking his lips softly, and I creep up to lay my hand along his jaw, sending him back to dreams of limitless ryki and the breasts of tavern trulls.

Cock's poxes, did I really just do that? Did I send two grown men into a sleep as deep as death? There's no time to pat myself on the back. The gilded door is heavy as I shoulder it open. No light shines from within and the chamber beyond is empty and dim. I can make out the shape of divans at one end, bookshelves along the walls, a large desk in the middle, and I realise this is the room in Azza's memory, the room where Brim and Phibia were reading maps.

Where *is* he?

I try another door. It leads to a high-ceilinged bedchamber. Inside, a warm breeze from the south stirs the night air and wafts the scent of sweet blossoms through an open balcony. Climbing stardew, Azza had called the vine when we'd come across the tiny blooms in the Kyder. "Poisonous," she'd said. How apt, then, that they frame Phibia's windows. How inevitable that it's her I find sleeping in a bed among their fragrance. The excessive four-poster matches the heavily carved door and is draped with golden sheers that ripple softly. Without a sound, I draw them aside.

Phibia's silver hair is unwound from her braids and kinks on the pillow, almost girlishly. She's thrown off the sheets in the heat and her night-gown is twisted around her. For a shocking moment, she looks utterly human, more vulnerable than I'd ever thought she could be. I imagine she might wake up, yawn and say my name fondly, like any normal mother – and the thought takes my breath away. I feel a strange longing, like something empty just yawned inside me, yearning to be filled. Is this the woman whose belly I grew inside, are those the hands that first held mine, the breast I suckled on? Can it be true that the one person I've longed to know, the answer to my origins and identity, is now the enemy I've pledged to overcome? It seems the cruellest irony of all – crueller than discovering I was branded, crueller than being matched against Brim in Orlath's fighting pits, crueller than freeing Osha only to find Orlath had already robbed her of freedom.

Phibia throws a hand above her head in sleep, startling me from my thoughts. When she stills again, I hover trembling fingers over hers and listen as she exhales a long breath, her mouth working as if at speech in her dreams. For a brief second, I want to run back to Azza, to Nixim. I want to remain blissfully ignorant of the truth, never testing myself against the measure of her. But then I remember the way she looked down on me at the feast, like I was a specimen to be dissected; I remember the flippant push of Osha's head after she'd read her in the Seer Circle; the hungry, controlling way she'd touched Brim's hand on the map table. But most of all, I think of her giving us away as babies, turning her back on us for the sake of her own ambition, for the sake of my imperfections, and I feel the bile rise inside me, the hurt and resentment prickling under my skin. The beat of her pulse thuds steady in my ear as if it's goading me on and, light as a whisper, my fingertips press to her wrist.

The quickening is no less sudden, no less violent than it was in the temple, except this time I'm ready for it, and she is not. I leap on her pulse, wrangling it to the rhythm of my own and I push. Asleep and vulnerable, the door of her mind doesn't just creak ajar, it swings wide open. And she shows herself to me, not as she is now, but as she was in her youth. She's dressed in Mass robes, sitting with the other Mor schoolgirls in the front rows of the Roundhouse, and I guess she's close to the age when her Pairing will be announced. But then there are hands around her arms, rough and coercive, and suddenly she's being dragged from the gallery by Warder guards and pushed to her knees before the Elix Council. The scene is so familiar, I might be watching myself being brought to account all over again. Except the charge that is spoken is different from mine. *Fornication before Pairing*, the Elixion pronounces – an Elixion I don't recognise, one from long before my time in the Settlement. *Exile from the citadel,* comes his sentence. But the Council leader falters, his focus distracted, as if he's forgotten his lines. Someone rises, removing the fingers Phibia has wrapped around the Elixion's hand in supplication. It's Mother Iness, standing tall without her cane, looming over the girl.

Did you think to better me, child? Iness says, her tone almost impressed. The Roundhouse is empty now, save for Phibia, still on her knees. Iness smiles but the intent behind it is not kind. *Perhaps one day I might have taught you how.*

Teach me now, Mother. Phibia begs, urgency in her voice. *Influence the Council to let me stay. I can learn from you, be your right hand. I'll do whatever you say.*

It's too late for that. You've inherited my gift to sway desires but what good is it if you cannot learn to master your own? You already carry a child, the spawn of a mere brandservant. Mother Iness makes a scoff of distaste in the back of her throat. *You disgust me–*

This child is no brandservant's! Phibia spits. *How could you think I would pollute myself so, that I would dishonour our blood?*

Then the gossips are right? It is Nils Oskarsson's bastard that you grow? Phibia closes her eyes in acknowledgement, a single tear tracking down her cheek. *He might have been a good match for you, child, if he wasn't already Paired,* Iness says.

He wants to relinquish that Pairing. He loves me. He's told me he will petition the Council so we can be together.

Perhaps he does love you… for now. But the life of a Pure is long and men's attentions are short. You have already given him what he wanted. His match is the Elixion's daughter and he won't give up such a powerful union so easily. Could you have been any more gullible, child?

Phibia's face is swollen and red, not just with tears. She grapples for her mother's hand, but Iness jerks away from her touch. *You dare to try your sway upon* me, *girl!* She laughs and the sound is acidic, burning. *Accept my offer to redeem yourself or take your chances with the Wastelanders.*

But must it be Reis? Phibia cries out. *You'd send your own daughter to dwell in the desert with barbarians, heathen dirt-bloods with no value for the Pure-born? Your offer is a punishment, not a redemption.*

How clear-sighted you think yourself in love, yet so blind in politics. The Reis capital is thriving, their lands beyond Cha Shaheer a cornucopia of plenty. I've seen it in my visions. Iness strokes the breast of a fleet-falcon perched on the Roundhouse altar, a predecessor to the ghosthawk, evidently. *Reis grows like the Old World risen from the desert. And one day you will be its mistress, supplying Isfalk's armies. That, too, I have seen.*

Phibia stands unsteadily, digs her fingers into her hair. *Mistress of some uncouth desert tribe,* she says with desperate vehemence. *I'm an Isfalki Mor. Blood of the Founding Four.* Your *blood!*

Don't be so blinkered, daughter. Pure bloodlines are useless if we cannot feed ourselves, even I know that. Expansion and colonisation is our only future, do you not understand? I'm offering you the chance to lay the foundations of that future. You will Pair with one of the Reis Kha and you will use your skill to build Pure sympathies there – Isfalk sympathies. If you succeed, you will be so much more than the plaything of a social-climbing Elix heir. One day you might command him and his armies.

A Warder enters the Roundhouse, young, tall and blue-eyed. The familiar forelock is longer, thicker, but still streaks his brow like lightning – even brighter now that his hair is the youthful colour of flax in summer.

Lars, Phibia says, almost disappointed, as if she was expecting someone else.

Nils sent me, Lars Oskarsson says with palpable awkwardness. *My brother wishes me to be your Warder escort. I've promised him I'll see you safely to Reis.*

Nils asked that of you? Phibia glances from Oskarsson to her mother. *He's casting me off? He wishes me gone, then?*

Don't look at me so, Iness says as suspicion narrows her daughter's eyes. *It was his decision. I had no part in swaying it.* And the old woman seems genuine, even Phibia can tell, for her face crumples. She shrinks over her belly as if the weight of what is growing there drags her down into a pit from which she cannot escape. *I told you, child, life is long and men's attentions are…*

The vision fractures. Suddenly another voice is in my head. "So… you return, little fec." Phibia has woken, her hand locked on mine, sharp as the tiercel's talons. But the pressure squeezes my heart too, drawing my pulse to hers. I try to fight it, but she's so much stronger than me, more experienced, and I begin to tire quickly.

"Tell me," I manage to choke out. "Tell me if… I'm… yours."

The shock of it makes her grip waver for a moment. She laughs, a sudden high peal, unexpectedly entertained. She's reading me, watching me listen to Takia's revelations. "So *that* is what brought you back here? *That* is what you burn to know? How delightful!" I feel her knuckles brushing my cheek, indulgent as a mother's, but her voice is hard, not a single note of maternal feeling in it. "Well then, if that's what the gossips say, it *must* be true."

I'd thought the knowledge of it might make me crack, might reduce me to a whimpering mess, but it doesn't. It only makes me angry, incensed with the injustice of it, burning with resentment at her ability to deny her own blood, her own babies for the sake of ambition and power. And when that rage has blazed through me, just as it did with Azza aboard the *Na'quat,* I feel scorched clean, fresh as the snow of the Fold in winter, peaceful as the Moon Pools. It means nothing, it changes nothing, that I'm her daughter. I want to survive her, as I've fought to survive everything else in my life. I summon all the energy I can to push her presence to the periphery of my mind… And I burst into her memories again.

Brim is there, dressed in sand scarves as if readying for a journey. Phibia's hands rest on his shoulders and she looks him over, solemn and intent. *He camps south of the Mallaka Plain*, she tells Brim. *But he moves soon to join his sister and your pet Brand – the one he took to his bed, the one who is in his thrall. Her love for him blinds her and he will use her skill to curb us, to crush the prosperity and advancement of Isfalk.* Phibia cups Brim's jaw tightly, making him look back into her pale eyes. *Everything you've tried to do for her has been thwarted by him, all her reason and loyalties – warped by him. You knew it that first moment you saw them meet – by the sled in Isfalk at Morday Mass. You've always known it in your heart.*

Brim's gaze flickers for a moment and then his lips thin with determination. He nods his agreement and Phibia slips something into his palm. It's a small vial, stoppered with the pewter head of a sand siren. I remember the wrangler using a similar vial when he killed the krait and drained its mesmer.

Hurry, Phibia tells Brim. *Find Nixim and do as I ask. Then bring the fec to me.*

Brim kisses both her cheeks, but it's the single word he says as he takes his leave that stops my breath and makes my heart trip.

Mother.

The shock snaps me out of the vision, and I reel backwards in confusion. As I do, Phibia's sway quickens over me once more, pressing into my throat, cutting off air to my lungs. "So, you see the truth after all, poor little motherless child. You and your sister were not the babies I carried across the desert. Do you really believe I would ever give birth to a *fec* and let it live?" I can't find the mental strength to push her away this time, for she already has me choking, my sway slipping from me like sand through my fingers. I resort to the only skills I have left – the ones I've grown up mastering since Brim first taught me to form a fist. Just as stars begin to shoot across my sight, I catch her with a jab to the stomach. Her grip on me falters and I make the mistake of bending over to suck in a breath. She grabs my hair between her fists and pain sears through my skull, sharp as the ghosthawk's tearing shriek in the night outside. Blood spurts from my nose across the tiles and I use the pulse of it, the dregs of my sapped skill to wrangle the tiercel to me. It settles on the balcony ledge, pinning me with that yellow eye, unmoving, and for a moment, I think all is lost, but then, talons first, it glides into the room. There's a suffocating confusion of feathers, the bird's wings beating frantically in the narrow space between myself and Phibia, but the pressure on my throat eases. The Khadib staggers backwards with a scream, the hawk attached to her face, shredding her cheek with its claws.

I take my chance and run.

A Mother's Love

Nixim is all I can think of as I flee Cha Shaheer, working the mare to near exhaustion as I retrace the route through the Kyder to Azza's camp. What if I'm too late? What if Phibia gave Brim the poison days ago and he has already reached the wrangler? I can't warn Nixim when I have no idea where he is. All I can hope is that he's mobilised his troops already. All I can pray for is to find him alive and well, planning strategy with his sister in our jungle camp before Brim discovers our position.

The mare gives me her all, her flanks lathered white from our pace, but even my sway can't prevent her legs from stumbling beneath me. She valiantly finds her footing again, but I know if we continue like this I'll end up flogging her until she drops. Reluctantly, I dismount, rubbing her down and watering her. The rest allows the vision to catch up with me. Phibia is Brim's mother, not mine. She wasn't pregnant with me and Osha when she arrived in Reis, she was carrying *him*. But what motive did she have for giving up a Pure son? Why did she send him back to live in Isfalk? Perhaps she wasn't getting rid of the burden of another man's child. Perhaps she wanted Brim to be raised alongside Isfalki Pure and take his rightful place among the other Elix heirs of the citadel. It makes sense, especially when I think of Mother Iness's tolerance of the Oskarssons – Brim's constant truanting at school overlooked, his uncle's frequent run-ins with the

Council resulting in nothing but rapped knuckles from Iness. Brim is her grandson, her blood, and Lars Oskarsson was privy to her secrets.

Phibia was in love with Lars's brother. But Nils sent her away when he knew she was pregnant with his child. He placed his ambition, his standing within the citadel, above her and his son. No one recovers easily from a wound like that. I can almost understand now why Phibia threw herself into Iness's plan to take over Reis – she wasn't just proving herself to her mother, she was getting back at her lover, playing him at his own game, raising herself through marriage and waiting for the time when he would see her in all her glory – as the leader of Isfalk's southern territories, the power behind its new empire. Having her son grow up in the Isfalk citadel, must have given her the added satisfaction of sending a living message back to her lover. Brim would forever be the scandal Nils Oskarsson hoped to be rid of, a constant reminder of what he gave up. Phibia wasn't to know Nils would die before the child was old enough to walk.

How pleased she must be that her son has returned – an instrument to do her bidding, an heir to the fruits of her plans and schemes. But without the influence of her sway, I wonder what Brim would think of his mother? Would his yearning to know her make him overlook her politics, her ambition? Back in Isfalk, he was always so keen to protect Pure bloodlines. Will he let his blood speak louder than his newfound morals, his knowledge of what is right… his loyalty to me? I need to find him. I have to release the influence Phibia has over him and bring him back to us before it's too late.

But more than any of that, I need to save the wrangler.

Mounting the mare again, I urge her through the jungle, my sway keeping her to a steady walking pace, despite our exhaustion. But when we finally stumble into the camp, my heart sinks to my stomach – everyone is gone save for the servants and cooks who are packing up tents and supplies to follow in the convoy's wake. Voices call out across the stragglers when I arrive and a tent flap opens suddenly to reveal Takia. I follow her inside with a mix of relief and trepidation.

"Takia, I–" But without saying a word, the servant shoves a letter to my chest. I recognise Azza's handwriting. Frantically, I scan the script.

I can guess where you have gone, Nara Fornwood. I hope saving your friend is worth the price of Phibia reading our entire campaign through your stupid head. My mind reels at your rashness, your irresponsibility. But you already know these things. If you are reading this, you have somehow survived Phibia and I will save my energy to tell you that Takia knows the location of my brother's army. Our troops must take the track, but she will show you the faster route so you can join us at Nixim's camp. But hurry. Tathar or not, our campaign will not wait on one foolish Solitary.

Your friend,

Azza Ni Azzadur

PS. You may have survived Phibia, but good luck with Takia.

Fecs alive. *Angry* doesn't even cut it when I lower the letter and take in the brandservant's face. Half of me – the cowardly half – wants to set off south and try to find Nixim myself without having to face her burly wrath, but I have no idea where I'm going, and I desperately need food and a fresh horse. Takia hisses something in Reis and before I know it her hand is on my throat. I brace, thinking she's about to slam me to the floor, but she shoves me backwards through the tent flap and I sprawl on my arse in the dirt. "Stupid, stupid girl," she spits. Squatting down beside me, she raises her hand to my face as if she's about to strike. I flinch, but no slap comes. "Stand," she barks and I jump to obey her. She scans me suspiciously from crown to boots, head cocked to the side, jaw muscles clenching. What is she looking for? I don't have time for this. I step away from her but she grabs my hand, wrapping it around her own. That's when I understand. Her warm pulse jumps to mine, but I do nothing more than listen to its quickened beat. I could sway her now, make my life so much easier by flattening her anger and resentment, ensuring her quick cooperation, making her trust me. But I don't. This is a test – Takia wants to see if I'll use my sway against her. She wants to see if Phibia has had her claws in me. I hold her hand as patiently as I can, waiting for her to realise she's just as livid with me as before.

Takia grunts and casts my arm aside. Returning to the tent, she fusses inside for some moments before re-emerging with stuffed saddle bags. She strides across the camp without looking back. Guessing I'm supposed to follow, I lead my stumbling mare after her. At the river a boy is watering horses. Takia mutters something to him in Reis and he takes my saddle and tackle, placing it on a muscular stallion, black as the night. The whites of the horse's eyes flash with excitement as the boy readies him and I'm reminded of the colt Hira gave me when we raced to Cha Shaheer.

Takia shows me the route I'm to follow by drawing in the dirt. There's the line of the river through the contours of the jungle and into open farmland. I get a general idea of key landmarks I'm to pass, praying to the Mother that the journey is as simple as her map. I have no sense of the distance or whether I'll be able to catch up with Azza, but I thank her anyway, touching her arm. "I'm sorry, Takia," I say hurriedly. I want to explain everything, but there isn't time. She throws off my touch, and just as I think she's about to turn away, she looks back at me.

"You hurt Nixim," she says, "I kill you myself." I nod, eager to show her I understand. She's not his mother, but she might as well be for the fierceness of the love I see in her eyes. She reminds me of Amma, the woman who mothered us in every way that was important – caring for us, protecting us, laying down her life for us. Shame creeps through me all over again for seeking out Phibia, for my selfish and destructive drive to discover the woman who gave birth to me, when I've known who my *real* mother was all along.

"Go, stupid girl," Takia repeats, slapping the horse's rump for good measure.

He lunges so violently into the sultry afternoon, I'm almost thrown. And I'm left wondering whose wrath I fear more – the brandservant's or the Tathar's.

A Coin and Lady Luck

The stallion comes into his own as we follow Takia's route out of the jungle and into the open farmland of the south. I feel his pulse through my entire body, so eager to join with mine that the distance seems to fly by without need for rest or water. It's me who finally draws the beast to a stop, my legs turning numb from hard riding. The light is failing anyway, and we both need food and water.

Drawing up to a sandy clearing on the banks of the river, I see footprints, trampled rushes – signs that someone else has used the flat access as a natural stop to water their horses. And they've done so recently, because the rockpool at the water's edge is still silty from being disturbed. Whoever was here is probably only minutes ahead of me. I cast about for clues, signs that it might have been Brim, signs it might have been Alrahim's scouts scoping the river before setting up camp, but there isn't anything conclusive.

The idea that Brim might be so near to Nixim gets me back on the stallion, following the tracks in the last of the light. As night falls, the path becomes rocky and starts to climb, but the horse pushes on, sure-footed and tireless, and I wonder why Takia selected such a mount for me when she resented me so. Evidently she mastered her jealousies far better than Hira did; I couldn't have chosen a better animal myself. It's as if he knows the route better than I do, and I find him strangely comforting. When I smell smoke and hear low voices up ahead, his ears twitch and he slows to a walk before I even have to rein him in. I dismount, trying to get eyes on the party, but darkness has descended and it's black as hell off the track. I sense a movement at my shoulder, but before I can turn, something hits me from behind. I'm still seeing stars when my arm is yanked over my head, a cold blade against my throat.

I know that body lock. It's the Maw's signature move. "Wait!" I yell. "Maw, wait, it's me!" My assailant loosens his grip, exhales. "Fecs in hell, I haven't come this far for you to finish me off by accident!" But when I turn around, it isn't the big man. It's Annek, re-sheathing her knife. The Maw is behind her, his grin flashing white in the dark. To my surprise, the Ringer pulls me into a bear hug. It almost suffocates me, but poxes, it feels good. At least one person isn't judging me for running off to Cha Shaheer.

"Nara, what happened?" Annek begins. "Fecs, you are in such deep shi–"

"There isn't time. Annek, I found out something in Cha Shaheer and I need to get to the wrangler as quickly as possible. Where is he?"

"His camp's still another day's ride away." She lifts her chin to the south. "The Maw and I are scouting the river in advance of the army. Azza and Alrahim hope to join Nixim by tomorrow night."

My heart feels like it's been stabbed. Another day's ride away? Brim could get to Nixim before me. He might already be there. I might be too late.

"What's going on?" Annek asks as I reach for my horse.

"Yes, Nara Fornwood, what is going on?" A figure calls through the dark foliage.

"Cock's poxes, Az!" I hiss in shock. She lowers her bow and arrow, clearly enticed to the river by the prospect of a dusk hunt. "I don't have time to explain now… Please, we have to hurry." But Azza grabs my arm, locking her fist around my wrist. As soon as our skin touches, the quickening crackles through me. I feel the invasion of her pulse in my ears and I understand. For once, I let go, freely opening my mind to hers.

She stiffens as she sees all that happened at Cha Shaheer. When she drops my hand, her breath is fast and livid. "Get your horses," she tells the Maw and Annek.

"How far?" I ask again as I remount.

"A day for an army; half, for a good rider." She eyes my horse. "Maybe less."

I gather the stallion's reins. He's my only hope. She must see the misgiving, the anguish written in the lines of my body. "Nara." She stops me, clutching my horse's bridle.

"Az, I'm so sorry…" My throat squeezes, threatening a sob. "I'm sorry–"

"No, you are not." I feel her shrewd eyes on me in the dark. "You are not sorry you went, Nara Fornwood. And now, neither am I."

"What if Brim gets to him before us?"

"You forget, we know Nixim's exact location. Brim must only guess at it." She swings onto her horse. "And you forget, we are Tathars. So shut up and sway that animal. Make your bull-headedness worth it."

We ride through the night, my stallion flanking Azza's. She sways her horse as I do, but it means that the Maw and Annek are soon left behind in the darkness. I can't slow down. All I can think of is Nixim. He might already be inviting Brim into his camp. He has no way of knowing Phibia got to him, that Brim is her weapon and can no longer be trusted. Images of that little vial keep returning to me. Brim's fingers round the krait-head stopper. I picture the wrangler's face the last time we parted, except now his skin is grey as ashes, void of all expression, his eyes tinged as blue as the snake's on the Wasteland Plains.

"Focus on your horse," Azza says, suspecting the bent of my thoughts. I do what she says for once – I sway the stallion so hard she struggles to keep up when our route becomes open grasslands and pasture again. Freed of the rocky terrain, our horses fly, and I count the passing of the miles on the drum of hooves, the suck of lungs, the frenetic pulse on my tongue. A light wind blows from the north, aiding our progress. But here in the open, I can't help the feeling of being watched. Instinctively, I look up, and there it is – the familiar shadow, a black diamond on the milky night sky. The ghosthawk's cry scores my nerves, still a little terrifying, but I let go of the stallion's pulse for a moment and open my heart to the bird. Its piping *kee-ee-arr* descends in a steady circle, until I slow my mount and its talons find my raised forearm.

The tiercel fixes me in its gaze. The sensation of falling through that bright yellow iris is growing familiar. When the images come, they're of a galloping horse, the rumble of hooves crossing grasslands that I know can't be far away. I can see the rider's blond hair in the darkness, the straight blade of a Warder broadsword strapped to his back. Suddenly, the mount rears, screaming in fear, eyes wild. Brim is thrown, rolling a few feet through the grass before shaking himself off. He manages to calm the mare, but whatever nocturnal animal spooked her must be on our side – as Brim tries to remount, she shies away, favouring a hind leg. Brim runs his hand over her cocked hoof, cursing. Leading the hobbling horse behind him, he continues on foot.

The perspective changes. The grasslands grow small now, the river thin as a string whipping loose from a bow. There, between two small patches of forest, campfires are dotted in the darkness, a vast spread of tents, pockets of corralled horses. The camp is sleeping, a handful of watch guards pacing the perimeter, waiting for dawn to break. But as the ghosthawk flies closer, my vision focuses on a fire still blazing, a single figure pacing before it. He stretches tiredly, cracks his neck as if sleep has eluded him this night, and I recognize the wrangler – alive and so close I could almost reach out and touch him, can almost breathe the autumn scent of his skin. I want to cry out a warning to him, but this is only the vision as the ghosthawk has seen it, and shout as I might, I cannot speak through it. I can only watch as he squats to the fire, pokes its embers and throws another log onto them. The flames cast his face in warm orange, just as they had that first night we camped on the Wasteland Plains all those months ago, the night I thought he had sold us out to Haus's crew. I study his expression as he runs the fingertips of one hand across his mouth and lazily knuckles the stubble along his jaw, that mole stirring in his cheek. Back then, it annoyed me so much I wanted to slice the damn thing out of his face with my skinning knife. Now all I want is to cover it with my lips, taste it with my tongue.

"Sleepless and thinking of me, Wrangler?" I long to tease him. But it's enough to know he's simply alive, closer than we'd thought, and that I might have the chance to get to him before Brim does. I'm about to draw out of the ghosthawk's mind when I catch Nixim's frown. He reaches into the pocket of his leathers and draws out something that winks in the firelight. With all the sharpness of the tiercel's sight, I recognise the coin I gave him when we parted, the one Lars Oskarsson had pressed into my hand the night I was exiled from the Isfalk citadel. He tosses it, swipes it from the air with his fist, then opens his palm to study the face embossed with the Halqa. He's playing *Lady Luck,* just as I said he should when we parted. Fecs, why did I taunt him like that? Why did I let him leave without admitting he'd never have to play a game of chance for my feelings? And now I might not reach him in time to ever confess them. Twice more he spins the coin, but he's too quick for me to make out the results. The twitch of that mole and his grin when it comes turn my insides messy. "The Fates are on your side, Little Scourge," he says to the fire, but his words are for me.

"What news? What do you see?" Azza asks when she catches up. The bird lifts from my arm and banks into the night on a soft beat of wings.

"Lady Luck is with us." My face is bright with hope and the flush of something else Azza doesn't need to know. Heeling the stallion, I shout over my shoulder. "Brim's horse has thrown a shoe. Come on, Nixim is waiting!"

The Elix and The Kha

We thunder into the wrangler's camp just as dawn is curling the edges of the night. Watchmen on the periphery block our path and catch hold of our horses' bridles, making demands in Reis. Azza handles them, while I frantically call Nixim's name at the top of my lungs. The guards let me pass and I race through the camp towards the largest canvas, Ghumes stationed at its flap – the strategy tent. "Nara?" the wrangler exclaims as I burst in, motioning for his soldiers to stand down.

"Nix–" I double over, hands on my knees. "Thank the Mother…" I pant in relief. But when I straighten, there's the outline of someone else behind him. Brim sits at a makeshift camp table, still grimed and windswept from his journey, clearly welcomed into the camp without suspicion. The wrangler must still believe Brim sailed with us. He has no reason to doubt him. I can smell fumes of ryki filling the ger as Brim leans back, taking his refreshment from a horn cup. That's when I notice a matching cup in Nixim's hand.

"Don't drink that!" I yell, knocking it from his grasp. Only a trickle of liquor spills to the dirt – he's already drunk most of the cup. "Spit it out!" I grasp his jaw and try to shove my fingers down his throat.

"Nara, wha–!" Nixim chokes, catching my wrists.

Brim rises, the whisper of drawn steel loud and out of place in the confines of the tent. I wrench away from Nixim with

224

a cry, trying for my sword, but Brim's fist is already in the wrangler's hair, his blade at his neck. I raise my palms slowly, warily, like Brim's an animal caught in a trap. "Stop, Brim! Wait…" Panic turns my voice pitchy and I swallow, trying to reel in my emotions. But that blade so close to the wrangler's jugular makes my throat tighten. "Brim, let's talk… We need to talk." I reach for his hand, white-knuckled around the sword hilt.

"Don't touch me," he says, edging backwards and pulling Nixim with him. "She said you'd try to do that."

"Brim… look at me." His blue eyes are clouded, restless, as if seeking some satisfaction, some reassurance he can't find, searching everywhere except my face. "*Look* at me, Brim!" The force of it startles his gaze to mine and I think he sees me, really sees me, just as he used to when we trained together in the Fornwood. "Is this truly what you want? The wrangler defenceless, his blood on your hands?"

Brim shifts his grip on the helve and cracks his neck like he's trying to realign his thoughts. "It's his fault," he spits, blade pressing deeper into the wrangler's skin. "*He* made you do all of this."

"All of what?"

"Everything! Running from Isfalk, putting ideas in your head so you forget who you are… so you forget about *us*."

"The wrangler didn't do that, Brim. *I* did. All of it. But this…" I reach out again but he jerks back, "this isn't your choice. I know you. It's not who you are." I keep my tone as gentle as I can, swallowing back a cry at the nick of blood trickling down the wrangler's neck.

"Remember when you left me on the Wasteland Plains? Afterwards you said you couldn't believe you'd behaved that way. Well, that was my fault. I swayed you then – just as Phibia has swayed you now. *She's* why you're doing this." Brim shakes his head again, as if to loosen my words from his ears. "You've seen the truth of what Reis is," I tell him.

"You've witnessed what Azza and her mother have built, the equality between the Brands and the Pure. Equality between you and me. It's the freedom we dreamed of in the Moon Pools all those months ago, don't you remember?" He blinks, the sword trembling in his hands. "Brim, don't do this. Come back to me."

Slowly, I reach for the cross guard of his weapon, careful to avoid his skin so as not to spook him. I turn the blade gently away from the wrangler. "If you want to punish someone," I say, "it has to be me, because I brought us all here." I draw the edge to my own throat. "This is my doing."

"Nara," the wrangler warns. But I keep my focus on Brim, scared to lose what little connection I have to him for fear of losing Nixim.

"No," Brim says. "No. You wanted to be a Warder, Nara. You wanted to join the citadel guards and fight for Isfalk. *That's* who you are." He's desperate for this version of me to still be true.

"That's who I was when I thought I was a Mor, when I thought Isfalk was all that was left of the civilised world. Back then, I believed Brands needed protecting. But now I see the only protection they need is from the tyranny of the Pure." I grip harder on the hilt of the sword. "If I've betrayed you so badly, if I'm such a traitor to Isfalk, then take your anger out on me."

The wrangler makes a grimace of protest. Still locked in the vice of Brim's arm, he says my name again, but this time no sound comes out.

"I know you'd never hurt me, Brim. Not me, nor anyone I love," I say, and his eyes dart to the wrangler. There's jealousy and resentment there, but then resignation, as if he finally understands he can't win a heart that's already been given. The Brim I know isn't cruel enough to destroy something from spite. Slowly, he loosens his grip on the sword. The blade falls to the ground with a dull ring and I rush for the wrangler.

Nixim holds his arms out to me for a moment as if all is well, but his skin is pallid and his breathing shallow. Plates clatter, a jug of ryki spills and the makeshift table behind him upends as he staggers. I'm too late to catch him. Nixim collapses in the dirt, mouth frothing, body twitching. I fall to my knees, trying to roll him on his side, praying the seizure might make him vomit up the mesmer.

"Help me!" I yell, sensing Brim hovering over us. "Help me!" But when I turn, Brim only stares at the fallen wrangler, a look of confusion contorting his face as he backs away towards the tent flap. "I need help, Brim," I say again, but the command has slipped from my tone now, my voice little more than a wounded whisper as I watch him push past the canvas and disappear into the night.

My fist clutches at Nixim's collar, the other hand feeling for a pulse under his jaw. When I don't sense anything, I rip open his shirt and frantically lay both palms over his heart, straining to pick out a rhythm. I can hear nothing but my own drumming panic. "Come on, Wrangler!" I plead. "Don't do this to me… don't you dare leave me."

But Brim isn't the only one who has slipped away.

Azza finds me desperate, still searching for a pulse. She drops to her knees, replacing my hands with her own on his skin, all the while muttering breathlessly in Reis. I watch – hopeful, heartbroken – as her fingertips skim over his neck, his throat and chest, reading each vein, each pore as if for some secret message embossed on his skin.

"Is he alive, Az? Is he…?" Her face is lined with concentration, giving nothing away. "For fec's sake, tell me he lives!"

She nods, a single dip of her chin, and I let out a shuddering sigh that becomes a sob. I hold in the next breath. I need to keep it together. I need to think. *Think, Nara.* Leaning up close to Nixim's face, I sniff at the froth that has bubbled from his lips, then pull back one of his eyelids. His brown irises are cloudy, that inner ring of bronze filmed with milky blue – just like the sand siren on the Wasteland Plains.

Azza confirms my suspicions. "Krait's poison... an overdose of mesmer turns the eyes that way." She calls to a guard, issuing orders in Reis, before turning back to her brother. Laying her hands more firmly on his chest, I can tell she's reaching for her sway because her pupils dilate, body falling still and quiet, as she yokes every other sense to the service of that sixth faculty. I watch her frown of concentration turn to deep fear. She grabs my fingers and presses them to the wrangler's neck, re-positioning carefully so I can catch the faintest tremor of life under his skin. "It is you who must try, Nara Fornwood. Perhaps yours is the heartbeat his will answer to." I feel the quickening at her touch and I take a breath. Closing my eyes, I try to draw out his pulse, strengthen it, command him back to us. The rhythm leaps, grows a little stronger, my heart soaring, before it stutters and is lost to me completely.

I turn panicked eyes on Azza, but she reassures me he still lives. Poxes, I wish Osha were here. She would know what to do. If anyone could save him, it would be her.

There's a commotion at the tent flap. A young girl in white robes steps under the canvas, rushing to Nixim.

"Saqira?"

"She fled Cha Shaheer and joined us yesterday," Azza explains. "Saqi says scouts spotted our ships. Phibia knows of our arrival and her forces mobilise to attack us here in the south."

I reel at the news – we're on the eve of battle, likely outnumbered and with our general barely clinging to life.

The wrangler was wrong, Lady Luck isn't with me at all. And Phibia makes her own fate.

Saqira aligns her palm with mine over Nixim's heart. Instantly I feel her sway beckoning like an invitation, a door to something mystical cracked ajar. Azza's skill is all power and control, and Osha's is warm and nurturing, like hot broth. But Saqira's? Saqira's is somehow mysterious *and* grounding, like stars glinting in a freezing night-sky, the depths of the roiling ocean, the creaking of glaciers beyond Tindur Hof. I feel stable in her presence, at one with something ancient, bigger than me, the way I always feel when I bathe in the Moon Pools. Under her touch, the wrangler's pulse grows a little easier to detect, but she surprises me when she moves her hand away. From her robes she fetches a small leather pouch like the ones I've seen Osha and Shessa use for their compounds. Saqira mixes the powdered contents with a finger-width of liquid from her water skin. Except it isn't water. I catch the heady fumes of dramur vit, the smell transporting me back to nights on the Wasteland Plains, the liquor like a fire warming from within.

"What is that powder?" I ask.

"An antidote," Azza says.

"Are you serious?" I don't dare believe it. "She just happens to have an antidote to krait's venom *in her pocket*?"

"It's not so surprising," Saqira says. "We Seers use mesmer to enhance our visions. We're trained to carry the antidote with us in case of over-ingestion."

Azza trickles the fluid between Nixim's lips. "I never thought I would be so grateful that my sister became a Seer," she says, glancing at Saqi with such relief it makes me miss Osha all the more.

I bow my head to Nixim's chest, thinking that perhaps I was hasty writing off Lady Luck. But when I look at him again – his ashen skin and milky eyes – I understand how he must have felt watching me fight the krait's poison aboard the *Na'quat*, how helpless and angry. How desperate.

"Nara," Saqira says cautiously, "you must understand that the mesmer we inhale in the temple is a fraction of what my brother has swallowed. The antidote I possess is only intended as a remedy for slight overdoses, and he has the poison in his stomach, not his lungs. He is very weak, and I cannot be sure he will..." She trails off, throwing herself suddenly into the solace of her older sister's arms.

"We can only wait," Azza tells me over Saqira's head, but what I read in her expression is the opposite – we have no time to wait. Phibia's armies will not delay.

The war machine has been set in motion and no one can stop it now.

That night, we strategize until dawn. I can barely think straight, imagining the wrangler breathing his last under Saqi's watch, but Azza keeps forcing me back into her discussions with Alrahim, making sure I'm distracted – a tactic, I'm certain. I envy Azza's focus, her determination, ever the composed leader, the mistress of her feelings. The tremble of her fingers on the maps of Reis is the only tell of her inner fears; the lingering glances she casts Alrahim the only hint at how much she relies on her Captain for emotional, as well as military, support. At least she *has* Alrahim. I have no one now – no Nixim, no Osha, no Haus... and no Brim. The thought of him is the final twist to my wrung-out heart. How much I'd relied on him to keep me grounded, to save me from myself. How much I'd relied on them all. I'm more alone now than I've ever felt in my life.

I slip back into Nixim's tent in the early hours, kneeling by the cot and nestling my forehead against his neck. The feathering of his pulse terrifies me – I've felt stronger rhythms in dying quarry caught in my Fornwood snares. But I try to steady its syncopated beat, try to boost it with my own. I stop only when I feel the trickle of blood on my upper lip, withdrawing my sway to find I'm sweating as hard as I used to when Azza first trained me.

"Your love for him makes you desperate." Her voice is gentle at my shoulder. "And desperation makes you lose your control." I sit up, turning to her. "You must wrangle these emotions on the battlefield, Nara Fornwood. Phibia will have no–"

"Fec's sake, Az, spare me the lecture for once. I'm in no mood." I swipe angrily at the blood with a cuff.

She backs away and I hear the trickle of liquid, sense her pouring drinks behind me. Shoving a cup against my chest, she knocks hers back in one gulp. "It isn't ryki," she says, perceptive enough to know I can't stomach the smell of that liquor anymore, perhaps never will again. The dramur vit burns as it goes down, but I'm grateful for the fire it stokes in my belly. It doesn't settle my nerves much though, and after a moment Azza forces me to stand, angling my shoulders so she can study my face with those dark hunting eyes. I feel like a snowjack breaking free of the treeline, nowhere to hide.

"I can't do this," I blurt out. "I can't go with you into battle. Not now. Not knowing he might never–"

"That is exactly why you must go," she says, fists tight around my arms. "To make it all worthwhile. He followed his instincts about you. He truly believed you could lead us."

"Lead you? How can *I* lead you? I have nothing to offer that you and Alrahim and the Maw don't already have. I'm not a strategist or a great warrior... I'm not even a very good Tathar."

Azza's expression is fierce in the dimness of the tent. "When my brother returned to Cha Shaheer, he spoke of Osha and the power he had sensed in her. But I could tell the person he really wanted to talk about was you."

"Complaints and criticisms, no doubt."

She nods. "Yes. *Stubborn as a bull to stable*, he told me. *Rash, reckless, no command over her impulses*, he said, *and yet strong, so strong inside*." Her mouth hitches at the corner, but her voice is still serious. "*She will fight for what she believes*, Nixim told me, *even if it means swimming against the current. I would follow her along the river to hell and she would bring me out the other side.*"

I scoff softly. "Well, that's a load of horse shit. The wrangler knows I can barely swim." But the joke doesn't ward off the threat of the tears that burn my throat.

"Nixim saw something in you, Nara Fornwood. Where is that woman now, I wonder? Will she lie down and curl up, simply because he is no longer here to goad her?" My heart drops into my stomach at imagining Nix gone. She must sense it, for she takes my hand. I feel the surge of her energy bolstering me, more warming than the dramur vit. "Tell me you are with me," she says.

I know she'd never sway my actions. I couldn't respect her if she did, and she certainly couldn't respect herself. But I almost wish she would. In the end, it's her hopeful face – so determined, so similar to Nixim's – that does the job. I realise I never want to let her down again. But there's also something else growing in my chest, hardening my resolve. Something feral and fearsome that makes me nod my agreement. She and the wrangler were right – I have no command over my passions or my emotions, and I'm not proud of the one I'm feeling now – but I know I'm going to need it when dawn breaks. For that feral thing is hatred.

It is hatred and revenge that will make me ride out tomorrow at Azza's side.

I am going to make Phibia pay.

Of Flame Hair and Steel Will

I stand on a rocky promontory overlooking an arid plain.

My stomach swoops and dives like a bird at the familiarity of it. The wind in my face is dry, my throat even drier, laced with the smell of fires, horse shit and sweat-stewed leather carried up from the camp below. This is the vista I'd seen when the Blood-wife touched me in her cottage on the Edfjall – all those miles away, all those months ago. It was the same one I'd seen when Mother Iness grabbed my arm in the Roundhouse and when I'd touched Phibia in the Seer Circle. This same desert tableland, this same camp of gers, horses and soldiers spread out below me. Except it is night now and this is no vision. It is real.

Our own insurgent army is a vast beast curled in the dark, keeping watch from the ridge. Azza leads Nixim's southern clans, Alrahim her Ghumes, and the Maw is at the head of Haus's Hrossi riders. I imagine the day to come – the ring of weaponry, the whinny of horses, the dust that will rise when the sun crests the eastern dunes and claims the sky. But for now, there's only Azza at my flank, sand scarves flapping against her armour, brooding silently as she studies Phibia's forces camped below. Save for the pacing of their night-watch, the enemy makes little movement, catching what rest they can on the eve of battle.

The morning after Brim poisoned Nixim, Azza had insisted we decamp, giving Phibia's scouts no time to discover our location. Instead of moving to meet her forces head-on across the Mallaka Plain, as the Khadib expected, Alrahim had broached a bold return north along the coastal desert. She argued we should secure as many of the landing points to the capital as we could along the coast, preventing Isfalk reinforcements from coming ashore. Azza might be sceptical, but Alrahim was taking my vision of the Isfalk host on the move as a serious influence on our strategy. And without any better plan on the table, Azza had given in.

Now, we've circled almost unhindered back to the plain of Cha Shaheer in an approach from the south-west, meeting nothing more than skirmishes with the Kham's old coastal guard. Clearly, Phibia hadn't predicted such a play, and it makes me see Alrahim as more than a respected captain, more than Azza's lover – I see her for the gifted strategist she is. And yet, even as I scan the desert plain, the trick fate has played is obvious. Alrahim's plan to defend against what I saw in my vision has ironically brought it to pass. Here I am, witnessing the same battle-camp on the same dusty terrain. Here I am facing the very image of the army I foresaw.

Nixim's absence aches like a wound, only eased by the knowledge that he's in his sister's hands. Saqira watches over him at our base camp, an hour's ride south along the coast, where Dalla has helped her set up treatment tents for our wounded, and organised supplies. Scouts deliver news of him regularly, not that they have anything to tell – he hasn't woken or stirred in five days. *No change*, Saqira writes. *No change*, Dalla says when she rides to the front to visit Annek, who still trains as a soldier under the Maw. Eventually, I learn to read each rider's body language as they approach me, until I don't even have to open their messages anymore. *No change*. Each night I lose sleep thinking of the wrangler's ashen skin, his cold body, his breath falling softer than a shed hair across my cheek. And when I do sleep, I have the same recurring dream – that he is nothing more than a carapace left behind in the dust of the desert, while his spirit calls to me from far away, in a place I can't follow.

"It is to be expected," Saqira told me before we marched out, feeling for my fingers on the wrangler's neck where I tried to read any change in him, any sign of progress or regression. "He told me you slept for three days when you took mesmer on the *Na'quat*, and you swallowed only a few drops. It could take Nixim weeks to regain consciousness." I'd sensed her sway then, the grounding of her energy against the volatility of my own – like a mountain, solid and steady against the vagaries of the sea.

"The visions I've had of the battle ahead – I always thought he'd be there at my back when the time came," I confided in her. "But now I think of them, it's always a woman at my side – Azza – not Nixim." I'd never paid attention before, and acknowledging it – his *absence*, his *lack of being* – made a shiver bolt down my spine. I'd squeezed his sister's hand, hoping for the comfort of her sway, but instead I read the fear sticking in her throat like a stone.

"You think we might lose him, Saqi?" She drew her hand from mine in answer, and I tried to ward off panicked tears with anger instead. "Fec – fec, fec!" Saqi stopped my pacing, wiping my cheeks, while her own eyes brimmed. "Tell me something hopeful, Saqi! Cock's poxes, lie to me if you have to!"

Her mouth worked a little, searching, not wanting to be untruthful. "His pulse still beats. That is hope enough," she said. "And it always seems a little stronger after you have touched him... I noticed it whenever you were near him in Cha Shaheer, you know."

Now, her words float in my mind like pieces of flotsam in a rising tide of panic. Azza scans the camp below the ridge, her face unreadable in the moonlight.

"Az," I prompt, wanting to hear her speak, to say anything just to distract me from the glaring fact neither of us want to acknowledge – Phibia's army outnumbers ours, a consolidated front we can't hope to beat. Alrahim's strategy had gambled on our meeting only the Khadib's defensive forces on the plain outside Cha Shaheer, the greater part of the Reis army marching to pursue us in the south. But news of the coastal skirmishes must have reached Phibia, allowing her to pivot and redirect her host. Now she awaits our move on Cha Shaheer with the full brunt of her militia at the ready.

"How bad is it?" I ask Azza.

"Two to one by my estimate…" Her horse grunts – a scoff in the night. "Alrahim would agree with my mare – she thinks I am optimistic."

"More than double our size," I whisper. I may be full of hate for Phibia and desperate for revenge for Nixim, but now the reality of what that entails is laid out before me. I realise this battle can be nothing but a blood bath. "We can't engage with those odds, Az. We have to negotiate."

"Negotiate what, Nara Fornwood? Negotiate the lives of Brands? Should I barter for your kind? Is that what you wish me to do?"

"But you'll be facing your own people on the field. Hundreds of Reis stand to die on both sides."

"Is that not what I asked of your Hrossi chief?" She lets out a bitter grunt. "Now it is I who must be the one to prove myself on that count. War is full of irony, is it not?" She throws me a sidelong glance. "Besides, one does not haggle with a sand siren. One either gets bitten or flees. And Phibia will not make me a coward."

I think of the krait on the Wastelands Plains, Nixim's horse rearing, the coldness creeping through me as I looked in the serpent's eyes. And a thought strikes me like a bell, resonating through my entire body.

"What?" Azza asks, sensing the change in me.

"You're wrong. About sand sirens. Nixim didn't run from that krait, and he didn't get bitten… He struck first."

"What are you talking about?"

"Your brother. I saw him kill a sand siren in the Wastelands. He lopped off its head."

Azza is silent but I feel her studying my shape in the dark. "Are you suggesting this as a strategy?"

"My gut is saying we go for the head. We aim straight for Phibia."

"Phibia will be safe in her fortress," Azza answers. "And, thanks to your last visit to her chambers, she will be surrounded by a wall of bodyguards. You and your *gut* should account for that, Nara Fornwood."

My cheeks flame. "Hey, hold on. I know my visit to Phibia could have been handled better, but without it we wouldn't have known about Brim... we wouldn't have treated the poison so quickly in Nixim. Sometimes my *gut* has served us, even you have to admit."

She chews the inside of her mouth, her silence telling me I've scored a point. Still, she's not ready to concede just yet. "If you think to mimic your Hrossi chief and sneak off in the dead of night on a personal vendetta again, I will have Alrahim put you in the stocks."

"That isn't what I was thinking."

"Was it not?"

"Alright, maybe it crossed my mind... but you're right. Breaking into her bedroom a second time could very well be suicide."

She scoffs. "Finally. You see sense."

"But I'm serious, Az – why wait? Why not strike now, before dawn? The Hrossi are masters of the ambush. The Maw and I could lead an advance unit into the camp and wreak havoc before they've even pulled up their pants from a morning piss. While chaos reigns, you and Alrahim can launch the dawn offensive from the western flank as planned."

Azza doesn't answer, the soft rise of her breasts her only movement in the saddle. "No," she announces finally, and without emotion.

"But–"

She turns her horse back towards our camp.

"Just hear me out, Az–"

"There is no need. This plan is rash, unpredictable and exposes our best fighters to the greatest risk of death. It is exactly what I would expect from you, Nara Fornwood." I open my mouth to argue, but she raises a hand to stop me. "It is lucky for you, then, that we are of the same mind for once." I hold my breath, wondering if I've heard her right. "I agree with this foolish strategy, except in one point. You will not spearhead such a desperate foray. The Maw will. He and Alrahim will select a unit of Ghumes and Hrossi. You will ride with me at the rear of the host."

"But I want–"

"I do not care what you want. You are a Tathar. An undisciplined and volatile one, but a Tathar nonetheless, and I will not risk one of our greatest weapons in a stealth attack." She stops her horse for a moment, squaring her shoulders to me in the dark and I know she'll brook no argument. "Like you, I value my *guts*, Nara Fornwood, and my brother will have mine for bow strings if I let anything happen to you."

In the few hours left to us before the attack, we try to rest. Despite my nerves, I must nod off at some point because I dream of the wrangler. He's watching me from the other side of a great watercourse, wide as the river that had hooked around Orlathston. His skin is still leeched of colour, as ashen as when I left him unconscious at the camp with Saqira, and his movements are ghostly between the trees.

"Wrangler, wait," I call out to him. "Wait for me to cross."

"You're a terrible swimmer, Little Scourge," he says, shaking his head. "And you can't follow where I'm going."

"Why not?"

"It's not for people like you," he says simply. And as I draw closer to the bank to question him, I see his face is no longer Nixim's – it has morphed into Brim's. He's serious, unsmiling, wearing that superior expression he'd get when he donned his Elix robes and took his seat among the Isfalk Council during Morday Mass – the look of an Elix Heir, blood of the Founding Four. "It's not for people like you," Brim repeats, turning his back on me.

I wake to my own whimpering and a sense of loss that descends so fast I feel like I'm freefalling. Brim and Nixim – I've lost them both. Perhaps I never really had them to begin with. Brands like me can't love Pures like them. Each beat of my heart is a great effort, as if my veins are full of sand. How easy it would be to lay back down right now and let this feeling carry me under. I imagine the weight of it pressing me into the dirt until I'm just another speck of dust blowing across the desert. But all around I can hear the noise of our forces preparing in the dark, blades being honed, armour and tack checked. I suck in a breath and reach for my cuirass, trying to shake off the dream and muster the energy to do something useful.

At the next campfire across, a Ghume fighter stares at me, head cocked. Perhaps she heard me cry out Nixim's name in my sleep, perhaps she recognises fear and hopelessness when she sees it. She must know who I am, even though I don't know her – another faceless soldier in a vast camp of them. I run a hand across my mouth, trying to school my expression, to set a good example, but she's already rising, approaching me with a water skin extended in her hand. As she draws closer, I can smell that it isn't water, it's ryki.

Forcing a smile, I shake my head. She can't know what it means to me, how such a simple gesture of solidarity puts a flint to my rage. Blood hammers in my veins once more, reliving the wrangler frothing at the mouth, the stench of spilled ryki in the tent, the pale shell of him on the camp bed... and I remember everything that Phibia has taken from me.

"Thank you," I tell the soldier. She nods and adjusts her armour, her branding dark on her hand, lacing her fingers and trailing her forearms in a constellation of dark blue swirls. Yet she is strong and healthy, taller than I am, and with shoulders bulked from wielding swords and shields. Not so long ago she would have taken my breath away – a woman warrior, a Brand so strong and fit and free. I would have been jealous of her and the wondrous world she came from.

But now I notice her hands trembling as she puts down the ryki skin – nerves for the battle to come. It makes me remember the branded sister and brother I'd seen in the Fornwood all those months ago, brittle as twigs from hunger, skin grey from sickness and malnutrition, the way the girl's hand had shaken as she snatched the snowjack from me – need and desperation making her brave. This soldier prepares herself with a similar determination, an unquestioning need to fight for her freedom, her survival. It shames me. Phibia has taken Nixim, and she has taken Brim. But she will continue to take from Brands like this soldier, and from so many more with *tainted* blood – my blood. It reminds me why I'm here, why I let Azza train me. Something deep inside tells me it's been my fate all along. I'll fight beside Azza and her Pure supporters for all their lofty principles, I know that now. But when the final swing of my sword comes, when I take my last gasp of breath as all hope fades – that thrust will be for *my* people, for the Branded, for vengeance.

Alrahim selects the best of her Ghumes for the vanguard attack and the Maw chooses his Hrossi. I watch Annek helping the giant with his armour, almost as sullen as I am about being excluded from the unit. Azza had told her she was not ready for such a mission, but I know Annek. If that look in her eye is anything to go by, I won't be surprised if she mounts up and rides out with them regardless. Dalla watches the Maw from the corner of her eye, as if suspicious he might encourage her to do it. Annek wraps the giant in a bear hug, much to Dalla's disdain, but when he sets her back on the ground and turns for his axe and shield, it is Dalla who holds them in her hands. "Here," she says, "bend down, you big oaf." He lowers his head as if Dalla might be about to kiss him. But she stops short with a sniff.

"What the pox are you up to, Dal?" Annek asks.

"Smelling his breath." She rubs her nose, nonchalantly. "Guess you're as sober as you're ever going to be." The Maw straightens, a twitch of amusement in his brow. "Might let you have these, then." She gives him his weapons. When he's buckled up, she stops him leaving with a touch to his arm. Kneeling at his feet, she re-buckles one of his shin greaves. I catch Annek's eye and she returns my astonishment, shaking her head in silent awe. Dalla Thorval, daughter of an Elix, blood of the Founding Four, and prized Mor of Isfalk, on her knees before a Brand. Not just any Brand, either – a southern mute with Brume markings darker than a moonless night and battle scars even darker. Back in the sleigh wagon crossing the snowbound plains, I'd fantasise about seeing Dalla humbled. But if someone had told me she'd do it of her own accord, I'd never have believed them.

"What?" she snaps, but she understands our stares. As if to compensate, she backhands the Maw across the chest. "Come back alive then, you brute," she says. "But mark this – if you let Annek follow you, I will hunt you down, do you hear me?" The Maw's grin flashes white against his ebony skin, and I'm still admiring it when he lunges towards me, grabbing my forearm so tightly in his, he almost cuts off my circulation. "Good luck, Big Man," I tell him. But the Maw doesn't let go, and much to my confusion, he closes his eyes. I cast about the faces of the group, looking for an explanation. It's Azza who holds my gaze. "What's he doing?" I mouth to her. She widens those big eyes and thrusts her chin towards me, and at last I understand.

The giant's pulse is almost torpid as I reach for it. It thuds deep within him like the sound of snow drifts falling from the trees in the Fornwood. I find it difficult to pick out his emotions at first. Perhaps they're tempered by drink or the habit of preparing himself to fight. But as I push harder, I sense something unfurling at his edges, fear like tendrils of a lana vine curling about his muscles, tightening his lungs. I let it thrive for a moment, tasting it, bitter and organic, on my tongue. When I have its measure, I smother it with my pulse, starving it of light and air, like a noxious weed. The Maw's breath eases, his shoulders relax, and I feel the crack of his neck like it's my own, the calm releasing with a satisfying rush of blood to the head. He lets out a vast exhale, opens his eyes and kisses my hands.

And then he's gone, his soldiers following him stealthily into the night with such zeal, I begin to suspect Azza has also swayed them – enhanced their courage, minimised their fears. We are about to mount and watch the Maw's progress from the ridge when two riders thunder into the camp. One dismounts quickly, pulling the other's horse to a stop. Pale sand scarves settle around the female form that descends – the white robes of a Seer Circle acolyte, too clean and bright amid the grubby mess of a military camp. My heart flips in my chest like a fish as Saqira approaches. I almost want to turn away so I can't see her tears, can't hear her say the words that Nixim is gone. But I don't. I keep looking because that's how I've always punished myself – staring down the things I know will break me inside.

Saqira speaks first to Azza in Reis.

"Tell me," I ask, my voice cracking, barely audible.

"It is not Nixim. Rest easy, Nara Fornwood," Azza says. "My brother lives." Breath fills my lungs again.

"I had a vision," Saqira says. "Forces from the north, flying the banner of Isfalk. Here in Reis." She offers me her hand and when I take it, I see the vision just as she did – the desert shore, not far from where we first landed the *Na'quat*, an armada flying the Warder banner from their masts. Soldiers, horses, weapons all pouring ashore. "If they cross the plain to join Phibia's forces–"

"We will be trapped between them and the krait," Azza finishes. She looks to Alrahim for her reaction.

"There is something else," Saqi adds, drawing her hand from mine as if she wants to protect me from seeing it. "The Warder captain–"

"What of him?" I ask, voice tripping over hers as I seize her arm again.

And there he is. Brim. Pale hair almost white in the sun, the raging battlefield before him, riding at the head of the Isfalki reinforcements.

Saqi drops her arm, nothing more to show. Brim is lost to me. What did I expect? Was I hoping I had broken Phibia's hold over him in Nixim's tent? That when he fled into the night, he ran away from me, but also from her? He's a Warder, an Isfalki through and through. He always has been and I've always known it. Of course he'd have joined the Warder forces. They are what he knows. They are his very identity.

"I am sorry," Saqi says gently, seeing my pain and reaching for me again. But I step beyond her touch.

"I'm sorry, too," I answer Saqi. "But sorrow isn't going to fight this battle." Something shifts inside me. All the grief and pain and fear flushes through my blood, white-hot as a sword from the forge, and when the hammer strikes I ring not with sorrow but with rage – rage and that burning need for revenge.

Something about the way I feel suddenly reminds me of the wrangler's words on the Wasteland Plains.

She of flame hair and steel will... shall rise a warrior of light in the dark... swaying her armies like a smith at the forge... to scorch the earth with the fire of regeneration.

Controlling my emotions be damned. I might as well try to harness the wind. *Anger, my old friend, burn through me. Go ahead, do your best.*

Sisters in Battle

The Maw leads the attack just as the moon is waning to a milky pearl in the east. Azza works her way through our soldiers like some armour-clad angel of the Old World, using her sway to boost their confidence and lessen their fears. I follow her lead, trying not to listen to their doubts. The time for doubting is over. *You guide me, my Na'quat. You've always guided me*, the wrangler had written. Now I need to guide these men and women, make them less fearful of the battle ahead. I guess that's all I can hope for.

Night still swaddles the plain below as Azza and I watch from the ridge, squinting through the dark and straining to hear the sounds of the vanguard's furtive assault. We can only imagine the muffled surprise of the ambushed watch, the draw of steel, the thuds as guards fall; we won't be able to see the Maw's progress until the sun breaches the horizon. Alrahim prepares our foot soldiers and riders for the assault from the south-west, keeping our lines open to the sea. The Ghume captain hopes to draw Phibia out from the plain, avoiding an attack on our tail should Isfalk reinforcements arrive. Despite my complaints, Azza keeps us to the rear-guard, watching the progress of the battle from above, like spectators.

By the time the sun's rays slant across the plain below us, the Maw's forces have already pushed deep into the camp, wreaking havoc. Azza's skub shows dead bodies in the throes of dressing or reaching for swords strewn on the periphery, the Hrossi and Ghume unit cutting a steady path through the unprepared enemy. But now the alarm has risen and there is light, the fighting starts in earnest and I don't know where to look. Everything seems chaos and noise until I draw my focus from small pockets of fighting witnessed through the glass and begin to read the more general push of our forces.

This may only be my second battle, but I've spent enough of my childhood listening to Brim regale me with accounts of the great Warder conflicts of history to understand the difference between shell shields, phalanxes and offensive wedges. I know our best chance against Phibia's highly trained Reis army is to strike before her units can organise themselves into regimented tactical defences. It would have been Brim's advice if he were here... if he'd been on our side. I can see Alrahim sending forays of her Ghumes to attack before they can make formation. But she is cautious, wary of releasing too many of her holding forces onto the plain for fear of opening our rear to attack from reinforcements. Meanwhile Nixim's southern clans forge ahead, over-eager and unruly, hacking their way through the melee with their curved swords swinging, or fighting back-to-back from the ground with a ferocity I haven't seen since my days in the Cooler. No wonder the wrangler wanted these tribes on our side. They may be untrained but they are fearless.

The stealth attack gives us an advantage... for a while. Our foot soldiers tear through Phibia's men before their captains have even emerged from their tents with their boots on. The Maw looms vast and supreme in the thick of attack, first on horseback and then hand-to-hand, his two-bladed axe cleaving a path of blood through the chaos. If anyone was born to do this, it is him; his vast silhouette is the epicentre of the conflict. But as Brim once told me, all heroes draw the attention of a challenger eventually.

The man who comes for the Maw across the gore-strewn camp is lean and rangy, wearing a golden Halqa on his armour and sitting on the largest horse I've ever seen. I narrow my focus through the skub, then pass it to Azza. "Phibia's champion, Captain Tahim Nal Dur," Azza says, her mouth a hard line as she tracks his movements. "A Pureblood glory-seeker, hoping to rise in more than the Khadib's military favours. It was only a matter of time before he sought out the Maw."

I take back the skub, holding my breath as I watch the rider charge the Ringer Champion, curved sword glinting. The Maw spins, ducking his blade and crippling his horse in one cruel blow to the foreleg. Tahim slides from the saddle before the horse falls, landing on his feet, weapon still trained on the Maw. He's easily a head shorter than the Ringer but, like Haus, he's agile, young and quick. Within the first five minutes of their dogfight, the Reis lands two hits on the Maw, one to the shoulder, the other behind his thigh – a blow that sees the giant struggling to walk.

"I can't watch anymore!" Gathering my reins, I turn my horse to the path down the ridge, but Azza pulls me short. "Poxes, Az, I can't just sit up here like a bystander! He needs help."

"We stay true to our plan, Nara Fornwood," she reminds me, her voice hard as stone. "Watching and waiting is what commanders do. Breaking strategy now leaves our rear-guard without updates or direction. It would rob them of the chance to retreat. Do you wish to shed *all* our blood?"

I know she's right, but my heart breaks over it. Grabbing the skub back again, I see only a confusion of bodies and weapons, the clash of metal, the battle cries and groans of the dying and wounded as I hunt for the Maw. It becomes clear we're rapidly losing our short-lived advantage. Scanning the melee, my scope catches a dark form, buckler raised above his head, more blade than shield. The giant has lost his axe and faces the Reis captain without a weapon. I taste blood. My tongue throbs in my mouth and I realise I've bitten it. Tahim spins under the Maw's shield, lunging for the kill, but then disappears from my sights. When I find him again in the eyepiece, he's on his knees, sword slipping from his hands. A second later he falls face down in the dirt. The figure behind him withdraws a bloody broadsword. "Annek!" I cry. "Annek... you crazy beautiful bitch!" I knew it. I knew she wouldn't stay behind cutting bandages with Dalla.

Azza snatches the skub and surveys the scene. "You Isfalki women," is all she says, before quickly moving the lens. Phibia's host marches out from the plain, just as Alrahim had wanted, engaging with our lines further west towards the sea, but now they are armed and organised into their formations and it is clear they are wresting control of the conflict. Azza's face is stormy, her brows tight and as she lowers the scope. She's conflicted. Now is the time to push my suit.

"Your lover is fending off three warriors at a time and you're going to stay up here and watch?"

I'm expecting a riposte, a counter-argument, a stupid Reis proverb, but this time Azza says nothing. Her throat works so fast I think she might be about to throw up in the dirt. She masters it, inhaling sharply, before turning to the guards who were to be our last protection if the battle was lost. There are maybe fifty riders, the reis-chafi masking their faces, curved swords sheathed on their backs. Their mounts side-step on the loose scree of the ridge, impatient for action and I know from the way Azza motions to the battle below, as she gives them their orders in Reis, that they will be riding into the fray – for the Maw. For Alrahim.

We hurriedly touch the hands of each rider as they pass, lessening their fear, boosting their confidence with our sway – just as we did with the Maw and his soldiers before the ambush, just as I imagine Phibia has done with her own commanders. I try not to let fear take hold – fear of her greater numbers, fear that they will out-manoeuvre us on the battlefield. I push it beyond all conscious thought, and in place of that fear I let my anger, my need for revenge flow freely.

I grab the pommel of my saddle and throw myself back onto my horse. A war cry erupts from my throat, answering the roar of the riders as they gallop down the ridge to join the melee... but it's a different scream that follows hot on its tail, ripping through my chest, high-pitched and predatory. Instinctively, I lift my arm for the ghosthawk and with a ripple of feathers, he comes to rest. What I see in the depths of his yellow eye raises the hairs on my neck. Isfalki Warders are riding from the ocean, a commander on horseback, mustering them towards the battleground.

"Brim is coming," I tell Azza, and I wonder how my voice can break over a name I used to say with such love and admiration. "He brings Phibia's reinforcements."

Azza masters her reaction, but her knuckles are white around my reins, our horses jostling. "How many?"

"Too many," I shout back at her. "We need to sound the retreat before they arrive."

"It is too late for that." Azza squints at the horizon. "They are already here."

I spot the dust trail of troops, the bright hue of fresh banners glimpsed between. "We have to go down there, Azza. Alrahim and the Maw need every sword they can get."

"No!" She yanks back my reins and my horse whinnies wildly. "You are a Tathar, Nara Fornwood. If we lose you, we lose one of our greatest weapons."

"And what good is a weapon if you keep it sheathed?" I bark at her. "I won't run any more, Az. I've been running ever since Warders killed my Amma in the Fornwood, and I'm sick of it. I'm not losing any more of the people I love to Isfalki Purists or that fecking krait."

Azza holds back my mount, looking me over. "He said you would be like this. Nixim said once the battle started, your instincts and hunger would drive away all fear."

I cover her fist on my reins, our skin tightly pressed. And she lets me do it. She lets me send my energy into her in a great surge of courage and conviction. *I* sway *her*. And the determination blazes in her eyes, dazzling as the sun. She clasps my arm in gratitude, in solidarity, before mounting her horse. "*Never let a sister go into battle alone,*" she says.

"Fec's sake, don't tell me – *Reis Proverbs*, volume twenty-five?"

"No," she shouts, heeling her horse down the ridge. "That one is from *The Book of Azza Ni Azzadur.*"

The Sand Siren

The fray is blood and noise and chaos in ways I could never have imagined. Worst of all, I know we are failing, outnumbered, the enemy drawing in before I have even begun.

Cutting through the brawl, I see the Maw towering above the heads of other fighters, beset by two of Phibia's guards. He staggers from his injured leg, and Annek covers his flank, face daubed with gore. I'm barely inside the real fighting when I'm unhorsed and dragged backwards by a rider latching onto the neck of my cuirass, nearly throttling me in the process. As soon as he slows, a punch to the side of my head makes me see stars. I must black out for a few minutes because when I come to, I'm outside the fray, on an open stretch of dunes. I stand unsteadily, only to be intercepted by a sword, not swung to injure but to stop me short. The soldiers circling me wear armour of pristine white, the enamel unchipped, a golden Halqa glinting on their tabards. These were the private guards of the Kham... now answering to the Khadib. I'm surrounded by Phibia's henchmen.

A kick to my back sends me sprawling. I realise I must have lost my sword when I passed out. I make for the dagger at my belt, but the soldiers close in. A boot on my neck shoves me to submission, blades glint near my face, but none draw too close. No doubt they've been briefed by Phibia to avoid my touch. I slump in the blood-drenched sand and close my eyes against the sound of the carnage behind us. What do I want my last thoughts to be? Nixim's grin, Osha's swollen belly, Haus squeezing my shoulder, Azza's husky laugh. The Maw, Annek, Dalla, Sigrun – all the faces of the people I love flash before me. And then there's Brim, running his hand up the stubble of his neck, about to give me a piece of his mind. The memory of his face is sharper than the sword at my throat.

Poxes, why don't they finish me and get it over with? Why are they dragging this out?

When I open my eyes the soldiers are parting, a horse stepping into their ranks. The stallion is white, utterly without blemish, its neck a graceful arc, hooves high stepping prettily. The beast is a vanity mount – a ride fit for a queen's victory parade, not a war-horse. The rider wears a breastplate and vambraces of white tooled leather, white braids snaking in a crown atop a face of alabaster. Backlit by the sun, Phibia might be the Elita incarnate, come to earth in all her pale and dazzling beauty. The only flaw in her terrifying perfection is an angry red welt on one cheek, the gash left by the tiercel's talon, still inflamed and weeping.

"My budding little Tathar," she says, eyes running over me with a mix of fascination and distaste. "And her *handler*, I see." I reel around. Azza is on her knees behind me. "Really, Azza Ni Azzadur, I knew you were jealous when I took Saqira into the Circle, but if you want for companions to take her place, I can at least find you one who isn't a dirty fec."

Azza remains silent, but her fists clench, as if missing the weapons Phibia's men have wrested from her. My blood starts to rush, an angry river in my ears. A pox on Azza's restraint. If we're about to breathe our last, I'm going out yelling.

"Hey, Phibia," I heckle. "Armour suits you. But Holy Mother, that gash–" I suck air through my teeth with a nonchalance my thundering heart lacks "–looks nasty. You reckon it's *infected*?" Phibia's mouth hardens at the jibe and the next thing I know I'm seeing stars again, my cheek on fire, backhanded by one of her guards. I get a small thrill of satisfaction that I've riled her, even if I'm swallowing blood for it. Azza grunts and I can't tell if she's acknowledging my guts or my stupidity. If we're about to die, I hope it's the former.

"Come, little fec," Phibia says, hand outstretched as if to a small child. "Let us finish what we started." Her face is so close to mine, I think she's going to kiss my cheek. The proximity is distracting, and I'm not aware of her fingers at my throat until they start to squeeze. The quickening of our joined skin is so intense I think I might pass out again. But Phibia's grip loosens a little and I understand why. She doesn't want to end me yet. For all her driving ambition, her disgust at my tainted blood, her fear of my potential power, she's simply too *curious*. She wants to know my past, how I came to be – this freak of nature, this Tathar Brand. I'm too intriguing to her.

Everything falls away – the din of the battleground, Azza's sudden shout in Reis, the flash of swords all around us. Images rush in a tangle through my mind. I see my first bow and the snowjack I felled with it, Amma blooding my forehead on the ice plains; I see Osha collecting feverease and heartwort, her lashes laced with snow as we chase falling flakes with our tongues. And then there's Lars Oskarsson telling Amma to give us up, her cottage roaring with flames, and Osha and I stumbling half-dead into the Settlement. But the most unnerving of all are the images I don't recognise, scenes that perhaps belong to me but I was too young to remember – a pregnant woman laid out on a bed, a mess of brown curls stuck with sweat to her face, bloody sheets twisted about her legs; Lars Oskarsson watching Osha take her first steps; his face again as I toddle after Amma's squawking chickens; and once more as we lie down in the drifts, arms outstretched to make the shape of fairymoth wings in the snow.

The pressure around my throat increases. There's a hiss, a bitter curse breathed across my face. "You bastard, Lars," Phibia grits out. No... that's not it. "*Your* bastards, Lars," is what she says. Leaping onto her distraction, I grab her wrist at my throat and press my advantage, feeling my own energy crackle under her skin. There's a fissure in her concentration and I wedge my will into it, prising open her mind. I expect nothing more than flashes, snippets of memory, but when Lars Oskarsson materialises again, the image of him is as clear as a summer morning. He holds a bundle of cloth in his arms and next to him is the dark-haired woman I'd seen in the bloody childbed. With her curls free of her face, I can see the branding on her cheekbone – a whirlpool of tiny stars, spinning towards her ear and into her hairline. There's something so familiar about her that my insides wring with longing, as if I'm looking at Osha after being parted for several years, her face ripened with experience. Except this woman isn't Pure, like Osha. She's a Brand, like me.

She carries a bundle of cloth in her arms, too – a baby wrapped in swaddling clothes. She and Lars Oskarsson are carrying newborns. Someone speaks. Phibia's voice. A younger version of herself, not much older than I am now, judging by her plump skin and unlined brow. *Do this last service for me, Lars,* she says, *and I will ask no more.*

The young Oskarsson stiffens at the request. Contempt thins his voice. *You'd forsake your own sons for your ambition?*

Don't judge me so, Lars, Phibia snaps back. *I only do what men do every day. I do what your own brother did. He sent me away. He turned his back on his sons.* She gives Oskarsson a defiant look. *Besides, I'm not forsaking them. I'm giving them the chance of a better life in the north, among the best of their kind – among Isfalki Pures.*

One of the twins is weak, Phibia, Oskarsson presses. *Roshana says he might not survive the night, let alone the journey.* He glances at the branded woman beside him.

Then Roshana will go with you to look after him, Phibia says archly. *They say she has a way with the sick. Useful… for a fec.* She scans the Reis woman with the same distaste she wore when she first saw me at the Kham's feast. *I've heard how much you like her company, Lars,* Phibia taunts, as if relieved to distract scandal away from herself. *How very undiscerning you've become since we came to Reis. You've turned quite... native.* She shrugs. *Love makes fools of us all, I suppose.* She reaches for his hand, perhaps intending to read the extent of his relationship with the Brand woman, or else wishing to encourage him to carry out her wishes. Either way, Oskarsson appears wise to the ploy, stepping quickly beyond her reach.

I'll take your twins to their father of my own accord. I need none of your convincing, Phibia. And if Nils rejects them, Oskarsson pauses, his face clouding for a moment, *I will raise them as my own. I promise this freely, as redress for my brother's wrongdoing. But know this – I pledge myself to these children, not to you.*

How very honourable you are, Lars, Phibia scoffs. *Perhaps I picked the wrong brother?* Her laugh rings out, as frivolous as the golden bangles that adorn her wrists, but when she turns from him, she struggles to mask the tremble of her mouth, to blink away the watery film that makes her eyes shine. She fights the very tears that would make her human.

Oskarsson takes the branded woman by the hand, regarding Phibia with the same defiance she'd directed at him. *Come, Roshana,* is all he says.

The vision blurs at the edges, then clouds completely as I lose grip of it, and of my advantage over Phibia. My breath grows laboured. "Enough!" she grits through her teeth. "I tire of this game."

"Then stop playing it," a voice challenges. Craning my neck, I see Azza standing among the Khadib's bodyguards. Her palm is wrapped around the hand of their captain where it rests on the pommel of his horse. He dismounts, relieving Azza's sword from one of his men and handing it back to her.

"What in Hell's poxes are you doing, man?" Phibia screams at him. She must have instructed the unit to keep me at sword's length, but said nothing of Azza. Ignorant of her skill, the soldiers had made the mistake of holding her back, focusing all their attention on me. While Phibia and I have been locked in a mental battle of wills, Azza was spreading her sway throughout the guards and commandeering their captain. Now they stand down, weapons lowered, waiting on the dark-haired girl as if she's the Khadib they've followed all their lives.

"No! This can't be," Phibia says. "How?... How did you keep it from me? I would have felt your skill." Emotions flit across her face quick as birds on a branch – first shock then panic and rage. I think she might dismount and rush for Azza, but there's a disturbance at our rear, the sounds of the conflict growing closer. Phibia looks up from her mount. "Brim!" she calls out in relief, and as I follow her eyes I see him, the Elix heir, as uncompromising as the Isfalki standard that flies above his head. Sitting astride his horse, he leads the new reinforcements of Warder troops just landed off the coast. And I know now our battle is lost.

Phibia snatches her breath suddenly, her pale cheeks turning bloodless. When I turn to find the cause, I discover Lars Oskarsson, riding alongside Brim. He squints into the dusty wind, the white streak in his hair catching the sun like he's still rimed with the frost of Isfalk. Has he come to do Phibia's bidding once again? Or is it Brim's command that he has answered this time? It hardly matters. "Call for Alrahim and the Maw to lay down their weapons," I yell to Azza, desperate to spare what lives we can. But Azza shakes her head, unbowed and far from broken. How can she not want to spare the massacre to come? But when I look back into the fray, I see the Isfalki forces aren't fighting alongside Phibia's. They are attacking them.

Phibia heels her mount with sudden violence. Her personal guard overthrown and turned upon by her own reinforcements, she makes a break for the desert. Azza throws herself into the saddle of the captain's horse and immediately gives chase. Torn, I take in the conflict raging before me. The remnants of Alrahim's forces, revived with hope, are surging forward to join the Oskarssons, pushing the enemy towards the Storm

Sands. Phibia, in all her pride, has allowed her forces to chase us too far across the plain and now she pays the price of leaving her citadel – its defence will be fatally weakened. But I'm not about to let Azza pursue the krait into the desert with no back-up. I find a horse and swing myself onto it, following the line of their dust trail.

Their route doesn't go far into the Storm Sands before I hear the scream of a horse. I discover their animals riderless and panting, Phibia's pretty parade stallion no match for the stamina of Azza's battle-hardened beast. Unhorsed, the Khadib rises to her feet between the dunes, facing the younger woman, finally seeing her for what she is – a Tathar. Her shock and panic have turned to fury now as she rushes Azza, hands raised, hoping to touch her skin first and press the advantage. Phibia's weapon has always been her hands. She forgets Azza's has been her blade. The glint of steel at her jugular stops her short. In sheer desperation, she grabs the nearest thing she can reach – my leg in its stirrup. Before I know it, she's dragged me from the saddle, slamming me into the sand, her fist at my throat. Her sway is a tidal wave, a wall of energy built from age, experience and bitter determination. "Lower your sword, Azza Ni Azzadur, or I'll bleed your little fec dry," Phibia grits out. I hear a grunt, a snatch of breath, and realise those sounds have come from me. The krait manipulates me as easily as a puppet, bending my will, leeching me of life, just as Azza warned she would. I try to turn my mind cold as the glacier at Tindur Hof, white and blank as the ice plains, but the effort of blocking her makes a familiar warmth fill my nostrils, the taste of rust flooding my tongue.

Azza curses Phibia in Reis, her voice growing distant. Blood slicks my chin and my vision starts to telescope, narrowing at the edges like I'm looking through Azza's skub the wrong way round. I'm no match for Phibia's strength, we both know it. I've been aware of my sway for barely a few months, whereas Phibia has trained hers over decades of latent wrath, a long and strategic bid for control, to prove herself to the mother, the lover, the citadel who rejected her. I flail for the dregs of my power, for a final push against the Khadib, but my only reward is another gush of blood. I spit it out across the sands.

Fec this! Phibia isn't the only one who's been rejected and exiled; she's not the only one who's had her heart broken, her happiness ripped from her. I think of Osha's bruised skin under Orlath's fingers, the scars on Haus's back from a childhood in the Cooler, and I remember Nixim, pale as a ghost on the other side of a river I cannot cross. All that pain and suffering washes back to me as fury. I can't match Phibia at her game, so I'll play her at my own. If she's distracted with bleeding me dry, then Azza has the advantage. But the Khadib is counting on the younger woman's humanity – a humanity she sees as a weakness. One clean stroke. That's all it would take, if Azza could risk it, if she was prepared to sacrifice me as I'm prepared to sacrifice myself.

I let my wrist go limp in Phibia's hand. "No!" Azza cries as she senses me giving up, disintegrating under the Tathar's manipulation. "Do not let go! Block her! Fight, Nara Fornwood!"

"I don't have to, Az," I tell her, voice a cracked whisper. I stare directly at Azza's sword. Her dark eyes fix on mine, understanding. "Do it," I mouth over Phibia's shoulder. "Do it!" Azza raises the bright blade again, pressing the tip to the back of Khadib's pale neck. I feel Phibia's assault of me stutter and ebb.

"Azza…" she says slowly, tone cajoling now. "Come. Let us talk. Haxim would have wanted us to reach terms for the good of Reis."

"You dare to speak my father's name?" Azza's voice is wolfish behind gritted teeth. "You dare to speak of the good of Reis while you stand amid the gore of a battle you brought to our shores?" Azza's trembling hands make her sword glimmer in the sunlight.

"I dare to tell you this – you are a Pure and a Tathar. Do you understand how powerful you could be? How I could train you to reach your full potential? We are the instruments that will bring back the prosperity of the Old World, a world without sickness and disease, without Brands."

"Nara Fornwood is a Brand and yet she is a Tathar," Azza says.

Phibia's forehead creases, her lip curling, as if at the inconvenience of me, like a fly in her ryki, marring the clarity of her vision for the future. "She's a feral and a freak – an anomaly. She has no bearing on what we could achieve together, you and I." Her grip loosens on me. "Take my hand, Azza Ni Azzadur. Let me show you the Continent as it could be – as I have seen it – for those with our blood." I sense she's about to turn and make a grab for Azza.

"Az!" I cry. But Azza's eyes are blacker and more unknowable than I've ever seen them, and for the first time since we met, I doubt her. Not her loyalty, not her integrity, but her ability to follow through, to use the blade. For all her fighting prowess, Azza believes in democracy and debate. She's yet to execute someone in cold blood to secure her own agenda.

But Phibia has. Phibia has taken many lives.

Do it. Do it! I chant in my head, wishing I could take the helve from Azza's hands and cut the krait's throat myself.

"You are right, Phibia Khadib," Azza says at last, tears shining in her eyes. "This *is* about what the Continent could be. This *is* about blood. It is about my mother's–" I hear a grunt, "my father's–" a soft sigh, "and my brother's." And finally, with perfect control over both voice and sword, Azza completes her stroke. "*E Frellah Husq'anan!* And this is for the blood of my people."

Phibia's head cocks, brow crumpling. But what pools in her eyes isn't shock or fury or puzzlement. It's sadness. She twitches as she falls, fingers still on my throat. And in that split second before she hits the sand, her mind opens to me, one final image flooding my thoughts. It's of Phibia as a girl in the Mor school, about the same age I was when I was exiled from the citadel. She's reclining in the stone casement of a window seat, the view overlooking the snowy Fold, clean and pristine as a newly laundered sheet shaken from the line. A young man rests his head on her belly and her fingers twine through his hair, the colour of ripe wheat. His face is so like Brim's, I cannot breathe.

You do love me, don't you, Nils? Phibia asks, her cheeks flushed.

Mmm? he murmurs, languid from lovemaking.

Do you love me?

Yes, he says.

Nils Oskarsson. Brim's father. The lover who spurned her and their sons. After all this time, Phibia's final thoughts are of him. Did he truly care for her or did her sway turn lust to love? She must have asked herself the same question again and again. And for a moment when I open my eyes, I see her not as the fallen tyrant, but as the girl she once was, the yearning lover, the spurned mistress... the woman who never wanted to doubt herself again.

Phibia falls at my feet, Azza's blade still tracing the arc of the stroke over her shoulder. One of her white coronet braids, marred by blood and sand, comes unpinned. I think of the sand siren Nixim had slain on the Wasteland Plains, the question mark of its body like the lopped curl of a seductress. Azza stares down at the dead woman's face, as if needing to process the truth of it. And for once, I can't look. I've seen too much of Phibia's life. Azza can have her death.

A Pretty Piece of Nothing

The battle doesn't end in a roar, as I'd always imagined great conflicts do. It slinks like an injured animal going to ground. Stripped of their leaders and attacked on two fronts, Phibia's army struggles to recover any strategy. Some of her soldiers surrender, but others flee. Our Ghumes push them far into the Storm Sands, leaving them to meet their fate at the hands of the elements.

In the evening, Azza and I pick across the gore of the battlefield, checking for survivors. The wounded are gathered onto carts and taken to the treatment tents set up by Saqira and Dalla behind our lines. In the distance, I see Brim and his men searching for the living, too. He must feel my gaze for he glances up at me, tormented, hopeful, full of things unspoken. I can't bear to look at him yet, can't stop my mind from seeing Nixim taking the cup from his hand, trusting him, drinking with him as if they were friends. Brim's actions were not his own, I know, but there had to be a vein of jealousy latent inside him that Phibia mined, a streak of bitterness and destruction, not unlike her own. He is her son, after all.

"This isn't what I thought a victory would feel like," I tell Azza. "No one warned me winning would feel so empty... All this bloodshed, all these wasted lives." My voice cracks as I survey the carnage surrounding us.

She takes me by the shoulder and leads me away from the worst of it, understanding what I need more than I do myself.

"Return to Saqi's camp." It's an order, not a suggestion. "My brother needs you now."

I hesitate and then, to my surprise, she slides an arm around my waist, drawing me in, holding me tight. The gesture, from her of all people, sends me over the edge. For the first time in my life, I admit something I've never said aloud to anyone ever before. "I'm frightened, Az… I'm terrified of saying goodbye to him."

She looks me over gently. "Nara Fornwood," she says, "when did fear ever stop you?"

The wrangler hasn't moved since I left for battle. Laid out on a pallet, his skin is still grey, lips dry, eyes sunken under their lids. For a moment I hold my breath, frozen at the flap of the tent, unable to go inside. I can only think the worst. "He still lives," Dalla hurries to tell me, but her eyes dart to Saqi, and I know she's not telling me everything.

When I kneel beside him, my fingers trembling over the skin of his neck, he feels cold, his pulse still faint and unresponsive. Saqi draws my hand away. "Give him time." She rubs her palm along my wrist, her energy comforting, warming when I feel chilled and as exposed as night on Tindur Hof.

"Tell me of the battle," Dalla says. I think it's a distraction, but when I glance up at her, my selfishness comes crashing in. Her eyes are wide, face blanching at the blood all over mine, the dents in my armour, the wounds and grime of war. She longs for news of Annek, almost shaking with the restraint of giving me time with Nixim before she asks.

"She's fine, Dalla." Her shoulders sink in relief. "In fact, I'm glad she didn't do what she was told because she saved the Maw's life."

"Shame," Dalla says with a grin, "because now I have to kill him."

After I've quickly recounted the battle, she rushes out to prepare tents and beds for the wounded. Saqi rises to follow, but turns before she leaves, eyes on her brother. "We will keep trying, but…" She breaks off, blinking away tears. "I think we need to prepare ourselves." I nod quickly, appreciating her honesty, but not wanting to hear the words.

When she's gone, I let my head fall to Nixim's chest, despair shredding my heart. The faintest scent of autumn and kasta nuts still lingers on him. It makes me sob, and sob some more, until all the fighting, all the bloodshed, all the struggle to get here, to this *victory* that feels nothing more than a crushing loss, is washed through me.

I fall asleep on the damp linen of the wrangler's shirt.

I wake to the warmth of someone's hand at my cheek. The memory of Phibia's fingers makes me rear up in fright, instinctively reaching for my sword. Lars Oskarsson wheels back from my weapon. "It's alright!" And then more gently, "Nara, you're safe."

It's the deep satisfying rumble of the voice I remember from Amma's hearth, a voice I want to trust. This man took us in from the Fornwood, protected me from the wrath of Mother Iness, and has just saved us on the battlefield… and yet he has kept so much from me.

He scans my face in silence, as if waiting for my reaction, uncertain where to start.

"You have some explaining to do, Elix," is all I can manage. He sits at the makeshift table, wipes his exhausted brow with a hand still bloody from the conflict, then looks at me standing before him, my arms crossed. "That expression, the set of your mouth…" He lets out a soft grunt of amusement. "You remind me of your mother, just before she'd dig her heels in."

"You knew her." Not a question, a statement, because I've already pieced most of it together, but I need to hear the truth from his lips. He pours us a shot of dramur vit from the skin on the table and knocks his back quickly. "Well?"

"Yes, I knew her."

"When I touched Phibia, I saw a branded woman in her memories – a servant. You called her Roshana. She was my mother, wasn't she?"

He nods, and a rush of air leaves my lungs involuntarily. "She was a brandservant, yes," he says, "but she was also a healer. She worked for the Kha that Phibia married after we got to Reis. I think Phibia suspected Roshana was a Sway, but she couldn't process such an aberration – proof that the skill wasn't the reserve of the Pure-born. So she sent her with me to Isfalk. She needed a carer for her babies, yes. But she also wanted rid of her. Rosh's very existence threw Phibia's beliefs in the supremacy of the Pure out of kilter."

"And how did she become my mother?"

He sighs, his eyes somewhere far away. "The journey back to Isfalk was difficult, prolonged by dangers and necessary detours. Rosh was courageous, practical, more determined than any Pure woman I'd ever met. I was already in love with her and unashamed of it. Reis taught me – *she* taught me – what the Branded could be.

"One of Phibia's twins had been born weak, beyond Rosh's power to heal. He didn't even make the sea crossing, but she blamed herself. That night I..." He pauses to look at me, awkward. "I comforted her."

"Say it," I demand. "Say what you should have told us all those years ago, when Osha and I walked out of the Fornwood into Isfalk."

His eyes are weighted as the ocean, full of regret. But he says the words steadily. "You're mine... you and Osha. You're my daughters."

His admission doesn't make it any easier to digest. He doesn't say the word *father* and neither do I. "Why didn't you tell us?" I hear the hurt and frustration, the longing in my voice.

"It was too dangerous. When we finally reached Isfalk, Roshana's pregnancy was showing. I couldn't bring her into the citadel – her brandings would have sent her to the village and I'd never have seen her. It was better that I hid her in the cabin in the Fornwood; close enough for me to visit, far enough away to keep her secret from the prying eyes of the Settlement. We'd brought a Hrossi wet-nurse with us to feed Brim on the journey north and she stayed with Rosh, delivered you. When your mother died, she became your carer, too – your Amma."

I pace the tent, taking it all in. I'd always thought Amma was a Solitary, but that lullaby she used to sing to us as children was so unlike Isfalki or Solitary songs. It had the same melody as the one Haus played on his lute on the Wasteland Plains. The wrangler had said it was a Hrossi ballad and he was right. Amma was a Hrossi. It all makes sense now. But as the puzzle pieces fall into place, it isn't satisfaction I feel. It's resentment thickening my throat and burning under my skin. "You took Brim into the citadel under your name and protection, yet left your own daughters to survive in the wilds of the Fornwood?"

"Listen to me, Nara." He holds his palms out, as if wanting to touch, his need to make me understand turning a little desperate. "Your mother got to hold you both before she died. She looked at the girls we'd made together – one Pure, one Branded – and she made me vow you'd never be separated. How could I take Osha into the citadel and leave you in the village? No." He shakes his head. "I wouldn't have you living a second-class life, feeling inferior, suffering all the narrow-mindedness and prejudice of the Isfalki. I decided I didn't want either of you in the Settlement, not after Rosh had taught me how Brands and Pures might live, how a colony like Reis could be integrated and still thrive. My plan was to take you back there, bring you up in Cha Shaheer, but when I returned to the citadel to deliver Brim to his father, things weren't as I expected. My brother had been killed in a skirmish with

Wastelanders. I was now the Oskarsson representative on the Council – a seat I thought I could use to effect change for the Branded in Isfalk. This was my chance to replicate what I'd seen in the south. I didn't know then how Iness would block me at every turn."

His voice falls away and he searches out my gaze, imploring. "You can't know how much I've always loved you, watched over you from a distance. Don't you think I knew about your antics with Brim as children? At first, I thought it best to keep you apart. But you made it very difficult. You were inseparable. When I found out Brim was training you, I realised how useful that might be in protecting yourself in the future, and I bribed the Warders to turn a blind eye to your truanting from the Mor school. If I couldn't be close to you, at least Brim could."

"Fec's sake, I needed a father, not just a friend."

"Nara, if I'd showed my ties to you, my true feelings, it would only have set tongues wagging and drawn Iness's attention to you and Osha. I was already walking a knife's edge keeping you in the citadel, under the shadow of the very woman who would exile you if she discovered who you were... *what* you were. I suspected you'd both inherited your mother's skill, but I didn't imagine it would be you, Nara, who would become such a powerful Tathar."

"Not powerful enough, it seems." My voice breaks as I turn back to the wrangler.

Oskarsson rises and crosses to the bed. He surprises me by touching Nixim's cheek. Despite my resentment towards the Elix, I feel a sudden longing for him to reach out and touch *me* like that, reassuring me I'm not alone in this... that I now have someone to turn to, even if I can't bring myself to call him father.

"I knew Nixim was the Kham's son when he came to Isfalk," he says, looking down on the wrangler. "Phibia wrote to me. She hoped a little hardship might make him see the error of his ways. Of course, it only achieved the opposite. Treated as the Brand the Isfalki took him to be, the Settlement only made him value his mother's ideals and what she'd achieved in Reis all the more. When you and Osha disappeared with him, my Warder trackers followed you, sending word back to me that you were heading to Orlathston. The Blood-wife told me the rest."

"The Blood-wife?"

He smiles at my surprise. "Iness might publicly condemn witches, but you'd be surprised how many Isfalki from the citadel still seek out their help. Frenka the Blood-wife told me about your growing abilities, of your vision and the battle ahead in Reis. I began to muster men from my Warder days, soldiers who trusted me, who were as disillusioned with what Isfalk had become as I was. Many of them had witnessed Iness's trading of Mor women with the Wastelanders in exchange for supplies, and they realised the Settlement was floundering, our survival hanging on slaving deals and immoral trade agreements to which the Council turned a blind eye. I organised our rebel army and sailed south. Just in time, it seems."

"I saw your forces leaving Isfalk in my vision, but I thought they came on Phibia's order... Frenka warned me the sight couldn't be trusted. I didn't really understand when I visited her with Nixim all those months ago. Now I know what she meant." I study Oskarsson's face, his grey eyes with their flares of green, his height and grace.

"What?" he asks when he sees me staring.

"You look like Osha. It's so obvious. I can't believe I never saw it before."

He smiles, watching me play reflexively with the pendant about my neck. He dips his chin towards it. "I bought those for Rosh in the suk before we left Reis. They were a pair of earrings originally, could you and Osha tell?" I shake my head, examining the gold. "Back then, I knew the icon was the Halqa," he says, "but I didn't realise the Elita prophecy wasn't universally upheld by the Reis. When I gave Rosh the earrings, she said she wasn't a follower, but that long ago, in the Old World, the symbol had a broader meaning. It represented balance, the cycle of light and dark, death and new life. And that, she said, was a good enough principle to live by. She wore them all the time, almost in defiance of the prophecy, and when she died, I made necklaces of them – one for each of you, a touchstone to your origins, to the land your mother came from. But most of all, a token of how much I loved her, how much we both loved you."

I swallow back the burn of tears in my throat. *A pretty piece of nothing*, the Blood-wife had called the necklaces. She'd been referring to the prophecy, the elitism and division Phibia's religion fostered. But the pendants themselves seem to offer a new meaning to me now. Suddenly they are a pretty piece of everything, everything that is worthwhile in this life, the only thing that's important.

Love.

I reach into the pocket of the wrangler's gilet hanging by his pallet, taking out the Reis coin I know I'll find there. "And this? Why did you give me this coin the night I was exiled in the Roundhouse?"

He frowns at the memory, sighing. "I guess I was a little desperate for you to make the connection, especially after all that had happened to you. I wanted to confide everything, but it was too dangerous. Even to be seen with you would have put your life at risk. You were safest away from me, far from the citadel." He runs a hand over that white streak in his hair, and I imagine the young Warder my mother fell in love with – kind, honourable, handsome. "I hope one day you might be able to forgive me, Nara."

I can't bring myself to answer yet. All I can manage right now is a grunt and a half-shrug. But I know I will forgive him. I'll forgive him because he did it all for the right reasons, and I understand now what I would do, what I *have* done, for those same reasons – for love.

I should be happy. I should finally feel some sense of fulfilment, kneeling next to the father I never knew was mine. But I only feel hollow as I sit beside the wrangler and take his cold hand in my own.

It might be hours later, it might be only minutes – I've lost all understanding of time – but I'm roused by a touch to my forehead, one I recognize now. It's the same hand I felt all those years ago in Amma's cabin as a child sleeping by the hearth. Lars Oksarsson's palm is big and warm on my chilled temple and this time I don't flinch. He stands next to me, calloused knuckles moving to stroke my cheek. And when I let him, I sense the loosening of his shoulders, hear his exhaled breath, drawn-out and shaky. "That might be the longest sigh I've ever heard," I tell him.

He looks down at his hands. "Well," he says. "It's been almost two decades in the making."

We stay there, silent, watching over Nixim for a long time, until one of Oskarsson's men calls for him on the other side of the canvas. He straightens, but before he leaves, he asks, "You'll forgive Brim too, in time, won't you, Nara?"

I give him a half-hearted nod. How can I not? Brim's my best friend. I just can't forgive him right now, not with the wrangler's life in the balance.

Lars offers a small smile that fades as he runs his eyes over Nixim. "You should try your own skill again with the boy."

"I did, before the battle. But it's Osha who's the healer, not me. I wish she was here."

"Your mother once told me some hearts will beat only to one rhythm and good luck trying to sway them."

"Sounds like the wrangler," I scoff. "I've never had any luck tapping into him before." I think of the first time I tried, my laughable efforts outside the Blood-wife's cottage on the Edfjall.

"Did you ever consider that perhaps you struggle because his heart is too similar to your own?" His green eyes glint as if remembering some private joke. When he sees me frowning, he says, "Your mother used to say the same of mine. But once she'd read the rhythm of it... well, she could have told me to haul the moon from the sky and I'd have killed myself trying." He runs a knuckle over the hitch of his lip. "She never even had to use her sway."

He leaves me alone then, and I touch my fingertips to Nixim's chest. His skin is cold and lifeless and makes me shiver. But when I close my eyes, my father's words strike home. I listen once more for the wrangler's pulse, breathing in so I can smell him – the memory of autumn, the spice of dramur vit when he first kissed me, and something uniquely Nixim – honed steel and leather and the desert wind. I feel his presence behind me in the saddle as we gallop over the steppe, the weight of him between my legs aboard the *Na'quat*, the clutch of his wet hands in the saman. The weakened beat of his heart trips a little, as if responding to the thrill of my own, before it quietens again, so faint and erratic I struggle to even hear it.

You've got a lot to learn about yourself, Little Scourge.

If I'd known you liked it dirty, we needn't have messed around with swords.

Not even a goodbye kiss?

"It wasn't goodbye," I tell him, voice growing raw as I remember the way we parted in Cha Shaheer. "That wasn't goodbye, Wrangler, you hear me?" My fists twist the linen of his shirt and I shake, blood beating a drum in my ear. "Do you hear me? If you've brought me all this fecking way just to abandon me, you lying, fickle son of a trull, I swear, I'll..."

My head sinks to his chest in defeat, angry tears squeezing through clenched lids. And slowly, so slowly, I feel it – the press of his pulse against my cheek, soft but regular. I raise my head, almost choking on a sob. His eyes are open, the ring of bronze around his pupils a little dull, but the milky glaze gone.

"What Sc-scourge?" The words are barely audible, tapped out dryly from the roof of his mouth. "What... will you do?"

"I swear, Wrangler, I'll damn-well kill you myself!" I'm blubbering like a child, wiping snot on my cuff, not sure whether to kiss him or call for Saqira to check him over.

He coughs a little, then winces, but his fingers twitch, seeking mine. Was it my sway or angry desperation that brought him back to me? I don't know and I don't care. He's alive and that's all that matters.

"Wrangler."

"Is that tenderness in your voice?" he rasps.

"It's bloody relief."

"Mixed with a dash of love?"

I can't help laughing through my tears, and for once I let him get close to the truth.

"Yes, Wrangler." I say. "Mixed with the tiniest dash of love."

PART THREE:
ISFALK WAITING

Sleepless Nights

"Fair winds, my friend," Azza observes as we stand shoulder to shoulder looking out at the open sea. We're on the deck of a ship much larger than the *Na'quat*, a vessel built for war, for troops and horses and weapons.

"I wish you were coming with us, Az. I'd feel a lot better about this venture with your sword at my side," I tell her. I've come to rely on her for far more than her sword.

"Don't worry," the wrangler calls from the bridge, "you've still got me, Scourge!"

"Hardly a comfort," I call over my shoulder. "You slept through most of the last campaign." He grins, but is distracted by a question from Lars Oskarsson – *my father*.

Azza sees me watching them at the wheel. "You are still resentful of the secrets he kept from you?" she asks.

I shrug. "I haven't been able to call him 'father' yet, even though I can see he longs for it," I confide.

"Such titles must be earned, not claimed."

I'm going to miss her trite wisdom. It's too soon in Azza's tenure as the newly elected Kham for her to leave on a war expedition, but Lars believes we need to push our advantage to Isfalk while we have allies in Orlathston and Reis to provide us with forces. By taking the offensive, he hopes to control the trade routes north, strangling Iness of supplies and giving us a good chance at a takeover of the Settlement.

Now Nixim is fully recovered and the Shadow City secure,

there's another reason I want to press north again so soon. I long to be with my sister, to be there for Osha when her baby comes.

"Saqira will miss Dalla's help in the new school," Azza says, watching the Mor girl oversee the crew as they winch the last trunks aboard. "She has become quite the administrator."

"Bossy organiser, you mean," I scoff. After the battle for Cha Shaheer, Azza and Saqira disbanded the Seer Circle and converted the Golden Temple to a secular school for the healing arts. Azza was adamant it should be open to healers both with and without the skill. She argued it was the only way to keep Sways grounded, to prevent elitism, and to ensure that apothek and herb lore from all around the Continent was recorded and kept alive for future generations. Dalla has been throwing herself into the administration of the school's archives, organising scribes to work alongside renowned Reis apotheks and tribal healers from the southern clans. Her scholarly passion is set to rival even Osha's. That's partly why Dalla insisted on returning to Hross with us – she says she has too much to learn from the Wastelanders about north-Continent healing and herblore to stay behind. The other reason, of course, is Annek, who would have cut off an arm rather than give up the chance to return to Isfalk and wreak her revenge on Iness. Where Annek goes, Dalla now follows.

"Any news of Hira?" I ask, wanting to be reassured that any threat to Cha Shaheer is under control before we set sail with a portion of Azza's army. Her face clouds at mention of the girl's name. Hira couldn't be traced after the battle, and is now the last splinter in Azza's thumb, a lingering memento of Phibia's rule.

"Alrahim had word from Ghume scouts last night," Azza says. "They located Hira's whereabouts. She has resurfaced among the eastern clans, still aligning herself with purists and spreading Phibia's elitist dogma."

"I don't like leaving when you've had that news," I tell Azza.

"I am not troubled by it. Without the skill of her mother, Hira's venom is hardly toxic."

"Why the eastern clans?"

"They are her father's tribes. I suspected she might return there. It is the only place she holds any status now."

"That makes sense. Someone like Hira couldn't contemplate life without status. The apple doesn't fall far from the tree."

The corner of Azza's mouth hitches. "I like this proverb, Nara Fornwood."

"Yeah, that figures," I say. "It's about as clichéd as *The Book of Azza Ni Azzadur*."

She laughs that husky, contagious laugh and I turn my gaze out to sea, pleased to have amused her. As I do, a ship passes ours, another of our fleet, its sails full, heading steadily out to open water on a favourable wind. My face falls as I recognise Brim staring straight at me from its prow.

"You will need to forgive the Warder Captain eventually, my friend," Azza says, big brown eyes too perceptive for her own good. "Phibia's sway would have made him lose sight of his own integrity, you know that. And I believe the punishment he gives himself is worse than any you can inflict."

"Maybe, but his jealousy, his hatred of Nixim… his belief in Pure superiority – all those feelings must have been latent inside him in the first place for her to have swayed them. You said even Tathars cannot create emotions that aren't there."

"And who amongst us has not felt emotions we know to be wrong, even as we have entertained them? Sometimes our faults rule over reason. I thought you of all people would understand that, Nara Fornwood."

I take a breath at her frankness, sharp as a grass cut. But I know she's right.

"I'll face him, eventually," I tell her. "But for now, I'm relieved he travels north on another ship. I need this journey to learn to forgive him."

"Well, then," she says, telling me it's time she went back ashore. I hold out my hands for hers and she hesitates a moment, still leery of letting anyone in. But when we clasp palms, the surge of energy between our skin makes our eyes flare in wonder. My mind connects with hers, reaching out, and as it does, she loosens her grip, turns my hand and brings my fingertips hesitantly to her lips. For the briefest moment, an image flashes before me. It's of a younger Azza, sparring with staves in the little arena below the saman. She takes a hit – I feel it in my own shoulder – but a laugh bubbles through her as she falls, and I know the training session is a playful one. A girl straddles her hips and Azza doesn't even try to fight her off. Her opponent's arms are toned and glistening with sweat and sand as she tosses away her stave. Azza sinks her fingers into her loose black hair, pulling her down. As their lips meet, I recognise the girl – Alrahim, as a young recruit.

Azza lets my hand fall and I offer her a single nod, a thank you of sorts. After everything she has seen in my mind, this parting image feels like a gift, a small but intimate piece of herself she entrusts to me, her fellow Tathar, her friend.

"Make sure that brother of mine looks after you, Nara Fornwood," she says.

"I can look after myself, Az."

"I know. But that does not mean he should not. Or that you should not let him." I roll my eyes at her, but only to distract from the heat in my cheeks, knowing that she sees it all and always has – how hopelessly in love I am with her brother, how vulnerable it makes me feel. "There is a time and place for armour, Nara Fornwood, and it is not in the bedroom."

"Oh, for fec's sake, just leave and take your terrible proverbs with you!"

"Sister," she says, one final squeeze of my shoulder. I turn to face the ocean, tears pricking. From the wind, I lie to myself.

As I watch the rowboat return her to the shores of Reis, I wonder how I'm going to manage without her.

* * *

That night, I stand at the porthole of my cabin watching the moon reflected in the inky ocean. Even with all that lies ahead of us, I can't help thinking of another night, not so long ago, when the silver light fell just so across the rough boards of a ship's deck.

It was my first time at sea, my first experience of a mesmer vision... my first time with the wrangler. So many firsts – including a broken heart. *Be careful of the boy. He's a good soul born of bad*, the Blood-wife had warned. But it wasn't Nixim who betrayed me. It was Brim. It's always been Brim, now I think of it. He Paired with Osha in Isfalk. He refused to believe Iness would trade Mor for supplies and then tried to force us back to the Settlement. And here in Reis, he must have still retained that latent suspicion of the wrangler, that narrow-minded Isfalki superiority, for Phibia to have swayed him to her side. The Blood-wife was right – he was born of bad. And yet somewhere, deep in my heart, I know he's essentially good. It's just going to take me some time to learn to forgive him, to be able to look in his face and not see Nixim's almost slipping away from me.

The latch on the cabin door hitches and floorboards creak. Hands snake around my hips from behind, the scruff of stubble chafing my neck, rousing me from my brooding. "Excuse me," I say, indignant. "I believe you have the wrong cabin."

"I don't think so," the wrangler answers, pulling the shirt from my waistband and slipping his calloused palms underneath.

"I'll have you know, I'm not that kind of girl!"

"Is that right?" His breath prowls my skin. "Those goosebumps... oh, and that little moan you just swallowed... I think you're entirely that kind of girl, Scourge."

He's right, my arms and sides are gooseflesh as he drags the shirt over my head and tosses it aside. The cold leather of his gilet against my skin makes me shudder even more. I seize a breath – a prayer, a curse, a gasp of wonder all at once – as his mouth and tongue leave trails of warmth all over me, stoking the heat already burning low in my belly.

I tug off his gilet, peel his shirt away, fingers tracing the tattoos I once thought were brandings, lips memorising his shape, his smell, his pulse. "I still can't believe you're alive – that you came back to me." The sound of my voice, somewhere between relief and wonder, shocks me and I try to cover it with a joke, mimicking the way he'd scolded me aboard the *Na'quat*. "Krait's venom isn't something you can *dabble* with, you know." His laugh is a soft stream of breath along my collarbone. "Always trying to outdo me, aren't you, Wrangler?"

At the nickname, he lifts his hands from my skin and steps away, leaving me suddenly cold and aching. "What?" I ask, reaching for his wrists, trying to pull him back to me, but he resists. One of his brows hitches expectantly, but he won't look me in the eye and his chin is stubborn. "Alright, alright," I tell him. "Come here, if you please, Nixim Ni Azzadur." His grin spreads wide and smug when I say his name, so I whisper it again in the shell of his ear. "Nix." And he lets me return his palms to my skin, grumbles a low moan when I push them up to my breasts.

"All that time I was recruiting troops in the South... all those weeks away from you..." he mutters between kisses, "and the only thing keeping me going was the thought of you... of what we did." He unlaces my leathers, pulls them down so I can step out of them. "And here you are now, back in the captain's cabin..." He lifts me so I can hook my legs around his hips. "Naked... and warm... and wet," he groans, pressing me to the wall, "against hard wood."

"Hard wood, huh?"

But he's too busy with his tongue to laugh, and the silken trail of it at my neck, between my breasts soon makes me forget all about jokes and teasing. "Nixim… Please." Five minutes in and I'm already begging. *Poxes, Nara, have some self-respect.* But I have no defences against him anymore. And neither does he against me, it seems. Nearly losing each other has made us desperate to make every moment count. "I want you now, Nix. Don't make me wait."

My admission, my vulnerability, makes him pull away for a moment to look at me. "My Little Scourge," he whispers, stroking my cheek. "Don't you remember what I told you on the ice plains? Your words, my hands." And the way his breath shudders as he says it, breaks the last barrier in me. He reaches between us, and I slowly sink down. The rhythm he starts mimics my heartbeat, his heartbeat, and I understand now how they are one and the same. They always have been.

"Yes… like that," I tell him.

"Here?" he asks, his hand between us, thumb circling that place of opposites, that jagged, exquisite spot that draws me together and breaks me apart. "Like this?" And I feel weak, exposed, vulnerable as the day I was born… and I don't care, because I know he will catch me.

"Holy fec… don't stop…" The words tumble out with each exhale as if they've bypassed my brain. "Nix, I love… I love this."

"You love this?" He slows his hand. "Just *this*? Is that all?" He threatens to pull out of me, so I hold his face between my palms, squeezing my legs around his waist, and rock him back inside me, fast and hard.

"Nara!" he curses. "When you do that, I can't…" And as he nears the edge, his arms tighten about me and he groans into my mouth. "Are you with me, my Na'quat?"

I might be his moon, his stars, but he has me freefalling through constellations. Soft as down against his ear, I whisper my answer, unable to give him anything but the truth now. "I'm with you, my love."

* * *

"Hell's poxes, is that smug grin going to be a permanent feature now?" I squint at the wrangler through a brash beam of sunlight tilting through the porthole.

"Yep," he says, tugging my leg over his hip, hand mapping rivers, claiming new borders down my back. "You cried out my name – my real name – at least four times last night. I think I have the right to be a tiny bit smug." I yawn in his face, just to nettle him, then snuggle into his neck, away from the prospect of daylight and reality.

"That's all the thanks I get, Little Scourge? So bloody rude." He tips my chin, forcing me to lift my head to his and, reluctantly, I crack one tired eyelid and then the other. After he'd drifted into satisfied sleep, I'd spent the rest of the night pacing the boards, my mind a melting pot of emotions about what lies ahead. "You're exhausted, Nara. How come you didn't sleep?"

"Well, there was this Reis sailor in my bed and he just kept touching me and–"

"Tell me," he presses, ignoring my evasion. "What are you so worried about?"

"You mean, other than sailing headlong into a campaign to control the north against the Purist regime that traded me and my sister as breeders?"

"Yeah, other than that."

I run my fingertips over his lips, swollen and chafed from the assault of my own, and draw him close, wanting to lose myself again in his kisses. But he puts a hand between us. "Tell me, Na'quat." And I can't help biting down on a smile.

"What?" he asks.

"*Na'quat*. That name used to get me so worked up, but now," I open my legs wider, folding them around him, "it still gets me worked up… just in a different way."

"Good to know." He grins then kisses me. But when he pulls away, his face is still serious. "Tell me what's wrong, love."

That word isn't much better. I can't defend myself against him when he uses weapons like that.

I run a hand over my hair, the regrowth soft and curling again now. "Oskarsson – my father," I sigh, "wants to win control of the north."

"That's not exactly news, Nara. You don't want to go with him to Isfalk?"

It's the question I've been asking myself all night. Why should I care for that remote Settlement? Is the citadel truly my home anymore? Cha Shaheer, my mother's city – the place I sense her presence most – accepted me more than the colony that raised me. Isfalk spurned and exiled me, then traded my sister and friends. Why should we go back when we could live in the Wastelands or Reis? What have I got to prove? And yet...

And yet I long for the solitariness of the Fornwood again, the Moon Pools, the fresh drifts of the Fold, frozen dawns hunting on the ice plains. Those places are woven like a tapestry in my soul, and I can't seem to unpick them.

"Isfalk raised me – it's who I am, I guess," I tell the wrangler, watching as his brows begin to crease, the real issue of what kept me awake all night slowly dawning on his face. "Of course I want to go back and make good. I want to correct all the wrongs and ills and injustices of that poxy Settlement. And I want to show Isfalki Brands that the protection the citadel offers them is nothing more than a prison, a half-life." I think of Frida and the children in the Sink who looked up to me for that short time, who saw hope and a brief glimpse at a better future because of me. "I want to show the village Brands their potential, what they could be. But if we're successful, as Lars thinks we have a chance to be, it will take time. There'll be schools and infirmaries to build, and a new integrated government to establish. I'll need to stay. And then what becomes of–"

"What becomes of *us*? Is that what you're truly worried about?"

"Well, facing down a Tathar like Iness is also a fairly large concern, especially without Azza by my side." I try for a grin, and fail. "But, yeah, I am worried about us, too."

"Why would you worry about us?"

I catch his face between my palms. "Isfalk calls to me. But you're a Reis, Nix. Your sisters are there, your people, your heritage. When you wore the reis-chafi and rode to muster the southern clans, I saw who you truly were for the first time and it was… wonderful. I remember, the Blood-wife called you *Child of the Sands* and I know why now. The desert is in your blood, just as the Fornwood is in mine."

He presses our temples together, breathing my breath. "*You* are in my blood," he says, and the conviction behind it scares me a little. "If Isfalk is where you need to be, then it's where I need to be."

"There's a sacrifice behind those words, Wrangler, and I don't want to be the cause of it."

"But the thing is," he says, his eyes dark now, complex as the depths of the moonless Kyder, "it's not your choice to make."

I lick my lips. "It could be. I could sway you. Did no one tell you I'm a Tathar?"

"Ah yes, I'd forgotten. So that explains why I'm so hopelessly under your spell. These long nights of endless pleasure… you've been swaying me all this time?"

The jest turns sour and I look away. The Blood-wife had warned me the skill could be both a blessing and a curse. "I hate the idea of that."

But it's the precise reaction he seemed to be looking for, because he smiles. "See? You could never sway me."

"Why not? You still think I'm not strong enough?" My pathetic attempt to influence him outside the Blood-wife's cottage only extended as far as his dogs, and I'm still not sure I had anything to do with his recovery from the krait's poison.

He chuckles. "You can't use your sway on me because you don't want me that way. You love that I'm crazy about you and it's all my own fault. You have principles."

"Principles? Me? You sure about that?"

"Why do you think I wanted Azza and no other Sway to train you? My sister only ever uses her skill as a last resort. And so do you." He tugs me closer. "Now, stop worrying over a future even you can't predict. Come back to me, here and now." He shifts his hips so I can feel him warm and hard between my legs. "I haven't finished being smug yet."

The Line of Forgiveness

Despite fair winds at the outset, our voyage to Hross is beset by storms. They're not violent enough to upset our crew but they unsettle me and seem to add to the sense of foreboding I feel at the prospect of our campaign in the north... the prospect of facing Iness. I wake regularly in the night from the toss of the ship and dreams of Phibia's voice calling to me. *Let us finish this, Little Fec.* The feel of her hand on my skin is so real in the dark, I jackknife upright, only to find the crone's blue-veined fingers locked around my wrist. I blink and cry out. "Nara," the wrangler says, "Nara you're dreaming." Those gnarled digits, sharp as talons, morph into his warm hand.

The worst of the dreams comes when we're only two days from Hross and the prospect of seeing Osha makes me restless enough to pace the decks. When I finally find sleep, I dream of my mother writhing in a bloody childbed. Roshana's screams become Osha's, my mother's sweat-matted hair turning into my sister's auburn locks. There's so much blood. A sea of blood. And as much as I clutch at Osha's neck, trying to slow her pulse, reaching out for her child's, my sway is useless. I can't stop her slipping away.

I wake to blood all over our sheets, my nose gushing. "Na'quat?" the wrangler murmurs, still groggy from sleep. The shock coupled with the heaving ship make me vomit over the side of the pallet. When he realises the state I'm in, he jumps up to help me.

"She was giving birth... and she called out for me... and there was so much blood but I couldn't help her. I couldn't use my sway. I'm useless. And Iness will know it."

"Hey, hey, slow down... it was just a dream," the wrangler shushes, folding me tightly in his arms. "What's all this about Iness?"

"I should never have left Osha. I promised Amma I'd look after her, that we'd stay together. And now she needs me most of all and I'm not there. I'm useless as a Tathar, but I could have at least been there for my sister."

"It was a nightmare," he says, wiping my nose with the sheets. "All these dreams are only natural. You're anxious about your sister and her baby, but most of all you're worked up about facing Iness. She's not just the Mother of Isfalk. You've made her the mother of all your demons – the mother of everything you oppose." He strokes my hair until I've recovered some semblance of calm. "Of course confronting her again scares you. But this time, you know who you are, you understand your skill and you have an even better weapon." When I look at him in question, he says, "*I'm* going to be there."

"Thank poxes for that, then," I say sarcastically, recovering a little when I see that mole jumping on his cheek. I look down at the bloody sheets, the pool of vomit at the side of the bed. "Bet you didn't think sleeping with me was going to get so romantic, huh?"

"Please, Scourge, if a little vomit and blood turned me off, I'd have left your sorry arse in Helgah's months ago."

I grin, remembering how he'd bailed me out of that drunken bar fight, cleaned me up and put me to bed. And I'm awed at how much he's stuck by me despite all the shit I've thrown at him. "Wrangler?"

"Scourge?"

"I think I'm going to keep you."

* * *

Fair winds may have carried our fleet from Reis, but the rest of the voyage is plagued by squalls and high seas. The crew take the conditions in their stride but the weather, so different from our journey south, only aggravates my unease. The real tempest waits until we're only a few hours out of Orlathston, hitting our fleet in the middle of the night with little warning. Waking from the frantic sweat of another nightmare about Osha and her child, it feels as if I've conjured the roiling ocean from the tumult of my own fears. Something is not right. I've been sensing it with every league we sail north and now even the elements are telling me so.

I venture on deck, only to be engulfed in a chaos of lashing rain and breaching waves. Clinging to the main mast, I squint into the gale, straining to see the lights of the Hrossi port, until one of the crew shoves me back below boards. I do what I can to help secure cargo and take turns on the bilge, but it soon becomes difficult to stand, and I can only stagger to my cabin and lie on the damp pallet, watching the leaking boards in terror and heaving up my guts in between. A drenched and green-faced Annek tells me the wrangler has the crew navigating us into the waves, following the fleet back out to sea, fearful of being dashed into the coastline. The news makes me feel farther away from Osha than ever. In moments of tortured dozing, the wrench of my stomach becomes her writhing pain during the siege of Orlathston, and the groan of the battered boards her moans. Amma told me to look after her, that she would be the one to need it. I should never have gone to Reis. Now I'm going to meet my end at the bottom of the ocean and I'll never see my sister again. I'll never know her child. It will always be that grotesque baby I held in the warped landscape of my nightmares.

But the storm does pass. By the time we make our landing off the coast of Orlathston, it is evening of the next day. Lars remains with the fleet to inventory repairs, but the wrangler reads my anguish and gathers a small crew to row me ashore.

I can barely sit still as we navigate the Heitval inlet and it seems an age before Orlath's fortress looms before us in the dark. "Haus has redecorated," Nixim says as we approach. I'm vaguely aware the walls are different somehow – the grotesque heads and rusting armour removed from the portcullis, sconced brands illuminating scrubbed stone. But I can't appreciate it as he does. The island fortress fills me with dread as it always did, except now for a different reason.

I jump to shore before the boat has even been tied, letting the wrangler deal with the watch and rushing straight inside as soon as the gate is raised. I meet Haus crossing the great hall. "Where is she? What has happened to her?"

He greets me half-dressed. "All is well," he says but I can tell it isn't. His drawn face, with its pallor of sleeplessness, the lines of worry mapped across it, make me ask no more. I run straight for Osha's chamber, leaving the chief with Nixim.

"Nara?" my sister questions softly when I enter her room. The sound of her voice, the confirmation that she lives, makes me weak with relief. Only a single candle is lit and when I turn to look for her, eyes still adjusting to the dimness, I see my sister lies in a vast bedstead draped with Old World damask. Her skin is pale, her hair unwashed, and she looks exhausted. But she's alive and that's enough for now.

"Holy fec, O... I had such nightmares... this terrible dread the whole way here... and then the storm hit and it was as if I knew something was wrong but I couldn't reach you... and I couldn't stop thinking the worst, like I was being punished for leaving you. Amma always said–"

"Breathe," my sister says, gentling me. "Nothing's wrong." I let out a long exhale, and it feels like I've been holding it in the entire crossing. She grins and there's an edge of quiet satisfaction about it. "Everything is just as it should be. See?" And drawing back the sheets, she shows me a bundle of swaddling – the baby, still newly wrinkled, nuzzling her breast.

"She came early, that's all. Shessa couldn't get here to help because of the storm and Haus was beside himself." She strokes the baby's cheek. "She's an impatient little thing... wanted to make an entrance... like her aunt."

I'm breathless again, but this time in awe. "A girl?"

Osha nods. "Here."

I swallow back tears as she places the child in my awkward arms. "How do I... is this right? Am I doing it–"

"You're doing fine." She laughs and it's like warm palms around a frozen fist.

"And is she... okay?" I scan the sleeping child but all I can see is her pink face framed in swaddling and furs. "Is she well?"

"We're both well, Nara." She takes the child from me, and I can sense her sudden pique. "If what you really want to know is whether she's a Brand, then..." She lays the baby on the bed to unwrap her linens, and her tiny arms – now free of her cocoon – startle and flail, a wail building. "There. See." Osha lifts the candle and I follow her fingers to a spot on the babe's jaw where a line of freckles, fine as blue thread, runs upwards and comes to rest under her ear. "It's all anyone wanted to know. *Is she a Brand? Is she Pure?*" Osha says, wrapping the child again. She shushes her back to sleep. "But did you see, Nara?"

"Yes... I saw her markings." I try to keep the disappointment from my tone. "She's beautiful anyway, O." I'm uncertain what she wants me to say.

"I mean, did you see their shape?" I study my sister. Even in the candlelight I notice her colour is returning, and her cheeks seem to glow from within. "They're the replica of Haus's." I look back at the child in her arms. I hadn't thought to compare, but as I pull back the linens from her cheek, I realise they are. "She's his, Nara."

"She was always going to be his."

"But now I can be certain of it." Osha presses her lips tenderly to the child's forehead, eyes brimming.

I'm happy for her. I'm happy for Haus. But I can't help the feeling of despondency that washes through me. My sister's certainty came at a price, and I suddenly realise how much I'd been hoping the child would be a Pure, like her mother.

"I know what you're thinking," Osha says, reading my face. "You're disappointed."

"Well, aren't you? Her life would be so much easier if she was a Pure."

"Really? Just as mine has been? Just as the lives of Annek and Dalla and Sigrun have been?" And I hear how self-involved it sounds, casting Brands as the only victims when these Mor women have had their own trials, their own traumas. Perhaps their lives have been harder than mine in the end.

"How can you even ask if I'm disappointed?" Osha continues. "Am I disappointed with Haus for being branded? Am I disappointed with you?" She reaches for my hand and I feel that energy calling to mine. "You are my blood. This child is my blood. How could I ever be *disappointed*?"

"I only meant because she could get sick... She could–"

Osha instantly stiffens, face hardening. There's a shift in her voice as she answers. "I won't let her get sick. And if she does, I'll heal her." Her conviction is like the crack of ice under snow. Something ominous and instinctive and fierce about it that I've never heard in my sister before. I understand, then, that she will protect this child with her life... even if she has to lie to me to do it. I know my sister – it doesn't *disappoint* her that the baby is a Brand; it terrifies her.

I scan the room – the journals and copybooks scattered across the huge bed, the quills and ink and scrolls covering the desk by the door, the pestle and mortar dusted with compounds, the basket of roots and herbs beneath. All of it tells me Osha still works late into the night, sacrificing sleep to find her cures. Not just cures, but *the* cure – a cure for the Brume. The baby mewls in her arms. Now she has a bigger reason for her obsession.

"There are things you need to know," I tell my sister. "So many things I discovered while I was away."

"What is it?" she asks, worried.

"Someone sailed with us from Reis. He'll want to see you very soon… He'll want to see his granddaughter." She startles, and the weight of everything I have to tell her bows me.

She lifts my chin. "Start at the beginning," she says.

Osha accepts Lars as our father far sooner than I am able to. Maybe the baby helps forge the bond of family between them. Lars makes a wooden crib as a newborn gift for his granddaughter, placing it in her parents' chamber. Despite the joy it brings Osha, the gesture conflicts me.

"He carved it with his own hands," my sister tells me. "It's thoughtful of him."

"No. Thoughtful would have been not abandoning us to survive in the Fornwood as children. Thoughtful would have been not lying about who he was, not starving us of his love."

"Nara, must you always be so harsh and unforgiving?"

I hate how resentful I sound, but I struggle to let go of it. "It's going to take more than furniture to win me over."

"He's a doting grandfather to Rosh. Can't you just be happy for that?"

My sister has named the baby Roshana, after our mother, which also gratifies Lars. She claims it was Haus's idea and I tease the chief mercilessly for trying to ingratiate himself with our father. Kidnapping his daughter to trade is not the best start in life for a son-in-law, after all. But it is obvious to me that Lars already admires Haus. His single-handed combat against Orlath prevented a drawn-out siege for the island and saved hundreds of lives, a feat that would be admired by any strategist and commander. And the fact that even Orlath's dyed-in-the-wool clansmen now bend the knee to Haus has raised him to great heights in Lars's estimation. Anyone can see how skilfully the young chief leads the river settlement, despite his youth. When he referees disputes among the clans, he satisfies both Hrossi custom and his own principles, not fearful of drawing his sword when he needs to, but making it clear he prefers to take counsel and consider problems carefully before coming to his conclusion. I notice Lars observing him with the pride of a father. It makes me yearn for Lars to look at me in that way... and then I grow resentful that I even want him to. I've lived for years without his praise. Why should I need it now?

Haus might rule like he was born to it, but I can tell he misses his old life. While Oskarsson, Brim and Nixim organise resources for the campaign north, I ride with the chief into the hearthlands, accompanying my sister and Dalla as they speak to Hrossi healers in the outlying clans. I notice the old wildness return to Haus's eyes, the exhilaration in his ruddy cheeks, and I understand how much he misses the freedom of being out on the plains and in the saddle. But he tells me there is so much work still to be done in Hross, and I know Haus is the last person to shy away from his duty. He recognises the chance to make the old capital so much more than it ever was – integrated, enlightened, civilised – the type of city he witnessed in Cha Shaheer; the type of city in which he'd want to bring up his daughter. And he knows he can use his position to help Osha bring about her dreams of treating the sick and researching cures here.

They'd set about doing so the moment the colony was brought to order. The stone-walled rooms of Orlath's harem and its outbuildings become the site of the city's first infirmary, the island a natural quarantine for controlling the outbreaks of fevers. Osha now continues the work, recruiting Sigrun and Dalla to help expand the wards and treatment rooms. Her plan is to establish schools, too, and a library, in place of the Cooler, around which they'll build an academy for apotheks and healers from across the Continent to share their knowledge. When I hear my sister's mastery of Hrossi, the way she talks to spae-wives and clanswomen like she was born on the plains, the way she burns the candle late into the night to record everything she's learned, I'm certain her dream will become a reality. Her eyes glaze over the quill and the candle wax gutters as she disappears into her own visions – not of birds and symbols and soldiers on arid plains, but of the very cause of all this conflict and woe. One day Osha will master something far more powerful than armies. One day she will master the Brume itself.

Work has already begun on rebuilding the Cooler and refitting its interior when Haus takes me to view the site. Almost a quarter of the tower's brickwork on the eastern side was tumbled by the fire, like a candle that has burned down asymmetrically in a draft, and the mason's tools, scaffolding and winches on this side, tell me the project will be one that spans years, not months. But what a legacy it will be, and how apt – a seat of healing sprung from the ashes of pain and death.

In the dusk, the tower and the training yard are nothing more than the ghost of what they once were. All the terror this place had instilled in me, the noise, the betting, the leering, the hurt and gore, feels scorched away, cowering in the ash-laced shadows. Images of sparring on these bloody sands, of sweating at the chipped practice poles, and drinking at the spot where the water bucket used to stand, play out like the memories of some other girl – naive, uncertain, unaware of herself. I'm not that girl anymore.

"It feels like a lifetime ago that we fought here, Haus."

He grunts. "Months only."

"You saved my life. You turned me into something more, someone different."

"Not so different," he says. "Stubborn still… angry still… mouth in the dirt…"

"You calling me foul-mouthed, you miserable son of a trull?"

His rare laugh makes me feel like I've won something precious.

"You still do not forgive," he says pointedly. His hand squeezes the back of my neck, turning me towards the entrance and when I look up I see Brim emerging from the shadows. The chief is already walking away, and I realise Haus has set me up.

"Don't blame him," Brim says. "It was my idea."

I shift, looking up at the tower's broken rim where the gulls have re-established their lofty nests.

"You can't even look at me, can you?" he says. I take a breath and force my eyes to his. "This is the first time we've been alone in weeks. You avoid me at every turn. You barely speak my name."

"Can you blame me?"

He shakes his head. "You of all people must know I wasn't myself when I was around that woman."

"That *woman* was your mother."

"Apparently…" He steps a little closer. "Are you going to make me carry her sins for the rest of my life?" He waits, as if it isn't a rhetorical question. When I don't answer, he says, "I had no more choice in who my parents were than you did, Nara. Lars is your blood and yet I notice you still don't call him Father."

"Titles like that need to be earned."

He nods slowly. "As do *brother, sister, friend… lover.*"

"Don't, Brim." I turn away, not wanting to hear his reasoning.

"There was once a time I'd earned some of those titles from you, Nara."

"Well, clearly you forgot them, otherwise you could not have done what that krait asked."

"She *made* me–"

"Tathars can't sway you to do things you haven't first imagined. A thread of the desire must already be there in your heart, Brim. As you say, I know better than anyone. Perhaps that's why it's harder for me to forgive you."

"Of course the thread of desire was there!" Brim snaps, his desperation echoing from the walls of the tower. "Don't you think learning that Phibia was my mother made me long to know her, to feel a mother's love, a mother's approval, just as other boys had growing up? You can't tell me you don't yearn for the same with Lars. I can see it in your face when you look at him. That was the weakness Phibia worked on in me."

"And what of Nixim, Brim? You sat with him as a *friend* and poured him enough poisoned ryki that he should have never woken again. You might as well have taken your dagger and run it through my heart at the same time." I try to stay calm, rational, but I'm already losing that battle. "Poxes, you must have hated him so much… You must have hated me." Brim wipes a palm behind his neck, studying his boots in the sand. His breath is agitated and I can sense his unsteady pulse, the conflict in it, even without touching him. He looks up suddenly and catches me watching.

"If you touched me now, you could see it all, couldn't you? You could feel what I felt?"

It's the first time he's asked me about my skill. Before the poison and the wrangler and Phibia, I was grateful he never asked, worried that it would make him forever wary of coming close. But now, as he holds out his fingers to me, it's far worse. The look in his eyes is full of awe, full of all the respect and admiration I've always ached for from him. But I don't want it for this. Not for being a Sway.

I shake my head and he lets his hand fall. "So you have this immense skill, but you won't use it?"

"No, not for trivial things."

"And I'm trivial?"

"You know what I mean."

I think we're about to fight over that, but he only sighs – a sound that says the time for lies is long past. "I did hate the wrangler," he says. "I hated him because he had you. He's always had you as I never have. And yes, perhaps once or twice when he looked at you, I wanted to gouge his eyes out and throttle the air from his lungs. But would I have acted on those impulses without Phibia? Of course not!"

I'm still wary and uncertain at the mention of that woman's name, even though she can't hurt us, can't harm any of us anymore. Brim steps towards me. "I'm not her, Nara. I'm not my mother. I know you're thinking of my narrow-mindedness in the past, how much of a Settlement man I've been at heart, and how that must align me with her. But I hadn't seen the world beyond Isfalk back then. I never knew what it could be. I needed to see that with my own eyes, for all those northern prejudices to be scraped away like scales. Surely you understand that, too?"

I do. But when I don't answer, he goes in for the kill. "You had feelings for me once, Nara, I know you did, and not just as a brother or a friend. When you watched me Pair with Osha, when you saw us join hands at the altar in the Roundhouse, didn't it feel like your heart was being ripped out of your chest? Didn't you want to make both of us feel some of that pain, too? And when you were exiled as a Brand and Osha was taken back to the Mor school to be examined, didn't a small part of you long for them to find markings on her, for Osha to be declared imperfect, rejected and spurned, just as you were?"

I grunt at him, indignant that he could voice such things aloud to me, could presume to put such emotions in my chest. But everything he says is the truth. It's exactly what I felt.

"You had all those awful thoughts, just as I did, but it didn't mean you would ever act on them. That was the line Phibia walked, that was the edge she'd discover and push her victims over."

He watches me, waiting, and I can't help but nod in agreement. I would never have done anything to harm Brim or Osha, even when it felt like they'd torched my heart, scorching it as badly as the Cooler walls all around us. I would need to be pushed beyond myself, just as he was.

"I'll admit it," Brim continues, "I hate that cocky bastard of a wrangler. But I will tolerate him for you. Because I know you love him and because I know he loves you... *almost* as much as I do."

I flick my gaze to his, but when the corner of his mouth hitches, I realise he's teasing.

"Are you going to forgive me, Nara?"

I purse my lips, thinking. "He has a name, you know."

"Who does?"

"Nixim."

"Mmm, if you say so."

"And it's *his* forgiveness you should ask, not mine."

He raises his eyes to the sky in frustration. "You're impossible, do you know that?"

"Why?"

"Because Nixim forgave me weeks ago."

While I know the Isfalk campaign is imminent, I'm still not ready to face the inevitability of leaving behind Osha, Haus and the baby. In the evenings, I am drawn to my niece. The yearning to watch her feed or sleep is greater than any desire for those needs in myself. It's a feeling that shocks me, something protective, nurturing, that I'd imagined would be natural in Osha but would never blossom in me. Back in Isfalk, before the wrangler and Reis, I'd have been horrified at such vulnerability, the weakness of it, the chink in the armour that loving something more than yourself exposes. But now I understand it, not as a crack or a flaw, but more like the patina that comes from a life properly lived, a depth of love that can only be known because of the knocks and challenges and bittersweet turns of fate.

Rosh stirs in her crib, mewls briefly, then resettles. Her eyes are a rapid percussion under blue-veined lids, lashes so thick and long they brush the rise of her fattening cheeks. Orlath never possessed lashes as pale and long as those. There isn't a doubt in my mind whose child she is. No one speaks of her brandings. They won't change the way this child is raised. She will have all the attention, care and education of any child back in Reis. She is the first generation of an entire colony of Hrossi Brands who will. I know her compromised health still bothers Osha, but it no longer concerns me. What I worry more about is something else in the child.

She starts to cry. "You can pick her up, you know," Sigrun tells me as she enters the chamber. She often helps Osha with Rosh's care while my sister studies. I lift the baby into my arms and she nuzzles eagerly, searching for milk and fussing again when she smells only leathers and fur.

"I'll take her to Osha," I tell Sigrun. "She's ready for a feed."

On the short walk to the infirmary, I hum softly, mainly to distract myself from the little hand that wrestles from the swaddling and clenches the air near my chest. I stop for a moment, sitting on a carved bench in the corridor. The song, I realise, is the one Amma sang to us as children, the Hrossi ballad Haus had played to Osha on the Wasteland Plains. Back then, I never dreamed I'd be singing a Wastelander lullaby to my half-Hrossi niece. I lay Rosh in the groove of my legs and watch her fists flail, mouth wide with angry cries. I've avoided touching her skin whenever I've held her, but now curiosity gets the better of me. I have to know. Azza would tell me it doesn't matter what she is, but I can't leave with that question burning at the back of my mind. And so, I take her tiny hand in mine and close my eyes. The quickening starts as the faintest warmth beneath my fingernails, but within seconds it floods my skin like the first hit of dramur vit. Her quick pulse calls to mine, plaintive as a pup abandoned in the Fornwood. "Here I am, little one," my blood answers. But when our rhythms meet, it is hers that wrestles mine into submission, hers that smothers my beat, my breath, my very soul with a force I have never felt before, not even in Phibia. I snatch my hand away.

"Is she awake already?" Osha asks, walking down the corridor towards us. "I thought I heard crying?" Rosh is silent now, gurgling up at me with eyes that haven't decided their colour yet. "But you both seem to be happily–" Osha breaks off, catching my expression. "Ah…" She sighs and looks away, guilty. "So you know. I was hoping–"

"What? That she wouldn't have the skill… or that she would?"

"I was hoping she wouldn't." My frown must be question enough, for she explains, "I just wanted a simple life for her, Nara. A happy, healthy life without that complication."

"This is the strongest *complication* I think I've ever felt, O," I say, lifting Rosh's fist as it grasps my finger.

"It isn't supposed to even be there yet. Azza said the quickening develops as the brain matures in late childhood. It's not usually felt at birth."

"Well, it's not going to go away, simply because you don't wish to acknowledge it." She won't look at me, so I stand, passing her the baby. "She's a Tathar, O."

"We don't know that yet."

"I do. I can feel it. Whether you like it or not, you have a duty to help her understand that, to train her when the time comes."

Osha mulls over my words, acceptance slowly dawning in her face. "Not me, Narkat," she says. "You're the Tathar. It's you who must come back and train my daughter."

Eyes and Ears

Haus pledges weapons, horses and those clansmen he can spare to Lars for our campaign in Isfalk. We cannot sail the journey because winter has begun to set in and the seas in the north are already beset with ice floes. Instead, we make preparations for the overland route, across the Wasteland Plains.

"I never thought I'd make this journey again," Annek says as she tightens the girth of her saddle.

"At least we each have our own horse this time," Dalla replies.

"Thank fec for that," I tell the girls. "If I have to listen to you two pretending to hate each other for the next twelve days, I might just dash your heads together this time." Dalla grins and I catch the wink that Annek gives her.

"Can you believe we rode south chained as cargo and now we're returning at the head of an army? Warder, Hrossi and Reis all banded together in the name of freedom." She fists the helve of her sword and her eyes shine hard and unforgiving as river stones. If I know Annek, she's thinking less of freedom than of vengeance on the city that cast her out, that traded her like breeding stock. We're too much alike in that regard. Except it won't be Annek that Iness hunts down when our forces engage.

Haus squeezes my shoulder one last time, a longing look in his eye. Once, there was nothing that would have stopped him coming with us, but now there are two good reasons – the child in his arms and the woman at his side. One day in the future, I know he will take Rosh on her first pony out across the Wastelands, teaching her the names of the constellations, the first chords of Hrossi ballads on his lute, how to heft the stock of a sword. And that's what takes me by the throat and threatens to choke my breath. Not saying goodbye, but the threat of never returning, never showing my niece how to hold her first bow, how to read scat and spoor, how to shoot and skin a snowjack. This rising we've set in motion, the political and social changes that might live as the great legacy alongside our names – none of it feels as important to me right now as the tiny human details my niece might treasure in her memory, the same way I hold Amma in my heart.

I don't kiss the child, I don't slap Haus on the back, and I don't seek Osha's arms one last time. I simply turn away from all of them, mounting up and riding out before the goodbyes are finished. Osha knows not to call my name and this time I don't look back.

A half hour later, when he has ridden the line of the troops with Lars and Brim, the wrangler catches up to me riding behind the Maw at the helm of the column. He doesn't speak at first, letting his horse pace itself against mine, giving me time to calm the shudder of my lungs and mute my snivels inside the collar of my furs.

"You'll see them again, Na'quat, I promise," he says.

"You can't promise that."

"I can, because I know you. I know you're scared of facing Iness alone. I know you're thinking the only reason you defeated Phibia was because you had Azza by your side." I look away, not wanting him to see the fear he's pinpointed so accurately. "What you don't realise is that Azza defeated Phibia because you were by *her* side. You're stronger than you think, Nara. She knew it and so do I."

"Keep telling yourself that if it makes you feel better."

"No." He smiles, shaking his head. "I'll keep telling *you* until you start believing it." He draws his horse close enough that he can brush my thigh. His touch doesn't send a rush of confidence through me as Azza's or my sister's would, but it quickens something else in my heart – something that helps fill the void Osha and Rosh have left behind. Nixim is another kind of vulnerability, but he's someone I'd fight for, and that is enough.

I straighten in the saddle, pulling myself together. "Don't worry about Iness, Wrangler," I say, hitching an eyebrow at him, "I'll protect you."

"Is that right?" He slaps my mare's rump and she breaks into a canter. I give her the reins, enjoying the simplicity of riding for a little while. It doesn't last long. Deep down, I know my joke isn't so far from the truth. Despite the armies, despite the military tactics and planning, the battle for Isfalk will come down to two people: me and Iness.

The journey across the plains takes far longer than it had when we came south as the cargo of Wasteland raiders. A fully fledged army is slow and cumbersome. Every evening our soldiers and horses must be fed, watered and rested, tents pitched for the Isfalki officers and gers for the Ghumes, as is their custom. The cold grows increasingly bitter every night, but I refuse a tent in favour of sleeping around the fire with a skin of vit. I wake in the early hours to find the warmth of the liquor has been supplanted by the heat of the wrangler's body wrapped around mine. The weight of Nixim's limbs helps ground me, but not enough to stop my worries spinning out of control like snowflakes in high winds, and I can't find sleep again.

The thought of facing Iness feels like something elemental, shored by decades of experience beyond anything I could conjure. Hers is the mind that moulded the Isfalk colony, that warped the petty desires of men to her own ambitions, all while letting them think they still held the reins of power. Hers is the mind that rid herself of other Sways and traded Mor women for supplies, that turned a remote ice-bound citadel into one of the strongest and most influential settlements in the Continent. Hers is the mind with enough forethought to exile her daughter to the south so Isfalk would have food supplies and trade routes for the future. And I've no doubt that hers is the mind that plotted the overthrow of Reis from thousands of miles away. Phibia may have executed the plan but it was Iness who pulled her strings, I'm certain of that now. How can I hope to match such a mind when I've known about my skill for barely a year, and wielded it for even less? How will Iness use her sway in the conflict to come? Have decades of experience made it even stronger than Phibia's, or dare I hope that age weakens it?

Restless for an escape from the cycle of these thoughts, I disentangle myself from Nixim and walk away from the campfires into the silvered darkness of the steppe. Iness read me in a matter of seconds on the Roundhouse stage and I've no doubt she will do so again if I let her get close. The idea of facing her, of facing my past, makes me feel like a child again. I have the urge to run, to convince Nixim to gallop away with me into the night, into the peace of the Fornwood, to a simple life of hunting and survival. But just as I'm imagining the wrangler as a Solitary, a cry rips through that brief fantasy. The ghosthawk spirals down a bruised dawn, his pulse drumming upon my tongue.

He'd followed me at a distance on the sea journey from Reis, occasionally swooping to the top of the foremast or jib of our ship to watch me with his yellow eye. He turned aside the morsels of salt fish I'd thrown from our supplies as if to say he was quite capable of hunting fresh meat along the coastline, as if to remind me he waited on the call of my sway, not on tidbits like some docile pet. Now his scream raises the hairs on my arms, a rebuke for not seeking him sooner, a challenge to spy on Iness and scout our destination for weaknesses.

Except I'm terrified to do it.

The closer we draw to Isfalk, the more I grow nervous around the bird. I think about who first trained him, as if he might answer the call of his former mistress, feel the greater power of her sway over mine. I have the overwhelming feeling that if I let the tiercel draw me in, it will be Iness watching me, not the other way around. But the chance to spy on Isfalk before we arrive, to see how much our strangling of trade routes has weakened the colony and to study its defensive preparations, is too great to ignore. Arm weak with nerves, I call him down to me. He answers with a piercing *chwirk, chwirk.* But before his talons can hook about my forearm there's a frantic flapping, a confusion of feathers and screeches of alarm. The ghosthawk veers suddenly away, banking skyward, and then his shadow splits, making two silhouettes in the dawn light, the much larger wingspan of another raptor baring its talons to my tiercel's back. I recognise the shape of an ice eagle. My ghosthawk barrel-rolls, meeting claw with claw, and the two embrace almost as lovers, before tracing a screaming corkscrew towards the earth. Loose feathers float about me and dance across the snowbound grass. And then flakes begin to fall – huge fat ones that obscure my sight of the warring birds. A long, high shrill rends my chest, clean as a heartshot from a bow, and a black shape folds in on itself, plummeting from the sky with a soft thud. I run to the mound of plumage, recognising my hawk, limp and unmoving in the drifts. Its yellow eye stares back at me half-open, the crescent of an eclipsed sun, its brindled throat a bloody mess of down. The ice eagle laps me slowly, twice, thrice, circles widening around the camp, as if taking in our numbers, our weaponry, our position. I try to listen for its pulse, but by the time I sense the long, even beat, the bird is already soaring towards the north on loping wings.

"Get a good look, you fecking crone," I yell to the sky, anger masking grief for my felled ghosthawk. The misgiving I'd felt about his loyalty, I realise now, was simply self-doubt, second-guessing my abilities in exactly the way Iness wants me to. "Take a good look at the army this little fec has brought to your doorstep. Because I'm coming for you." But my voice is dampened by the falling snow, my bluster lost in the vast steppe. I feel powerless, just as I did when I knelt before Iness on the Roundhouse stage, baring a shaved head and a branding I knew nothing of. I bend to gather the ghosthawk in my arms, its feathers still warm in my freezing hands.

I'm easy pickings – a blind and mewling cub, just emerged from the den. Iness has just stripped me of my eyes and ears.

Fortresses and Fears

"You should eat," Brim tells me. I'm poring over the map of Isfalk, rehearsing once again the play of Lars's strategy for the attack at nightfall tomorrow. "You've barely eaten a proper meal since we left Hross." I take the bread from the plate of cheese he pushes towards me, and tear a mouthful from it, if only to shut him up. Our relationship has cemented again in the days trekking north, and Brim has fallen into the role of annoying older cousin with alacrity. It's not so different from the way we always were as children, as if the cold and the landscape and getting ever closer to Isfalk is rolling back the years.

Under the table my leg hammers with nerves. I want to understand the assault plan, studying the coins Lars and Brim have placed upon the map, representing the position of our forces at the outer fortifications of Isfalk. Lars believes Iness would be a fool to offer us any resistance in the open field. He told me a decent number of her best fighters and captains defected to join his cause, and he thinks we can smash the outer defences of the Settlement and overrun the Brand village with brute force. "It's the inner citadel that poses the problem," he said, patiently describing the ancient defences to me. "No army has ever been able to get a foothold on its ramparts. Its ports have never been cracked." And yet, that's exactly what Lars is intending – to batter down the southern and western gates of the citadel under the shield of archers and flame-throwers. It feels wrong to risk so many lives, but he and Brim argue the Settlement has never faced a siege force the size of ours, or one made up of its own highly-trained Warders with insider knowledge of the walls and their defences.

"Do you think perhaps we might be overlooking the northern gate?" I ask Brim. "It leads straight into the citadel from the ice plains and the Warder barracks are right inside it. If they exit there, couldn't they come round and attack our rear?"

"Relax, Nara. Lars is stationing units there to engage anyone who flees. *Warder* units. The wrangler believes his Ghumes aren't up to the task." Brim gives Nixim a baiting grin over the lip of his kornbru.

"My Ghumes are only just getting used to wearing furs and you want them to attack over the glacier? No, you Isfalki can freeze your balls off in the wind chill from Tindur Hof, thank you very much."

"Thought you liked getting up to tricks on the ice, Wrangler," Brim says. "Shame you don't have your dogs right now, eh? You might have taken your troops on some sled rides."

"Well, they were certainly very popular with the ladies." Nixim offers a smug look.

"Cock's poxes!" I snap. This is Nix and Brim's relationship now – an almost companionable dick-swinging that drives me to distraction. They're never as bad when Lars is around, but he's off briefing his captains. "Can you two shut up and concentrate on finding common ground?"

I get up, leaning over the strategy table to stare at the map, running my finger over the outline of the citadel. "You're really not happy with Lars's plan, are you?" Brim says.

I shrug. "I know I'm not a trained soldier and I've no experience of sieges or fortress defences, but I do know Isfalk's gates. I am a little familiar with sneaking in and out of them, after all." Something wordless passes between Brim and I that reminds me of old times.

"You're thinking of the eastern gate. It was always your favourite," he says. The eastern gate was the port I'd use to sneak in and out of the citadel to hunt, disguised as a brandservant. Brim rubs a hand over the cropped stubble of his neck. "Nara," he warns. "If you're thinking of trying to get inside the walls so you can confront Iness alone, you can think again. I'm not an idiot." He shakes his head. "There's no way I'm letting you do a Haus."

I turn away, not wanting him to see how utterly he's exposed me. Deep inside, I know it's why he hasn't taken his eyes off me since we got within two days' ride of Isfalk. Part of me is relieved that he's saved me from my own impulsiveness – I'm terrified of facing Iness alone. But taking her out of the equation is surely what I'm here to do, the reason I've been training my skills all this time. Why wait to do it while others spill their blood?

Brim can't help a self-satisfied glance at the wrangler, proud to be the one reading my mind. His look says: *I still know her better than you. I'm the one who will shield her from the greatest danger – herself.*

The wrangler is unfazed. "You're good, Pretty Boy. But you're not that good. She isn't thinking of going to the eastern gate alone." He rises to refill Brim's cup with kornbru. "She wants you and me to go with her."

"Fec's sake!" I bark at them. "You do realise I'm sitting right here? I can speak for myself. And frankly I could do without the two of you circling each other like a pair of bucks about to lock horns."

Brim's cheeks redden, but the wrangler laughs out loud. "I've hit the bullseye, though, haven't I, Little Scourge?"

I don't answer, and he raises his glass to Brim with a wink.

"The guards on the eastern gate get lazy at handover time," I say, ignoring them. "It's not that difficult to get in and out... I did it often enough."

The wrangler mulls it over. "I suppose once we're inside

the citadel the three of us could take the watchtower alone, if we did it in the small hours when the guards are sleepy and unprepared. Then, we open the gate to our waiting troops and by dawn we've overrun the citadel from within."

"Sounds good in theory." Brim leans his arms over the back of his chair. "But in reality, it's impossible."

"Why?" I ask.

He stares me down, as if I've lost my wits. "Iness knows we're here, Nara. You already said she's been watching us through that eagle of hers. She knows Isfalk's surrounded and she'll be preparing the fortress for a siege. Every port to the citadel will be guarded tight as a Mor on her Pairing night."

I look to the wrangler. "He's right," he says, reluctantly. I cross my arms and turn away in grudging defeat.

"That's why we don't go through the gates," Lars' voice says. "We go *under* them." Standing in the tent's entrance, he's clearly been listening for a while.

A small, hooded figure follows him though the canvas. "Mor Nara! I knew you'd make it. I knew you'd come back for us!"

"Frida?" I cry, as the woman lowers her hood.

She reaches for my hands, bending to touch her lips to them. "I told my Jarl you'd return one day… that you'd be the reason we could hope for better things… I knew it!"

I fold her in my arms, too pleased that she's alive and well to care much about the way she's pitching me as the returning champion of the Sink-born. "What the poxes are you doing here, Frida? How were you allowed past the outer walls?"

"I wasn't… exactly," she says, then bobs a courtesy towards Lars. "Perhaps the Elix should explain?" She looks up at him nervously, as if she's standing before the Council on the stage of the Roundhouse again.

Lars offers her a seat at the table, and she sits uncertainly, his deference clearly unnerving her. My focus turns to him, his voice coming low as he speaks, as if from deep inside his memories. "All those years ago in Reis, Rosh had told me stories about the Cha Shaheer catacombs – Old World myths of fabled heroes getting in and out of the Shadow City through secret passageways – the very tunnels you used to flee, as it turned out," he says, glancing at me and the wrangler. "Back in Isfalk years later, I was visiting the Mor school archives. I'd learned Osha went down there often and I wanted to keep an eye on what she was up to. When I discovered the crypts, it occurred to me that similar tunnels might exist underneath the Isfalk citadel. I had little time to indulge my curiosity, and I forgot about it until I was gathering my supporters and preparing to head south to come to your aid in Cha Shaheer. We stashed weapons in an undercroft beneath the Roundhouse and I asked Frida if she'd investigate the extent of this vault while I was gone to see if my suspicions were founded. I didn't think much more of it until an hour ago, when she stepped into our camp."

"What do you mean, she *stepped* here?" I ask.

"I walked out, Mor Nara. That crypt turned into a long tunnel leading from the Roundhouse. It split in two directions, one south under the outer fortifications to The Fold, and the other north right inside the citadel."

The tent falls silent for a moment, only the canvas sucking softly in the wind.

"I'm struggling here." Brim is the first to speak. "The Isfalk fortress has never been breached. It's one of the most impenetrable Old World citadels in the Continent, and you want us to believe that you walked through a tunnel that leads straight inside it?"

Frida studies her feet, as if having her word questioned by an Elix heir overrules the evidence of her own eyes, as if the truth can only be curated by the Pure. Memories of us both on our knees before Elixion Fjall flood my mind.

"What's so difficult about believing her?" I turn on Brim. "Someone tunnelled under Cha Shaheer centuries ago, and that's an impenetrable fortress too, apparently. So why not Isfalk?"

Brim has no answer for that.

"How did you discover the tunnels, Frida?" I ask.

"Once the Elix put the idea in my head, I recruited Jarl and his friends to go snooping – no one pays much mind to Sink kids," she says, encouraged by Oskarsson's nod. "Some of the older buildings of the village had vaults that led nowhere. But then we discovered an ossuary off the vault below the Roundhouse. Jarl came across the opening to the tunnel by accident in the end. The little skelfs were mucking about putting the wind up each other tossing bones in the dark and there it was, a hollow space, hidden behind a stack of remains. It branched off in different directions, some passageways overrun with rats..." she shivers visibly, before continuing, "... and others dark and ancient, as if waiting for something. Or someone." She casts a glance at me, and when I look away she draws out a parchment from within her cloak, laying it on the table before Lars.

"We've been mapping the passageways for weeks now. I've done my best to draw the routes but... well, I've not had much practise with a quill, so..."

I reach to squeeze her hand, shaking my head at her to stop apologising. The map she's drawn shows crude pictures of Isfalk's outer fortifications, the Roundhouse and village marketplace inside them, and then the walled citadel. The ink work is crude and smudged but it's readable enough. I feel a swelling of pride for Frida.

"See this one here." She points to a long shaky line. "It leads right under the citadel and guess where it comes out?" She looks at me, eyes sparkling. "Mor Osha's favourite place."

"The Mor school archives?" I ask, and she nods. It all comes together now. Osha's precious corridors of trading records and maps, of almanacs and codices, weren't the only things hidden within the ancient foundations of the citadel. I imagine the passageways like arteries and veins under the city's battlements and I marvel at the human mind, that it can be the architect of unassailable fortresses and yet construct within them the very means of escape. I understand better than anyone that fear of being walled in, imprisoned, confined. Perhaps this is our fatal flaw – our fear of being trapped becomes the means by which we are assailed. Azza would like that. I'll try to remember it for her.

Brim cranes over the map, eyes working fast, still digesting it all. "You're saying we can access the citadel itself through the Mor school, without going past any watch?"

"She's not saying it, Pretty Boy, she just proved it," the wrangler says.

"How wide are these passages, Frida?" Lars asks gently, and I'm grateful for the lack of command in his voice when he speaks to her.

"Wide enough for a person to walk through…" She eyes the Maw, a silent and watchful presence near the tent's entrance. "Although some might struggle."

"Too narrow for troops to access at any speed," Brim says to his uncle.

"We don't need troops to access them, though, do we?" I say. "We only need a few of us to ambush the watch and open the gates from the inside." I arch an eyebrow at the wrangler.

He lifts his chin to me, grinning, then turns to Brim. "See, Pretty Boy, she's talking about the eastern gate – me, her… maybe you, if you've got the stomach for it."

What Lies Beneath

The tunnels are worse than I imagined, far narrower than the Reis catacombs.

I curse myself for thinking I could handle this. Frida leads us to a tumble of snow-covered boulders in a dell of the Fornwood, just where the trees skirt The Fold. She slips between a mossy crevice and we follow her down steps so dark and narrow, I have to gird myself to carry on. Brim, the Maw, Annek and a dozen other fighters – the best of our joint forces – creep single-file, making steady progress up ahead, and every time I feel the walls close in around me, I try to focus on the light of their torches, the shame I'd feel if, after everything I've been through, I lost my shit in a tunnel. But it's not long before the walls around us shrink even further and turn to packed mud, occasional stone lintels crooked between root-bound earth. We're forced to bend double to carry on, and when my torch gutters out, I'm one breath from hightailing it back to our camp to ready our troops with Lars as he'd wanted me to.

It's only the presence of the wrangler behind me, the reassuring warmth of his hand on my hip, that stops me bolting. When I turn, his eyes roam my face in the light of his firebrand. "One breath at a time, Na'quat," he says. But the softness in his voice makes me crumble.

"I... I can't... I don't..." My lungs suck at the dank air like I'm drowning. On the verge of passing out, I squat on the dirt floor, but he sets down his torch and catches my shoulders.

"Look at me," he commands. "Hey. Look at me."

But my eyes are squeezed tight and I shake my head vigorously. "No... I... small spaces..."

"I know," he says, thumb tracing gentle circles on my cheek, somehow understanding I can't be held right now. "I saw the way you were in the wagon on the Wasteland Plains. It's why I worked so hard on Haus to let you out."

"The fec you did!" I bark back. "We were in that box for five nights. You didn't work that hard, Wrangler."

"Well, if someone hadn't tried to slit the chief's throat with his own sword–"

"You'd just ambushed and kidnapped us with no explanation. What did you expect me to do? Roll over and play nice?"

"You? Play nice? Hardly, Little Scourge. But I flattered myself that you might have trusted me a tad more."

"Trusted you? Wrangler, trusting you back then was like climbing into a barrel of shit and thinking I was going to come out smelling of roses."

"And what about now?"

I don't answer, so he draws nearer until I'm breathing the fog of his breath, until I can see the want dancing in his eyes, as warm as the light of the torch at our feet. He takes my mouth suddenly, tongue sliding deep and slick against mine, and when I can draw breath again, he finishes with small kisses to the corner of my mouth, my jaw.

"See?" he whispers. "All better."

"What is?"

He smiles and I realise my voice is steady now, and my lungs don't feel like they're clawing out of my body for breath. His baiting and the kiss, as much as he meant it, was a distraction and it worked.

"Let's catch up with the others," he says. He must see my face tensing again, because he puts his hand on my hip once more. "I'll be right here behind you, just in case you need more *moral support.*"

I manage a smile. He suffered Brim to take the lead, settling for bringing up the rear because he knew I'd spook. He wanted to be there, at my back. Knowing that is enough to keep me putting one step in front of the other.

It feels like we walk for hours through the damp and narrow dimness, The Fold spread out above us.

When the passageway becomes wider, the excavation more refined, I imagine we've passed Isfalk's outer fortifications, the Sink slums and the Brand village after that.

The tunnel splits and veers off, but Frida reassures us of the route. "That way leads to the Roundhouse." She points through the bone-cold gloom. "We follow this direction. Not far now and we'll be under the citadel."

Eventually she brings us to a set of steep and crudely hewn steps, so narrow the Maw has to climb them sideways. At the top, a small iron grille door opens into an undercroft. Blinking in the moted light of the torches, I recognise a space that would once have served as a niche chapel where an altar might have been, except now it's obscured by mildewed piles of ledgers and inventories, rat-eaten scrolls of trade routes, and endless bills of carriage. We've made it to the Isfalki archives.

Out past the alcove, we reach a part of the crypt that is familiar to me. It's where I used to find Osha studying, the place I'd search first when she wasn't in her bed at midnight. The desk she worked at remains untouched, a quill stained with ink still resting in the open pages of a codex. *Anathomia and Physik.* "It's as if everything's still waiting for her return," I tell Annek, my stomach clenching with longing at how badly I miss my sister, how much I fear not seeing her again. I close the tome and brush the water-stained vellum.

"Dalla's already lectured me about salvaging these books," Annek says. "Osha's influence has made her obsession worse, you know." She scans the dim shelves, unimpressed.

"Promise me something?" I say. "Do what Dalla asks. Take

these books back to Hross. It would mean a lot to Osha – and to me." The implication in my voice glues her gaze to mine.

"Not happening," she says flatly. "I return without the books, that highborn princess won't dine with me for a week. But I go back without you, she'll feed me to the vuls. You think I have a death wish?" She rubs at her nose in the dusty air. "Besides, I can't carry these all by myself."

I see her lopsided grin. I know what she's doing – making light of the situation, making me believe this mission is simply a normal day's soldiering in a long campaign to secure the north, reassuring me I'll survive this. But I can't pretend that Iness isn't waiting for me somewhere in the citadel above. Ever since we entered the tunnels, it's felt like her sway is calling to mine, raising my pulse, working my muscles and bones, forcing me to put one foot in front of the other. My head has been pounding, my skin clammy with sweat, my breath short. I can deceive myself as much as I like that this is just my old fear of small spaces, but I know it's more than that. When we surface in the priests' vestry behind the Mor school chapel – into the fresh air and silver light through frosted windows – those symptoms don't go away. In fact, I feel worse.

Brim orders the torches extinguished, and Annek and the Maw join him to scout the dark church beyond. At the all-clear, we gather at the altar where Father Uluf would assail us with prayers three times a day. Brim takes the lead. With hushed orders he readies the unit to steal out across the quad, through the alleys of the citadel towards the eastern gate. I hang back, my vision tilting as if I'm at sea again, and Frida catches my shoulders. She pulls me back into the vestry and sinks me down on one of the old carved benches set before a dressing glass. "I'm *fine*," I tell her before she can ask. "Need to get my breath after those poxy tunnels, that's all." But as soon as the wrangler realises I'm not with them, he returns.

"Na'quat?" He takes my chin, angling my face to the moonlight through the small window.

"I'm good," I tell him.

"You're pale and dripping with sweat!" Fist around my forearm, he tries to drag me up. "You're sick. I'm taking you back to camp."

"Nixim." And the way I say his name, the utter fatigue in my body as I slump back down makes him stop. "I thought I could manage the tunnels, but they've exhausted me. I'm not moving. There isn't time. You have to finish this for me."

"What is it? What's wrong?" I can hear the panic in his voice now. "I'm not leaving you. I need–"

"You need to go with the unit. I'm too tired to go on. Help Brim take the eastern gate and show Lars the signal."

"Lars can wait."

"No, he can't. He'll have started the assault on the outer fortifications already. That was the whole point of this, wasn't it? Speed and the element of surprise. Attacking from both inside and out." I lean my elbows on my knees but when I swallow, I taste blood. Poxes. I sit up again and prop my head against the wall. I need to get the wrangler away from me. If he sees me bleeding he'll never leave. And then I won't get the chance to face Iness. Because I know she's coming for me. It's just a matter of time. Now I'm close and I can sense her sway: I'm as certain of it as the winter snows, the melt of ice in spring, the constant underground flow of the Edfjall. But I won't risk anyone I love near her when she finds me.

"Go... Frida will stay with me." She nods at him in reassurance. "Go, Nix. Come back and get me when... when Isfalk is ours." I can't help the doubt surfacing in my voice, and he hovers at the door of the vestry, ignoring Brim's frantic whisper from inside the chapel.

"Na'quat?" Nixim asks, torn.

"Go. You heard what Lars said about timing being key... and you're always fecking late, Wrangler."

When he's gone, I spit up blood across the flagstones. Frida grabs one of the embroidered priest's stoles hanging behind me and presses it to my mouth. "You're sick," she says, and I only nod. She doesn't need to know the truth of it – that I'm so faint I can barely stand, that my pulse is deafening in my ears and the shirt under my leathers is so sweat-drenched it feels like it's turning to ice in the draught from the quad.

Frida gets up to look for water, cursing softly under her breath. She finds a jug and pours it into one of the hammered chalices used for mass. The metal is icy cold in my hands and when I drink, the chill of the water revives me a little, clears my mind, so I can think what I must do.

"Frida," I say, resting my palm on her wrist. "The Brands in the Sink will rise up and join Lar Oskarsson's attack against the citadel. You said so, yes?"

She nods, certain of it. "Some of the Burg Brands might take up arms alongside Iness's Warders, but not many. Most are too hungry now. I think they'll sit tight when they see Oskarsson's banner. But the Sink is already ours. I've told them what's coming and they're ready to rise."

"And Jarl?" I can feel her pulse trip at mention of her boy's name, growing faster as my fingers squeeze hers. "You know what he's like... so eager to grow up. He'll want to join the fighting. All those little skelfs will... but they're still children, Frida. Someone needs to watch them, to hold them back." I can taste the fear that washes through her. Weak as I am, it's easy to swell in her because my own heart is already full of dread – dread that something will happen to Brim or Nix at the eastern gate, dread that Lars will be hurt, dread that too many innocents will die in this uprising. "Go to the Sink, Frida. Protect Jarl and the others." Her eyes flicker briefly and I think perhaps my skill is failing me, but then she rises, wraps her cloak around her and slips through the dark church without a backward glance. I hear the groan of the double doors, a whistle of wind and then nothing.

I'm alone in the Mor school chapel.

Waiting.

A Parting Gift

Patience has never been my strong suit.

Sick as I am, I can't bear the idea that Iness will find me weak and cowering in the very place I spent so much of my childhood, forced to follow her ridiculous rules. I've a good idea where I might find her. There's a spot along the parapets of the main keep where she would release the ghosthawk, a place where the whole Settlement spreads out below and you can see The Fold and the edge of the Fornwood rolling beyond. My hunch is Iness will watch the attack of Isfalk from there. I push to my feet and shuffle through the door of the vestry, stopping under the chapel's small dome to steady myself against the dark altar. I can feel the wind whistling through the door. In her haste, Frida must have left it ajar. For a moment, I think she's returned because the oak creaks on its ancient hinges and there's an icy blast of snow up the aisle. A shadow crosses the threshold. The ice eagle makes a circuit of the dome in a whirlwind of snowflakes and beating feathers. There's a clatter as one wingtip knocks a wrought-iron candlestick to the flagstones, before the bird comes to rest on the altar's brazier. Swivelling its head, it fixes me with its pale grey eye, almost luminous in the dark.

I look to the doorway again, suddenly terrified the eagle is the herald of Iness herself, but no one's there. The urge to flee makes my guts watery, but I'm not sure I can summon the energy to crawl, let alone run. Iness already knows I'm here, there's no question of that now. The eagle has me in its sights. I have nowhere to hide.

It's what I wanted, after all – to face her alone. But not in this state, not so weakened, the priest's stole sopping at my nose and blood starting to drip through my fingers. Am I really sick, as Frida says, or is this Iness's doing – the force of her ancient sway? I can't be sure. All I know is I'm barely strong enough to unsling the bow from my back, to ready an arrow from my quiver. I lay them down inside a row of pews, hands trembling at my nose.

The eagle studies me. Snow flurries through the open door, branches tap at the window, but I keep my focus on the fine calibrations of those eyes. The bird's pulse is sturdy and imperious over the tripping beat of my own. If I was stronger, I might have used my sway to call to it, to win it over as I did the ghosthawk, but the time for spying and games is long gone. Now, all I can do is imagine what the creature sees – a pasty Brand still slumped helplessly in the pew of the Mor chapel after all these years. I close my eyes for a brief second and there's Brim, poking his tongue out at me through the window, pointing to the sunshine and his riding whip. And there I am, rolling my eyes at Father Uluf's endless droning, miming for Brim to wait for me. The memory unfurls a tendril of warmth in my chest, and that's when I realise I'm cold as death and shivering to the bones. When I open my eyes again, the church is still, the doors shut against the snow and candles have been lit. Small flames lick inside the altar brazier. The ice eagle has gone. I must have passed out. But for how long? I still have the stole in my hand, half pressed to my weeping nose, and the tree's branches still tap at the dark window. No, that's not the sound of tree branches. That tick, tick, tick is inside the chapel, coming up the aisle.

"Good Father Uluf will not be pleased with you," Mother Iness says, lifting her cane in my direction. She comes to stand before the pews, unsurprised to find me sitting in one of the rows, as if waiting for the sermon to begin. "I believe that was his favourite Mass stole." She jabs at the bloodied cloth, resting her stick accusingly on the kneeler rail dividing us. Her ancient forehead crinkles where her eyebrows used to be, silver wisps of hair thin as night vapours curl under a white fur hat that matches a floor-length coat. She looks somehow frail and fierce at the same time, unstoppable – the embodiment of winter itself. Her misshapen knuckles grip the cane handle, skin thin as parchment. She's so old, so fragile, I feel like I might cough and blow her over. But it's me without the strength to rise, bleeding out like a sacrifice on the altar of her power... and she hasn't even touched me yet.

"Oskarsson's young Flamehair," Iness muses. "The Sway who got away." She tilts her head and inspects me with a surgical gaze I know all too well. Phibia had looked at me in the same way. It strikes me now how similar the two are – matriarch and daughter – the same cruel curiosity in their eye, and that blinding self-assurance born not of others' approval, but from some dark and unflinching sense of entitlement.

"I'll confess, I underestimated you, Nara Fornwood," Iness says. "A Brand with the skill? Shockingly unexpected, a curious anomaly... and yet, hardly threatening. Not to me." The strained sound in her throat might be amusement. She can be as arrogant as she likes now – she might be old but I'm the one cowering and reduced, unable to move. My hand falls uselessly to my quiver on the pew beside me, the stole still bunched in my fingers.

"If I'd known your skill would become so bothersome, I might have spent more effort hunting you down across the Wastes."

"Or made sure your henchmen did a better job of burning innocent women in their homes?" My body may be useless but my tongue still works.

"I see," she says. "How touching. You still grieve the woman you called your grandmother." Heat rises in my throat but it barely touches the terrible cold that cripples me. I wish I could reach my bow. Perhaps Iness has seen it behind the kneeler rail, perhaps she hasn't. It makes no difference – with blood flowing freely down my front, I'm too weak to nock a shaft, and she knows it. My body is no longer my own. I can only flick my eyes away from her in fury... in fear.

"My Warders took care of the Solitary we understood to be a spae-wife healer," she continues. There's a note of annoyance in her voice, but she reins it in, reaching for a smile. "I'm not a fanatic, like Uluf. I do understand that most of those forest witches are harmless enough... even useful, to a point – peddling dreams and hope for the Branded. Uluf forgets he's little more than a peddler himself, selling them his True Faith and his Coming of Elna." She tuts at the icon of Holy Mother's daughter carved in painted wood beside the altar. "But when rumours reach my ears of gifted healers, I must intervene. In my experience, that gift is likely to be the skill. And I cannot risk the rising of another Sway."

"You made a mistake, though, didn't you," I say thickly, swallowing back blood. "My Amma wasn't the Sway in the Fornwood all those years ago. Osha was."

Iness doesn't like hearing that. Her hands tighten on the cane, knuckles white. She could simply lift a finger to my cheek and finish me right now. So why doesn't she? The answer becomes obvious the longer she stares. She's trying to understand my existence, trying to comprehend that Morday Mass months ago when I'd reduced her – a Tathar at the height of her powers – to a breathless old woman cowering in her sedan chair on the Roundhouse stage. Like her daughter before her, she's curious, she cannot bear not knowing.

"A branded Sway is so very rare," she says. "Once, in my youth, some village whelp was brought to my attention for her skill with animals. She wouldn't have lived long anyway – the Sink-born never do. But you, a branded Tathar strong enough to overthrow my daughter? I might never have believed it if I hadn't seen it with my own eyes."

"Not exactly your *own* eyes," I say, gaze settling on the ice eagle which has returned to perch in the stone arch of a window. "I imagine you're near blind these days without your birds. Must be hard when they turn tail and don't return to you." The gibe is worth the coughing that follows. I bring up a clot of blood and the noise, the smell, makes the eagle loose a screech. Osha's voice in my head scolds me. *Don't provoke her, Nara. Save your breath to stay conscious.* But I've never had my sister's control, or her common sense. What's the point now? I can't fight Iness. I can only hope that Nixim and Brim have opened the eastern gate, that Lars's army is surging through the citadel as we speak, that one of them will do the job and finish the crone once I've failed.

Numbness becomes an ache that wracks my body and steals the air from my lungs, but with every last effort I can muster I reach trembling fingers towards Iness's resting on the carved head of her cane. I want this over. I want her to finish it. She jerks away.

"You still hope to use your skill against me, little fec?" Iness says, her voice all cold amusement.

"You still afraid of me, old witch... even with all your Tathar power?" *Stop provoking her, Nara.*

"You talk of fear like it's a weakness, girl. But not fearing you enough was the mistake my daughter made. So yes, I took measures to reduce you, as she never did."

"Reduce me?"

"My Tathar skill is great, but not so great that I can make you bleed to death at a distance, however much I might wish it." She looks down at the sodden stole in my lap, and I follow her eyes to the clots collected there, thick and tinged black, as I've never seen them before. "Eiter fungi are fatal... eventually. But first they curdle the blood and cause paralysis of the limbs. The caps are tasteless when ground into bread flour."

Bread? When did I eat bread?

And it comes to me in a surging rush. That last meeting in the strategy tent, Brim had been worried I wasn't eating enough before the mission, pushing the plate of cheese and rye towards me on more than one occasion. But surely not. It isn't possible... I won't believe that he could.

Iness confirms my suspicions before they can even form cogent thoughts in my head.

"I'd hoped the boy might have completed the task before it came to this." She gestures to me slumped in the pew before her.

"Shame I wasn't hungry."

"You were hungry enough." There's a soft chafing noise as she rubs the palm of one hand across the knuckles of the other on her cane, warming her fingers in the cold chapel. "I think I can manage the rest."

"You swayed him... like Phibia did."

"Would it be easier to swallow if I said I did?" She laughs, shaking her head. "No. Brim has never required my sway. He shares my vision for the Settlement of his own accord and he's prepared to make the sacrifices Isfalk needs to become the ruling power in the Continent." To my horror, there's a note of pride evident in her smile.

"Ah, do I sense some doubt that Brim would betray you so?" she says. "Or is it a little heartbreak that he didn't love you after all?" She's clearly entertained as I struggle against tears. "I'll admit, he has his weaknesses. All men do." And she runs her eyes over me as if I'm a flacon of dramur vit or a trull from Helgah's. "He's made mistakes because of you, girl. From time to time, he even believed his childish infatuations and loyalties were worth the risk to our legacy. But in the end, he always came back to me. My grandson knows who he is. He's a Pureblood through and through – not just an Elix heir, but a born Elixion who will return this Continent to the glory of the Old World. A Pure world."

My heart breaks, not because she's won Brim, but because, once upon a time, I might have... had I understood myself, had I understood him more. In the end, I wasn't enough. "Lars Oskarsson is attacking as we speak," I say desperately.

"The Isfalk citadel has never been breached and it never shall be," she replies, her conviction making my heart sink. "Here. A parting gift." She reaches across the prayer rail and finally takes my hand, fingers light and fragile on mine. "See for yourself." The numb ache recedes, warm breath floods my lungs, and I close my eyes at the relief of it. The shriek of the eagle makes me open them again, only to find I'm high above the citadel streets, watching dark silhouettes stealing through the shadowed alleyways. It's Brim, leading our small unit to the eastern gate, Nixim bringing up their rear. As they reach the port's arches, Brim halts the group and slips silently into the watchtower to scout its stairwell. A single cry cuts the silence – not surprise or alarm – but a command. And then arrows are whistling from the battlements, Warders streaming from the tower, torches flaring, shouts and grunts and thuds as our squad, surrounded and outnumbered, drop like cornered game on the citadel street. I search for the wrangler. Where is he? Where's Nixim? But I can't control the vision. I can only see what the eagle has seen circling over the still shapes of our fallen. And then I catch the flash of a sword in the moonlight, golden rings glinting in dark locks – the wrangler facedown in a puddle of melted snow. Hair slicked to his neck at one side, he doesn't move. Because it isn't a puddle of snow. It's a pool of blood. His own.

Memories of Amma make my head spin and my lungs seize. This can't be happening, history repeating itself again and again, like some tired old joke – Brim, the poison, the church altar, a Tathar gripping my hand, the shared vision, and now Nixim bleeding out across the snow just as my grandmother did. All because of me. I forced the wrangler to leave, I made him follow Brim. I was arrogant enough to think I could handle Iness alone, but all I've done is drive him straight into the sword of all her plans. I want to stop seeing, to get out of Iness's head, out of her eagle's view, but I'm trapped there, the feeling worse than any physical confinement I've ever railed against before. I barely have time to process it before my stomach dives and I'm swooping up and over the parapets.

The eastern watch looks out towards the village and I can hear the sound of Lars's oncoming assault. Ahead, I smell burning, see fires blazing along the outer palisades of the Settlement, the chaos of ramparts stormed and defence units overrun. A thrill of hope flares inside me. Lars's troops are surging through the southern streets of the Brand village, the Sink alive with activity, slum-dwellers joining forces with our army and meeting little resistance at barricades in the Burgs.

But slowly my joy turns sour. Our progress is too quick, too easy. When I spot the dark unwieldy mass gathered on the southern expanse of The Fold, I know what it means well before the eagle banks and dips, spiralling closer. Mounted Warder cavalry form a vanguard to a horde of armed foot soldiers, among them a few faces I remember from the village taverns, branded burgmen like the miller, Heygor Lysson, and his narrow-minded cronies. Leading them is a face I could never forget – Elixion Fjall, and far more disturbing are the Hrossi who boost the company – northern clansmen, perhaps disaffected by the overthrow of Orlath, living too far north to feel the benefit of Haus's rule, but close enough to Isfalk to fall under the sway of Iness's bargaining. As the eagle loops the host, a single horseman gallops across The Fold, coming to a stop before Fjall, his mount blowing steam into the night. The raptor's focus homes in on red-stitched boots, leather buffed to reflect the torchlight, silver furs teased by the wind. Brim's jaw is proud, his pale hair almost luminous in the darkness, his shoulders squared – the bearing of an Elix heir protecting his Pure privilege, defending his legacy.

The horde mobilises, following Lars's route through the broken defences, and Iness's strategy suddenly becomes clear. She knew of the tunnels all along – they allowed Brim access to the citadel to plot with her, to prepare the eastern watch against us. Without that gate compromised from within, Isfalk can't be broken. Lars's force is about to be trapped between Warders defending the walls and reinforcements advancing on his unsuspecting rear.

A sound rips through my chest. I'm not sure if it's the eagle's cry or my own. I regain consciousness in the chapel, choking on a slew of blood. Iness still has my fingers in her bony fist. I try to shake her off but my hand feels like it has no more life than the wood of the pews. The crone holds my gaze but doesn't speak. There's nothing left to say. I won't give her the satisfaction of seeing my despair, so I close my eyes.

The force of her energy washes through me, her pulse calling to mine. It's self-assured, inevitable, as ancient stories so often are, weakening the last shreds of my own. I understand now. I can finally give up. I can slip towards that smoky light where all is gentle and still – the lamplit windows of our cottage in the Fornwood at dusk, Osha's familiar song drifting to me through the trees, the smell of the ice plains, sharp and boundless, still carried on my furs.

But Iness won't let me go, at least not so peacefully. "It was clever of Oskarsson to keep you in the Mor school – hidden in plain sight," she says. "But it won't be long before... on his knees ... blood of so many Brands on his hands... looking up into the face of his nephew... see the final ruse is mine." Her voice drifts in and out of my consciousness. Why is she still bothering to speak? *You've won*, I want to tell her, *and I'm too far gone to even care.* "Lars... sentimental fool... thinking to out-manoeuvre a Tathar..."

"Is that right?" A different voice startles me back to lucidity.

Another woman, the sound of someone I recognise but can't place. "Don't you go believing everything this one says, child."

I try to focus, but the chapel is dim and my eyes won't stay still, rolling between candlelit shapes and darkness.

"You!" I hear Iness snatch, and her grip weakens, fingers freeing mine. The eagle screeches, shocking me awake. And with it comes a rush of warmth through my limbs, reviving as the Moon Pools on an icy morning. Blinking away the fogginess, I see the Blood-wife standing beside Iness, her face painted as if for war, cheeks and jaw white as the snow, a streak across her eyes the colour of fresh blood. One of her stained hands is around mine, the other wrenches Iness's wrist away. The two Sways lock eyes and I feel the clash of their energy, as physical as two swords grinding, refusing to give ground. I try to muster any last dregs of skill left in me to help Frenka, but I'm fighting my own battle now – between warmth and numbness, between memory and forgetting, between consciousness and sleep.

A crash rouses me – Iness's cane falling to the flagstones. The crone staggers back towards the altar, the Blood-wife pursuing. Frenka still clutches Iness's wrist but they grapple and Iness grabs Frenka's throat. Locked in a mental stand-off, they grow still. I leave them to ransack each other's memories, slipping away to my own – a wide river, the wrangler on the far bank. Except this time, it's he who cannot cross and I who must journey on alone.

All I want is to be left in peace, but the voices drag me back. "Of course I knew you lived," Mother Iness growls at the Blood-wife. "I didn't hunt Solitaries simply for the sport of it."

"How many did you kill, all for the sake of one Tathar who didn't want to be found?" Frenka says sadly. "Was it truly beyond your comprehension that any Mor with the skill could content herself living as a hermit? I made a life on the lava plains of the Edfjall because, unlike you, power did not interest me, my–"

Iness chokes her words with a squeeze and the pair pit sways once more. The Blood-wife begins to struggle for breath. Her eyes grow wide, her legs threaten to fold beneath her. Iness cannot bear her weight, but she won't let go either, bending over Frenka as she slumps against the altar. For an instant, the Blood-wife's focus returns to the chapel, searching. And when her eyes find mine, there's such sadness, such apology in them, I know she's losing the fight.

"Frenka," I cry, but it's more a gurgle than her name, blood filling my mouth. I spit it out across the pew – the very benches where I once sat, where all young Mor would sit to be preached at by Father Uluf, to be shaped and controlled by Iness. The memory sparks a spasm of fury in me. Heat rushes my skin. I wobble to a stand just as Frenka buckles to the altar steps, Iness standing over her. I crack my knuckles, fingers brittle as frozen wood. I've been cold and stiff so many times before, hunting on the ice plains. My hands know their work by heart – a skill, an instinct that's nothing to do with being a Sway. This is about survival.

The string thrums loud in the quiet chapel, the shot a soft *pock*. Iness turns with aching slowness. Confused, her fingers probe the arrowhead that punctures her throat, mouth working to swallow the blood bubbling from her lips. Behind her, Frenka pulls herself up along the altar, and staggers to stand between us. Iness grasps for her, but Frenka steps beyond her reach. The ancient Tathar of Isfalk sinks to the flagstones, a bag of frail bones inside a carcass of bloody fur, her rheumy eyes as sightless now as river stones.

I cough and spit. "Frenka?" I say, panicked.

"It's alright, girl," she croaks, catching my shoulders before I hit the pew. She lays me down. "Rest now."

Two Crones

The Blood-wife lays her palms against the skin of my neck. "Breathe... that's right, just breathe." Her sway feels so good coursing through me that when she lifts my chin and asks me to open my mouth, I dumbly comply. "Swallow," she says, thrusting a ball of paste onto my tongue.

It disintegrates immediately, leaving behind an aftertaste so bitter it makes my eyes stream.

"What the fec–" I choke out.

"Got your tongue back, then?" She prods under my jaw, feeling the glands there, and I flinch, still a little wary. "Have some faith, girl. I'm a Tathar, not some spae-wife peddling nostrums of snowjack shit." Her eyes flash for a second before growing faraway, just as Osha's do when she's healing with her sway. "It's an emetic. You're going to purge." She steps back and I vomit almost instantly, all over the pew. "That better?"

I nod at first, sensation returning to my extremities. My skull no longer wants to float away like a seed clock, and I've stopped bleeding. But then I change my mind, shaking my head because I still feel like Iness's claws are squeezing my heart. "The wrangler, Frenka. He's dead. Brim betrayed us... and Lars, my father–" The tears flow freely, shock and grief too much to bear.

"Oh, hush now," she says, her skill slowing my pulse, and soon my breath. "What did I tell you about visions? You shouldn't believe everything you see. Nor should you trust Tathars like that one." She jerks her chin towards Iness's body, now nothing more than the shell of a sad old woman, long past her time. "For all her grand-scale scheming, even Iness couldn't sway the vagaries of fate, the random effect of the individual will."

"What the pox does that even mean?" I say, barely able to focus on breathing in and out, and in no mind for esoteric talk.

"It means I was camped at the Moon Pools last night, waiting to trade my dye with a citadel seamstress, but the threat of the siege kept her away. I hadn't known about Lars's army until Iness's eagle came hunting overhead." As if aware she's talking about him, the raptor spreads its expansive wings to circle the chapel, before coming to settle on my pew in a draft of feathers. "You answered when I called, didn't you, my beauty?" Frenka strokes the eagle's flawless breast. To my surprise, it chitters softly in answer. "My animal sway is stronger than Iness's – the benefit of having creatures as my only companions for so long on the Edfjall, I suppose. That's how I knew you were here," she says. "My feathered friend laid out Iness's plans to me, clear as dawn. He wasn't her eyes and ears during the attack on Isfalk – he was mine. And when he returned to the citadel I made him show Iness what *I* wanted her to see."

I struggle with it at first. "But the wrangler... and Lars and his forces trapped against the citadel walls? You mean, none of that was real?"

"Some of it was real. The boy betrayed you as I warned he would, and I'm sorry for it."

She frowns at my pained expression. "Perhaps you need to see the truth for yourself." Taking my forearm, she holds it out, and I realise she means it for the eagle. I flinch. "Steady, now. Have some faith and let him settle." The bird swivels its head and preens briefly, before coming to perch upon my sleeve, fearsome and magnificent. His breast is as white as the melrakki I felled with the wrangler on the ice plains, his iris bright as a honed sword. "Now, let him know what you wish to see," the Blood-wife says.

The eagle's restless eye stills, engulfing me first in liquid silver and then a tunnel of blackness. I emerge above a snow-crusted street, dark figures moving through the shadows, the vast bulk of a soldier blocking the reflection of moonlight on the snow. The Maw follows the shape of Annek and Nixim making for the eastern gate, the rest of our unit darting erratically behind. The soft glow of torches illuminate the arch of the watchtower, the murmur of guards playing cards within. It's Brim who reaches the gatehouse first. With the eagle's precision, I notice the dull gleam of his blond hair catching on his eyelashes as he blinks. The unit waits for him in silence while he scans the stairs, just as we had planned, except Nixim follows him inside, changing the protocol. What's the wrangler doing? There's a scuffle, a soft cry and two figures trip from the shadows. Brim is in the wrangler's arms, mouth gagged by his forearm, dagger pressed to his neck. In an instant, the rest of the unit are running up the watchtower. Swords ring, voices cry out and two bodies are launched in quick succession over the wall. They land twisted and misshapen in the street below – watchguards, by their uniforms. And then, to my relief, there's Annek up in the tower, frantically waving a burning torch. A reciprocal flame is traced somewhere in the Sink – Lars's answer.

The eagle's focus shifts to the two men this side of the fortifications. The wrangler and Brim tussle, and Nixim loses his dagger, hissing a curse. He backs away to inspect his forearm, making me think Brim has bitten his way free. When they face each other again, it's sword to sword.

"You're really going to do this, Pretty Boy?" Nixim says, tone too cocky as he makes a lunge for the Elix heir.

"And you're really going to risk Isfalk because of some sentimental guilt towards the Branded?" Brim ducks, his parry narrowly missing the wrangler's shoulder. "I'm not about to let that happen. The Branded are weak... Poxes, half of them are already dying!" Their swords lock, grinding.

"With careful planning, they could be bred out of the future of this Continent within a few generations."

"And what of Nara?" The wrangler grunts as he throws Brim off. "You grew up together... you say you love her... but you'll do this to her?"

"Nara's different. The others are diseased cattle, but she's..."

"She's what?" Nixim circles Brim, one moment in the shadows, the next in the moonlight.

"She's a Tathar. She has the skill."

"Doesn't that disprove your point about Brands being useless?"

Brim lunges but it's lurching and hasty. He's losing his patience; I've seen it before when he gets riled.

"Let me get this straight," Nixim baits. "You say you love Nara, but you don't tolerate Brands?" He trips backwards, regaining his balance from an overhead block and I want to tell him to shut up and concentrate. "She's worthy of your love but not worthy enough to have a normal life, or to have children who might be branded?"

Brim paces a circle around the wrangler, shaking his head, as if he recognises the distraction for what it is. "You can't hack it, can you, Wrangler? That she wanted me before you. That I'll always be her first love." He feints a jab, but the wrangler predicts it with total composure.

"I'll confess, it used to bother me," Nixim says. "But, at night, when she's moaning my name, I don't think she even remembers who you are."

It's the final straw for Brim. "I should have ditched that rkyi and cut your fecking throat while I had the chance." He launches at the wrangler with a two-handed upthrust, but Nixim dodges, and Brim is unbalanced. When he stumbles, Nixim takes his shot – a slice straight to Brim's cheek, then a backslash to the neck of his cuirass. Brim freezes mid-step, sinking to his knees, body twitching. His hand goes out to the wrangler, and Nixim hovers as if to steady him, his expression full of conflicted emotions – remorse, sadness, relief. Watching Brim pitch face-first into the snow, I feel those emotions, too... and so many more. Except anger, strangely. That reaction has faded in me. I'm worn out by anger, and I'm tired, so very tired.

I exit the eagle's vision to find the Blood-wife squeezing my fingers, flooding me with warmth, as if she knows the truth I've seen is double-edged – sweet relief underscored by a terrible heartbreak. We're quiet for a moment, Frenka letting me process it all. Nixim is alive, but Brim is dead. It's like I've survived a sinking ship, only to be smashed against rocks. I'll never hear Brim's voice, never be able to look him in the eye and ask why he chose Isfalk and Iness over me, over everything he witnessed in Reis and Hross. He's gone and I feel like I never truly knew him at all.

"What of our forces? What of the breach?" I ask Frenka, suddenly remembering there's more to this campaign than Brim. "Are they safe?" I try to rise. "I need to find Nixim... I need to fight."

"You need to sit down before you fall down, child." And once again she catches my shoulders just before my legs give way. "You lose any more blood and you may not live to tell the tale. I'm a healer, but I cannot raise the dead."

"The forces on The Fold were about to attack... What has happened to my father?"

She cants her head at me. "Lars Oskarsson," she says slowly, and I realise that she might already have suspected who he was when I first met her all those months ago in her cottage on the Edfjall. "Oskarsson's uprising fares as well as any other where the defenders turn coat to join the rebels."

"But I saw Iness's reinforcements – her Warders joined by village burgmen and Hrossi riders. They were set to attack from behind our lines."

"I know. I'm quite the Tathar when I set my mind to it, even if I do say so myself." Her laugh is wheezy and cracks in her chest. She hocks unapologetically towards the altar. "Damn Uluf and his clearfrage incense. Forgot how much it sets off my allergies."

"The horde on The Fold didn't attack us, then?"

"Keep up, girl," she tuts. "They rode out in support of Oskarsson. Your father always did underestimate his popularity among the Isfalki Warders. I can't imagine the burgmen took much convincing, either, given the food shortages. The citadel has been too greedy for too long."

"And the Hrossi clans I saw?"

She shrugs, but I don't need her answer. I can already work it out myself. "Haus. He must have convinced the northmen to support us."

I try to get to my feet again, opening my mouth to argue with her, but she beats me to it. "Fecs alive, you're a pain in the arse, girl!" She grabs my forearm and we shuffle towards the door of the chapel, two crones, not quite on our last legs.

Moon Pools and Memories

Lars Oskarsson doesn't place Brim's ashes in the Oskarsson crypt, nor does he want his nephew resting with his mother's family in the Mikkelssen vault. When he asks my opinion, I ride out with him to the Fornwood, to one of Brim's favourite places – the clearing where he'd taught me to fight. The practice post still stands there, the moustachioed face Brim had drawn on it now comic and sad all at once. Our sword chips in the wood are like tree rings, marking the passage of time. The day is bitterly cold and grey, winter already settled deep in the forest. But when our private ceremony is over, the ashes scattered under the snow at the base of a greenock tree, a weak sunshine struggles through the branches.

I lay a wreath of cylla vine woven with skeggan moss over the spot that is now Brim's. New life. New beginnings. Free of pain. For all of us, I hope.

"You're good to honour him, after everything," Lars tells me. We've waited two months to lay Brim to rest, and he's invited no one else to this ceremony, perhaps thinking only I could understand his conflicted grief, how we're both sad and angry, mourning and hurting in equal measure.

"He was still my best friend... long before he was my cousin, long before he became my enemy."

Lars sighs. "I'm ashamed of the Purist he became. Perhaps it was my fault. Perhaps he grew that way in opposition to me, to set himself apart from who I was."

Maybe there's some truth in that, but instead I say, "As a boy he was essentially good... and I loved him." I think of the Blood-wife's prediction – a good soul born of bad. "I still find it ironic he was the person who taught me to fight and ride, to believe I could be so much more than the citadel expected of me."

Oskarsson runs his hand over that white streak in his hair. "I should have been the one teaching you those things."

"Yes," I say without apology, making him shift his boots in the snow. "But that doesn't mean to say you can't make up for lost time. You're teaching me now – how to be a good leader, to listen and be patient and kind. You have your work cut out for you, but we're both trying. And you're teaching me to trust again." He looks up at that, wanting to see if I mean it. I tap the side of the woollen nab hat Frida made me, the place under my hair where my branding sits. "And... it's my job to keep you accountable in reshaping this new Isfalk." He rubs his jaw, bites back a smile. I can tell he's pleased, hopeful now that I want to stay in the north and not return to Hross. When I slip my arm through his, walking to our horses, he startles, then almost blushes with pride.

"What?"

"You remind me of your mother."

"Really?" I fiddle with the thong of leather at the neck of my furs, the pendant warm against my skin. "Don't tell me she was a contrary, foul-mouthed, grudge-holder, too?"

"No... but she made me laugh." And the sound of him, that low rumble in his chest, the sight of his green eyes lit with amusement, goes a long way to replacing all those memories missing from my childhood.

Before he turns to mount, I touch the streak in his hair. "*Bar'quan*," I tell him. "It means lightning in Reis."

"I know what it means."

"Okay, then," I say, rolling my eyes at him. "*Mehib*."

"I understand what that means, too," he says, and he crosses his arms at me for calling him a know-it-all. "I was in Cha Shaheer for quite a bit longer than you were, remember? And your mother was a good teacher."

I watch his face carefully as I say, "You are too, *Kharam*." And I know he's understood because his eyes turn liquid and then he starts to blink rapidly.

"That is the best name you could have called me, my Nara," he whispers, catching my hand and bringing it to his lips.

It's the first time I've called him Father.

"You ride on ahead," I say, as he swings into his saddle.

"You're not returning with me to the Settlement?" he asks, surprised. Osha is bringing Rosh for a visit at month's end and I have a great many changes to oversee before her arrival – the Mor chapel, which Dalla is turning into a library; the infirmary to set up in our old dormitory quarters; the Roundhouse school in the village square to organize with Frida. I have a task list as long as my arm. But there's something I must set straight first.

I remember a time when riding alone in the Fornwood would have earned me a lecture from Brim or required a full Warder escort. Now, my father only lifts his chin in acknowledgment, something knowing about the hitch of his lip. He heels his mare towards The Fold without question. "Be careful," he says over his shoulder. "Make sure that bird goes with you."

When I reach the Moon Pools, steam rises thickly in the freezing air. The ice eagle circles up through the mists to a vantage point somewhere high in the canopy, where his screech tells me he's already found some small victim for his lunch. I'm never quite sure whether he's my eyes or ears, or if he remains the Blood-wife's, but I like the idea of having a connection to the old Tathar. I'm still uncertain of my skill, wary – a *healthy scepticism*, as Frenka calls it. And, in her own way, she's helping me master it, continuing Azza's work, but making me explore new directions with my energy, too. She's a busy woman in Isfalk now, helping with diagnoses, remedies and treatments, and I can't wait for her to meet Osha, to see how much they might teach each other, both in traditional healing and sway. But Frenka still refuses to live permanently in the Settlement and disappears from time to time in the wilds. I understand that need more than most.

At the Moon Pools, I shuck off my furs and leathers on the rocks and submerge myself in the sulphurous heat. I wish it felt like old times, but it doesn't anymore. Bathing here both comforts and unsettles me, a mix of joy and sadness, like coming home to find everything has been rearranged, changed forever, that the places of childhood only exist in memories.

The wrangler's shape emerges through the mist. He's been exercising his dogs across The Fold, the whip still slung at his hip. His thighs flex in his leathers as he navigates the rocks.

"You look flushed," he tells me.

"It's the water temperature."

"Right." He grins and I gesture for him to come closer. Squatting at the edge of the pool, he leans in to kiss me, only to get a face full of water squirted from my mouth.

"Nice," he says, sitting himself on the rock edge and drying his face on my shirt. But he doesn't take off his boots or undress. He never does, even though I can see his cheeks and fingers are raw from the cold. When I wrap my warm hands around his, he hums with pleasure.

"Wrangler?"

"Mm?"

"Why don't you ever bathe with me here?"

He doesn't seem surprised I've brought it up, only shaking his head a little. "You've never asked me to."

"Are we back to needing invitations?"

He tips his head, and I'm expecting some retort, but his face is serious. "This is your place. Yours and Brim's. Figured you needed the time alone here to remember him... at least as he used to be."

Slowly, I rise from the water to cup his jaw in my hands and bring his frozen lips to my warm ones. "You know, it's hard for me to say this, but... thank you for that."

He pulls an impressed face. "Gratitude. And not even a sword at your throat. We're making progress."

"But, Nix?" I begin to open his furs, pushing them down over his shoulders.

"Na'quat?"

"As much as I have memories of him in this place..." I untie the laces of his undershirt and drag it over his head, "the Brim I knew as a child left the Moon Pools a long time ago." He holds his gaze fast to mine, as if to judge whether I mean it. To banish all doubt for good, I loosen his leathers, slipping a warm palm inside. "Get in the water, Wrangler."

"Why, Little Scourge?"

"Because I want to make new memories here – with you."

Acknowledgements

Thank the Mother for the skilled crew of women who've worked on this series with me. I'd like to thank my agent, Catherine Drayton; the Angry Robot sister squad, Gemma Creffield, Caroline Lambe, Amy Portsmouth and Desola Coker; and the Pantera Seer Circle – Ali Green, Kajal Narayan, Katy McEwen, Lucy Barrett, Melissa Snook, LinLi Wan and Lauren Draper. You are Sways, one and all. Most of all, thank you to my editors who I suspect burn the candle late into the night making sure my manuscripts don't sound like the flim-flam of spae-wives: Lex Hirst, Kirsty van der Veer, and Anna Blackie you are Tathars at the height of your powers. Thank you for quickening my skill and knowing where to find the pulse of my writing. Dan Hanks and Steph Hanlon, thank you for swooping in with eagle eyes.

Debra Billson, you make my books covetable objects with your cover designs. I can't tell you how much praise *I* get for *your* art. You need no ghosthawk because you already have vision. Juliette Marillier, your time and kind words meant so much to this tragic fan girl, and Bronwyn Eley and Stacey McEwan, thanks for the thumbs up and for keeping me laughing when it all gets a bit serious. Ever a vit skin for you at my campfire.

To my writing group, Suzanne Brown, Sam Milton and Barbara Hatten (Lucy Lever), thank you for being visionary critique partners, the best of advisors and precious friends. I wouldn't want to plan any writing campaign without you in my strategy tent.

Thank you, Michelle Barraclough, Donna Cameron and Fiona Britton, for navigating the high seas of publishing with me, for filling my sails with writerly advice and filling my glass when in doubt. Pam Cook, thank you for risking me with a microphone and letting me talk shop with some great fantasy writers on the Writes4Women podcast. I'm learning so much. Thank you, Paige Belfield, for much support and fun at Supanova. Your hunting skills are expert (pasta-by-the-metre was definitely the best of the bag). To Dan O'Malley, thanks for teaching me how to shoot a pithy pitch and the power of a well-timed cocktail. May your ryki be iced and shaken (but never with krait's venom). Maddie Te Whiu, Tim Tam slam mentor extraordinaire, thanks for keeping my energy levels at Nova so high.

Writing fiction for a living can sometimes feel like hunting the ice plains of the tundra alone, so I'd like to thank all the OG A/NZ readers who contacted me with messages of appreciation or beautiful posts about *The Branded*. You stoked my fire and warmed my fingers at the keyboard when I was wrangling *The Rising*. It's in big part down to you that I'm now thanking an international crew of bookstagrammers and booktokers who have also championed *The Branded*. You know who you are. Publishing is a numbers game, but you guys make reading and writing a community, a place to belong, and I'll take that dopamine hit, thank you.

To my hearth clan and true warriors of the sands, Cris, Ceci and the SBT School – thank you for making sure I get off my arse and look up from the page at least three times a week. You keep me sane. Sorry for the shit backhand, though. What can I say? I'm a novelist – I favour a good hook.

I could not have finished *The Rising* without the help of my UK family. Thanks to Suzanne and Marcus for letting me keep the torches burning all night up in the attic and for feeding me when I finally came down; to Vana and David for the second office and coffees at the elbow; and to Aunty Sylv and Uncle

Luci for the trusty steed. Lydia, Maisie Knight and Jo Luker, thank you for making me take that weekend in Amsterdam immediately after structural edits. Sometimes we need fun more than sleep. Next time, let's try the mesmer.

Thank you, Henry, for the procrasti-memes and pesto pasta. Couldn't have written those battle scenes without a few *Office* bloopers. Thank you, Lydia, my constant inspo for concept art, animation, and thrift-store scavenging - we now have enough boots and leathers to clothe the Warder army. Both of you inspire me every day. (Please make sure you tell me when my proverbs get cheesy.)

Last but never least, to my lovely GJ, thank you for having the patience of Haus with this all-consuming obsession of mine. You are my lyfhort, you ground me and I couldn't do it without you.

About the Author

JO RICCIONI graduated with a Masters in Medieval Literature from Leeds University, where her studies included Icelandic saga and the Arthurian and Robin Hood legends. Her short stories have won awards in the UK and Australia and have been anthologised in Best Australian Stories. Jo's first novel, *The Italians at Cleat's Corner Store*, won the International Rubery Award for fiction and was long-listed for the New Angle Prize in the UK. *The Branded Season* is her first epic fantasy duology.

We are Angry Robot, your favourite independent, genre-fluid publisher, bringing you the very best in sci-fi, fantasy, horror and everything in between!

Check out our website at www. angryrobotbooks.com to see our entire catalogue.

Follow us on social media:
Twitter @angryrobotbooks
Instagram @angryrobotbooks
TikTok @angryrobotbooks

Sign up to our mailing list now: